MY NAME
IS LEGION

A. N. Wilson

MY NAME
IS LEGION

FARRAR, STRAUS AND GIROUX
NEW YORK

To Sarah Sands

Farrar, Straus and Giroux
19 Union Square West, New York 10003

Copyright © 2004 by A. N. Wilson
All rights reserved
Printed in the United States of America
Originally published in 2004 by Hutchinson, Great Britain
Published in the United States by Farrar, Straus and Giroux
First American edition, 2005

Library of Congress Control Number: 2005922159

ISBN-13: 978-0-374-21742-6
ISBN-10: 0-374-21742-4

www.fsgbooks.com

1 3 5 7 9 10 8 6 4 2

And always, night and day, he was in the mountains, and in the tombs, crying, and cutting himself with stones.

But when he saw Jesus afar off, he ran and worshipped him, And cried with a loud voice, and said, What have I to do with thee, Jesus, thou *Son of the most high God? I adjure thee, by God, that thou torment me not.*

For he said unto him, Come out of the man, thou unclean spirit. And he asked him, What is thy name? And he answered, saying, My name is Legion: for we are many.

Mark 5: 5–9

MY NAME
IS LEGION

The body which lay beneath the thin white linen sheet was in pain. Only occasionally did groans or whimpers come from the bed. Then, one of the women would try to dab his lips with water, but though he sucked the moisture with the desperation of a baby, his face remained tormented. The torment, however, was a controlled torment, and this was what struck all who saw it as so powerful, so strange. One of the younger monks said that he knew now what it must have been to witness the Crucifixion. The agony on that bed appeared, to this young observer, to be offered to God, and shown back to them: a pattern of how to die. But much of the agony was spiritual. None of them could doubt that, as he lay there, he underwent mental suffering which matched the wounds in his body. Sometimes, he opened his eyes and looked up at the crucifix which hung on the wall opposite the end of the bed. His large blue eyes, full of tears, gazed at the figure on the Cross.

He had sinned much, though quite what those sins were, only God knew – God, and the monk who had been to hear his last confession. There were others, evidently, prepared in their different capacities to rush to judgement.

The police had suggested that he should be taken to a prison hospital and held in custody until the various allegations and counter-allegations could be investigated. He stood, as far as they were aware, suspected of a string of terrible crimes: the abuse, and the murder, of a minor; involvement in terrorist activity; possession of illegal firearms; conspiracy to murder.

A lawyer, the family lawyer of his brother, the Earl of Longmore, was able to point out, however, that he had not been charged with any of these crimes, and that there was no evidence against him. Yes, they had seen him shoot the boy. There were dozens of witnesses to that. But though he was illegally in possession of his old service revolver, his shooting had saved another human life, and would certainly be defended as a justified homicide.

The tall, military gentleman – a brigadier working for the Ministry of Defence, but clearly an intelligence officer – had, against the better judgement of the infirmarian, been allowed into the room to sit beside the bed to interrogate the dying man.

The questions had all been, if not ignored, then quietly sidestepped.

'Can you hear me, Father, Father Chell?'

The Brigadier's upper class voice was gentle, but insistent.

'I'm sure you would want the truth to be known.'

From the bed, a murmur, perhaps an expression of pain, perhaps an 'mm' of agreement.

'Did you know anything about the plan to assassinate the General? The bomb in the hotel?'

'Mm.'

'You did? You knew who was going to organize the attack? Was it Thimjo, or one of the other Albanians? It wasn't an Irish device.'

'Mmm . . .'

'The bomb in Bermondsey was defused – the one in the newspaper building,' said the Brigadier. He spoke in such a quiet tone that he might have been relaying cricket scores. 'We've a fairly clear idea who planted that one. But please, Father. You have made your peace with God, man. If you know something which can prevent any more innocent people being killed . . . The bomb in the hotel didn't just kill the General, you know. There was the waiter. One of the women lost an arm – the women who were with him in his room. Surely you don't want to die with that on your conscience. If there's anything you know, anything at all . . .'

There was silence from the bed. Then the great blue eyes opened again.

'Mother of Mercy,' said Vivyan Chell quietly.

'You're talking about Mrs d'Abo? The mother of Mercy Topling?' asked the Brigadier.

The old grey head on the pillows nodded slightly but then murmured, 'Hail, Holy Queen, Mother of Mercy, Hail our life our sweetness and our hope . . .'

The Brigadier looked sheepish. The prayer was obviously unknown to him, but he was respectful – more than respectful, evidently awestruck in the presence of the monk's stoicism. The dying man was not just a monk. He had been awarded the Military Cross for valour when a major in the Coldstream Guards.

'To thee do we cry, poor banished children of Eve . . .'

'Quite,' said the Brigadier, quietly. 'Perhaps, anyway, if any names occur to you . . .'

'Mother of Mercy . . .'

'We would offer them amnesty in exchange for the explosives, the weapons.'

'Is Joshua dead – little Joshua?'

'Yes – General Bindiga is dead. There has been a régime change in Zinariya.'

'Lennie dead?'

'Lord Mark is alive. General Bindiga is dead.'

The monk on the bed closed his eyes, and for the first time in days, a smile played on his face. The interview was over, and the Brigadier never heard him speak again.

There were rules in the house about women; ever since Kelvedone, a cavernous, ugly brick mansion, had been turned into a religious house in the early twentieth century, women had been banished from most of its rooms. They were allowed into a small chamber near the front door, to seek advice or spiritual counsel from one or other of the monks. No woman had ever dined in the refectory since the house became a monastery. None had ever entered a monk's room. None had entered the infirmary.

But now it was the twenty-first century, and the figure lying beneath the white sheet was no ordinary man. The Superior of the community had not even consulted with his brother-monks. When Father Vivyan's body had been brought back to the mother-house of the order, groaning and bullet-wounded, the young, dark-haired, intense woman had been with him in the ambulance. It would hardly have been possible to turn her away at the door. Later, when the black woman had arrived, it was equally difficult to think of a good reason why the rules should not be broken. The black woman was the mother of the boy Father Vivyan had killed.

'How many more parish women are going to follow?' had been the weary misogynistic question of one of the older fathers. It was a rhetorical question, though. The monks had no intention of allowing crowds into the sickroom of a mortally ill man. It was necessary, apart from anything else, to keep out the press. One of the papers – the *Legion*, inevitably, against which he had waged his lonely war – had asked, on the day after Father Vivyan was shot, IS THIS THE MOST EVIL MAN IN BRITAIN?

The dark-haired, intense young woman, Rachel, had wept

when she saw the headline. The Father Superior, who was allowing her to stay in one of the guest houses, said nothing. Later in the day, he pointed her to a passage in one of Father Vivyan's devotional books:

> *The Cross does not make us despair, as Darwin might do. It says, rather, 'The only sort of God worth worshipping would be a God, not of Absolute Justice, but of Absolute Love. You only find out whether such a God could be, not by arguing, but by living the life of Christ; by dying with Him to self, and by rising with Him to glory. Then we have to become the loving gods of creation. We have to animate the pitiless universe with love, endow the impersonal infinite with personhood. Then the human waste, whom Nature casts aside as statistics – a million famine victims here, a thousand killed here by flood or earthquake – becomes the mass of individuals, queuing with rice bowls or sleeping bags at our doors, calling in our hearts for the love of Christ.*

Rachel, the intense young woman, handed the book back to the Superior without a word. Later, writing to thank him for allowing her to be with Father Vivyan to the end, she confided that she was an incurable atheist, to whom such words meant nothing.

The other woman, some ten years older, Mercy Topling, was a very different figure. When the monks discovered who she was – the mother of the dead boy – they had feared that she had come to cause trouble. She was a plump, sensual-looking person, whose face, all the time she sat beside the bedside, was wet with tears. She did not sob. She wept silently. Sometimes, in spite of protests from the Brother Infirmarian, she stroked the brow of the semi-conscious monk. Sometimes, she placed her hand beneath the sheet.

'Oh, Vivyan, Vivyan, we've lost our boy . . . we've lost our darling boy,' she would whimper. Sometimes her hands moved beneath the sheet with the words 'my lovely, lovely man'. None of the monks who had ministered to Father Vivyan discussed the implications of these words at the time. They did not wish to do so. The truth was that Father Vivyan was viewed at best ambivalently by the rest of the community. Though a monk of their order – the Community of the Holy Redeemer – he had hardly spent any time at Kelvedone since joining them. After his initial period of training in the mother-house, he had returned to his beloved Africa, where his life-work had made him famous. Lately, as almost all newspaper readers by now knew, he had returned to Crickleden, to run a parish in south London.

No small community, college, family, monastery takes completely kindly to one of its members becoming a star. Father Vivyan's fame brought lustre to the order, and in this the monks to some degree basked. Most of them, however, had been known to say that 'there are over a hundred and fifty members of the order worldwide, and it is a pity if the only one who ever gets mentioned is Father Vivyan.'

Rachel Pearl, the one whom the Superior thought an intense young woman, realized in retrospect that the scene of Father Vivyan's dying in the monastery had parallels with the death of the *staretz*, Father Zossima, at the beginning of *The Brothers Karamazov*:

Though the late elder had won over many hearts, more by love than by miracles, and had gathered round him a mass of loving adherents, none the less, in fact, rather the more on that account, he had awakened jealousy and so had come to have bitter enemies, secret and open, not only in the monastery, but in the world outside it.

8

Had Father Vivyan been killed by his own pride: by his belief that he could 'save' a dangerous and mentally unstable boy? Had he been killed by his own fanatical political posture, his alliance with those whom the rest of the world saw as terrorists? That was clearly what the old Brigadier felt, the tall, genial man who sat beside the bed, trying to pump Vivyan for information. Or had he been destroyed by the popular press, and in particular by Lennox Mark, the proprietor of the *Legion*? Perhaps by a bit of all these things.

The time of watching beside the bed was seemingly interminable. When the end came, as it happened, there were quite a number there. It was dawn. Old Monty Longmore, Vivyan's brother, knelt beside the bed in an attitude of prayer which would not have been out of place in a medieval altarpiece. Mercy Topling knelt on the other side, holding Vivyan's hand. Rachel Pearl, Brigadier Courtenay and a number of monks stood at the end of the bed. When the whimpering from the body ceased, and with it the breathing, the Superior began to recite the prayer 'Go forth upon thy journey, Christian soul'. There was a moment of intense calm which all present would recollect for the rest of their lives. It was a calm broken, seconds later, by the insistent ringing of the front door-bell.

It was a young novice who opened the door. He saw the Bentley pulled up on the gravel. The paunchy, short figure in a light grey suit smelt of the frankfurter sausage with onions which he had been consuming in the back of his limousine.

'Tell me I'm not too late,' he gasped. 'Tell me I'm not too late. I must see him, I must see him.'

'But . . . there must be no more visitors . . . the Father Superior . . .'

So it was that within minutes of Father Vivyan's soul leaving its body and soaring God alone knew where, to purgatorial shade or celestial bliss, the silence of that religious house was broken. Even in the infirmary, which was at the back of the house and yards away from the front door, they could hear the coarse accents of Lennie Mark shouting, 'Don't you realize – you CUNT – don't you realize who I FUCKING am!'

PART ONE

ONE

There had been no witnesses, but it was easy enough for the police to reconstruct what had happened. Whoever perpetrated the outrages – the attack on the delivery boy, the unlawful entry, the thefts, the threatened assault on Mrs Mark herself – must have been watching the house for several days. They would have seen the same delivery boy, on the same motor-scooter, arrive from the same large Knightsbridge shop at the same front gates on three successive afternoons.

Granville Stoppard did not reckon to operate a takeaway or same-day delivery service; but Mrs Mark was Mrs Mark, and this had been an emergency. Okay, she had agreed on the first day it happened, she was ringing after the Food Hall had closed. Surely that did not stop the fool of a man from getting her a pint of milk. And while he was about it – lobsters. Three lobsters. A dinner party? What the fucking hell had it to do with him if she was giving a dinner party? As it happened, the lobsters were for her husband to eat in the bath before they went out to dinner. Oh, and she had run out of cigarettes.

More to the point, she had run out of servants. So, the first day, and the second, and the third, Granville Stoppard had been on hand to supply Mrs Mark and her household needs. They would not open up the Food Hall after hours for Everyone. But Mrs Mark was Someone. And the manager knew what view would be taken in *The Daily Legion*, *The Sunday Legion* and *Gloss* if the capriciously ordered deliveries were not supplied. No lobsters (whether or not available after the closure of the Food Hall), no semi-skimmed milk, no Dundee cakes and Vacherin cheese ('My husband likes to spread Vacherin on Dundee cake') and it was easy to imagine the damaging publicity which would ensue.

Mary Much, the editor of *Gloss*, would plan the long-term damage: articles in the opinion-forming glossy dismissing Granville Stoppard as the John Lewis of the new millennium, a place for suburban aunties, where the truly chic would not have been seen dead. Meanwhile, in the women's pages of the *Legions*, *Daily* and *Sunday*, articles would remind readers that only has-beens went to Granville Stoppard. The paid gossip columnists – 'Creevey' of the *Sunday*, 'Dr Arbuthnot' of the *Daily* – would bristle with stories of famous people closing their accounts at Granville Stoppard. It was even possible to imagine them commissioning L. P. Watson to write one of his 'outrageous' columns about the venerable old store. The manager would not put it past them to infiltrate reporters from *The Daily Legion*, posing as members of the human race, to enter the shop as customers and engineer situations in which they had been insulted by the lift boy, ripped off at the *parfumerie* or kept waiting inordinately long in Accounts.

Easier by far to send off the required lobsters and milk – at seven p.m. the first day. She had the decency, on following days, to ring slightly earlier with her requirements. On the day that the delivery boy was attacked, she had added a cold chicken to the order at the last minute, two jars of pickled herrings, and not just Dunhill cigarettes. She wanted menthol. No – as well as Dunhill. As well. As well. Did not the fool know English? Menthol as fucking well. She knew that the Food Hall did not stock cigarettes. This she had been told on the first day and the second, but if a motorbike-rider did not have the intelligence to stop at a corner shop and buy forty menthol cigarettes was it any wonder the country had become a fucking laughing-stock in the world? Oh, and bread – they needed bread. What kind of bread? What kind of a question was that? Brioche, sun-dried tomato, pain au chocolat, any of those, anything except fucking wholemeal, which gave her husband the squits.

Ahmet Hussein will not play a large part in our story, though strangely enough, he too had his connection with the world of *The Daily Legion*. His father, Ali Hussein, a newsagent in Crickleden, rose early each morning to slice open the bales which were dumped on his doorstep by the wholesalers' vans. The *Legion* was his biggest seller, and it was the newspaper he read himself. In future, Ahmet – aged eighteen when the attack occurred – would always feel queasy as he watched his father hump the heavy parcels of newspaper and jab with the Stanley knife at the plastic tapes which bound them.

As he was able to tell the police, after he had been treated at the Chelsea and Westminster, Ahmet had parked his Honda City Express (50 cc) beside the kerb in the leafy street, Redgauntlet Road, SW7, somewhere behind the Brompton Oratory. Darkness was falling. It was about four in the afternoon. He took the plastic bags containing lobsters, cold chicken, pain au chocolats, pickled herring and menthol fags from the plastic tub on the back of his moped and approached the twin brick pillars which sustained the ten-foot-high reinforced gates. On the previous days, he had rung the buzzer and spoken into the entryphone. He was just about to do so on this afternoon when an arm came from the shadows behind him and he felt something sharp prick his throat.

It was somewhere in the Brompton Road that a passer-by stooped to find him. Before that, he had run, then staggered through half-lit streets, feeling blood and the capacity for coherent attention drain from him. He passed out in the gutter. They never were able to find his ear, but – though he carried a scar in his throat for life – the wound came nowhere near his jugular. As a nurse remarked in Casualty, he'd been lucky. The doctor who gave evidence to the police said it was almost as if someone had been playing. Whoever manipulated the knife would appear to have shown, not pathological violence so much as heartless frivolity.

TWO

'The first question,' said Lennox Mark, 'is this. *Why is there anything at all?*'

Lionel Watson did not overtly sigh, but he felt a lowering of the spirits. During any meal with the proprietor, there would in all likelihood come a moment when the Eternal Verities were debated.

'You haven't,' added the proprietor, 'finished your steak.'

They had already had the roast of the day (which was lamb) as their starter. Then some potato soup – with extra croutons. Double helpings of smoked salmon. Then Lennox had asked for the steaks. With chips.

Lionel tried to keep up with his paymaster on these occasions but at a certain point his body simply refused to take in any more food. It was not, especially, that he felt sick. That would come later. It was that the colloquialism about feeling full really was true. He believed that if he were at that moment put under anaesthetic and cut open, the surgeon would find a stomach stretched to capacity with potatoes, chewed meat and fish. Something like a queue of the stuff had formed in his oesophagus; every yard of intestine felt as if weighed with it, while beyond the stomach the colon filled with the processed reject.

Just as some women, lunching with Lionel, would know that there would be a point in the meal when a hand would begin its exploratory work beneath tablecloth and skirt-hem, so Lionel himself knew that when he was almost breathless with the proprietor's hospitality, the question of God would be placed on the table, as unwelcome at this juncture as another bowl of spuds.

'May I?' asked Lennox Mark, taking Lionel's cold sirloin and slithering it on to his own plate.

'You would concede,' he insisted, 'that existence itself is fairly mysterious. There doesn't *need* to be anything.'

He cut the steak into manageable mouthfuls, placed the knife sideways on the side of the plate in the American fashion and with his large, pudgy right hand brought a forkful to his lips.

Seated, Lennox Mark had a certain dignity, since his markedly short legs were not in evidence. He wore expansive double-breasted suits of a pale grey suggestive of summer wear or tropical kit, whatever the season. His face was fleshy, but not especially fat. He had a very big head, with a massive jaw. White hair was swept back from an apparently untroubled, anyway unwrinkled, forehead. In the massiveness, even monstrousness, of his skull, the eyes, always seeming slightly sore, as if mild conjunctivitis could not be banished, looked small. His nose was blubbery, and had a suggestion of the later, more syphilitic portraits of Henry VIII. Lionel Watson had more than once pointed out the likeness of their proprietor to a Holbein: it was one of the jokes he shared with Mary Much.

'It depends,' said Lionel, 'what you mean by *need*. Existence is what there is. For many of us that's tautology, but – literally, it goes without saying. You don't need to speculate about whether it is necessary, nor whether it has a cause. We are not looking for explanations.'

Lionel Watson, at fifty-three, was the same age as his proprietor, but in various ways he had weathered less well. There was a tremendous weariness, an ennui, in his face — which was meant by nature to be the face of a thin man. The heaviness around cheek, jowl and chin hung superfluously and reproachfully. He was not a healthy colour — the veins in his cheeks were burst, many of them. His brow was furrowed. He was half bald, and a great quantity of dandruff and scurf fell on to the dark pinstripe which was his habitual wear.

'You would admit,' said Lennox, 'that it would be easier if there wasn't anything at all?'

'How do you mean?'

'Neater.' He spoke with his mouth full, so the word was semi-audible. 'Less bother.'

'To whom?'

'Ah!' said Lennox with a gleam.

The disconcerting thing about these discussions was that they were not random. Lennox Mark, huffing and panting through a thousand luncheons, was in quest of the person who could persuade him that God did not exist. The Hound of Heaven pursued the proprietor of News Incorporated, down the nights and down the days.

Lionel Watson remembered reading a Graham Greene novel in which the hero was in love with a married woman. He believed she had another lover, and he set a detective on her. In fact, she was going to visit a professional atheist to convince herself that there was no God. If she could only convince herself, she would be free to disregard a vow she had made to God that she would stop seeing her lover.

Lennox Mark was fatter — Lionel imagined — than the woman in the book, and it was hard to imagine him having a love affair. Lionel had not fathomed from what moral hook the proprietor would exempt himself if he could embrace total unbelief. They had often, over the cheese, the puddings and the savouries, run round Dostoevsky's contention that if God did not exist, anything would be permitted.

In what sort of moral universe *The Daily Legion* would be permitted, L. P. Watson, its leading columnist, did not like to speculate.

THREE

While Lennox Mark lingered out luncheon at the Savoy Grill with Lionel Watson, his wife, at home, was about to have an afternoon bath – when the front door buzzer interrupted her.

Since the Filipinos had staged their truly unpardonable walk-out four days ago, Martina Mark had run the bath herself. Well, whatever anyone might suppose, she was capable of turning a tap. Half-dressed, she was still an impressive sight after all these years, as half a dozen mirrors attested, while she drifted from bathroom to bedroom and pressed the device on an adjacent landing to answer the peremptory entryphone.

Carefully coppered hair, so skilfully done by Franco of Sloane Street that even the most malicious of women had taken it for genuine chestnut, clustered round that pale, clever face. The eyes had worn their expression of frozen surprise for some years now, rising to positive astonishment after a second lift was deemed advisable by the brilliant Mr Aziz of E. 65th Street. Her lips were frozen in an everlasting scarlet *moue*. The nose was at least a centimetre shorter than it had been during a wretched adolescence and young womanhood. Had the surgeons left that nose in the state in which first Nature, then a brutal man, had shaped it, Martina's face would have told, rather than concealed, its story; one would have read dignity and sorrow rather than the studied pertness, both of cartilage and manner, which was presented. Some years ago, almost imperceptibly, the face had passed through the stage where it might plausibly deceive the short-sighted to one where it made no pretence at reality, as such. Rather, it challenged the observer: so – which would you rather? A woman who let herself *go*? Yes, it's art. So have almost all fashions, whether of coiffeur or couturier, for the previous five centuries been art. It was a hauntingly intelligent mask through which eyes caught an approving glimpse of themselves in a mirror, as all-but-motionless lips said, 'Yes?' into the entryphone.

She was lighting a long American cigarette as she spoke.

Cigarettes, by the way, were no more harmful than crossing the street, as the *Daily* and *Sunday Legions* both reminded readers on a frequent basis. (They made no mention of the extensive tobacco farms owned by Lennox Mark's family in the northern region of Zinariya.) The Puritans who wanted to interfere in people's lives with their bogus statistics and sob stories about Auntie dying of cancer should just SHUT UP. It was the God-given right of every English man and English woman to smoke cigarettes. What else in hell's name had Magna Carta been for? Okay, L. P. Watson went too far in his columns, advocating 'Fags for Kids' in primary schools, but Christ, that man was bloody funny.

'Yup? Yup?' she said impatiently into the device.

When the police interviewed her, they asked why she had not noticed, on the tiny screen identifying callers by a concealed camera, that this was a different delivery boy. She was damned if she was going to explain to a policeman that without contact lenses she could hardly see the fucking screen, let alone make out the smudged little figures on it. Besides, she had learnt early in life not to make too much distinction between one visitor and another.

So, bare-legged and bare-footed, she had said, 'I'll be down' into the receiver. Then she drifted down to open the door.

FOUR

'No money? Whaddya mean, no money? There can't be no money!'

Lennox Mark was shouting. He'd left the Savoy Grill, and L. P. Watson, and was alone in the back of the Bentley, which purred eastward. He eschewed a receiver, using the type of mobile which allowed him to speak aloud without an instrument. It gave him the appearance of a madman talking to himself.

The words were a yelp of despair: they were also his creed, this howled double negative. There couldn't be no money – just as there couldn't be no God. Money had always come from somewhere. Always. If not hard cash, then something more important: the capacity to reassure someone else to part with some of theirs, some punter, banker, some stupid bastard, some sap.

The mobile mumbled back its devastating words. Kurtmeyer at his least helpful.

'But you told me the Scouse deal was in the bag!' yelled Lennox, adding in a whisper, 'In the bag!' because he had suddenly met, in the driving mirror, the eyes of his driver Tom. It was intensely painful, suddenly, that this man, a driver who was paid £14,000 p.a., should have heard those words 'no money', and, with a glimpse, *seen through* the rich man who leaned against the flesh-coloured leather seats in the back of the limo.

'We – that is News Incorporated – never tied up the details . . . Sky . . . Moon . . .'

Kurtmeyer was saying that all the other production companies had a pre-negotiated deal with one of the more prestigious football clubs . . . Arsenal . . . Man U . . .

Scouse TV, which News Incorporated had bought as a shell two years before, had actually no hope of outbidding any of its serious rivals.

'But I bought a fucking football team – Scunthorpe Athleticals . . . You made me go to Scunthorpe, and get myself photographed in the local paper.'

'It's one of the NI titles, boss.'

Kurtmeyer chose Lennox's most vulnerable moments to call him 'boss'. He quietly reminded him that the purchase of Scunthorpe Athleticals had been his own idea, foisted on him by the editor of *The Daily Legion*. Both Spottiswood and Kurtmeyer himself had been against the purchase.

Lennox allowed whole weeks to pass in which the complexities and details of his financial affairs were blurred in his mind. Kurtmeyer or Spottiswood, or their combined genius, usually saw him out of the worst crises. For the past ten days, in spite of their giving no indication that this was the case, he had allowed himself to think that one of the two men would produce a miracle. The money from the Scouse deal – a television franchise which would give them exclusive rights over some of the key FA fixtures – would have compensated some of the horrendous losses at the *Legion*s.

'Another option . . .' Kurtmeyer was saying, 'would be to abolish the *Sunday* as of now – just merge the two titles.'

'Jesus.'

'You'd be saving the salaries of two hundred overpaid fuckers.'

'Okay,' Lennox shouted, 'okay.'

Kurtmeyer said what everyone always said about Blimby, the editor of *The Sunday Legion*.

'Then let's sack Blimby.'

'The drawback,' Kurtmeyer's gentle voice reminded him, 'is that you have yet to announce the sacking of Tony. If you sack the editor of the *Daily* and the editor of the *Sunday* in one week, it might look like panic.'

'I haven't told Tony he's sacked,' said Lennox.

'But you've offered his job to Worledge. You're dining with Worledge next week – no?'

'And Blimby. Christ – maybe we don't need to sack Blimby?'

'But you could tell them at the dinner – about the merger of the titles. Get Worledge to wield the axe – he's a cruel bastard. He'll enjoy the sackings.'

He wanted to yell at Kurtmeyer – It's all right for you, it's not your buggering money that's going down the pan! Such moments, however, brought the dreadful sense of void – it wasn't his money either. There was no money. In the pit of his stomach he had the sense, like the knowledge in childhood that he had angered his old man, that a Reckoning approached. Kurtmeyer was burring and buzzing about printing bills unpaid, overdrafts extended to pay *Legion* salaries, advertising revenues down. Lennox Mark thought not of this or that creditor refusing to wait any longer. Instead he was possessed by a generalized sense of doom.

'Are there really . . .' his voice croaked as he asked it, 'no funds . . . anywhere?'

Pudgy fingers shook as they reached for the emergency comfort-bagel, oozing cream cheese, which he had been balancing on a trouser-knee. It was between fat thumb and stout white forefinger. That swooping emptiness, that horrifying sense of putting his foot on what he had supposed firm ground and finding nothing but air . . . that falling, falling . . .

The bagel was gone in two mouthfuls.

Now, what in hell was he going to eat? The Bentley was wedged in traffic, approaching the Tower of London. They were quarter, maybe half an hour from LenMar House, the penthouse office, the fridge, and the caviar.

'So now – Kurt – are you listening?'

Kurtmeyer was listening as Lennox Mark spoke the hateful truth to the back of his chauffeur's head.

'Incorporated – News Incorporated – the TV company, the fucking football club – all my newspapers – *Gloss*, the magazines – they are all dependent on what we can get out of Africa? From Zinariya, from Bindiga?'

Kurtmeyer seemed to think this a fair assessment of things.

Jesus, what would his old great-grandfather have said, Lennox Mark the First, he who first gouged out the red earth of Kanni-Karkara and opened the copper mines? What would the old patriarch have thought about a Lennox Mark, in the third millennium, going cap in hand to a crooked nigger like Bindiga?

Lennox rapped Tom on the shoulder and said, 'If we pass a food shop – any kind of place – I need something to eat.'

'Of course, sir.'

'Why not sell Scouse while we're at it? Sell Scunthorpe Athleticals?' he bellowed to the air. He knew the answer before Kurtmeyer had given it. Spottiswood had been trying for months to find buyers for the crap TV company and even crapper football club.

Twenty minutes later, LenMar House, all twenty-five storeys of it lit up in the murky Bermondsey afternoon, came into view. Tom had stopped the Bentley outside a takeaway in the Jamaica Road, and bought three meat pies for the boss to chomp during the final leg of the journey. Lennox Mark's mouth, though not for long, was full, as the Bentley swerved into the forecourt, and he could ask, of no one in particular,

'What the fuck?' The smooth progress of the chairman and proprietor of News Incorporated towards the automatic glass doors and the uniformed commissionaire was being impeded by a group of angry demonstrators – a crowd of between fifty and a hundred people. And head and shoulders above the crowd was the tall, scrawny figure of the man whom Lennox saw as his nemesis, his guilty conscience, his visitant from a disapproving God.

FIVE

'Granville.'

That was all he said.

'What's that?'

'Granville. Gottya food. Innit.'

The voice was the parody of rough cockney; but then, so were the voices of a million others in London. It was only when Martina quizzed him again that she became puzzled.

'You mean, you're from Granville Stoppard?'

'That's right, madam.'

This appeared to be spoken by another young man, an officer in the Brigade of Guards, a public schoolboy.

'I'll be right down.'

Martina's suspicions – how did she put it to the police afterwards? – were hardly aroused by the way a delivery boy spoke. She had other things on her mind.

She would lie to the police. She would have to. Yet it was true that, as she drifted downstairs towards the boy, she was not interested in his personality. She had, while running the bath, been concentrating her mind on the newspapers in which she took so much more intelligent, so much better informed, an interest than her husband did.

It need hardly be said that it was her decision to sack Anthony Taylor and put in Worledge as editor of the *Daily*. The little coterie known as Martina's Court made those sort of decisions, while Kurtmeyer – sometimes Spottiswood, sometimes the pair of them – bleated about the boring stuff. Lennie, who owned over forty periodicals, knew hardly any journalists, except those, such as L.P., procured for him by his wife or by Mary Much.

Lennie met everyone, or rather, Everyone: those in his own terminology who were Big Hitters. Yet while meeting Everyone, he knew No One. He had no intimates. This was one of the first things about him which Martina had intuited: the knowledge from the first gave her enormous power. She marched into virgin territory to colonize and plant her flag, rather as his forebears, having the geological flair, and the sheer cheek, to understand the meaning of those red hills in an unclaimed part of West Africa, had proclaimed themselves lords and owners of the mines of Kanni-Karkara.

Through the reinforced iron gates, which she had just opened for the young psychopath, had strode others whose psychopathic tendencies, creatively used, had taken them to triumphant heights: the present Prime Minister, and the one before that; the new Leader of the Opposition, and the two before that; any number of Foreign Secretaries, Chancellors of the Exchequer, ambassadors and peers had trodden the short gravel path between the little row of tubbed bay trees and listened patiently while Lennie and Martina told them what to think about the world. Film stars, television luminaries, foreign heads of state, playwrights – even novelists of a certain type – had trooped in to the fashionable evenings up the very steps now trodden by the youth with his bagful of lobsters.

It was all Lennie's fault anyway – and this, apart from the new editor of *The Daily Legion*, was her other chief concern as she girlishly skipped down the carpeted stairs – that the Filipinos had gone away. By Christ, she had given that fucking agency *hell* about it on the telephone. The bloody woman had had the cheek to say there were *limits*. Lennie had enemies. One needed enemies. This had been one of Martina's most useful discoveries about life. A few enemies here and there served as grappling irons to assist one's ascent up the sheer rock face. Lennie, though, had made enemies pointlessly, just by being a shit. She had forced him to offer a lot of money to that agency, she'd gotten them to sign injunctions the minute the little Filipino shits walked out on them forbidding them to say one word about their experience. Otherwise, it was easy to imagine the headlines in the rival titles. Gone were the days of decency when stories about proprietors were not carried in newspapers owned by rivals. In the scurrilous gossip columns of other rags, and in *Private Eye*, there had already been inaccurate jokes about Lennie's servant troubles.

The world knew — or that part of the world which enjoyed reading shit — about Lennie's uncontrollable rages with drivers, cooks, maids, butlers. The shit-eaters had all read about Lennie picking up the Chinese — Korean, actually, which shows how much you can believe of this total crap — maid by the scruff of the neck and holding her out of a first-storey window; and similarly garbled stories had appeared of the coffee pot that got hurled at the little Eye-tie's head, or the scrambled eggs deliberately thrown, then heeled into the sheepskin rug. He did *not*, however, shout, 'Now suck it' — he'd said, '*Lick it.*' But these bastards got nothing right. Of course, they never stayed long, these agency servants. Never before, though, had all five walked out en masse and without notice.

It was obviously to punish the Marks — Martina wasn't a fucking idiot — that the agency had not supplied replacements at once. If the Queen's staff all left Buckingham Palace, if the German Embassy found itself without a single person to wash a teacup, then the agency would have temps round there and —

aber dalli. Why did this fucking agency not send someone at once to empty Martina's kitchen trash-can, which was starting to stink, make a meal, tidy a bed? Because they were making a point. So tonight's dinner – which was to have been a buffet for thirty – was now a smaller sit-down affair at Diana's, the Court's favourite restaurant. The couple promised by the agency would not start for another week.

Martina thought of these things, and not of the personality, or appearance, of a delivery boy bringing a few supplies, relief to the house of siege. So – no – afterwards – to the police – she could not give any very accurate vision of what he looked like.

As she fumbled with the key which opened the last Chubb lock on the front door, she asked, 'You remembered the cigarettes?'

The visitor was six feet or more, a gangling boy in a loose black blouson and enormous trainers. Of his features, a balaclava helmet hid all but his eyes, which were smoky-grey.

'What cigarettes is vat ven?'

The cockney had returned, replacing the Guards officer. It was a flattened, slightly anxious voice. He walked past her carrying the plastic sacks. That was her first intimation that something was amiss: he did not, as the real delivery boy had done on the two previous afternoons, put the bags down by the front door, and present a chit for her to sign before scampering off again into the dark. This boy stepped inside and slammed the door shut with the swivel of an elbow.

'You're on your own, right?'

The throaty fear was all the more evident in his tone now, but she also sensed, with his fear, an excitement.

She was so taken aback by the impertinence of his question that she answered it.

'What's that to you?'

'Quick. Money.'

'But the shopping is always charged to our account. You're not expecting me to pay on delivery?'

'Money.' More insistent.

'What is this? If you think you're getting a tip simply for doing your job . . .'

It was then that she saw the Stanley knife in his hand. Its blade was already moist with blood. In his grey-blue eyes she read a combination of emotions which she had seen so often before in her visitors in the old days: triumph and terror.

SIX

Towering above the other demonstrators, the bony skull and grey hair of Father Vivyan Chell were unmistakable. Though Lennox Mark had seen the priest on television and sometimes in the newspapers, it was nearly forty years since he had seen him in the flesh. The short hair, which had been dark in those days and was now silvery, was brushed back from the brow in the identical military manner. The high cheekbones and hawk-like nose both seemed more pronounced. He was even thinner, like some alarming bird of prey in his black monk's habit and cloak. Yet, despite the peculiar rig, he looked, as he had always looked, more like a brigadier than a padre.

In figurative and actual terms, Chell stood head and shoulders above the other demonstrators. These displays were a regular occurrence outside LenMar House. Some of the bleeding-heart newspapers had begun to notice the situation in Zinariya. One of the lefty rags had a cock-and-bull story about the Kanni-Karkara mines: it raked up the old sob-stuff about cruelties in the days of white ownership, the supposed responsibility of Britain to intervene because Britons – that is, great-grandfather Mark – had first thought to extract copper from the mountains of southern Zinariya, the setting up of the West African Mining Organization after independence, the alleged abuses continuing after African control, the stories of corruption, of Western businesses forming unwholesome alliances with the present régime. Time was, the Western busybodies who presumed to interest themselves in these complicated affairs had supported General Bindiga because he was supposedly a Marxist-Leninist. Then, the earnest old hags in ankle-socks and the corduroyed college lecturers discovered that, like Lenin, Bindiga was not afraid to kill people who got in his way. Then, some of these bearded cretins put two and two together and realized that Lennox Mark's business interests continued in West Africa while he built up a media empire in Europe. So, when they wanted to make themselves feel smug and warm inside and they had momentarily forgotten the plight of the poor little foxes being hunted by dogs, or the Tibetans being persecuted by the Chinese, or prisoners of conscience languishing in Turkey, the professional minders of other people's business would come and demonstrate at LenMar House. Lennox did not reckon much to their chances of interesting the great British public in their moral preoccupations. The great British public would weep buckets over the plight of poor little foxy-woxy, but it frankly couldn't give a shit about some tribesman in northern Zinariya having his balls shot off by one of Bindiga's guerrillas, nor about the so-called slave-labour employed on the cocoa farms in those regions. Jesus, most English people did not know the difference between West and East Africa, wouldn't be able to locate a big country like Kenya on a map, let alone point to Zinariya.

Father Vivyan was something rather different. When Lennox Mark was still a little child, the story of Father Vivyan had gripped the public imagination: the gallant young army officer who went to Lugardia, as it then was, in the last days of colonialism, became embroiled in the civil war, and then, as a result of a profound spiritual experience, renounced the soldier's life, and joined a religious order, and lived among the poorest of the poor. He wrote a spiritual autobiography which was an international best-seller. Vivyan Chell had become the voice of the African oppressed, persuading the missionary order which he had joined – the Community of the Holy Redeemer – to identify itself completely with, first, the Zinariyan struggle for independence, later with the most radical of its political figures. Chell's voice and influence were heard beyond the confines of Zinariya. He visited South Africa and Rhodesia, from both of which he was expelled, and he formed friendships with several African heads of state. He had become himself a symbol of the European capacity to remake itself, in penitence, and assist a new and independent Africa on its way: a symbol, more generally, of Christianity's surviving power to challenge the values of this world.

Lennox Mark was a boy of fifteen when he read Father Vivyan's *Lift Up Your Eyes!* The book came as an extraordinary revelation. It had never before occurred to him to question his father's and grandfather's right to be rich and powerful. Their 'ownership' of farms, tobacco, cocoa, of copper mines, of large houses, of stocks and shares, seemed quite natural, just as the servitude of the black house-servants and farm-workers was simply a given, the way things were.

At Queen Alexandra College, the bogus public school which he and the other white boys attended in its well-mown grounds outside Chamberlainstown (now Mararraba), the life of the huge majority of Zinariyan citizens was unseen, unimagined. Lennox edited the school magazine. Somewhat to his surprise, the headmaster acceded to his request to go down to the slums of Louisetown, the shanty district of Mararraba, which huddled near his grandfather's copper mines, and interview the famous Christian troublemaker who lived there.

Within the first five minutes of stepping from that dusty old bus, the pudgy schoolboy Lennox had known that he was to have his entire vision of the world changed. He had seen and smelt the life of the poor for the first time. And above the rags and the dust and the squalor of the red mud-houses soared the brick church, built with their own hands by the Community of the Holy Redeemer, a building which, since the coming of Vivyan Chell, already symbolized in the eyes of many Africans the hope of freedom.

Vivyan Chell was fifteen years older than Lennox, so on this encounter he was little more than thirty. So many times, in the intervening decades, Lennox had closed his eyes and seen that street in Kanni-Karkara, a gust of wind blowing a dust-cloud along the road; shoeless children running, clutching the skirts of this enormously tall, gaunt Englishman, who wore a white cassock like the Pope's.

And here he was again, forty years on, in Bermondsey, bellowing, 'Justice for Zinariya!' The crowd, which was about half African, took up the cry, and then Chell began to chant '*Alkawari!*' – the name of the opposition party, whose leader, Professor Galwanga ('The Zinariyan Gandhi'), was regularly lampooned in the *Legion* newspapers.

'*Alkawari!*' drawled Vivyan Chell's unmistakably aristocratic tones. '*Alkawari! Alkawari!*'

That adolescent encounter beneath the great brooding brick church of the Holy Redeemer was something which Lennox Mark had been trying to forget for his entire life. He had fallen completely under the priest's spell. The headmaster had given him permission, for the purposes of collecting information for the magazine article, to stay one night in Kanni-Karkara. In the event, for nearly four weeks the boy stayed and worked in the mission in the shanty towns. He had slept on a straw pallet, as the priests did. He had risen earlier than dawn to pray with them, and to wait for God in the darkness and silence of the

African night. Then, before first light, he had served Father
Vivyan's mass, an unforgettable, highly charged spiritual experience, and the day would begin, the exhausting and unfolding
life of a poor parish in an African industrial suburb.

The monks helped to run a hospital, many of the patients
young men, wheezing and dying from emphysema or pneu-
moconiosis – now, Lennox had heard, forty years on, full of AIDS
patients. There were two schools, run largely by volunteers.
There were the makeshift houses where mineworkers lived with
their families; all these hovels were tiny and none had proper
sanitation. There was no flush lavatory, as far as Lennox ever
discovered, in the whole of the township; the monks, like the
mineworkers, squatted over earthen holes when the need came.

'You have been given a great gift,' Vivyan Chell had told
him. Lennox could still remember the bony fingers of the priest
on his own fleshy shoulders, and the penetration of those iron-
grey, terrifying eyes looking into his own.

'Christ sent you here.'

In spite of Vivyan's short back and sides, there was something about the monk's long face which recalled certain images
of Jesus, those on the Turin shroud, for example, or of El
Greco, which made it possible, when he spoke, to believe that
you were actually in the presence of the Word Made Flesh.

'You did not come here by chance. Christ sent you. You
must go and tell your father what you have seen. Your father
is not a bad man. He is something very like a bad man, though –
and that is, a rich one. It is easier for a camel to pass through the
eye of a needle than for a rich man to enter the Kingdom and
know God. You want your father to know God? Well, it is for
his sake that you must go and tell him what you have seen here.
Tell him what these mines are doing to these people . . .'

This speech so fired the adolescent Lennox with a vision of

Christ's Kingdom that he did pluck up the courage and tell the old man. Not long afterwards, he found himself on a plane crossing the Atlantic. He did work experience in a merchant bank on Wall Street, stayed with some cousins at the Hamptons in the summer, lost his virginity, and entered MIT, slightly young, the following fall. He had never seen Vivyan Chell from that day to this, though he had followed the monk's career, his political agitations, his return to England.

Forty years on, Lennox Mark did not know whether he still possessed a conscience. He sometimes wondered if Martina's function in his life, the secret of his dependence upon her, was her capacity to numb his few remaining tendencies towards heart, towards feelings, towards what the sentimentalists called decency. He could not resist the superstition, it had been with him ever since his first encounter with the priest in Africa, that Vivyan Chell could reawaken all the bleeding-heart nonsense. This was because, try as he did to convince himself otherwise, Lennox Mark believed that the universe was indeed run along lines where moral laws were as invariable as those of physics. God was always there behind the curtains.

'Get that crowd cleared away before I get out of the car,' Lennox told Tom.

'*Alkawari!*'

The old ladies and corduroyed lecturers had taken up the African cry.

'*Alkawari! Alkawari!*'

'Get rid, I say, get rid . . .'

The commissionaires were emerging from the automatically opened glass doors of the building, but it was hard to see what two bottle-nosed old pensioners in white peaked caps could do against a crowd of a hundred, nor why the police need be summoned to disperse an entirely peaceful assembly.

Lennox Mark did not mean to get out of the car until the crowd had gone away. He certainly did not mean to address them. No sooner, however, did he hiss at Tom to get rid of the demo than he found himself opening the door of the Bentley and facing them.

'I assure you . . .' he heard himself calling to them, 'there is absolutely no . . . If you have a grievance . . . I am more than happy to discuss . . .'

Corduroy, beards, black faces, ankle-socks, like waves of the Red Sea falling back before the rod of Moses, filed against the plate glass of the building, leaving alone Father Vivyan Chell, as if before that modernist construction of the late 1980s there had been translated, as in some pious fable, the carved statue of a saint from the stone niche of a Gothic cathedral, standing there upright, gaunt and tall.

'Then, Lennox,' said the monk, 'I should think that after forty years there would be things to discuss – wouldn't you?'

'Father Vivyan.'

He stood there, the silver-haired proprietor of that great enterprise, once more a gauche, overweight teenager.

'I don't know quite . . . what it is you want . . . what . . .'

'You could invite me in,' said the monk, 'for a glass of whisky.'

SEVEN

Martina's steadiness surprised even herself. It visibly surprised the boy. She could see the eyes peering from the balaclava for signs of distress. Even her voice betrayed only the hint of fear, its tremolo disguised by the habitual foreign lilt.

She knew that he had stepped into a world where he would find nothing familiar, and she traded on this weakness. Even her un-Englishness was chic, sophisticated. He had probably never heard a voice like hers unless he had hung round the bigger tourist hotels in London.

She returned his stare and just above the eyes saw a few centimetres of honey-brown skin.

'What do you want?' she asked.

'Money,' he repeated huskily. 'Jewels.'

A long-fingered hand, also honey-brown, reached for the diamond in her right lobe. It was a large stone for so small an ear, and it was a stud, fixed by a small screw. From the way in which he held the ear, as a clumsy child might grab a flower on a delicate stem, it seemed possible that he was deciding between two quick methods for removal, either tearing the ear from her head with his fingers or doing a slice with the bloodstained Stanley knife.

'Let me help you,' her voice said.

Early in life, she had learnt to detach herself utterly from what was happening physically with a man. Only thus had she retained her sanity. Those early days of unhappiness served her in good stead now.

'Don't try nuffink.'

It was the parody voice again.

EIGHT

'You don't drink?' asked the monk, who had taken a swig of the single malt offered him.

'I'll stick to Seven-Up – no, I don't drink. Are you sure you don't want . . .'

Lennox leaned forward, offering the plate of turkey sandwiches, and seemed relieved when, with the wave of a languid sacerdotal hand (almost as if he were blessing them) Father Vivyan rejected the chance to share.

'I'll stick to your excellent whisky. Well, you are a busy man, Lennie, up here in your eyrie, looking down on the kingdoms of the world and the glories thereof.'

They were at the very top of LenMar House, and outside three vast plate-glass windows London stretched, a shimmering drizzle of street lamps and neon. Behind the sleek coiffure of Lennox could be seen the distant Tower of London and beyond it the floodlit dome of St Paul's. From the window to his right the river wound seaward past the twinkling tower of Canary Wharf. Behind the monk's head was the sprawl of south London – Streatham, Balham, East Dulwich, Sydenham, all indistinguishable in the murk.

'You didn't answer my letters, Lennie.'

'I didn't know how to.'

'Do you remember meeting little Joshua Bindiga when you spent that month with us at the Redeemer?'

'Of course.'

How much did the monk know about Lennox Mark and Bindiga? Lennox had expected, after the 'demonstration' in the forecourt, that the old man would take the chance to preach a sermon, but he was simply sitting there, with a huge slug of whisky, staring at Lennox with a slightly whimsical smile.

Of course he fucking well remembered meeting Bindiga as a schoolboy. That was the extraordinary fact about his month with the monks in Louisetown township: it could have made him a Christian saint − as it was, it gave him the crucial piece of good fortune which had enabled him to move from being a comfortably rich businessman to being a hitter, big indeed.

All manner of rumours circulated about how Lennox arrived from Africa, apparently from nowhere, and was able to buy *The Daily Legion* and the *Sunday*, the glossy magazine *Gloss*, a host of smaller publications including the surprisingly profitable *The Seedsman*, as well as a handful of local newspapers in England and Scotland. The prosaic truth was not (as rumour wished) that Lennox had a connection with the Mafia: nor that he had been adopted as the toy of a Texan heiress with a fetish for fat boys; nor that he had struck oil in the South China Sea. (All these stories found credence where two or three London journalists were gathered, and alcohol consumed.)

The Lennox Mark money came from copper: it was as simple as that: but he would not have held on to it, nor would the old man have been able to die on the family tobacco farm (when so many other Europeans were driven off their confiscated land), had he not befriended the General. In the civil war of '81, which ended in a victory for Bindiga, the control of the copper mines at Kanni-Karkara had been the single most important factor in Zinariya's economy. The prodigious, princely wealth of Lennox's grandfather, and of the great-grandfather who had first sunk the shafts and sent African miners down into the red rock of the southern province during the 1890s – this vast wealth had evaporated. The old man, Lennox's father, inherited none of the business acumen of his paternal line. The vagaries of the world stock markets before the Second World War ate into his huge capital. After the war, gin and frequent divorce made him sink from the princely class to being merely a man of means, Lennox's various stepmothers managing to run up colossal debts doing nothing in particular in Monte Carlo, Nice, the Greek islands and London. His holdings in WAMO made him a key player when the future of the copper-mining industry was in question, but he had no subtlety, no foresight, no practical intelligence. By the end of the civil war, the old man was on a bottle and a half of Gordon's each day and the fourth (or was it the fifth?) wife, as leathery and as foul-mouthed as her predecessors. Marooned on their farm in the northern province, they inveighed against the 'fucking commie' and against Lennox for 'siding with the niggers' against his own kind.

This had been Lennie's real stroke of luck, genius, or both. He openly sided with the man who seemed to be intent on the destruction of all the European settlers. The last time Lennox had met that final stepmother, her stringy brown arm had stretched forth for the umpteenth cigarette of the afternoon and she had gluggled more poison from her tumbler.

'Bin-digger' – she evidently found it stylish to mispronounce the General's name – 'is a fucking commie.' False teeth clinked against ice-cubes in her glass. 'Red, nigger, *bastard* – right? And that white bastard – yes – *that* one' – a long scarlet talon jabbed from the end of the nicotine-orange index finger – 'that father of yours has done nothing – NOTHING – to stop it.'

The old man's tendency to marry women who abused him, usually verbally, sometimes physically, had been one of Lennox Mark's reasons for delaying marriage. The old man had spent his life in various pleasure spots which gave no obvious pleasure, numbing out their irrational angry whinnies by matching glass for glass their appetite for the sauce. Cirrhosis, which was an inevitability, was deemed by the final shrew a 'relief'. Many a vsitor to the hotel bar in Eastbourne would hear, before her own liver gave out, how she'd got out of Lugardia in time; how it would have broken Jim's heart if he'd lived to see what the niggers had done to his beloved Africa.

Lennox Mark's own attitude had always been different. He was happy to see Lugardia die and Zinariya be born. He was not a defeatist. He saw in Bindiga a kindred spirit, a fellow scrambler up ladders, sailor near winds, cutter of corners.

'You came in those days – no white boy from Queen Alexandra College came among us: but you came. For that month you came and lived with the fathers. You shat in a hole like an African. You taught me rugby. You remember? Drop goals?'

The General had grinned. This had been almost his first word to Lennox when he granted him an audience, after the revolution. The General's advances in life had begun in that missionary school: his decisions to pass exams and get to Sandhurst had been made possible by the chance of being taught by the former Major Chell MC – now Father Vivyan. This was some feat – of push by Bindiga, of stringpulling by Chell. The strict requirement of the Zinariyan army was that soldiers be five foot six inches or above. The General was five foot four. This Napoleonic truth about him could be seen as a paradigm for all his further defiance of the fates. He knew how to take chances, when to change tack. All his advisers, LSE-trained, urged upon him the out-and-out nationalization of the mines in '81. One last meeting at the Presidential Palace in Chamberlainstown (as it still was then) had clinched the matter.

'Take over those mines, General, and all your international investors will pull out: *tomorrow*.'

Lennox knew that this was probably false, but he said it without a quaver in his voice. It might after all have been true.

'Keep WAMO up and running, with its Dutch and American mining engineers, its British–Zinariyan management team working in partnership . . . and you'll be able to fund a new Zinariya. Nationalize WAMO and the socialist experiment will never have a chance.'

So the bargain was struck and the General never had reason to regret the friendship he had forged with Lennox Mark.

As if Father Vivyan read the mind of Lennox Mark, and had himself been tracing the history of an African tragedy, interwoven with their personal destinies, as they sat in silence, the monk said:

'We both supported Bindiga at the beginning.'

'You more enthusiastically than I,' said Lennox.

'Look,' said the monk, putting down his whisky glass and clasping his hands together. 'You have read my letters to you. And you know why those people out there are staging a small protest. Last week the editor of the only liberal paper in Mararraba—'

'The ex-editor of a paper which went kaput,' corrected Lennox.

'The paper was *suppressed*.'

'It closed because no one bought it – because that kind of liberal horse-shit might go down very well in Hampstead but it means nothing in Africa.'

'Hasirye was *hanged*,' said the monk calmly. 'Before that, he was almost certainly tortured. You are the only Western newspaper proprietor with a first-hand knowledge of the situation in Zinariya. I am asking you why the death of Hasirye in a prison cell in Mararraba was not reported *at all* in *The Daily Legion*. On the day he died, your newspaper had the divorce of a young American film star on its front page.'

Lennox ate a sandwich to give himself time. He wanted to see whether the old monk still possessed any power over him: power to disconcert, to worry, to undermine.

Little by little, since Lennox's first meeting with Joshua Bindiga twenty years ago, his dependence on the tyrant had increased. The Zinariyan government now effectively owned the mines. Lennox had never withdrawn his support. He supported Bindiga's policy of sacking the British managers, then supported the policy of deporting all non-African engineers. When the first major disaster occurred – the collapse of the shafts which killed two hundred workers, some as young as twelve, Lennox Mark went in person to the chairman of Reuters News Agency and promised him, on his oath, that the story was a pack of lies put about by Bindiga's political enemies. By the time Lennox Mark had acquired newspapers he was able to give enthusiastic support to Bindiga when he abolished the opposition. When the Alkawari! party was made illegal, L. P. Watson wrote a learned analysis of how 'opposition' in the Zinariyan context was really sedition; and he asserted that 'the Zinariyan Gandhi', Professor Galwanga, was really a crypto-terrorist. The *Legions* never missed an opportunity to dub the Zinariyan opposition in exile a nutcase. Dangerous. A traitor to his country.

'Can there ever be a justification for printing what isn't true?' asked Father Chell. 'What you know to be untrue?'

The silence was broken only by the squelch of mayo on iceberg as the proprietor chomped on his sandwich.

'Lennie,' the monk's voice had sunk to the low murmur with which he spoke to women in his confessional, 'Lennie! You know what that man is doing to Zinariya – to your country.

You and I know more than ever gets reported in the papers here – the massacres, the tortures . . . You know better than I, God knows, what a sheer bloody mess he's making of the economy.'

Lennox's voice was husky in reply.

'You supported him once. You educated him. You put him where he is.'

'Don't you think I have that on my conscience – every hour of every day?'

'So my newspapers have to change policy to satisfy your conscience?'

'Lennie, you know that's an absurd remark.'

'The President expelled you from Zinariya because you were plotting against him.'

'That is also an absurd assertion – as you know.'

Now the bony jaw of Vivyan Chell jutted angrily.

'The Happy Band of Pilgrims – wasn't that its name? I remember it when I worked with you in Louisetown. In those days it was a youth club – kids came and learnt football. In the last decade or so' – Lennie pronounced the word 'decade' in the American manner. There was a very faint twitching of disgust at this in the other man's lips – 'you've been teaching them some other things, those boys. The Happy Band have learnt bomb-making, commando tactics, sabotage . . .'

'So, Bindiga's Gestapo have been keeping you well supplied with propaganda.'

'I notice you don't deny making those kids into criminals.' Lennox Mark grinned. The spell was not quite broken for him; he still felt the monk's power to hypnotize him, but it was much weaker than he had feared. Once the words had begun, they flowed. He told Vivyan Chell that the disruptions in the mines, the industrial unrest, the small explosions in one of the shafts, the home-made bomb found on a public train pulling into Bindiga Central, Mararraba – all these had been traced to Happy Band activists.

'My job is to be a priest,' said Chell with a sort of eruptive energy. He boomed the words. 'And let me tell you, while you mouth all this rubbish, if an assassin killed Bindiga now, this minute – if they held a knife to his throat' – he mimicked slicing movements against his own throat with an index finger – 'they'd be doing God's work.'

NINE

In Lennox Mark's house, five miles westward in Knightsbridge, his wife Martina reached to her right lobe and cupped the long honey-brown fingers in her own small white hand.

He now spoke to her in Checkpoint Charlie officer's English.

'Don't try anything. Okay?'

The voice reminded her of the courtesy, and above all, of the cleanliness of her clients who were British army officers. That was after the move to Frankfurt. They were good payers, and sometimes they'd take you for a meal afterwards. Their shyness on arrival did not last once they were naked. She associated that army voice with the combination of social diffidence and urgent, thrusting action. It was while watching their white public school arses go up and down that she had formed to herself a notion of the world they came from. She literally lay back and thought of England, seeing quite clearly, like something vouchsafed in a vision, that this land would give her a new life. She had moved to London in '66.

'You can have my ear-rings,' she said to the boy.

'They're diamonds. Right?'

'Mm.'

'Right?' Her failure to give full verbal authentication of the genuineness of the rocks made him yank one ear roughly. For a moment she imagined that he would remove the ear-rings by force, without unscrewing the studs. One thing was for sure. She was not going to give him the satisfaction of showing fear.

She was not going to plead with him. Instantly, the situation recalled those many experiences of being manhandled, the worst days when she worked the Russian sector in East Berlin. She had known sometimes that this was what the bastards needed, to hear her whimper, cry, beg. Then they'd be close to getting off and she could be left in peace. Sometimes, though, they wanted more than just to pull her hair, to wrench her shoulders, to rape her. They really needed, some of them, to cause damage: cuts, stitches, bruised or misshapen lips. She remembered a businessman in Frankfurt: no action, until he'd pummelled her face with his fists; then the shy, shrivelled little cock burst into life as she wept and bled. (The nose job, anyway the first, had been a surgical necessity.)

If those years taught one lesson it was that the more fear you showed, the more excited the bastards became.

'Here – you can have them.'

She drew another hand up to his. She actually held his fingers for a moment. After she had unscrewed first one, then the other ear-ring, she held them out and looked into his eyes.

She sensed he was a good-looking boy under the hood, the cagoule, the jeans; but, oh no – he wasn't going to have that.

There was a burglar alarm button by the front door. Upstairs, beside her bed, there was a 'panic button' which rang in the nearest police station without making any noise in the house. She knew that if he suspected her of raising an alarm, then he would panic – and in fear he might become more violent. She found herself, even while she plotted to press one button or the other, liking his strange eyes. And those hands. Those hands were very beautiful.

'Rings,' he said, seizing her hand roughly. 'Now, the rings.'

She wore the plain gold ring which had been placed on her hand ten years before by Lennox Mark. There was also the large engagement ring clustered with diamonds and sapphires.

'If you pull like that, they're not going to come off.'

'I'll suck them.'

'No!'

It was a command from her lips, not an imprecation. He disobeyed it, pulled his woollen mask down beneath his chin and lifted her small hand to his lips. She closed her eyes while he slurped and she felt her wedding ring disappear into his mouth. The insistent sucking sensation was not unpleasant. She tried, as the diamond ring slipped off too, not to like those lips.

'Where's the safe?'

'I don't have a safe.'

'The safe with the other jewels. Necklaces. Crowns.'

'I don't have a crown.'

'A house like this?' He stared about incredulously at the expanse of polished parquet, the marbled pillars; the enormous Empire looking-glass, the bust of Pitt the Elder on its vast black plinth. 'In a house like this, there's gotta be a safe.'

The voice had changed yet again; the English officer had seemingly been replaced by any south London youth playing truant from a remand home. (For, yes, she was coming to the realization that he was very young: a boy, not a man. There was something . . . she could not explain it to herself . . . something about the voice which was not right.)

'Up!'

He was waving the knife at her now, directing her to the staircase.

She began to speak very loudly and very distinctly.

'So you want to go upstairs and steal my valuables – my belongings.'

'Where you from, then?'

'How do you mean?'

'That's not English, how you talk.'

'I'm from Switzerland!'

She almost shouted this.

'I'll give you any valuables you ask for, but I promise you, there's nothing valuable UP HERE!'

In spite of her best resolutions, she could feel her voice, as she projected it, cracking with fear.

'Don't make me drag you, lady. Don't make me cut your cunt.'

Obediently, she led him up the stairs.

TEN

'Wasn't Jesus a pacifist?' Lennox asked.

'But Saint Peter cut off the ear of the High Priest,' said Father Vivyan approvingly. 'I'm a soldier of Christ, Lennie. We've been waiting two thousand years for His Kingdom. I'm an old man. There isn't much time left to me.'

'So you'd sanction wars? Terrorism? I don't believe I'm hearing this from you.'

'I'm not sanctioning anything. I'm telling you what is inevitable. If you have injustice on the scale it exists in Zinariya, people will protest, they'll *fight*, man!'

'And what about this country? What do you think of dear old Blighty since your return?'

'You're wrong about my being expelled from Zinariya – though I'm sure I'd never get a visa to return. Not since I became friends with Gabriel.'

'Galwanga the Loon!'

'I was invited back to England by the bishop. St Mary's Crickleden has long associations with CHR. Our founder, Bishop Guiseley, was vicar there before he went off to Kelvedone with four friends to start the community. St Mary's was a big Victorian parish – what they used to call a slum parish – and the bishop thought I might be able to get back some of that energy we seem to have lost in the church. It's a problem area . . .'

'Largely thanks to your black friends.'

'Lennie, that's not worthy of you.'

'I know what Crickleden's like – for God's sake, it's only three miles south of here. Those sink estates down there – they're muggers' universities, schools of rape. I suppose you think they're making a violent protest against all the injustices in English society?'

'In part – yes, that is what I think.'

'Jesus!'

Lennox kicked out his short legs, at the end of which were pale blue mohair socks and very small, highly polished Italian loafers.

'As you say,' said the monk, 'Jesus! When I left this country, the best part of forty years ago, England still seemed to have a soul. It had pulled together after the war and committed itself to a welfare system . . .'

'Jesus, it was the welfare system which drained this fucking country of its soul – can't you *see* that? The dependency culture destroyed any sense of having to do something for yourself. Do you think those violent, criminal bastards in your parish would have *time* to be muggers if they had ever been *made to work*?'

'Made? By whom? When I came home after forty years away, I found an England I hardly recognized. It seems to have no values at all. An African friend came to stay with me in the vicarage when I'd been there a few months. I tried to explain to him what an "old folks' home" was. This Zinariyan friend knew that in a few very sad cases there might be old people in any society who had outlived every member of the family and needed residential care. But he simply could not grasp the notion that British families wait until their parents or grandparents are in greatest frailty and need and then discard them, put them with a lot of other old people to be cared for by someone else. In this man's village in Zinariya—'

'And why was he here if it's so marvellous in his village? To sponge off the British welfare state . . . ?'

'He was here because his wife had been raped, then killed by government troops. His house was burnt down. His permission to work as a lecturer in Mararraba was revoked.'

'Lovely African community spirit.'

'He stayed here a few months only. Now he lectures at the university in Lagos. I envy him. I have become an African. You seem to have lost your African-ness, Lennie. You can't really think much of England? It's entirely Americanized – hamburger joints in Crickleden High Road, KFC, rowdy violent films, expensive drugs and cheap music the normal entertainment. This isn't the England Clem Attlee and Nye Bevan set out to build.'

'In Clem Attlee's socialist paradise you'd be lucky to get a margarine sandwich. You're a snob, Father! KFC or Burger King give poor people cheap food they enjoy. You want them to be at a church social playing ping-pong; they'd rather go to a disco, see a movie – what's wrong with that?'

'England's lost its way – lost its values, lost its identity.'

'Too many immigrants – but again, you'd favour that.'

'I don't know – maybe I would, maybe I wouldn't. I want Britain to be the decent, humane place it was in my boyhood. When I was a child we were fighting a world war against racialists, we were welcoming refugees – now everyone is so mean-spirited, so unwelcoming. The church is inward-looking, squabbling about gay bishops when it should be preaching the Gospel. But what about you, Lennie? You still believe in the Gospel – I know you do.'

Lennox looked sheepishly at his Gucci loafers.

'I believe,' he murmured.

'Then, for God's sake, stop supporting Bindiga!'

The monk knew that this was the end of the interview. He stood, an enormous beanpole of black cloth.

'I'll show you out, Father.'

They made a strange pair, descending in the glass lift through twenty storeys.

'And all this is yours, Lennie?' The monk shook his head at the greed of it. Lennox tried not to notice the reproof; took the enquiry at its face value; replied in a tone, almost, of detachment, speaking either to himself or to some imagined guest, rather than to a man who had expressed such blanket disapproval of him and all his works.

'These floors are let out. They are the offices of ZA — what was Lugardair . . .'

'And do you own Zinariyan Airways, Lennie?'

'They're owned by the state. You know that. With some private investment obviously. This is WAMO.' He nodded at another wall of plate glass, more yards of fitted blue carpet tiles, stenographers staring patiently at VDUs.

'I spit on your Mining Organization, your mines, your greed . . .'

'Then these floors' — as the lift whooshed downwards, but not fast enough now for Lennox in his embarrassment — 'are devoted to some of my magazine titles. *Gloss* has its own premises in Mayfair, but here we've got *The Seedsman*, some motorcycle mags, a Formula One racing magazine which is doing rather well . . .'

'And where do you produce the iniquitous newspapers?'

'We're passing Floor Six — that's the boardroom for the two *Legions* — now on Floor Five that's the legal department and the reference library — Floor Three — if you like we could look round the offices of one of the *Legions*?'

'No, thank you.'

'That's *The Sunday Legion*!'

He pointed to the large open-plan office, taking in at a glance the wisdom of Kurtmeyer and Spottiswood's advice: if the same editorial team could be used to produce *both* titles . . . Each head, glimpsed through the plate glass squinting at its computer screen, was costing him thirty, forty grand a year.

'And then we have the *Daily* . . .'

An identical office – same toneless grey laminated desks, each with its grey computer, same carpet tiles, same strip lighting. There was more activity here, however, and a larger staff. The priest could make out employees bustling, even running about.

'And then we have Classified Ads and the whole advertising department: the whole lifeblood of a newspaper. These guys' – he indicated through the windows the workers in the advertising department – 'actually make all the money which these fuckers' – he jabbed with his finger in the direction of the editorial offices – 'spend.'

The monk closed his mouth like a rat trap and actually closed his eyes when the lift came to a halt. They emerged on to the large marbly landing known as the Atrium. A London plane was planted there and stretched its branches upwards to about half the height of the building. A tall cascade splashed on to a goldfish pond.

'This is where we part, Father.'

'So it would appear. You haven't heard the last of me, Lennie.'

Suddenly, this tall Englishman with bony grey socks sticking out beneath his black skirt was not simply ridiculous, but extremely annoying to Lennox, and he burst out, 'Just who the *fuck* do you think you are?'

'Goodbye, Lennie,' said Father Chell.

Lennox watched the silver head disappearing down the silver escalator, disturbed by his own loss of control.

'Don't let that man in this building again!' he shouted at the commissionaire.

The man was assuring him that he wouldn't when beside him the receptionist leaned forward from her desk. 'Mr Mark – an important telephone call from your wife . . .'

'I'll take it upstairs!'

He could not stop shouting.

'She says it's urgent, Mr Mark. There's been a—'

'Upstairs – didn't you *hear* me?'

ELEVEN

While Martina Mark in Knightsbridge was telephoning her husband with her version of that afternoon's events, and while Lennox Mark in Bermondsey was yelling in response at the plate glass of his penthouse and while the lights of London became visible out in the darkness beyond, two women in Crickleden were entering the gates of a large comprehensive school for an interview with a psychiatric social worker.

Lily d'Abo was a neatly dressed woman in her early sixties. She wore a crimson coat, trimmed at the collar with soft cotton velvet. It looked, and was, a coat which had been well cared for for over thirty years. She wore a small black felt hat which, covered with a multitude of tiny drops of moisture, glistened in the evening drizzle, as did the short curly white hair which protruded from its rim. From the hem of her coat could be seen two stick-like legs descending into shoes which proclaimed that like their owner, they were sensible. Other metaphors were suggested by the brown lace-ups which, like the coat, dated from her early nursing days in London: they were feet planted firmly on the ground, they were her own and she stood on them; whichever was the best, she was going to put it forward.

Her daughter, Mercy Topling, was four inches taller and at first sight excited an altogether different set of assumptions. If Lily d'Abo's appearance suggested immediately a person who could restore order and common sense to a troubled scene, Mercy looked in the merriest sense as if trouble of a frivolous sort could easily ensue at her arrival. Someone had once told her that she had the figure of a woman on a saucy seaside postcard. She was not sure that such postcards even existed any more in these serious times, but she had taken the observation as the compliment intended. She dressed to please – though in the periods of gloom when her husband Trevor was beyond pleasing, it was hard to be specific as for whom exactly the pleasure was intended. The truth probably was: everyone. This evening, a short skirt of black leather revealed massive, shapely calves swooping to the slenderest of ankles, a gold ankle bracelet and patent leather shoes. Her generous bottom had many admirers, both at the office – she worked for the planning department of the local council in a clerical capacity – and in the streets of Streatham when she did the shopping. The bright cerise woolly jumper emphasized large breasts. The rain caught their mounds, so that she seemed to carry before her two great fluffy globes adorned with dewy sequins beneath the open PVC mac which only partially served to keep out the weather.

Compared with the two women who had come to meet him, in a bleak interview room on the first floor of the school, Kevin Currey – the psychiatric social worker on Peter d'Abo's case – had made markedly little effort with his appearance. He was the same age as Mercy, thirty-eight, but already (balding head, bad teeth) he was going to seed. While the two women, like the great majority of civilized humanity throughout history, had taken trouble, every day of their adult lives, to clean and to adorn themselves in readiness for what that day would bring, Kevin Currey belonged to that large number now alive on the planet who had never seemingly possessed this instinct.

With his lack of dress sense went an absence of any sense of occasion, formality, or order – either in individual lives or in society. Though his work exposed him daily to those whose lives were malfunctioning, he felt no calling to restore individual lives, let alone society itself, to order or workability. He had never, in fact, thought through the implications of his work at all. He took each case as it came: seemed, when he met the parents, to be gormless, if kindly by the lights he had presumably acquired at a college. When one interview was over – on to the next. When one problem had been investigated – chewed upon, aired or acknowledged – on to the next.

Kevin Currey did his share of listening while teachers or parents wept. He did his share of attending juvenile courts, sitting in on police interviews as a 'responsible adult' when his young clients were in trouble, and he was reasonably conscientious at visiting homes, or – where the case had been moved from a domestic situation – remand homes, detention centres or prisons. He had never once thought through the state of things to the possibility of a solution, either for individual dilemmas or for more generalized social ills.

In his job, he arrived in a mess, to find more mess, and he left it a mess. His function was to stir up the mess a little and if possible give short-term consolations, offer friendship. Hence, perhaps, the appropriateness of his clothes – the trainers, the white though not markedly clean socks, the Levi's against which his expanded belly protruded a flabby protest, the sweatshirt emblazoned with the name of an American university which he had never visited.

'So – Mercy, Lily! Great, great to see you!'

With sweeping arm movements – suggestive of an all-inclusive attitude to the world, perhaps disappointment that it was just the three of them and that the two women had not brought a party of friends to discuss Peter's case – he indicated two plastic stacking chairs with the munificent air of one proffering luxury.

Mercy, who had been loyal to Trevor since her wedding day, was by nature a coquette. When she looked at a man the thought of sex was never absent – what he'd be like naked, what sort of lover he'd be. Not only did Kevin Currey score low. Something wasn't there. This disconcerted her from the beginning, but it did not stop an automatic habit of flirting, of flashing her very round, and very slightly squinting eyes.

'Thank you!' She injected into two words the exaggerated impression that Kevin or the stacking chair made her feel a real woman, and her smile, gap-toothed and brought on by a mixture of nerves and natural good-heartedness, seemed like a come-on.

Her mother's exaggerated 'Tanks' and her complaint about 'Dee rain it nairver stop, I'm telling you' seemed to be offered as a correction to Mercy's nonsense. Lily spoke normally with the rhythmic lilt of her native Nassau, but in real life her accent was simply that, a lilt like the gentle movement of a fishing boat bobbing on a light breeze through Exuma Sound, not like a white person parodying a West Indian bus conductress on some television sitcom. Mercy had noticed over the years that in situations of seriousness, especially those which threatened the family, her mother exaggerated her West Indian voice. It was the equivalent of an old cat arching her back and standing her fur on end, this underlining the difference between themselves and Kevin.

Mercy was born in Crickleden and she spoke with the voice of an intelligent south Londoner who had left school at sixteen and worked in minor clerical jobs for twenty-two years. She often imitated her mother's voice and those of older Caribbean friends, just as she enjoyed imitating the African voices of colleagues or friends from church. In the face of teachers, doctors or officialdom, Lily d'Abo's 'dats' and 'disses' were a retreat behind the Bahamian stockade.

'So!' Kevin with both hands patted the file, perhaps for good luck, and opened it. He drew out some papers, at the top of which was written the name PETER D'ABO.

'First things first. How's it been at your end?'

Lily looked at Mercy. It was an example of her maddening capacity to combine quite opposite qualities – bossiness and diffidence; tolerance and bigotry: hardness and kindness. She meant, by a pause, to convey a politesse. Peter was Mercy's son. Mercy should be allowed to speak first.

'No – you go first, Mum.'

'Well,' said Lily in her sing-sing, 'he's been helpful round the flat. He's a clean boy. He helps me wid arl de cleanin' and tidyin' – he polished the bath till it shone, I'm tellin' you. And he's bin better gettin' up in the marnins now, and I give him a proper breakfast mind you, an amlet, a plate of fruit – mango, pineapple, none of your tinned.'

Mercy, who loved, revered and loathed her mother, felt all this was torture. She knew that if Lily were not volunteering to shoulder the burden of Peter at this very difficult time, it would be impossible to cope. To leave Peter at home with her husband Trevor was not a possibility – nor could their sons, Bradley and Lucius, be expected to cope with it.

'None of dem carnflakes!' Lily's aggressiveness on the subject might have been appropriate if Kevin had been a member of the Kellogg family, but, for all his faults, the social worker could not be held responsible for the Western world's deplorable breakfasting habits.

'No one can say he go to school without sometin inside his belly.'

Kevin consulted his file with pursed lips.

Mercy knew what this meant. Peter – of course he was – was still playing truant. Mercy understood her mother's elaborate games with life. The boring recitation of the boy's nutritious breakfasts was not an exercise in faux-naiveté for its own sake. She put it forward like a counter in a game. Peter was *their boy*. She did not want her lips to be the first to speak of his continued truancy. So she made herself seem slightly idiotic, in order to get something out of the social worker.

'The trouble is,' said Kevin Currey on cue, 'no one can say he's going to school at all. He leaves you in the mornings, but he's not turning up for register.'

'What you sayin', den?'

'Mum!' – for this last bit of demotic was carrying self-parody too far.

'I'm saying that sometimes he goes to school, but much, much more often he doesn't.'

'He will be sixteen in August.'

'I agree he's nearly old enough to leave school . . .'

'And he's a big boy,' said Mercy proudly.

'But you see, it isn't just truancy, is it? There have been these incidents in the school.'

'I do think it's hard,' said Mercy, 'just because Peter's going through a difficult phase, that, when something goes wrong, everyone blames him. Mrs Rajagopalachari admitted that the fire in the laboratory was a complete accident.'

'She did,' said Kevin. 'Even though she was locked in, after the fire started. If it hadn't been for Mr Gallagher hearing her screams through the window . . . But we went over all that some weeks ago now. Water under the bridge.'

'But don't you *see*,' said Mercy, 'you just assumed.'

Kevin shrugged, stretched out jeans and trainers at an angle of forty-five degrees.

'Assuming isn't what I'm about at all.'

'But this was what was happening at home, right – this is just how this whole thing got started. Things went wrong, and we all started blaming Peter. Okay, so he's not perfect, no one is. But we weren't wanting to face up to all the other things – my husband's illness, the tensions that's causing, tensions between me and my other two sons . . . And Peter kept saying, "Mum you're always *picking* on me . . . Trevor, he does nothing except pick on me . . ." And, like, I was getting angry with him all the time and trying to keep the peace between him and Trevor, him and the other boys . . . But he had a point, Peter. When things went wrong, we all blamed him. And that's why it seemed a good thing for him to go and live with Lily, move to a new school . . . And it really, really *is* getting better, it *must*.'

'But then,' said Kevin, 'the behaviour patterns have started up again.'

There was no need for the three of them – Lily, Mercy, Kevin – to rehearse the list of offences. Peter d'Abo weighed on his mother's heart. Within weeks at the new school, similar complaints were being made. Once again, as at Streatham, Peter had gathered around him a gang of admiring and much younger boys who followed him slavishly. In order to prove themselves tough enough to belong to the group, these little thugs performed minor acts of vandalism, the theft of motor-scooters being a favourite. Windows had been smashed on a regular basis. Then there was the craze for eggs and spray paint which had been aimed at the front doors and windows of all the houses down one side of the road adjoining the school.

Much more disturbing had been the capacity of this Crickleden gang to victimize or persecute teachers, or other grown-ups, apparently selected at random, but often with deadly effect. A few weeks before – it had all been front-page news in *The Daily Legion* – an old-age pensioner in Crickleden had reached the point where he could bear the taunts and abuse no longer. Whenever he teetered out of his small flat to buy a newspaper or toddled towards the pub, a group of these young boys would be waiting for him. They kept up a vigil from early morning until late each night, sometimes just two or three of them, sometimes as many as ten. At first, the persecutions were of a trivial, even a comic, kind. They would walk behind him blowing rhythmic raspberry noises and holding their noses. Satisfyingly, this old man, Bill Hacklewit, would turn and shake his walking stick at them.

Little by little, the boys increased their levels of offensiveness, sometimes threatening old Bill with words, sometimes mouthing dreadful insults about his wife, who had died about a year previous. No one knew how these boys had managed to learn his wife's name. Since being widowed Bill Hacklewit had been in a state of periodic depression. During one such day of uncontrollable sadness he came home to find the words EDNA CUNT sprayed in paint on his little Fiesta. These words were then shouted through his letter-box for several hours.

One day, when a group of the boys had been crouching on the landing outside his flat, one of them with a firecracker in his hand, ignited and ready to post through the letter-box, Bill had opened the door in a rage and run at them, brandishing an old service revolver. It was then that Peter d'Abo, who happened to have been present at this dramatic moment, immediately used his mobile phone to summon the police.

It had never been proven that Peter was the ringleader of this troublesome group. His own story was that he was worried that these boys, some of them as young as eleven, were getting up to mischief, but not realizing that by so doing they were endangering their lives. He said that he lived with his grandmother on an adjoining estate in Crickleden and they were in fear of various unpleasant right-wing groups who had posted literature through their door. He claimed to have reason to believe that Bill Hacklewit had links with one of these extremist organizations, and had seen him posting British National Party leaflets through the doors of black people: hence his anxiety for the boys' safety. No one ever corroborated this claim. He also asserted that he had often heard Mr Hacklewit utter violent or threatening abuse to the children, and that this abuse was always of a racist tinge.

When the police apprehended Bill Hacklewit, he did not deny shouting at the children, 'Get out of here, you little black bastards! God, if I had my way, I'd shoot little niggers like you!'

The police had decided to press charges. The revolver, which contained no ammunition, was confiscated. Bill Hacklewit, who, as readers of *The Daily Legion* were reminded, had served in the Desert Rats and fought against the army of Rommel, was found hanging from the light-fitting in his one-bedroomed council flat on the morning that he was due to appear at Crickleden Magistrates' Court to answer charges of illegally possessing a firearm, and behaviour likely to incite racial hatred and a breach of the peace. His neck was held tight by the new plastic flex. On his brown acrylic cardigan he had pinned his service medals.

Mercy Topling did not merely suspect, she intuitively *knew*, that her son Peter had in some way orchestrated the persecution of old Mr Hacklewit. She knew, because she had watched her own cheerful, well-adjusted husband Trevor lose his job and his will to live, even lose his capacity to get up in the mornings, through Peter's unique gifts of unkindness, and manipulativeness.

Peter was no ordinary disruptive or disturbed adolescent boy. That was why they'd made the decision – for Mercy, a heartbroken one – for him to leave her house and go and live for a time with his grandmother. That was why these two stoical and level-headed women had consented, though with some scepticism, to the involvement of a psychiatric social worker. At the same time her deepest maternal instincts wanted only to protect the boy. She wanted to ask Kevin Currey now, as she had all but destroyed her marriage by asking Trevor and Lucius and Brad, Why pick on Peter – why not just let him be the way he is?

If Kevin, with his slob's clothes, was an accepter of human incurability, Mercy was eternally an optimist. Her birth, her youthful love affairs, her work, her marriage, her every working day had been the recitation of a joyous Yes to Life. She believed in Redemption. She thought that Peter, who had so many extraordinary qualities (not simply good looks, but charm and pleasant manners and a sense of humour), could be made better. Sometimes she thought that this might come about through prayer. (Lily had re-introduced him to churchgoing; he had even served mass – a fact which filled Mercy with a number of complicated feelings – for Father Vivyan.) Sometimes, however, Lily's excessive piety made the daughter place her faith in more modern varieties of the occult. Hence, Kevin Currey, and the endless burrowing back into the past, in the belief that there might be some twist of the darkened corridor where they might stop, and locate the precise moment where the life of her son had begun to go wrong. At other times, her optimistic heart shunned both prayer and psychoanalysis in favour of a gentler hope that time alone could cure many things, especially the character deficiencies of the young.

That was why, quite often, she could not concentrate as Kevin pressed embarrassed palms against his plastic files and tried not to meet her gaze.

'I'm not at this stage using the word "schizophrenic" . . . frankly, it doesn't matter what words we use . . .'

'How d'you mean, it doesn't matter?' Only in her defensive

mood Lily said, 'doesn't martyr'. 'Course it martyr. Are you saying he's not in his right mind, that he has evil demons?'

'Mum!'

'We must face the poss— Look, let's be frank . . . We haven't, formally, as such, *assessed* Peter . . . but what I'd like . . . maybe explore with you the possibility of . . . a psychiatrist.'

Trying to focus on the enormity of what was being said, Mercy tremblingly spoke. 'It was a mistake – is that what you're saying now – to talk to him about his father?'

'You remember what I told you, Mister Kevin,' said Lily aggressively.

'Mum, don't.'

'Don't come Mum don'ting me, Mercy. I tink it were a big mistake to go telling him. Dats what I say, Mister Kevin, when you say to Mercy that the boy was disturbed because he was trying to get in touch with his real father . . .'

'Often,' Kevin's toneless intonation, in such marked contrast to the bobbing lilt and sway of Lily's Exuma Sound smack, was the repetition of a mantra; the delivery of a sacred doctrine more than the utterance of an opinion, 'as a lad . . .'

Mercy bridled – it was 'lad', the way he said 'lad': something was giving her the creeps about this man.

'. . . as a lad moves through puberty and his body starts to show all these very visible signs of manhood, he starts fighting with his dad. And if the lad's adopted or he doesn't know who his dad is, he's looking around for him – and the aggression, the testosterone's building up inside him . . . And some of that aggression which should have been directed into rows with Dad gets repressed. It doesn't know where to go – and that's alarming for the lad.'

'Mercy,' said Lily, 'she never told *me* who the father of that chile was. She told *no one*. And you wait until this boy, this chile's going rarng . . .'

'Oh, Mum.'

'No, listen. We're all in this – me, I'm his grandmother, I live with him. Mercy – she's his mother. You. Mister Kevin, you know nutten at ahl about this. You jus' said out of some textbook: disruptive chile, so he wants to know his real father. Fifteen year, nearly sixteen year he live in this world without knowing. No one knew, 'cept Mercy. The minute she came back from the doctor and knew she was with chile, she shut up like a clam, dis one. Dat's a woman's right. No one's not saying she didn't do everything right by dat boy. He's always been different. From a little chile. You remember Joan of Arc. Saint Joan.'

'Yes, Mum . . .'

Mercy had hoped her mother would keep her Saint Joan memories to herself. At this rate not only Peter but the whole family was going to end up sectioned under the Mental Health Act.

'Joan?' Kevin's expression conveyed total ignorance. He looked on the verge of asking whether she lived locally.

Mercy explained.

'I've always read a lot to my children,' said Mercy. 'Peter loved being read to, especially in the days when it was just him and me. And when he was a little kid, we had these books – you gave them to us, didn't you, Mum?'

'I read dem to Mercy when she was a little girl – *A Chile's Book of Saints* – and den dere was *A Chile's Book of French*, *Italian*, all de different contries and so on and so fort.'

'Well' – Mercy took up the tale – 'the story Peter wanted over and over again was the story of Joan of Arc. If you didn't read it to him there'd be a tantrum.'

Lily laughed at the recollection.

'One day I bought a Noddy story for him to read and oh with what strong arms dat little man hurled dat book across the room – I don't want Noddy I want Saint Joan, Saint Joan – really screaming and yelling it, man.'

'And then,' said Mercy, 'you know the story of Saint Joan?'

'I didn't know you were all Catholics . . .'

'Who said nussin about *Roman* Catholics,' said Lily, adding to the confusion. 'Isn't the High Chorch good enough for you then?'

Kevin shrugged idly and murmured, 'I don't do saints.'

'Joan of Arc,' said Mercy, amazed at the ignorance. 'She was a medieval peasant in France, she fought against the English – they burnt her as a witch – anyhow, when she was a little kid, she'd hear these voices, angels and saints *talking to her*.'

'De angels talk to me, Mam, dat what he say,' burst in Lily, thereby spoiling Mercy's punchline.

'The angels *speak* to me,' Mercy corrected. 'He's always spoken well. I've never had to correct him, like I correct Brad and Lucius all the time. Peter's always been in a world of his own. Like, he'd want to *be* lots of different people. I know all kids are like that, you take them to a film and they come out saying they're the Lion King or whatever. But with Peter, it was always more than that. He really became another person. Like he was . . . I dunno . . . like he'd been taken over. By some other personality altogether.'

'Another personality,' said Kevin, who had begun to make copious notes.

'Frankly, I don't think sticking labels on people helps all that much,' said Mercy. 'I've met people who've been described as a schizophrenic and they're nothing like Peter. Look, he's a perfectly decent, clever, good-looking boy – much of the time.

But other times, he's someone else – and then he's someone else again. He's gifted. A lot of gifted people are like this.'

'But I hadn't finished,' said Lily, 'telling you, Mister Kevin, man, about this psychiatric approach to the problem, and I'm a nurse. I've got my head screwed on the right way round, man. And you keep on at my daughter she must tell him, she must tell him who his father is! And I'm telling you, man, it's too much to saddle a boy with dat knowledge when he has dese other problems. Why now? He didn't need to know now. If his father was someone from round here, no offence, someone like yourself, a teacher, a clerk, okay, so we'd all live with that. Believe me, man, no one ever screwed my head round the wrong way but it would have it spinning like a top to be told *my* daddy was a big, famous billionaire, owning *De Daily Legion* and all dat, while I was living wid my old granny in a council flat in Crickleden and grumbles about how to buy me a new pair of Reeboks. Do you see what I'm saying? Do you see what you did?'

'Maybe we should've spent a little more time thinking through the implications,' said Kevin.

'But you told me,' said Mercy, 'tell him who his dad was – give him the chance to get in touch with his inner self.'

'And what a dad – eh?' – it was Kevin's first smile of the interview; a particularly revolting smile in Mercy's eyes, since it seemed unduly impressed by the notion of having on his book the case of a son, albeit illegitimate, of Lennox Mark.

TWELVE

The first thing Lennox Mark noticed, when he entered the kitchen at 16 Redgauntlet Road, was the smell. When, desperate with hunger, he had padded into the room at breakfast time, the pong had been dreadful: an overflowing rubbish bin, beside which an open black plastic bin bag told its own tale, with its used teabags, its Seven-Up tins by the score, its eggshells, sandwich wrappers, pizza boxes and foil containers to which the remains of curry were encrusted. The sink had been full of unwashed cups and mugs and the draining-board had been piled with unemptied ashtrays. Now, the odours of decomposition had been replaced by the stringent atmospheric effects of bleach and that faintly nauseating smell which in the fantasies of detergent-manufacturers bears kinship with a lemon. Metal, enamel, wood and laminated surfaces shone spotlessly. The chrome garbage-can glowed, as if simonized. Who had done this? Surely the old woman, who had never performed a menial task since living there, had not donned rubber gloves and set to? And it beggared belief that Martina herself was personally responsible. On the very rare occasions he had seen her wash up a single cup and saucer it had appeared to enrage her that she had been demeaned into such a chore, and violently obscene expletives spat themselves from her lips for as long as it took to wipe a saucer, and remove a few grains from a cup with a much-cherished, creamed and manicured finger.

Certainly, both Martina and her mother defied their national

stereotype. Though they wanted the house spotlessly clean –
and this might be considered a Teutonic virtue – they both
preferred to suffer smells and dirt than exert any effort themselves with Dyson, J-cloth or squidgy-squeezy.

The only explanation, therefore, for the immaculate state of
the house was that Martina had somehow worked her magic on
the agency after all, and that a cleaner (at least) had been found.

This thought, the knowledge that the five long days without
domestic service were at an end, filled Lennox with such relief
that it almost neutralized his fear and anxiety about the break-
in – Martina's calm but clearly troubled voice on the telephone;
the agonizingly slow drive to Knightsbridge through evening
snarl; the police cars and blue lights in Redgauntlet Road; the
tapes to prevent him or anyone else walking on the pavement by
the gate, and the bloodstains; the forensic experts scouring gates,
gravel, steps, hall, stairs, every inch, it would seem, of house
and garden. When he had negotiated entrance to his own house,
by the servants' flat in the basement area, the place seemed
awash with police. He hoped and believed the cameramen were
engaged in forensic not journalistic processes.

'Olga?' he asked his wife when he came into the kitchen.
Having smelt the clean smell, his next consciousness was of his
mother-in-law's absence. This was something you could not
rely upon. In some moods, Martina agreed that Frau Fax should
keep to her own quarters on the second storey. Catch Martina
on a bad day, however, and she would ask furiously why she
should be compelled to treat her mother as a guilty secret.
Then, however grand the dinner or party, there was only one
thing for it, and Frau Fax, whose appearance was quite a shock
to those who had never seen it before, would be brought down,
and placed at table next to the distinguished ambassador or
government minister. Martina had relished as much as Lennox

had loathed her mother telling the Chancellor of the Exchequer that he was a 'fucking fool' for some fiscal measure over which he had no control.

'Mummy is tired, she's lying down,' said Martina; but Lennox could tell from the shocked expressions of the young officers in the kitchen that they had set eyes on Frau Fax.

There were three police, who introduced themselves to Lennox Mark. It had evidently been communicated to them by some higher authority who Lennox was. Equally clearly it was not a name which rang bells in any of their heads. Martina claimed afterwards to read into their attitude a spirit of truculent egalitarianism, a suggestion, particularly by the young female officer in mufti – a CID sergeant – that if you lived in such an opulent style you were asking to be murdered.

To Lennox, the young woman seemed as polite as could be hoped for, from a person whose generation had never been taught manners.

'It's just a bit of luck yer wife got the saliva of one of the men on her fingers,' observed this officer. 'It's hopefully going to make a DNA identification that much easier.'

The police were clearly puzzled, and when the evidence of the original delivery boy, Ahmet Hussein, was collated with that of Mrs Mark and Frau Fax, it was harder still to build up an accurate picture of what had happened. Whereas Ahmet believed he had been attacked by one black youth wielding a knife, Mrs Mark was insistent that it was a twenty-five-year-old white man with a moustache who had invaded her property, accompanied minutes later by a short tubby man, possibly Asian. Frau Fax believed both men to be older, perhaps in their thirties, and she asserted as something beyond doubt that they were Turks. When pressed on the matter, she said she had heard them talking Turkish, or a language which sounded very much like it.

So the police were on the look-out for three men – perhaps two Turks with an African, or Afro-Caribbean accomplice.

The other puzzling thing was the timing of the intrusion. Ahmet Hussein was found unconscious in the Brompton Road at 4.50 by a passer-by. It was estimated that he had been attacked about quarter of an hour or twenty minutes earlier. Yet the alarm button at 16 Redgauntlet Road was not pressed until ten past six, at the very moment the police were calling at the house anyway, following the trail of Ahmet's blood.

It was unfortunate that some of the areas which might have yielded forensic evidence had been cleaned. Brasso'd door-knobs gleamed and banisters shimmered with Pledge. Mrs Mark's bathroom, which had been chaos when Lennox half glimpsed it that morning, was now scintillant – the scrumpled bathmats stowed in a laundry basket, clean new towels folded on the heated rail. It seemed more like a bathroom in an hotel than a private home.

'I'm sorry – we have no staff this week and I was doing some housework when these men burst in.'

That was Martina Mark's explanation.

'And you'd say the men were in the house ten minutes?'

'Less, less,' Frau Fax had interrupted with her thick accent. 'As soon as I pressed ze buzzer zey were gone like birds.'

This, the CID thought, was truer than she could know, since they had left no muddy footprints on the carpets in spite of the dank drizzle of the evening – no fingerprints anywhere.

Lennox – lordly, benign, concerned – found his manner with the three police officers becoming more conciliatory. (When they'd finally gone, Martina privately asked him what need there had been to stick his tongue up their arses.) The more puzzling their story and the clearer it became that Martina had lied to them, the more ingratiating he became, offering them glasses of Seven-Up, Jaffa Cakes, sausage rolls, biscuits, all refused.

'Obviously now we've got statements from your wife and,' the CID officer looked at the floor, 'her mother,' she swallowed before continuing, 'we'll proceed with our investigations. The great thing is, your wife had the foresight not to wash her hands, so as I say, hopefully the DNA tests should show up something.'

Lennox could see that his attempts to be amiable with the police were irritating Martina, and that he would pay for this later with a tongue-lashing. His chief emotion, in spite of being puzzled – and in spite of dreading her sarcasms – was relief. Lennox Mark loved his wife, he was in love with her. The thought of her being in danger had reduced him to utter misery. In the long traffic-jams in which so unbearably the Bentley was delayed on his way there, Lennox had contemplated the possibility that Martina might have been badly injured, even killed. He had realized that the death or non-existence of this woman whom, presumably, everyone else on the planet regarded as a monster of rudeness and selfishness would be unendurable. The grief would be terrible, beyond bearing.

He therefore spoke truly when he said to the police, 'The main thing is that my wife is safe – safe and well.'

He put his arm around Martina as he spoke and she managed to move the sewn smile into an approximation of a grin as she rested her beautiful copper locks against his pale-grey lapels.

THIRTEEN

Mercy felt uneasy in her mind about discussing with Kevin Currey *her past*. In quite different ways and for quite different reasons, it was hard to revisit those days with her mother. The past was simply that: *passed*. She had momentarily believed Kevin: thought that by giving Peter's unknown dad a name, she would help the boy to become more rooted and settled. She had blurted out the name, almost at random, for a number of reasons which seemed good at the time: one reason was that Lennox was certainly the richest of the candidates, and if Peter were to have a father, why not choose one who would provide some good material compensations? Another reason was that she wanted to spare Lily the knowledge of the truth: namely that as a young woman, her daughter had been very promiscuous. Thirdly, more specifically, there was one possible father whose identity Mercy wanted at all costs to keep secret: the knowledge would break him, destroy Lily. So, the words 'Lennox Mark' had come most readily to her lips when asked to supply Peter with a dad: especially when she recollected how both she and Lennox had behaved at the time of her pregnancy becoming known. She had been resolute in her ungraspingness. Vengefulness was no part of her open nature. But Justice was another thing and if money might help Peter, was there not a case for calling in the chips?

Now, Kevin was telling her that maybe it had not been such a good idea after all, telling her son the name, or a name, of his father.

'It's not a question of being judgemental . . .'

That was one of the words in the armoury of Kevin's claptrap. Mercy wondered how it could be a question of anything else. We make judgements all the time. Mercy, as the only daughter, and for much of her childhood the only companion, of Lily d'Abo, had grown up in an atmosphere of judgements. Lily judged everything and everyone, finding almost all wanting: ward sisters, doctors, greengrocers, hairdressers, teachers. (Only in the case of priests did she suspend disapproval.) As she sat beside her radio or TV set, Lily would sound as if the newsreaders, weather-forecasters, actors in soaps, presenters of natural history documentaries were all performing a series of auditions: that their future in broadcasting was contingent on her approval.

'You'll have to speak more distinctly if you're going to get me listening to you mumbling away at the news,' she would admonish Richard Baker.

To the man from the Met Office – with many a chuckle – 'Call that a tie to tell me the weather in!'

Similarly, just as the cast of the TV soaps would be constantly talked over, corrected, interrupted by Lily as she watched, so the morals of her neighbours in Crickleden were under constant review and surveillance.

'There she goes, off to the Baptist church, and that's a heresy for a start!' Laughter. 'But I ask you, what's the point in setting yourself up as an elder of the Baptist church and leaving your dustbins in that kind of a state? That's what I'd like to know. She swears blind she did not steal our dustbin lid – but how come our dustbin lid disappears one night and hers appears the next morning? Answer me!'

Of another neighbour, a clerk in British Rail who commuted each day to Clapham, 'He'd be dog-whipped if we had fairness in this world. Just look at him now, walking down to the High Road! It's disgusting. Forgiveness of sins? No, excuse me. Let Almighty *God* forgive that man's sins if He has a mind, but there are some sins no woman should be expected to put up with.'

These were the daily, the repeated judgements of Lily. Mercy grew up with them constantly sounding in her ears.

'Look at that one' — as she moved aside the lace curtains for a better view. 'Look at that hemline! Why not put up a red light bulb in her bedroom and have done with it? Her husband's a fool to put up with that.'

As Mercy herself grew up and flowered, Lily's censures were perpetual. Mercy learned to live with them, and she also learned almost by a necessary survival instinct how to absorb and believe the value-judgements while also ignoring them for the most part in her own life. Naturally, with just two women sharing a small flat, there were repeated spats in which Lily declared that she would not leave the house, come shopping, go to a cinema with a daughter wearing *that* or with her hair, lips, nails, ears, shoes or neckline in *that* condition. Lily seemed eternally to disapprove, but beneath the surface quarrels there existed friendship between the two of them. Lily did allow Mercy to have boyfriends. She seemed to recognize that in her early teens, her daughter had blossomed into a beautiful young woman who was overpoweringly attractive to boys and men.

Lily went back to nursing, first part-time, then full-time, as Mercy flowered. The mother could not be the daughter's policewoman. Between them, there had existed a fiction that Mercy, however many admirers she might have had, was still a virgin. When the two went to church together each Sunday, Mercy still approached the altar to receive Holy Communion. Mercy did not feel shy with God about this, though she sometimes felt guilty about the deliberate deception of her mother.

To God, she'd said, 'You gave me this body. What did you expect me to do with it? Wrap it up in cellophane until I met Mr Right? Then why didn't you create men who treated women a bit better? Eh? Answer me that, Lord God! Or am I meant to wait until I fall in love? Oh – puh-lease!'

He'd seemed to take it on the chin, her candour. Not so many people believed in Him at all these days. Maybe He couldn't be so choosy about who His friends were. Maybe once upon a time He could say He'd only be friends with those who offered the right sacrifices, or said the right prayers, but now He had to put up with a few sinners to believe in Him. Mercy cherished in secret the reverent hope that God might be earthier than Lily and the Puritans imagined. Supposing the Indians were right, with all their erotic deities? Suppose God had given us sexual appetites because He actually liked the idea of us enjoying them?

That had been Mercy's uninhibited decision, made some time during her teens. She'd never since allowed much of a conflict in her mind between sex and religion, though she continued to make examinations of conscience when she said her prayers. In her teens, she still sometimes followed her mother's custom of going to confession: but if she did so, she'd confess to being greedy, or to minor acts of dishonesty, or to malicious talk about her friends. If she'd been clubbing, though, and the night had ended up, as in ideal circumstances it would, between the legs of a man she'd fancied, she wasn't going to give the priest cheap thrills by telling him about that.

Nevertheless, as she and her mother went to church together and she joined Lily kneeling at the altar, she knew that she was deliberately sending a misleading signal to her mother. Mercy knew that Lily was the old-fashioned type of Anglo-Catholic who thought that if you were in a state of mortal sin, you had to go to confession; otherwise, when you next knelt to receive the bread and the wine, you would be eating and drinking your own damnation. That was what Lily had learnt from old Father Richardson, who had prepared her for confirmation in Nassau, and it was what she believed still.

If Lily had so much as French-kissed a man, she would have been off to confession before she dared show her face at mass again. Not that such a thing was imaginable. Mercy's dad had done a runner when she was still a little girl. She had grown up without him – seeing him at first occasionally. Then never. (He went back to the Bahamas when she was six.) She had never especially felt the absence in her life and wondered whether the psychiatrists had exaggerated the necessity of belonging to a two-parent household. After all, during most periods of history, children grew up when men were away at war, or working all day long. They survived.

When Lily was left, she formed no new partnership. Over thirty years later, she was still a handsome woman. Never in her whole life could Mercy remember her mother responding to the attentions of a man. If flirtation or condescension (both manifestations of the same attitude of mind) were offered, Lily, normally a polite and warm-hearted person, would be glacial. A curled lip and a sniff were all she had ever offered in response to male attempts at charm, whether from smoothy hospital-doctors, vicars or neighbours.

To such a mother, seventeen Christmases ago, it had not been easy to break the news that she was pregnant.

'You aren't going to midnight mass in that skirt! Kneel down in that and the people behind you will see – everything.'

Or – next morning when they were dressing up, before spending the day in Lambeth with some cousins – 'This flat smells like a courtesan's boudoir . . . What's that scent you've got on? . . . You're not wearing those shoes?'

Even by that Christmas Day, Mercy knew. The period was two weeks late; but she let another month pass, realizing that she would by then be eight, nine weeks gone. Then, quite suddenly one morning before she left for work, she had blurted it out.

'It's a freezing cold day and you think that strip of leather skirt's going to keep out the cold? You'll get chilled in the kidneys. What's it supposed to be – Puss in Boots outfit?'

(Lily was incapable of innuendo.)

'Mum, I'm pregnant.'

There'd been the longest silence in the history of the universe, in fact lasting about forty seconds.

They were washing up in that flat in Crickleden where her mum still lived and where Peter had now taken refuge.

Lily was four inches shorter than Mercy, even in stockinged feet. When the mother was wearing fluffy bedroom slippers, and the daughter was wearing big high-heeled boots, the difference in height was more like seven inches. They had stared deep into one another's eyes and for one bleak, deep second, Mercy had feared that Lily would smack her face.

'Come here!' said Lily.

Somehow, in spite of the disparity between their heights, she had felt her cheeks being squeezed vehemently against Lily's, and she was enfolded in her mother's arms. It was the warmest, and the most accepting of embraces.

Mercy realized that her mother's love was unconditional. It had never been anything else. She could not, however, bring herself to shock Lily with the truth, namely that she did not know who the father was. How, without deeply hurting a mother who had reposed in her such trust, could she be open about the way, during that heady year, she had been living?

Trained in secretarial skills, Mercy had worked at a West End temping agency which brought in higher wages, even less the agency commission, than an ordinary humdrum office job. She was sent from week to week to different offices, sometimes working as a receptionist, sometimes as a typist, sometimes both. There was hardly a week when she was not propositioned by a man in one of these offices. She had her pick. Joyously, rapturously, greedily she enjoyed the attention and, for the most part, the sex. Boyfriends as such came and went: their possessiveness bored her, and though she shed a few tears, and felt tenderly about many lovers, she was never seriously in love.

About six months before Peter was conceived, Mercy had landed herself a permanent job. The agency had sent her as a temp to the offices of *The Daily Legion*. She worked in the Deputy Editor's office answering the telephone and doing minor secretarial chores. She was an instant success, and they asked her to stay on permanently.

Lily, who read *The Daily Legion* each morning over her elevenses and regarded its pages as only a little less authoritative than those of Holy Scripture, was overjoyed that her daughter was working for her favourite newspaper, in its last days in the old *Legion* building in Fleet Street. Within days, Mercy was thrilling her mother by saying that she had actually seen, or more excitingly still, spoken to some of the legendary writers on the paper. Old 'Dr Arbuthnot' the gossip columnist had held open for her the cage of the creaking lift. She had seen Philip Warrener the astrologer seated at a desk, and presumably casting horoscopic predictions for the next day. She had taken messages to the strange cigarette-filled room where 'Stan' the cartoonist sat swigging champagne from a bottle and composing his stereotypical vision of England (he'd pinched Mercy's bottom but that she did not tell her mother); she'd seen Peg Montgomery, interviewer extraordinaire and expounder of Women's Problems. She had seen the famously acerbic younger columnists – Martina Fax and L. P. Watson – and overheard the gossip (once again, not repeated to Lily) that Martina, who was Swiss, was conducting a lesbian affair with the fashion editor, Mary Much.

Mercy had loved the whole world of the *Legion*, adapted immediately to the camaraderie of the shared life of a large office, and felt as if she had been adopted into the crew of a vast, jolly piratical ship. She quickly formed gossipy friendships with the other secretaries. She enjoyed the flirtations of many of the men in the building. There was no obvious racism. The whole experience, she felt in retrospect, had sent her, not crazy but something which is almost the same, euphoric. Going to work each day felt like going to a vast and slightly naughty party.

Anthony Taylor, the Deputy Editor, who was her immediate boss, did genuinely appear to be an example of that rare species The Happily Married Man, but nearly all the other men flirted with her, some tried it on, and some succeeded. Within six months, she had – while trying to avoid behaviour blatant enough to get her labelled the office bicycle – a list of conquests. Most of these were regular dates which took place out of office hours. A gorgeous lad on the sports desk was the first to take her out; Wilf, who worked in Classified Ads, was another lovely man, about her age. One week, when she had slept with both of them on successive nights, she was aware of an enormous increase in her own libido. She'd made Wilf late for work by insisting, before they left his flat, that they do it again, even though they had done it all ways, all through the night. Euphoric now, not simply with the piratical jollity of the old *Legion* in its Fleet Street manifestation, but with sex itself, she knew that she was like a tigress on heat. She felt so randy that within hours of arriving in the office, she had deliberately gone into the cartoonist's room with a trumped-up excuse, and for the first time, she had let the old goat do just what he'd been panting to do for months, drop his trousers to the office floor and slip easily into her from behind as she sprawled over the unfunny drawing on the board.

It was her belief that men didn't *talk* in the way women talked. She did not think that old Stan, or Wilf, or the boy on Sports whose name she could not sixteen years later remember, had passed round the word. Rather, an atmosphere was given off. When L. P. Watson – a bit of a by-word among the secretaries, though chiefly for lewd talk and wandering hands – invited her out for evening drinks at the American Bar at the Savoy, she was not surprised, even though, when she was still a temp at the agency, if you'd told her she'd be swanning off to the best hotels with journalists who, if not household names, were known by their followers, she'd not have believed it. What had changed was not her status – she felt no snobby excitement (or not much) about the fact that her lovers, or potential lovers, were now richer, older, even in some cases more famous than before. What had changed was her attitude to life. For these months she lived in an erotic cloud, passing from orgasm to orgasm with impatience, and now seeing any man who smiled at her or flirted with her in much more specifically erotic terms than she had ever imagined possible. Previously her imagination had followed her giggly conversations with other women. She'd talked about fancying men. With spluttered mirth she had occasionally itemized this or that skill as a lover, this or that physical characteristic in a bloke which had caught that fancy. Now she had thoughts about the men she met which could only be spoken softly, in their ears, in bed.

It was while she was in this phase of highly charged sexuality that Mercy was asked to do a week's stint working in the Chairman's office – the old boardrooms at the top of the *Legion* building. It was a period of great change in the industry, and the *Legion* knew greater changes than most. The Dutton family, who had founded the paper (it had begun as a local paper in Leicester and moved to London during the crisis over the Corn Laws in the 1840s), had lost grip and no longer had the money or the vision to run it competitively. The last of the Duttons, Lord Charnwood, had been unable to resist a takeover, and the new proprietor, a rising tycoon from West Africa called Lennox Mark, was clearly not going to leave the paper as it was. Rumours abounded – that Lennox was going to move the paper to a tower block in Bermondsey. That the editor was to be sacked. That a new paper, *The Sunday Legion*, was to be inaugurated. (Most of these rumours were true. The only ones which were untrue were that Lennox Mark would turn around the financial situation of the newspaper or introduce a lot of new journalistic talent. He tended to use the same old team of journalists, and the circulation had been in fairly steady decline since poor old Lord Charnwood, a broken man, retired to a house in the country.)

At twenty-one, Mercy d'Abo had not been much concerned with the minutiae of these developments, though as a member of staff in a small and highly distinctive organization she could not avoid being affected by them. Everyone expected her, after a week in the Chairman's office, to return if not with pieces of industrial espionage, photocopies of letters or contracts, then with the 'low-down'. Very few members of staff had actually met Lennox Mark at this stage and Mercy was a proficient, indeed an incurable, chatterbox.

It was obvious to her from her first glance of him – his sleeked-back hair, blond then, not grey; his complexion the same even tan; the pale grey double-breasted suits of a design he'd still be wearing two decades on – that he fancied her. Even so, she was taken aback by the speed with which the pair of them conveyed, within a few short flirtatious conversations, that she would be on for it.

The cliché in her case was true; power worked as an aphrodisiac. There had been something quite extraordinarily exciting, and flattering, about the very act of doing it with the boss-man, with Mr Big. The power which had been able to wrest *The Daily Legion* from the control of the Duttons, which could move the whole caboodle from Fleet Street to Bermondsey, which could sack the editor and appoint a new one, which could control – or so she, with the rest of the world, supposed – millions and millions of pounds – this power was laid at her feet. They made a strange Cophetua and the Beggar Maid, as he knelt before her, naked, in that large old panelled room. The dome of St Paul's was not floodlit in those days, but it seemed so large and so brooding, this great voluptuous tit defiantly erect and randy on Ludgate Hill, that she could almost have reached out and touched it as Lennox Mark's tongue slurped up the inside of her thighs.

'I'm doing it – I'm doing *this* – with the boss!'

The encounters with Lennox were in fact sporadic. She was moved from the deputy editor's office to the top floor of the building, and she missed her old friends on the paper. Some days, if she brought in the letters or came to take dictation, he would treat her with indifference. At other times, a meeting of the eyes would tell her that she was needed for sex. It went without saying that she never made the first move, and it probably also went without saying that she was never in love with him. Nor did she feel the smallest obligation to be loyal to him. In one week, she had slept with her sports desk friend, with L. P. Watson – who took her to an hotel for the afternoon – and with Mr Mark.

And then – she found herself asking – 'Why? What in hell am I doing? What *is* this – this writhing about on top of, or underneath, people I don't really know?' It was not a visitation of guilt. There was nothing, as far as she could see, to be guilty about. The erotic obsession had passed, though. She no longer *wanted* these men and she was at a loss to understand what had been taking place in her own soul, both during the phase of the erotomania, and during the day or two in which it lifted.

At about this time, Lily, who had been working during each night at the intensive care department of the local hospital (and thereby allowing Mercy's nocturnal escapades to pass unnoticed), announced that she was taking a week off work to attend the parish mission at St Mary's, Crickleden. The mission was to be conducted by none other than the famous apostle of African liberty, Father Vivyan Chell.

This was fifteen years or so before Father Vivyan left Africa and returned to England, to become parish priest at that very church. The set-up at St Mary's in those days was much more conventional. A celibate priest, a secular, with his curate shared the large clergy-house, which no parishioner ever entered. The services were conducted in the old-fashioned way which Lily enjoyed, with perhaps fifty or so coming to the high mass on Sundays, and a handful – which included, when possible, Lily – to the low masses on weekdays. The sick, the old, the imprisoned were all dutifully visited but there was little sense of the place being of much interest to those outside the Anglo-Catholic fold. Those who did visit the parish from outside came because they believed that it was the site of a medieval place of pilgrimage – though the Shrine of Our Lady of Crickleden, which formed a separate chapel or side-aisle to the barn-like brick church, had not in fact been built until 1911, its ornamental ironwork being among the best work of the Arts and Crafts architect and designer Oswald Fish.

The parish still retained loose connections with the Community of the Holy Redeemer. Monks from the monastery at Kelvedone sometimes came to help out when the vicar was away or to conduct retreats or quiet days.

The fact that Father Vivyan was to be conducting a parish mission, however, attracted considerably more excitement. His books – first the paperback about the church in Africa, *Lift Up Your Eyes!*, and his later books about the spiritual life – were popular with a wider public. He was one of a handful of Christians throughout the world whose voice was attended by the secular press. As Lily had predicted to Mercy, the conferences which the monk was to give each evening in the large church would be packed out.

The mission, which lasted three days, took a set form. After an evening mass at seven p.m. each day, the preacher spoke for about half an hour. He would then be available for an hour afterwards to speak to anyone who chose to see him privately. In the morning, he would say the morning prayers with the parish priest, and he would again be available for anyone who wished to hear him. At midday, beside the clock tower at the end of the High Road, the missioner would speak in public. In the afternoon, he would again be available for confessions, private consultations and the like from individuals.

Mercy did not accompany her mother to the first of the evening conferences, though she heard all about it when Lily returned to the flat . . . 'Beautiful . . . such beautiful words.' While being hard to please, Lily also had a need to venerate. She appeared to believe in the sanctity of almost every priest she had ever met, though this did not stop her pulling holes in their sermons. Given the theme of the mission – 'Liberation' – it was surprising that she had such an enthusiasm for the preacher. In all senses, Lily was a conservative.

This was, as we have seen, a time when Mercy was passing through an emotional change, and wondering why she had been so completely out of control in the previous months. Did it conceal some fundamental lack of self-confidence: or was there some need to meet the father who had deserted her and her mother during her early childhood? Confused in her mind about this, she had overslept one morning and telephoned the office to say that she was not coming to work.

She was in two minds about whether to attend any of the mission. On the one hand, she would like to see the famous monk. On the other, it irked her at that stage of her life to do anything of which her mother would have wholeheartedly approved.

To walk towards the High Road at about noon and see whether Father Vivyan had collected a crowd by his open-air preaching would be a compromise between hovering around the church with the devotees and missing him altogether. After- wards, when she tried to remember how many had collected near the clock tower to hear the monk, she could not. All she remembered was him. This tall, emaciated figure, his eyes sunk low in his skull giving something of the effect of a bush-baby, the nose beaky, the hair brushed back like a matinée-idol in a 1940s romantic movie.

'Jesus Christ came into this world to make us free! But we do not want freedom, we men and women. So, everywhere we make shackles for ourselves. We tie ourselves down – to jobs, to mortgages, to pointless conventions. We persuade ourselves that we want the things on offer in the shops. That we won't be happy until we have had the holidays in the brochures . . . And we find ourselves imprisoned, going on journeys not of our own choosing, wanting to escape. But it takes courage to be ourselves, to be free . . . It takes courage to break loose . . .'

It was not particularly the words of Vivyan Chell, it was his manner of delivery, his urgency. He made Mercy feel that whatever shackles were binding most of his hearers, he had broken loose. He spoke of religion, 'Not as some voodoo trick – believe in Jesus and you'll no longer be responsible for your own actions! Believe in God and He'll let you off the punishment for your sins which you deserve. No! That's not what Christian freedom is! That's making Christianity into voodoo, it's superstition. Believe in the law of Christ and you will be free to do as you want. Love is the fulfilling of this law. Follow the law of love and all the other laws become pointless . . .'

He told his hearers about life in Zinariya. They were hopeful days. The old days of colonialism were over. The country had a new leader. Father Vivyan knew him. Joshua Bindiga had been at his parochial school as a little boy in Louisetown. He had gone on to Sandhurst, and though General Bindiga no longer claimed to believe in the Gospel, that Gospel was more powerful than we as individuals understood.

'Bindiga is a minister of the Gospel – oh yes, my friend.'

A man with a strong cockney accent was yelling that Bindiga was a savage, who had killed hundreds of people in the civil war and would kill hundreds more.

'Jesus Christ preached liberty to the captives, and the people of Africa have been captive too long . . . from the early days of slavery, through the period of European colonization . . .'

This got the audience going. Mercy remembered that, though what, precisely, was said on either side, she forgot. In the light of what happened later it was not surprising. She went along to the parish church afterwards and joined the queue of those who were waiting to have private interviews with the monk in the vestry. There were many, many people waiting to see Father Vivyan and afterwards she found it hard to explain to herself exactly what had drawn her there. When she eventually found herself at the head of the queue and entered the parish vestry-room, she simply felt within her an urgent need to talk. Almost before she had sat down opposite the monk, she had begun to talk.

During this interview, Father Chell was wearing a long cassock which buttoned down the front. Mercy was wearing a red fluffy jumper which greatly emphasized the shape of her breasts, and a black mini-skirt, black tights and knee-length black leather boots. She found that she was talking about the last few months of frenzied sexual activity – and wondering aloud whether it was an example of the 'freedom' of which the monk had been speaking in his public speech, or whether sex itself had become a slave-master.

'It must be wonderful to be like you – to have put all that away from you.'

She said the words, but as she did so, she was aware of an extraordinary psychological moment having passed between her and this tall, slender and in his angular way fascinating-looking man of fifty. She knew that although she was speaking, or intending to speak, as an anonymous parishioner to a man of God, she was in fact allowing her toothy smile, and her come-to-bed eyes, and her sex-appeal to work their spell.

In a half-choked whisper, the man was replying, 'You must know, it never leaves you – never – the need.'

'But – you're' – she said the words meaning to dampen him down but she knew they would be bound to have an opposite result – 'you're a holy man – you're a monk.'

'I'm a man,' said the choked voice.

94

This was all too obvious from the tumescence beneath the cassock.

'Oh, you poor man!'

And wordlessly, she knelt down in front of him, and he allowed her to unbutton the cassock.

What followed lasted about ten minutes. She heard herself muttering words she had often used – 'Oh my sweetheart, you need it, you need it so *much*' – but never had she felt it to be so true. While she said these words, the priest had murmured in a language which was not English. She guessed, in after years, that it was Hausa, and wondered how often, in the course of his African ministry, such moments had occurred. She knew also, at the time of the fuck, with something like mystic certainty, that this was her very strange and distinctive way of saying goodbye to a phase of her life when she would be an erotomaniac. Thereafter, she would be in quest of a man for domesticity, children, hearth and home. This last frenzied fuck was unlike any other which had gone before in her life, and it would be unlike any thereafter. When she felt him come inside her, she felt explosions of joy and ecstasy which she had never imagined would be possible.

She attended the two mission sermons on the last two evenings, and after the final one, there was a 'bun-fight' in the parish hall. Father Vivyan's words, as so often in his life, had been taken up and quoted in the newspapers. Never before had 'liberation theology' been so radically applied, by an Anglican, to the world political scene, to the English political world, to the church. There were therefore many from outside the parish clustering around the priest in the hall afterwards, while others shoved forward for sausages, egg sandwiches and fairy cakes, which had been spread out on trestle tables by Lily and her friends.

'We must have a short word.'

Somehow, in the middle of all that crowd, Father Vivyan had broken away and managed to walk back with her into the church. They paced along side by side in the darkened empty brick aisles.

'I'm ashamed about what happened,' he said.

'Don't be. Your little treat.'

'Is that really how you see it?'

He turned and looked down at her – her face reached the middle of his chest – and took her long fingers in his own.

'Yes – but it's changed me.'

'How has it changed you?'

'It's made me serious,' she said. 'No' – with a giggle – 'I mean it. I'm gonna go straight – I'm not gonna sleep around no more.'

'I abused my position . . .'

'No, you didn't.'

She tiptoed up to him and kissed him gently on the lips. They never had another intimate conversation until years later, when Father Vivyan had come back to England permanently. He left the parish the next morning and returned to the mother-house at Kelvedone.

By the time he was back in Zinariya, two weeks later, Mercy was beginning to fear that she might be pregnant.

She did not want to marry any of the men with whom she had slept in the previous month. There were four possible fathers: Lionel Watson, the boy on the sports desk, Father Vivyan Chell and Lennox Mark. The notion of settling down with any of them never passed through her mind, and she had no intention of humiliating herself by admitting that the father could be any one of four.

In his very nearly sixteen years of existence, Peter d'Abo had been an object of such unreserved and unqualified love that the question of his father's identity had rather faded in his mother's mind. There had been bigger problems – such as, after she had married, and had children by Trevor Topling, how these new males in her life could come to terms with her first great love, her primary love for Peter. And there had been the behavioural problems, which had begun to cause such anguish.

If, after a few interviews with the boy himself, and with the mother and grandmother, Kevin Currey had not suggested that a remedy would lie in a frank declaration of the name of Peter's father, Mercy would never have considered disclosing it. Since Father Vivyan had returned to London, to be Lily d'Abo's beloved parish priest, there was no possibility of Mercy upsetting everyone by naming him. She could not remember the name of the boy on the sports desk, and she hardly wished to saddle Peter with a hopeless old roué like L. P. Watson as a father. That left – assuming that she went along with Kevin's idea, and assuming that she told the truth – only one possible candidate. (She thought of stretching a point and naming Stan, the cartoonist, who was now dead, or one or two other friends on the newspaper, but honesty compelled her to admit that she'd had a period since making love to any of them.)

Lennox Mark's behaviour, when she had first realized that she was pregnant, was one of the many secrets which Mercy Topling carried in her heart. It was during the first week that her condition was obvious to her, when she was feeling very friendless and frightened, that the buzzer went in the inner office, and she heard Lennox's voice on the intercom.

'Mercy, would you mind coming' – pause – 'in. I have – something to show you.'

He had used exactly this form of words before, and she knew therefore exactly what she could expect when she went into the office. The thought passed her mind that she could send a message to the senior secretary, Mrs Claydon, that the Chairman needed her to step into his office; but Mercy was not a vindictive person; she did not want to punish Lennox particularly, merely to indicate that her affair with him was over. It would have been rather cruel to Mrs Claydon, a somewhat haughty individual with grown-up sons, who took the train in each morning from Sevenoaks, to make her enter the Chairman's office and see that few inches of overexcited chipolata signalling for her attention above the blotter. So, Mercy had gone in to see him herself, and, sure enough, there it had been.

Lennox was eating caviar out of a jar with a spoon, and as he stepped out of his trousers to see her, he dolloped some of the grey sludge on the top of the erection.

'Have a little beluga!' he suggested, with his mouth full.

'We have to talk,' she said, realizing as she did so that she had burst into tears.

Both his immediate reaction and his behaviour over the next few days had been shaming. When she allowed herself to think about it, she pitied him. Even as, with furious imprecations, he was wiping the caviar off his floppy little knob with a piece of tissue, he was accusing her of being a blackmailer. There was no tenderness in him at all as he zipped up the trousers and tried to reclaim his dignity; just anger, and behind the anger a tangible and woefully unstylish funk. She immediately wondered how she could conceivably have fancied, or told herself she fancied, such a tub of lard, but she felt no malice, only bewilderment, as the smallest vestiges of sexual love drained between both of them, leaving only horrible distrust and mutual self-loathing.

When he had sworn – using every swear word in a variety of surreal orders, and then again in a different order – he had produced a cheque-book from his pocket.

'That's not what I want, Lennox.'

It was the first – indeed, the only – time she'd used his name.
'That's not what it's about.'

'Then what is it sodding, fucking, cunting, buggering Jesus fucking Christ about?'

Behind his fat head and his smoothed blond hair and the heaving shoulders of his tropical pale grey suiting, the great dome of St Paul's, and the City of London which stretched behind him to the east, proclaimed the Kingdom of the World, but not the glory thereof. She saw him in this painful few seconds as the king of this world. She saw him as ruling and owning it all, with his cheque-book, his bespoke suits spattered with food and semen, his cars, his companies, his dodgy deals which as a secretary she had heard him hatch, with his employees, his wage-slaves, his rolling, furry wobbling belly and his stupid little prick. She remembered the one time – on that sofa over there – when he had actually removed all his clothes. *The Naked Ape*, hadn't there been a book with that title? She saw his dominance over herself and his employees on the newspaper as something as deeply basic as that of a great primate in a patch of jungle. He was some tremendously powerful, angry gorilla and she knew that the only thing to do was to get away from him, fast.

'I don't want the money – I do not want . . .'

She had run from the office during another stream of expletives.

As soon as the interview was over, she went down to the personnel manager and gave her notice. A P45 form and a month's salary were forwarded a few weeks later. Before that, however, she received a solicitor's letter. It was an abominable letter, sent by one of the grander firms in Lincoln's Inn Fields. It stated that their client did not, and would not at any time, acknowledge the paternity of the child in her womb. It libellously and untruthfully stated that she had tried to extract money from the Chairman. It said that if she presented herself at Number —— Lincoln's Inn Fields, and signed the appropriate documents, she would be committed never to repeat the claim that their client was the father of the child. She would, on signature, receive a sum of £20,000 which would be a one-off payment, never to be repeated . . .

No one in Mercy's family had ever possessed a sum even approaching £20,000. After she married, especially after Trevor became mentally ill, she had sometimes thought with some wistfulness about the letter she wrote back to the lawyers, with its suggestion of a suitable destination for the cheque. She had never exactly regretted refusing the money, though. Lennox had tried to buy her silence, as if it needed purchase. As the years passed, and particularly after her marriage to Trevor, she was sure that she had as much desire as Lennox did to bury the memories of earlier escapades and follies.

For years, in fact, the question of Peter's paternity had been put aside. She had stopped thinking about it, until the boy began to attend his sessions with Kevin Currey. For all her initial scepticism about therapy, she was half persuaded that some of Peter's troubles might stem from not knowing his father. So, these meetings with the psychiatric social worker had forced her, in the secrecy of her heart, to gouge out the sixteen-year-old memories. She could not face the truth any more: namely that she did not know who the father was. That sex-crazed twenty-one-year-old was a different person from thirty-seven-year-old Mercy. To shock her mother by recalling the incident with Father Vivyan was impossible. The boy on the sports desk – he'd be married himself, with kids by now. It was as well she'd forgotten his name: she could not endure the idea of Peter wanting to meet him and claim him as Dad. As for old L.P. – well, it was not as embarrassing as having slept with her mother's favourite priest:

but Lily liked to chuckle over the columnist's extreme views as she had her coffee and biscuits . . . It was somehow imaginatively impossible to suggest that Mercy remembered anything more about the man personally than that he once bought her a Manhattan in the American Bar at the Savoy. What happened after the cocktail had been consumed could safely be forgotten.

That left her the choice of lying about Peter's father – saying, for example, that he had been killed in a motor accident years ago, or naming Lennox Mark as his father. For a couple of weeks she had vacillated between the two options, while Kevin pressed the point home: Peter was unrooted. The 'lad' had tried to come between his mum and his stepfather and the tactic had failed. He had gone to live with Granny. The deep-seated hunger for Dad – for Dad's love, Dad's encouragement . . .

'It's Lennox Mark,' Mercy had blurted out one day during one of these tirades of Currey's. 'My old boss from the days I worked at the *Legion*. Well – the owner . . .'

She did not think, when the name had been drawn from the air, that it made much impression. She hoped for a day or two that this would be the end of the matter. Perhaps the boy himself – who had appeared indifferent, almost sullen, when told – would be unconcerned, and show no desire to make contact with Lennox. Kevin had told him not to do anything hastily, not to get in touch with Mr Mark on his own. Peter had to realize, said Kevin, that they were all right behind him. As Kevin squeezed Peter's shoulder and called him 'Good lad' in the presence of Mercy and Lily, it really seemed as if that might be the end of the matter. But now Lily, as they rose to go, after this week's meeting with Kevin, was saying, 'He war better ahf before, I'm telling you, before you made Mercy tell him. You say she owed it to him. He's on the verge of manhood, you said: he could presently be a father himself, you said, well Lordy,

Lordy, keep us from dat . . . But did you really, truly think it through? What it was going to mean to Mercy to have to tell the boy? What it would mean to Peter himself, to the two other kids? She'll have to tell dem too, you know. So far, so good. Peter's keeping shtum, but dey've met it hard enough in dat family, man. Don't you tink Trevor and Mercy have enough problems? When she tell him now, he's quiet; he run off down de street and doesn't want to know 'bout it. But one day, I know dat boy, he'll come in and want to get insultive, throw his weight aroun' and he'll say, "Brad, Lucius, your dad's a failed secondary school teacher who can't do nothing, 'cept sit round all day staring into space wid de depression, and my dad? You know who my dad is? He owns *The Daily Legion* . . ." Have you thought what that's going to do to our family? And don't you think my Mercy was right not to tell us all those years ago, and right to keep it to herself? You know what I tink? I tink that boy will get all sorts of hopes and dreams and it won't make nothing better. He'll go out a jonnycake and come back a dumpling.'

They were halfway down the stairs when Lily delivered herself of this prediction, and Mercy took her mother's arm as they teetered out into the dark and the rain.

FOURTEEN

Long strides, hare lopes, carried him away. The women had kept their word, and let him go out through the garden, over a fence, and, by means of climbing another wall, back to the streets. They'd kept the fuzz talking.

What if they now broke their word — what then? How much did they have on him? Nothing. No names. Jus' a bit o' spit on her fingers — but that couldn't prove nothing.

But if he went back, like she say he must? Which one come back then, man? Inside the boy's head, a cluster of different characters were to be found. As often happened at moments of crisis they all jabbered for attention. There was the strutting, streetwise sex maniac:

Chrise, when he'd sucked her fingers, he'd got a hard-on, thought he was in there with a chance. Like, she was gagging for it. Oozing. And, like, whether she said yes or no, he'd have given it to her once she took him up those stairs.

'You'd better come upstairs.'

That was what she'd said. She'd slithered up the stairs in that white silk thing. He'd looked forward to ripping that off her, wrenching her bra, grabbing those tits in his teeth before down come his zip and out come Big Joey wanting to stick in that juice-jar of hers. He'd have given it to her, hard, hard. Then taken a few diamonds, a bit of money. Then taken maybe jus' one thing of *his*. A toothbrush, maybe: a hairbrush? A tie?

Maybe one of those really expensive cufflinks he'd watched him buy in Bond Street, like, last week?

So up the stairs they'd gone. Martina. That was her name. He'd followed that wiggling ass up the staircase. Nice one. Seen her walk over to her bed, and then she'd turned. He'd seen in her strange expressionless smile something like recognition.

So she knew? She knew who he was, and why he'd really come there? Knew he didn't give a shit for some pizza delivery boy, not a shit for the jewels or the money, but – Jesus.

Fucking Jesus.

In that split second of confusion, he realized that she wasn't looking at him. He'd turned round and there she was – that hag. Was that a dyed blonde? Or was it a wig on top of that face? Oh, Jesus Christ, that face, or what was left of it: Whatever happened to give her a face like that? On one side there was one eye. The other was just an empty socket, and the scar went right down where the cheek would have been; only there hardly was any cheek, and the white scar-tissue contrasted horribly with the sun-tanned skin – it was like streaky bacon, that flapping bit of non-face! And the nose half there, half not there, and the mouth so twisted, and more scars in the neck. And she was jabbering in some fucking language, man, while she waved a fucking gun.

Sex Maniac had gone. Frightened Child took his place.

And Martina was saying, *Nein, Mutti, nein.*

And in her other hand the old hag had a knife. Not a little knife, a fucking great Sabatier kitchen knife. And she was shrieking something about *kastrieren den Neger.* And Jesus, you don't need GCS fucking Es to know what that meant as she released the safety-catch on the revolver, and moved the knife towards him.

She looked, the one-eyed witch, like she'd used big carvers on men before. Often. Ate cocks like other people ate hot dogs.

And then he didn't know what was happening, but they'd got him in the bathroom, which led off the bedroom. Jesus, man – that bedroom was bigger than the whole of Grammy's flat put together! And they were jabbering in Spanish, Russian, whatever the language was, right, and his one, Pussy-Glamour, pointed at the edge of the bath; like, at the cloth, and the cleaning-fluid?

'Get scrubbing.'

He'd been so surprised at first that he had not understood what she meant. Then the older woman had waved her gun and he'd thought it was a good idea to do as he was told. So he'd cleaned the bath with Jif. Then he'd cleaned the toilet, and the floor, and tidied up the towels. And then she'd made her deal with him.

'You're good.'

'My grammy,' – the terrified child had begun the sentence, but one of the others finished it for him, one of the ones who could speak posh – 'my grandmother needs help. I do the cleaning for her,' he had said.

'Now, listen.'

She spoke, the beautiful lady with coppery hair, very distinctly, in her foreign accent: not very foreign, just with a bit of a lilt to it – whereas the one-eyed monster, when she spoke English, it was, like, a joke, the accent was so strong.

'You have a choice,' said Beautiful. 'You can clean this house – from top to bottom: or we call the police, now.'

Before he was taken at gunpoint downstairs to the utility room, and shown the cupboard where the Filipinos had left mops, J-cloths, rubber gloves and plastic buckets, she'd opened her palm to him and insisted, 'My rings. If you please.'

He'd given them back to her quite meekly.

Once the whole strangeness of the situation was, if not

forgotten, put to one side, and once he stopped shaking, he found it quite interesting, seeing that fucking great palace. They in their turn, the two women, gradually trusted him more. While he did the kitchen, the old woman insisted he still wore that studded collar which they'd fitted round his neck, even yanking his chain a little if he failed to spot a tea-leaf or a smear of butter. By the time he had finished washing up the dishes, cleaning the floor, emptying the rubbish bin and tying knots in the black plastic sacks, swabbing the tables and surfaces, and mopping the floor, they unclipped his chain.

He had emptied the Dyson, cleaned the drawing room, the study and a small inner sitting room, and then brushed down and hoovered the main staircase.

'You're a good worker,' the Beautiful One had conceded. 'If you come back tomorrow, I'd pay you . . .'

The old hag tried to interrupt with a stream of abuse in her language. Martina replied in that language, then added, 'Trust me. I know what I'm doing.'

'If you come back,' she repeated, 'I'd pay you. If you tried to steal one fivepenny piece, one envelope, one crumb of bread . . .'

He had stammered general agreement to her terms. If he would consent to become her house-slave for a week, then she would protect him from the police. There was not time to fine-hone the contract. At that moment the police had rung the front door-bell.

'Leave this with me,' she had commanded him. 'Get out of the back. And fast.'

The old hag in a yellow wig had escorted him to the back door and pushed him in the small of the back, projecting him into the darkness of a yard. He could hear police sirens wailing at the front of the house. So, they'd found the kid he'd knifed.

The women had got the Stanley knife, covered in blood. The old one made him drop it into a cellophane freezer-bag, like it was forensic evidence. So they could, probably, get some evidence on him, if they wanted.

As he paced along, the memories and impressions of the previous few hours were shaken up inside him. In Brompton Road he jumped on a double-decker and stepped coolly off it again in Piccadilly when the conductor asked him for a fare. Suddenly, he was Bertie Wooster.

'What ho!' he said to the conductor. 'What ho!'

FIFTEEN

Mercy went home. There was no knowing where Peter had got to. Presumably, he would turn up at his gran's flat and express surprise that anyone had been worried about him. (His mother did not altogether blame him for boycotting the sessions with the psychiatric social worker. Kevin's meddling was doing no good. Mercy shared Lily's wish that they'd never started with the man, who, in some nameless way, gave her the creeps.) So, she went back to Lily's flat for a coffee, and then took herself off – a journey which involved two buses – home to Streatham. On the bus, she read her public library book, Zola's *Nana*. Its sauciness fascinated her, as much as its jaded tone shocked. Could human beings really be as depraved, as cynical, as money-centred as the French novelist depicted them? But – what a novel! She turned the pages eagerly, and nearly missed the stop in East Dulwich where she changed.

If only Trevor could bring himself to read once again. When she had first met him (he was seven years older than she was) Trevor had been a teacher in a secondary school. He taught English literature to children between eleven and thirteen. His love of teaching and books, his seriousness, quite as much as any physical attraction, drew him to her in the first place. She loved his kind, earnest face. They'd met at a party given by some friends in common. She'd dressed herself up to kill, as usual. She'd been to Afro-Styles in Crickleden High Road (Julie, the stylist there, was one of her best mates) and had her hair straightened and flattened against her head – very Josephine Baker. She had purplish-red lip gloss, a bright cerise top with a plunging neckline, and a skirt which was split up one side to reveal lots of fleshy thigh. Her throat and ears jangled with glister. He wore a grey open-necked shirt, a boring tweed coat, brown trousers, crinkly pale-brown socks and the sort of shoes which looked like Cornish pasties with a pastry-rim round the toe. Yet, when they met, he did not assume, as so many clever people would have done, that good-time girl equals airhead. He spoke earnestly about the books he was asked to teach the children, while – most satisfactorily – not being able to take his eyes off her chest. Although Mercy had not been serious at school, and had therefore been stuck in a series of boring clerical jobs for the previous decade, she was a person who enjoyed books and reading.

Trevor said how boring the books were which he had to teach: stories of children supposedly like his pupils – of mixed race, or with single or gay or divorced parents.

She calmly replied that she was the single parent of a mixed-race child. Instead of insincere apologies, he'd said, 'But he – it is a boy? – he wouldn't necessarily want to read about himself in a book. A book should release him into a world of fantasy, of other realities! As soon as we get through these boring books on the syllabus, I tell the kids about King Arthur, Merlin, Lancelot. We also do tales from Greek mythology, and Hindu and Norse legends. These are stories which nourish a child.'

Later at the party, they'd danced, smooched, kissed a little, but it was several months before they had become lovers. In the light of all that had happened since, it pained Mercy to remember their first dates, when he would come to her flat for a meal, and tell Peter, who was aged five, stories.

'They're so good you should write them down,' she had

urged him – and he had confessed that he was trying to get something on paper, a version of Homer's *Odyssey* for young children.

Mercy could still see Trevor in her mind's eye, with Peter on his knee. That was an alert Trevor, with dark hair, and a clean-shaven, clever face, his bright eyes shining as with the hypnotic knack of a good story-teller he spoke to the boy as if imparting a special secret known only to the two of them.

'Tell again,' was something Peter often said to Trevor.

'Tell what again, son?'

'Tell again about the Old Man of the Seals.'

'The Old Man of the Sea and his Seals? He is a very special sea-god, and he lives in a deep, dark cave down under the sea, with seals for pets. And when he is sure no one is looking, he and the seals come up and sit on the rocks, and he counts the seals, like a shepherd counting—'

'Tell again, tell how he *changes*,' Peter would insist.

'Now the old man hates anyone to see him. And if anyone does catch him, or tries to catch him, he hates them asking him questions. So what does he do?'

Peter, entranced, wide-eyed, would stare at Trevor.

'You say,' the child prompted.

'No – you say first.'

'He changes shape – he's one person and lots of different people!' said the boy with glee.

'That's right, because he is a water-spirit – and water runs through your hands, you can't hold on to it. So every time someone tries to get a hold of Proteus, he'll be someone completely different.'

Peter had always been a presence in their lives, Mercy's and Trevor's. Of course, Lily was a mother in a million, and she had often had the little boy to stay with her overnight, to give the pair time to be alone. It had felt quite strange, their first night in her flat, without the presence of Peter. They'd become a little tipsy on red wine, laughed a lot, made gentle, tender love to one another.

'She offered her honour, he honoured her offer, and he was on and off 'er all night long,' she had murmured. He'd never heard that one, and it made him shake with laughter. Oh Trevor – your laughter! She missed that so much now.

As time went by, Trevor and Peter seemed like perfect companions. Like Saint Joseph, Trevor was a just man and he asked no questions about Mercy's earlier life, nor about Peter's father. Peter sometimes called Trevor 'Dad', though he had never been asked to do so.

Mercy and Trevor married. Their own sons, first Bradley, then Lucius, were born. Peter changed from being a delightfully cheerful toddler into a gifted but highly disturbed and disturbing child, given to extreme swings of mood, to naughtiness and rages. Sometimes, he was violent towards Lucius or Bradley, and on these occasions, rows flared between Mercy and Trevor. He said she always sided with her mysterious first-born against the younger children, that she was always making excuses for Peter, even when, as quite a tall eight-year-old he did dangerous things such as holding his two-year-old half-brother upside down. The deep bond between Peter and Mercy was something Trevor resented, and their two sons breathed this resentment from their earliest years. They grew up with it, learnt it, absorbed it, shared it. Mercy greatly feared that she had contributed to Trevor's mental breakdown. After all, her husband's worst fears were based on a reality. She did love Peter with an all-consuming passion which was quite unlike her fondness (deep and sincere as this was) for Bradley, Lucius and Trevor. They had cause to be jealous. She did her best to conceal her emotions, and she tried not to be too open about loving Peter more than she loved them. It was simply a fact, however, that she adored her first-born in a way that she had never loved another human being, and a part of the reason for this lay in his very Protean character which Trevor had so presciently noticed very early: his ability to be first one person, and then another person, to be a whole variety of characters, depending on his mood or his company.

As she returned to the flat, Mercy felt real anger against the whole pack of them – Kevin Currey and his bloody theories of how to get real with the real Peter; the teachers who were, most of them, wimps who could not see the point of an original clever boy like Peter; Brad, Lucius and Trevor for having driven him away, driven her son from home.

The Toplings' maisonette occupied the first and second floors of an Edwardian house down a leafy side street in south London. They had lived there since their son Bradley was two – that is, seven years. (Lucius was actually born there in the flat.) It was home. Mercy had made it as cosy as she could, though 'the boys', a phrase she used to indicate not only the younger children but also their father, did their best to mess it up.

Since giving up smoking herself some years before, she was especially conscious of the smell of stale cigarettes, which hit her as soon as she'd come through the door of the house, and before she had as much as opened the front door of the flat. The door opened grudgingly against the boys' anoraks, which had fallen to the carpet. She hung them up again and in the little glass beside the hooks she checked her appearance, and gently shook the braided hair, which was moist with raindrops.

'It's still bucketing down out there . . .' she told her own face, not sure that there would be an answer.

From the sitting room came the sound of television. She had hoped the boys would have been in bed by now.

'Still up?' she asked with a weary smile.

The sitting-room door opened on to more floor-strewn detritus – Lego, a variety of other toys, some books, three Action Men, one in combat gear, one with its right leg snapped off. The two boys were lolling on the sofa. A box containing the remains of a pizza was on the carpet.

Trevor was sitting in the armchair. His posture and expression were unchanged from three hours before, when she had left him in charge of the children. Presumably it was Trevor, and not Brad, who had extravagantly ordered a pizza to be delivered.

Anger at the scene – the boys so unwelcoming, their dad so stiff and still, the mess all over the floor – flared in her head, then died. It was all so pitiable.

'Hey!' she said with a smile. 'You guys've got school tomorrow. Come and help me clear this lot up, then into bed with you.'

'Oh, *Mum!*'

But the boys did help her make the place neater. The toys were stowed in a green wooden box painted not unlike a canal barge with floral patterns. The telly, to cries of protest, was switched off.

'Okay?' She heard her voice becoming the cooing noise appropriate for addressing the very young, or the very sick. 'I'll see the boys into bed, then make a cup of tea. Eh?'

He was forty-five years old, but he could have been twenty years older from his appearance. He was thin, bespectacled, prematurely grey, not only in the hair of his head and the stubble which was always sketched over badly shaven cheeks, but in his very complexion. As well as being sunken, his stubbly grey cheeks, heavy smoker that he was, were scored with wrinkles. There was something wraith-like about him, and many of the pat phrases from the common parlance which Mercy's friends used about him were quite true. He really did seem like a shadow of his former self. Nor was he 'all there'.

'Read the paper?'

She waved *The Daily Legion* in front of him to see if she could at least make his open eyes show some recognition or response.

'He came round,' he said quietly. 'Came round here.'

'Peter came here? But he was meant to be with us, seeing Kevin Currey. Had he forgotten?'

'He bought the boys a pizza.'

'When?'

Trevor shrugged, indifferent: perhaps frightened.

'He was gentle,' he said in a quiet, dull voice.

This could not be relied on. Mercy sighed, thinking of the wars which had taken place in that flat. When Peter was ten, he had mutilated some of the exercise books brought home by Trevor to mark. They had contained a whole term's project on the *Odyssey*. Most of the children's work was poor, but some of them had taken real trouble with colourful illustrations of triremes, helmets, spears, goddesses or the Cyclops. Peter had spared the dullards, and ripped the books of the best children. Trevor had become wildly angry, chasing Peter around the flat, shouting. Mercy had come in from work to find Trevor pummelling the boy with his fists. She had screamed and dragged her husband off him.

She dated the first real onset of Trevor's depression from that day. When he got to school next morning and opened his briefcase, he found, nestling among his books and pens and the unmutilated exercise books, a dog turd which had been neatly collected from the pavement.

Thereafter, he developed something very like persecution mania. If kids at school misbehaved, he believed that they had been put up to it by Peter. Some of the girls in his class – egged on, Trevor believed, by Peter – had taken to calling him 'Perv Topling'. The parents of one of these girls came to see the headmaster with a bundle of anonymous letters, pasted together from newspaper and magazine cuttings. These alarming productions accused their daughter, aged twelve, of being 'the nigger's tart' and alleged that she performed disgusting 'services' for Trevor. Of course no one believed the letters, but they upset all concerned. No sooner had the memory of that incident faded, than another outburst of bad behaviour was capable of plunging Trevor back into depression. Racist abuse, or blatant sexual filth was written on his blackboard. Sometimes the perpetrators were caught, sometimes not. No one ever traced this back to Peter's influence, but such was Trevor's certainty that his stepson was behind the persecutions that he all but persuaded Mercy that some, at least, of the outrages were the fault of her eldest son.

There was something, therefore, all the more touching about Trevor's quiet surprise this evening.

'He was . . .'

'What was he, sweetheart?'

'He was . . . nice.'

'Come on, you guys!' Mercy said to the boys. 'Upstairs with you!'

She clapped her hands at them as if they were pigeons whom she wanted to scare into the air.

She wanted to make Trevor fly. He was quite visibly *sunk* in his gloom, slumped in it. Mercy had known many days of grief, fear and sadness in her life. Peter and his troubles were a constant, gnawing worry. She'd never, however, suffered from depression. In spite of reading books about it and talking about it to doctors, and living under the cloud of Trevor's depression for seven years, she still did not understand it or even, really, know what it was.

'Listen to your tapes,' she suggested to his languid, drooping body. 'Here – you like these, it's that actor who makes you laugh.'

It was the actor who made Trevor laugh in the happy days; they'd loved his renditions of P. G. Wodehouse. Now – was this person she lived with Trevor? She'd bought the stereo, and the tapes, for him, hoping to raise the flicker of a smile on his ashen features.

'Put on the headphones – go on.'

She did it for him, fitting the phones over his grey hair. He sat quite still while she did so. Then she switched on.

He leaned forward with a sudden spasm of agony and burst into tears.

'Oh, oh . . .' he moaned.

'What? What, for God's sake?'

Her sympathy had given out. He wrested the phones from his ears and leaned forward clutching his knees. She pulled the headphone connection from the socket in the player. Instead of their favourite comic actor reading about Jeeves, a loud violent voice:

> It's no use, bitch, dat you scream an' cried
> Cause your nigga's gonna fuck you an' he's comin inside

The music and the accompanying voices to the rap were harsh and violent. It felt as if the room had been invaded by a gang of young demons intent upon inflicting spiritual pain.

SIXTEEN

Tall, in his hooded cagoule, Peter kept moving, easiest way. The drizzle had turned to driving rain, so nothing was clear; all London was a smudge of car headlights reflected in raindrops, of orange street lighting glistening on wet pavements, of lighted windows and of spaces which were impenetrable, pure darkness. Cars, bikes, buses, pedestrians kept moving, beneath improvised head-covers made from folded newspapers, wind-blown small umbrellas whose spokes were askew, hoods and hats. In such a night identity and identities were swallowed in the glare and the blackness. Keep moving, keep walking. Keep calm.

Peter had been on buses, off buses, down the underground, up again. He'd paced the High Road, and caught an overland train to Clapham, then changed trains and came back.

In the train he'd played his Walkman and quietly repeated its phrases to himself. 'London in August rather tends to give me the pip . . .' 'Having a corking time . . .' 'What ho, Jeeves! What ho!'

Out in a high street somewhere, a parade of shops, he turned up the volume.

'Relief was surging through me in great chunks . . . I prowled about the neighbourhood all afternoon and evening, then I had a bit of dinner in a quiet restaurant in town and trickled back to the . . .'

Bally good show. One of the others, the characters inside him, had picked up the words, read by the actor on the tape.

Even though he had turned up the tape to full blast, he could not blot them out.

He paused in a shop doorway, leaned back against the plate glass of a window selling electrical goods, and breathed deeply.

She'd been his slave, right?

I made Martina clean that kitchen floor with her tongue and she loved it – this from the Guards officer in a drawly voice.

Then she lick my dick, then she lick – this was the moron, the violent one who liked knives.

Then, drawled the major in the Coldstreams, I want you to hoover the drawing room.

Gee, the old woman – those scars! The kid was nearly wetting hisself with fear. Pity they had to drag the kid round with them all the while. The kid just wanted a kiss and a cuddle, wanted Martina to hold him, tell him everythin's gonna be fine.

She knew without being told. She knew – he wept when he thought of it – why he couldn't meet Mr Currey in the presence of his mum and his granny. The others all talked big, but you didn't want to believe all they said. They hadn't had no sex. It was him who'd had to.

'If it crosses your mind to tell anyone . . .' said Mr Currey.

'Oh no, I wouldn't, I wouldn't tell no one,' whispered the kid.

'Only I can get you sectioned – know what that is? Taken away. Locked up with other nutters. And they wouldn't be gentle like I am.'

They all believed his threat – Jeeves and Bertie Wooster, the Coldstream major, the murderous moron, the kid and any of the others who had tagged along. Whenever Mr Currey had said it – and he'd said it each time he had Peter alone with him – they'd known it was true. Mr Currey could tell the school authorities, the police, the doctors that they had started the fire in the laboratory. He'd say that Peter was schizophrenic.

Murderous Moron talked big, said what he'd do to a brown-pipe engineer like Currey, cut that four inch of nuffin' off him for starters, cut his face too. But even MM feared Currey, feared his powers. And the others, besides, were aware that MM was a liability. Take all that stuff when they was all on their way to Redgauntlet Road to meet Martina.

He'd said how he'd burst into a flat the previous week. Just for practice. Knew the slag was alone. Saw her bloke go to work, then strolled over, nice 'n' slow and rang her bell jus' as she was washing up the breakfast 'n' that. Said he was come to read the meter. She opened the door, no problems. No questions. She'd peed herself when she'd seen the Stanley knife. Literally wet herself as she simpered and emptied out the contents of her handbag.

No bally class, old boy, said Bertie.

Well then he'd tried an older bitch, in them flats down Wigan Road? She'd whimpered 'n' all – while he ripped up her pension book, made her empty out the contents of that bleeding teapot. Lots of pound coins and a few dirty fivers. Twenty-seven quid. He'd smirked. He could see the headline in *The Daily Legion*: MURDERED FOR JUST TWENTY-SEVEN POUNDS.

Not that he had murdered her.

Or had he?

Pressing his wet forehead against the cold plate glass of the shop window, and looking at the row upon row of refrigerators, Peter *did not know*. He tried deep breathing. He tried to be calm.

He knew that MM was a bullshitter. He bullshitted the rest of them about sex. Talked as if he'd fucked everything that moved. Peter knew – or thought he knew – that this was completely untrue. He knew – or thought he knew – that he had had no sexual experiences with another human being until the school had insisted on his beginning those sessions with Mr Currey. These experiences left him feeling angry, ashamed – bitterly ashamed, at having consented to them – and unclean. He felt literally unclean as well as in pain when the man had finished each time.

Now – he thought that if he took this slowly, he could have the thought without the others interrupting – if MM was wrong about the sex, was it not possible that he was also wrong about the crimes, the murders, the pranks, the cruel practical jokes, the arson . . .

But this cool, rational, still linear progression of thoughts inside his head, which were as refreshing as the cold wet glass pressing on his face, could not control them all. There was, like, this whole crowd looking through *his* eyes, each one of them eyeing up one of the fridges in the window. And MM had broken up, like he sometimes did, into two of them – little Aggro-boy who liked stealing and Bullshitter who wanted sexual sadism as part of his kicks.

And Tuli – who was gang leader and could control even Peter himself – could only just control them all and say, Hey, gang! Guys, guys! Cool it there, inside that skull of mine. Have a little patience!

Tuli was wise. He was older than the rest of them – he could think for them all. Time will come, he thought, when that big house in Knightsbridge will all be his. He'd explain to Martina. And she'd smile that surprised baby-doll smile (why didn't her features move?) and when she knew, she'd say, Tuli, welcome. Welcome, my son!

After all, it was his home. The large gates, the front garden, the hallway with the swanky chairs and pictures like the ones in the National Gallery (which Trevor, with his everlasting desire to improve people, had taken him to see). And the smell of fresh lilies in vases everywhere. And springy carpets which, like, bounced under your Reeboks. And those shiny polished wooden floors. All his, his.

And the Bentley was his, and Martina's Volvo. And LenMar House, down Bermondsey – that was his, too, and when that fat fucker was good and dead every plate of glass in that building, every iron girder, every tread on the moving staircase, which gleamed like silver as it went up to heaven. Like in the story Mercy read him when he was a little kid, about the angels of God ascending and descending while Jacob slept and dreamed his dreams.

Oh, he'd dreamed dreams all right, Tuli had, since Mercy told him the truth, and he'd seen angels, 'cause that was what he was himself. You know, like it say in the Bible, there's good angels and bad angels? There's one like who say, Holy, holy, holy, round the throne of glory, all that shit, and then there's the others who say, Let's have a bit of action, let's go through this world seeking whom we may devour, man. And they're both angels.

And you remember in the Bible where it say, Jesus, he was coming round the lake, right, and he found this guy. And everyone said he was like a headcase, a nutter. Everyone 'cept Jesus. And he came round the shore of the lake to those tombs, it's like he's hanging out in Crickleden Cemetery 'cause there's nowhere else to run. And he's cutting himself with stones, and he's like, in these chains and he's shouting and swearing. And Jesus says, Who are you, man? And he's, like, going, 'My name is Legion, for we are many.'

And Father Vivyan can say those words in Hausa or one of those crazy African languages he knows. *Sunana Tuli ne; gama muna dawaya*. But Tuli doesn't want no African crap, man, it was bad enough in junior school being Bahamian when all the other kids were either Jamaican or wanted you to think they was Jamaican. Africa ain't cool — but that's not the sort of thought you could expect Father Vivyan to get into his white old nut. Anyways, Jesus, right, he's going to the guy, right, C'mon outta there, you fuckers — Murderous Moron, yeah both of you, Aggro-boy and Bullshitter, and the Major, and Bertie Wooster — all of you, come the fuck out. And oh, one minute it's like the inside of your head's exploding, like with heavy metal. And then you, like, look up at Jesus, man, and the noise stops, and everything goes, like, calm and beautiful. And you're free, and you're looking into a pale blue sky and butterflies are winging the mild, blessed air.

SEVENTEEN

London goes to sleep early, and in bad weather – it had been bad weather for months – Londoners keep indoors. By ten o'clock, even the West End was deserted, its shopping streets empty of traffic. Outside the nightclubs in Soho a few determined revellers lined up, as festive in appearance as a dole queue. A handful of foreign visitors trickled from the theatres in Shaftesbury Avenue and Charing Cross Road. But the population's capital was indoors, watching television or preparing for bed. All the way from Buckingham Palace, where the Queen was having a disturbing telephone conversation with the President of South Africa about the crisis in Zinariya, across Horse Guards Parade and Downing Street, where the Prime Minister was reading the Bible, across Westminster Bridge, and down the rain-swept windy river that rippled like shaken ink in the night, the thoroughfares were almost empty. Those still walking the pavements or waiting at bus stops seemed like wayfarers in the Deluge who had failed to talk Noah into letting them board the Ark. Desolation, alienation and darkness settled over a city which might be preparing not merely for night time but obliteration.

Where the suburban sprawls of south London began, the air of absolute desertion outside was complete, though tower blocks and, in streets lined with trees, upstairs windows still burned their electric bulbs. Five miles south, and west, of the Queen and Buckingham Palace and Westminster lay the unplanned ugliness and sprawl of Crickleden. Go past the deserted clock tower at the end of the High Road, walk as if you are going to Crickleden Junction and you will come to a huge Calvary, the white, tortured figure of the crucified Christ disturbingly realistic in the neon street-lit glare; and beside it, a noticeboard which reads SHRINE OF OUR LADY OF CRICKLEDEN. And behind it, looming up into the rain and the blackened sky, is the huge barn-like church. Beside the church is the large Edwardian rectory, built of blackened stock bricks. It is connected to the church by a brick cloister. In the drive are several camper-vans and caravans. We shall wait until it is light before we try to make out what these are doing here, and who is living there. The rectory and its grounds now have a floating population of about thirty, sometimes more. The front door of the house is always open. There are two public rooms downstairs – a large dining room and a sitting room. These are both deserted. One of the rules of the house is that the Greater Silence is kept: that is, after the night prayers have been said, there should be silence. Given the mixed population, this silence is never total. From different corners of the large house there are varieties of human sound: murmured conversations in Hausa, Kanga or other African languages – or in Albanian, Polish, Czech. Snatches of boozy song come from other quarters, interrupted by the occasional 'Shut up in there!' But if the silence is not complete, there is, as it were, a blanket over the house. It is subdued.

In the large bedroom on the first floor – what would have been the master bedroom when it was a 'normal' house – Father Vivyan Chell was sitting alone in the darkness. He had discarded the monkish habit which he had worn to the demonstration at LenMar House. In his early days as a monk in Africa, he had always worn the cassock and scapular of his order. Now, except when on public display – and he had gone to the offices of *The*

Daily Legion as a representative of the Church, so wore his uniform – he had rather dispensed with the fancy-dress side of religion. He usually wore black, but the clothes were taken from jumble sales. Those who wear soft raiment dwell in kings' houses. Beneath his ragged black jumper, his shoulders and elbows made sculpted twigs. His long hands lay on the black corduroy knees of his jeans. The light from a street lamp, the only light in the room, fell on his bony knuckles and the high veins on the back of his hands. Anyone who saw him in the shadows might have mistaken him for a jagged statue made of hard wood. His hair, cut quite short, was brushed straight back from the brow. He was very thin, so the shape of his skull was discernible beneath the skin. His large nose and ears gave him the appearance of some primitive mask.

He sat with patient hands outspread, waiting for God, as he had been waiting for forty years. During one period of his life, as a young army officer at the time of the civil war in Lugardia, he had known God's presence. When the campaign began and he was sent to Lugardia with his regiment, Chell had assumed that an army career stretched ahead, as it had done for so many of his relations. An uncle and one of his grandfathers had both been, like himself, Coldstreamers.

Then had come the bloodiest phase of the war, during which his platoon had run into some heavy fighting. Before that, he had never been a man of prayer. When he emerged from the anaesthetic in that field hospital, he had heard the voice of God. He had not heard actual words, but his awareness of the Presence was calm, certain, quite unambiguous. Perhaps it was easier to be aware of Him in Africa. In the thirty years he spent on the continent, he had often come to think so.

The hospital was some way from the fighting. A few days after he recovered consciousness, Chell had been looking out across Lake Alexandra, where a few rhinoceroses lazily wallowed, and where ibises swooped over the steel of the water's surface. The evening sky was a vivid orange. No words had needed to be said, but in that moment he had known the Presence. When he had insisted, against his doctor's advice, on rejoining his platoon, Chell was aware of God *within him* day and night for several days. All his previous life now seemed like a dream, a preparation for his new state of awakening.

The intensity of the experiences, perhaps heightened by adrenalin, pain, morphine, and then by more adrenalin when he was fighting – he won the Military Cross – never returned. He did not know it at the time, but he was to be required to 'bank' this deep serious experience and draw upon it for the rest of his life. Much later, when he had become a priest, he read that Saint Teresa of Avila never had any consolations in prayer, never had a sense of God's presence given to her when she prayed. The rest of his life, the long years in the dusty slums of Louisetown, was to be a daily living out of the incarnational theology which the Holy Redeemer monks had made him read when he joined their order. The years of his novitiate – at the mother-house of Kelvedone on the North Sea coast – had been cold, emotionally unsatisfying, boring. But he had been obedient. As he saw it, he had joined up and was under orders. He had left one regiment, the Coldstream Guards, and joined a new one, the Community of the Holy Redeemer.

It had been a huge relief when, after his ordination to the diaconate, he had been sent back to Africa. He had been there a lifetime, and Africa became his life.

Then, after nearly forty years in his beloved Zinariya, he had been called back to England. The Bishop had written to him and offered him the parish of St Mary's Crickleden, a 'problem' parish in many ways, with much poverty and many differing ethnic groups. He had not thought much about it. He was past sixty years of age when the Bishop's letter arrived from England. His life had been punctuated by sudden decisions, by commitments which it sometimes took years to unravel or comprehend. He knew that most men who reached his age were beginning to think about retirement. He mysteriously felt inside him a powerful hunch that he had some great job to do in England. He took this hunch, this feeling, to be the closest thing he was ever going to feel of God's voice – will – what was the right metaphor? Was it his own sinfulness which made God seem silent? Or was he so in tune with God's will that he did not need to have 'revelations' any more? Anyway, the matter was settled for him when the Superior of his order not only agreed to his coming back to England but said that the appointment of an African to the post of parish priest in Louisetown was long overdue. So – he came home, and for the last two and a half years he had been in this house in Crickleden.

The move into the sprawling house in the south London suburb had been easy since Vivyan Chell had few possessions. He had unscrewed the locks and bolts on his doors within hours of arrival. For the first few weeks, he had lived with packing cases and a deckchair. Except for the years of his novitiate in the monastery, he had not slept in a bed since the Call. Part of his vocation from the beginning was to follow Christ in a path of dispossession. Foxes have holes and the birds of the air have their nests, but the Son of Man hath not where to lay his head. Gradually, he accumulated enough sleeping bags and mattresses to accommodate the itinerant, floating population of the house. (The local authority were happy to make use of him and there were sometimes young families living rough in the house, either asylum seekers, or simply those whose lives had fallen into chaos – an easy thing to happen when no money was available.) Usually about twenty people slept in the house.

Now, as he sat alone in the darkness with hands outstretched, he prayed for them all.

'My time is in thy hand; deliver me from the hand of mine enemies . . . Shew thy servant the light of thy countenance . . .' Sometimes he prayed silently, sometimes he used words from the Psalms, in English, or in one of the African languages in which he was fluent.

Raina yana jin kishin Allah, Allah mai-rai.

The darkness was conducive to prayer, and to those rambling semi-coherent thoughts which sometimes were his nearest substitute for prayer. He bathed in the dark, wrapping its silence and shadows around himself like his shabby black clothes. Sometimes he dozed. Since army days, he had learnt to survive on cat naps, and he always felt sleep-deprived.

He prayed for Lennox Mark. The encounter with the tycoon had taken Father Vivyan by surprise. He had agreed to take part in the demonstration at LenMar House, wearing his black monastic robes, in order to draw attention to the cause in which he passionately believed. He had not hoped to meet Lennie himself, and now, with *l'esprit d'escalier* the older man felt he had bungled their interview. He wished he had confronted Lennie with more statistics, and he wished he had made a more direct appeal to the boy Lennie, who must have been cowering somewhere inside that rich businessman, and reminded him of his youthful hunger to follow Christ. If Lennie were to turn again . . . if he were to put pressure, through his newspapers, through personal contact, on the politicians . . . there might be the chance of a peaceful solution in Zinariya.

Father Vivyan was realistic enough to know how unlikely it was. Three of the house guests for whom he prayed were boys who had run away from Bindiga's tyranny. Two had escaped the lives of slaves on a cocoa farm where they had been badly beaten. You could see the welts in their shoulders and backs. They had joined the rebel forces in the northern mountains and had been fighting against General Bindiga's army. Chell knew the exact terrain; as a British soldier, he had fought there himself forty years before. Their stories of unforgettable horror, their courage, were awe-inspiring. Another Zinariyan boy, Akule, also in the house, had come from Chell's former parish in Mararraba. The African monks had spirited him out of the parish just in time, and he was now doing a course in computer technology at a former poly called the University of South Crickleden. This boy had been part of the Happy Band and he had helped to found a similar youth club in Crickleden, with Father Vivyan's help. The authorities in Zinariya had claimed that he had been manufacturing the explosives detonated in the Kanni-Karkara copper mines, which had destroyed so many lives since they were first opened in the 1880s by Lennox Mark's great-grandfather.

Lennox's newspapers, in so far as they allowed their ill-informed English readers to know anything about West Africa, had represented the Happy Band as dangerous anarchists. Bindiga had no alternative but to crush these people – that was the line spun by *The Daily Legion* – just as it had been the duty of the British Army to fight the Irish terrorists.

Things were much less clear cut to Father Vivyan's mind. He did not regret giving those boys training in basic survival skills while he had been a parish priest in Africa. (Well, what did he *imagine* they were doing? Playing table tennis?) In 1940 Churchill started the Home Guard in Britain. Nowadays, in the minds of many, it was almost a joke. At the time, it had been seen as necessary to national survival that young boys, and old men, should learn how to shoot people, how to blow up railways, how to render telephone lines and electricity supplies useless.

There was a vital war to win in Zinariya against Injustice. Father Vivyan Chell worshipped a Soldier Christ who came to bring not peace but a sword. It was for this priest a simple blasphemy to claim to worship the Incarnate Christ, but to hinder the coming of His Kingdom by supporting wickedness and selfishness.

Then shall he say also unto them on the left hand, Depart from me, ye cursed, into everlasting fire, prepared for the devil and his angels: For I was an hungered and ye gave me no meat: I was thirsty, and ye gave me no drink: I was a stranger, and ye took me not in.

Vivyan Chell believed that the human race was judged by these words. In forty years, the only God whom he could see or hear – after the first mystic certainty of the Call – was in the eyes of the hungry and in the crying of the poor. The copper mines in southern Zinariya were responsible for forty per cent of the country's wealth, but that wealth never reached the workers in the mines, whose lives were ruined by the conditions underground. Was it any wonder that boys like Akule, now asleep upstairs in a sleeping bag, wanted these mines blasted out of existence? If that meant killing a few of his fellow-workers, these numbers were only a tiny percentage of those enslaved, first by the Mark family, then by WAMO over the decades. Zinariya could never be a rich country. Perhaps it did not want to be. If every man, woman and child returned to simple farming, would that be such a bad thing? Such an outcome might result if the mines were destroyed. Those workers who had been killed would go straight to God. If the mines were closed, foreign investment could be withdrawn. 'Investment', as Chell had learnt very early, was colonialism under another name. Who but international capitalists wanted to teach a Zinariyan woman to feed her baby with powdered milk; or her farming family to rely on artificial fertilizers which systematically killed crops from year to year; or her children to become addicts of Coca-Cola?

That was why, when Akule told Father Vivyan that he had received another e-mail, recounting a successful blast in the mines, the monk said a quick prayer for the souls of those slain, and thanked the Soldier Christ in his heart.

Now, in the darkness of the Crickleden night, he prayed that Lennox Mark should be converted, should return to the condition of heartbroken penitence which he had known when he saw the conditions of those children in Louisetown forty years ago.

Chell prayed in the darkness to the invisible God – *My tears have been my meat day and night, while they continually say, Where is thy God?* Somewhere glimmering in the darkness of this world there was a means – so he believed – by which each human being could seize the capacity to fulfil the Divine Will. Throughout his ministry in Zinariya, he had felt himself hindered by his own sins. He believed himself – or 'believed', for he knew it was a superstition, and he was almost able to see it as a superstition of very great egotism – that the whole furtherance of Christ's Kingdom in Zinariya had been hindered by his, by Vivyan Chell's, besetting sin.

He had tried to abstain, but some specious argument inside his head had always corrupted him in the end, combined with an overwhelming physical need. If any would condemn him as much as he condemned himself, let them know how over-powering this lust was.

The most corrupting thing the devil ever told Father Vivyan

was that this erotomaniac indulgence kept him humble, by reminding him continually of his need for grace and divine forgiveness. The most realistic thing the priest found to say in his own defence was that he would never have raped someone, or forced himself on them against their will. The women had only to say no. The trouble was, they had seldom done so. He thought, for example of Mercy d'Abo when he had come to St Mary's to conduct the parish mission sixteen, seventeen years before. Her mother Lily was one of the most faithful members of his congregation – what old-fashioned clergymen would call a 'pillar'. She came to daily mass. She helped to arrange the flowers. She polished candlesticks. She visited the sick and the housebound, while still working as a nurse at the local hospital, and assisting Mercy with the upbringing of a 'difficult' grandson. When this good woman came to him to make her confession, revealing thereby her innocence and goodness of heart, Vivyan Chell felt lacerating self-reproach. *What would she think* if she knew what had gone on between the priest and her daughter?

As often happened with his 'brief encounters', he had blotted out the memory of what, precisely, had taken place, but he would always remember Mercy's smile when he met her eyes, and her evident enjoyment of the sex, and her kindness when they met afterwards. He would compose speeches to her in his head – *If I have done you any wrong or caused you any hurt, I am so sorry*. But he rejected these words as patronage and con- descension. The women were grown-ups. They enjoyed it as much as he did. And those who were not his 'brief encounters', but who had had long-standing affairs with Vivyan, had remained on good terms with him.

'You're just a randy old devil and you need it,' one of them had said, as they went to it.

No doubt it squared oddly with his profession as a monk,

and he would love to have been rid of it, this overriding, addictive lust for women, especially for black women. During his last days in Africa he had enjoyed a particularly intense and happy relationship with a woman called Nontando. Parting from Noni had been deeply painful, and he had wondered, in his prayers, whether all the public and political rows with Bindiga, his campaigns on behalf of the mineworkers, his faithful following of the summons home, his acceptance of the parish of St Mary's Crickleden – whether all these outward obediences to God were a preliminary to the real renunciations which were required of him. God was perhaps preparing him for a great ordeal. Could it be the case that his great work for Christ was not as a public campaigner on the part of the oppressed, but as a private human soul, renouncing with great difficulty a lifelong vice? Since coming back to England, Father Vivyan had been chaste. For two and a half years he had seen the response in women's eyes; he had feasted, visually, on the sight of their hands stretched out for Communion, on the shape of their breasts, their thighs and bottoms, and although the sight and smell and sound of them had sometimes made him almost pass out with lust, he had been loyal to his vow.

In the darkness of his night prayers, he had offered all this frustrated lust to God, and the extraordinary sense had grown in him that he was being prepared to follow in the Via Dolorosa. In Africa, his role, and that of the Community of the Holy Redeemer, had been that of John the Baptist, preparing and making way for the Lord, unpicking as much as they could of the colonial attitude from their African pupils, preparing them mentally – thirty years after political independence – for true personal independence, enabling them to become Africans again.

He had believed at first, when the Bishop offered him a slum parish in south London, that a similar role of leadership was required of him. That was, indeed, how he conducted the parish life, trying to make the church a centre of political activity, a microcosm of the coming Kingdom where all should care for each. But in the moments of aloneness, and sometimes when he slept, the text came into his mind:

From that time forth began Jesus to shew unto his disciples, how that he must go unto Jerusalem, and suffer many things of the elders and chief priests and scribes, and be killed, and be raised again the third day . . .

He owed it to his people, to the people of Zinariya, to help them continue with the struggle, and he would do that until his dying breath – through speeches, and campaigning, and raising money. All available collection money at St Mary's went to the freedom fighters. He had no qualms about getting money from his brother and his richer relations for the 'missions'. Nor did it trouble his conscience that some of the 'asylum seekers' in the vicarage – the two Albanian medical students, for example – helped train the Happy Band. But something told him . . . was it merely the onset of old age which made him feel this? . . . that his own personal journey was to be detached from this great cause.

Let us go into the next towns, that I may preach here also: for therefore came I forth. He had preached from that text at his first mass in Crickleden – and had often preached from it in his African ministry. So did we all come forth, bringing Christ into the world, making him flesh, in our own town, our own village, our own settlement, till the earth was full of the glory of God.

He still waited in the darkness for an explanation of these two apparently contradictory movements in his life, the calling to lead the fight for freedom, not only in Zinariya but in poor, benighted Britain – stinking, corrupted modern Britain with its subservience to America, its sheer material greed – and the calling to suffer.

Surely, before the first steps were taken on the Way of the Cross, God would allow the Christian warrior one last tussle with the High Priest's soldiers before the arrest in the Garden of Gethsemane? (What good cause had ever been won without a fight? Did not the Prince of the Apostles cut off the ear of the High Priest's servant?)

Then – guided by one of those psychic hunches or imaginative leaps which had led him throughout adult life – then he could surrender to the Divine Will. But first the struggle! Would not God let him have one last fight with Lennox Mark – expose the filthy lies in *The Daily Legion*, denounce the paranoid dirt which it peddled every day about asylum seekers, about poor people, about Africans and Europeans? *O Lord, let there be one last battle before I surrender myself into your will, let that extravagant Tower of Babel, LenMar House, fall even as Babel fell into confusion . . .*

In the darkness, he fumbled beside the deckchair for a whisky bottle and took a slug. The house, with its many inhabitants, murmured and groaned, snored and muttered as Father Vivyan's stream of thoughts swam prayerfully in the shadows of his room.

Downstairs, he could hear the front door opening, as it often did during the night. Wanderers of various kinds, in different stages of inebriation or none, blundered in. Someone was usually there, often Father Vivyan himself, to look after their needs. Two of the young monks from Kelvedone were staying in the house at present, and part of their job was to attend to such vagrants, where necessary offering tea or sleeping bags, and leading them, where possible, in the direction of lavatories.

(This was not always successful, which explained the mingled smells of urine and carbolic in the house.)

'Where are you going?'

He could hear one of the novices whispering the question urgently.

'It's bally urgent,' whispered back Bertie Wooster.

The priest could hear the long strides of the boy as trainers took the uncarpeted stairs three at a time.

The door of his room opened.

'Is it all right if I come in, Father? Father?'

'Tuli.'

'Oh, Father!'

The door had closed, and the tall youth, a shadowy wraith in the dark room, took shape as he stepped into the light shed by street lamps, a somehow flat light, so much less luminous than that of the moon, but enough to show the boy's face, the wide, large, frightened eyes. The distinguished straight nose, the well-cut sideburns, the firm line of his jaw.

'Is it all right to visit you, Father?'

The monk stood up and hugged the boy.

'Come and sit beside me, Tuli. Sit on the floor while I sit in my chair.'

For a while they were silent in this posture, the older man returned to his sitting posture, the youth leaning against the priest's knee. Father Vivyan's hand rested on the youth's shoulder and stroked his thick springy hair. Slowly, the anxious, very rapid breathing slowed.

'I've been out, Father. I've done bad things.'

'Tuli – Tuli, my son.' He rubbed the hair with a rapid playful gesture. 'What bad things? Tell Father.'

EIGHTEEN

All night long the rain fell on London – on Knightsbridge, where it washed the blood off the pavement in Redgauntlet Road, on the great serpent-shaped brown river, on the Tower of London, on St Katharine Docks, on the waters of Docklands, and far beyond, a mile down river on the Surrey side, on the unresting bright lights of LenMar House. The rain echoed on rooftops, waking and tormenting such insomniacs as L. P. Watson in Clapham or Trevor Topling in Streatham. At half past five in the morning it splashed the windscreens of the delivery vans of the wholesaler, which set out across south London to take the bales of newsprint to the innumerable newsagents in those few square miles.

By six, Ali Hussein, who had been awake all night, came from the flat above his small shop, drew back the bolts and dragged the cellophane-wrapped parcels inside.

With automatic gestures, he stabbed with his Stanley knife at the thick cellophane, then at the plastic ribbons which held the newspapers in place.

His wife, crushed, weighed down with fear, worry and tiredness was upstairs. Ahmet was asleep. They had not even kept him in the hospital overnight. Just a bandage, some pain-killers . . .

The Stanley knife broke the last tape, and Mr Ali reached for *The Daily Legion* – MARTINA THE BRAVE! A doll-like woman, her head resting against the shoulder of a fat man with grey hair, smiled out at Mr Ali. 'Police yesterday evening praised the courage of Martina Fax, *Legion* columnist and wife of the proprietor Lennox Mark, when she fought off three masked intruders into the couple's Knightsbridge house . . .'

Mr Ali scoured the story for some mention of his boy – his frightened, maimed boy who lay upstairs in a narcotically induced state. What sort of example would this set to Ahmet's younger brother and sister? He was doing so well, studying computers at university, Crickleden University, and working to pay his way. The job for Granville Stoppard made them all delighted. No ordinary delivery boy, their Ahmet, no pizza bikes, no takeaway curry for him! The fact that so many of the shop's clients lived in SW7 or SW3 or W8 had made both parents sure that it was quite safe. Only the rich lived there. And now some bastards had . . .

He stabbed furiously as he thought about the revenge he would like to take. Three *Times*es, three *Guardian*s, twenty *Sun*s, twenty *Mirror*s, seventeen *Mail*s, ten *Express*es and thirty *Legion*s. The *Telegraph* had a picture not of the Markses as a pair, but simply of Martina, smiling at the cameras. This paper, and the *Mail*, actually noted that the delivery boy had been attacked. Presumably Ahmet's name had been given by the police, since both papers said that Ali Amit had been attacked. At least these papers had tried to give some account of what happened. *The Independent* reported some doctor who said the boy's condition was satisfactory and that he had been discharged from hospital.

'Try having your own ear sliced off by a fucking maniac,' said Ali Hussein, 'before you tell my boy it is satisfactory!'

The Times had 'Wife of Newspaper Proprietor Held at Knifepoint'.

The *Daily Mail*, quick off the mark with a comment piece, wondered whether the 'gangs of marauding Turks' who now roamed the cities of the old East Germany were not straying over to England? How many more delivery boys get stabbed in the eye in London before the Home Secretary admits that his policy on asylum is insane?

The Guardian did not mention the incident at all on its front page, leading instead with a story about the copper industry in Zinariya being threatened by gangs of youths, who marauded and rioted in the mines, and who were believed to be responsible for the recent destructive explosions.

NINETEEN

Having grown up in a police state, Martina knew the strategic usefulness of misinformation. It had helped openly to lie, even – or especially – to members of the Court. 'Dr Arbuthnot' went round in a twitter for days believing that they were going to appoint a woman to succeed Anthony Taylor as editor of *The Daily Legion*. The household of L. P. Watson had been thrown into excitement by the prospect of him succeeding. (Mary Much had maliciously telephoned his wife, Julia, to ask if she thought he'd be *interested*, and although neither Lionel himself nor Julia thought of him as an editor, there had been a few days of thinking about the substantial salary, the chauffeur and other attractions of the post.)

The Prime Minister himself was interested to the point of obsession in the appointment. His press secretary had rung Tony Taylor for clues, but the outgoing editor was kept in the dark as much as anyone. (He guessed, correctly, though, that Worledge had been offered the job – the brutal Worledge, editor of an extremely downmarket Sunday tabloid.)

When Lennox saw the PM – it was on the last morning of Taylor's editorship, and the announcement was still not official – it was clear that the man could think of little else. He wanted Lennox first to confirm that the new editor would be Worledge, next that Worledge would continue the present very harmonious relationship between the *Legion* newspapers and Number Ten. Lennox, who liked nothing better than to

watch senior politicians gasping for his favours, was not going
to offer the Prime Minister any comfort until he'd got a few
reassurances about other matters. There was the little matter of
the Commonwealth, which Lennox wanted nobbling, and, not
being in a position to do it himself, he thought the Prime Minister
was the likeliest nobbler he could find.

Shirt-sleeved, sweaty, jet-lagged from a recent trip to
Pretoria, the PM shuffled uncomfortably in his chair.

'It's not gonna be easy, y'know, Lennox.'

Lennox produced a cigar from a case and began to roll it
about between thumb and finger, sniffing and caressing it while
the politician stared in alarm. The difficult matter under discussion, Britain's defence of Zinariya's continued membership
of the Commonwealth – was outweighed by this new crisis: the
impending disaster if the cigar were to be lit. To the pure, all
things are impure. In that Cabinet Room, where Churchill had
incinerated a thousand of Havana's finest, the air was now
unpolluted. For a visitor to ignite a cigarette or a cigar would be
to defy an almost sacred tenet; why, the poisonous blue clouds
might hover in the air, drift down corridors or staircases, seep
through connecting doors and, most horrible, reach the nostrils
of children.

'Doing right is never easy,' said Lennox, 'that's what the
leader in this morning's *Legion* emphasized, Prime Minister.'

'And I'm grateful for what you said, Lennox, very grateful.'

The mercurial sheepishness in the PM's face could, if viewed
from another angle, look like slyness. Lennox enjoyed this
shadow-boxing. Martina, discussing the matter the previous
evening with her husband, expressed a conviction that 'in the
end the little turd will cough.' The displeasing mixture of
metaphor summoned up a spattered lavatory-pan in the mind.
She meant that the PM would eventually give Lennox a peerage,

or as she said, laying prior claim to the honour, 'his peerage'. Meanwhile there were motions to be gone through. If the entire Commonwealth decided to gang up against General Bindiga, what could Britain do? The *Legion*s both had an unambiguous answer to that. Britain should remind the Commonwealth that if a country were expelled for the gross abuse of human rights, there would not be many heads of state left to dance the cha-cha-cha with Her Majesty when she had them all to dinner at Windsor Castle.

Let's avoid gesture politics [The Daily Legion *had urged*]. *It's a rough old world and no one is pretending that President Bindiga is a saint. But is it really worth putting at risk the economy of one of the most prosperous West African countries . . . The Prime Minister has so far shown real leadership . . . In this election year, let us hope . . .*

On page three of the *Legion* there were some unsubstantiated stories about Professor Galwanga, leader of the opposition Alkawari! party running up huge hotel bills in Park Lane.

'The President . . . er . . . the fact is, I spoke . . . is frankly unhappy . . . I have to tell yer, Len, I spoke ter the President frankly this morning.'

This was said in estuary English, the PM's previous utterances having been spoken by an Elder Statesman.

'You spoke to President Bindiga?' There was disbelief in Lennox Mark's voice.

'To the President of the United States.' The Elder Statesman pompously came to the rescue of the Barrow Boy.

Lennox waved the cigar-weapon.

'And we all know,' he said, 'what the Yanks mean when they start talking about democracy and fair play.'

'Ur read yer leader, Len.' Barrow Boy took over again. 'Um hearing yer. But Um bound ter say . . .'

As if the opposite had been said, Lennox regurgitated the salient points of that morning's editorial.

'What's important about Zinariya? The fact that in common with almost all African countries it is a one-party state, or the fact that it is one of the world's most important copper-producers? We all know the Americans would like to take over WAMO. Democratically, of course. Fairly.'

The prime ministerial brow furrowed in pain at the cynical tone of the tycoon. Elder Statesman and Barrow Boy stood to one side while the Concerned Vicar said a few words.

'It isn't just the Americans who are worried about Bindiga's human rights record, you know. Surely' – he pronounced the word *shoe-early* – 'we all care about human rights.'

Especially those of us married to highly paid human rights lawyers, Lennox thought silently.

'Your own paper admits that the situation in Zinariya is frankly appalling.'

'No it doesn't.'

'I'm sorry, Lennox – the excellent piece on the features page by Sinclo Manners.'

Lennox felt himself blushing, and an overwhelming lust for a bacon sandwich possessed him. He did not like admitting the truth, that he had not read every page of *The Daily Legion*. What had Tony Taylor been playing at – on his last day as editor?

The Prime Minister, who had the newspaper open in front of him, shoved it across the table to Lennox. This was tantamount to an accusation that Lennox had not read the article. His eye took in at a glance what sort of article it was. There were four photographs – one of emaciated mineworkers, one of some boys from the cocoa farms wearing their manacles, one of General

Bindiga in his uniform resplendent with medals, looking like the judge of a beauty contest with two tall, large-chested Scandinavian women standing beside him, and one, inevitably, of Father Vivyan Chell. Lennox had heard of Sinclo Manners – Mary Much thought she was in there with a chance – he was some public schoolboy with a conscience who had been to Zinariya. Unlike most *Legion* readers. What in the fucking name of glory was Tony Taylor playing at, printing this horse-shit?

'It makes my point,' said the Elder Statesman again, elbowing the Vicar out of the way and capitalizing on the advantage. 'Of course there's a case for not rushing to judgement, but there's no gainsaying the truth of that article. Sinclo Manners isn't some liberal intellectual. He was in Zinariya as a soldier.'

'Was he?' Lennox unguardedly asked, adding with an assumed shrewdness which in the circumstances seemed absurd, 'I mean, you take his word for that?'

'Green Jackets, wasn't it? Part of the UN peacekeepers sent in two years ago.'

Shit and fuck Sinclo buggering Manners. Lennox felt like grabbing the telephone from the Prime Minister's elbow, ringing the little arsehole now, this minute, pronto, and telling him to clear his desk at once and get the hell out of LenMar House. While Mary had a crush on the man, however, Martina would want a share of the action. They hunted in pairs, those two. He could not sack Sinclo Manners because he dreaded the contempt of the two women, and because he knew they were clever about people in a way that he was not. They would get him his peerage. So he had to lick a bit of ass while, an anatomically challenging exercise, kicking it.

'With very great respect, Prime Minister – and that's why the *Legion* has consistently praised your robust stand over this issue – we all care about human rights just as much as it suits us to care. We at the *Legion* don't want to sweep anything under the carpet, which is why we were prepared to run Sinclo's piece. But at the end of the day the editorial line is clear. Zinariya's a small country so we can boss it around, tell it what to think about child labour, homosexuality.'

'Excuse me,' said the Vicar, pointing to the paper which now rested on Lennox's blotter, 'but public castration? Assuming that story is true, it's simply unacceptable . . .'

'Assuming. But let's be clear about this – we're all prepared to strike deals with China and ask not one awkward question about what they do with their political dissidents, their unpaid child-labourers, their female babies murdered at birth, their secret police, their . . .'

'As zmadderfac', Len, yer wrong there,' said Barrow Boy. 'Behind the scenes, we've made a lodda progress.'

He's so far up the American asshole, thought Lennox, that he's started to pronounce the word 'progress' in the Yank way. Though he pronounced it this way himself, Lennox despised the PM for doing so.

'But I take yer point, Len. We can't let the Americans out-manoeuvre us on this one, and yes' – a schoolboy full of sheepish pride at having won all the cups showed he'd absorbed the flattery with which that morning's *Legion* had larded him – 'there are times when a guy's godda get tough. That's why Britain's gonna say to the Commonwealth – look. Either *we* work out a solution in Zinariya or we hand over to the Americans.' Gratifyingly the Prime Minister was now mouthing, almost word for word, the views e-mailed to the *Legion*'s leader page by Martina the previous evening. 'Bindiga's methods may be rough and ready, but this is a guy who went to Sandhurst. We can do business with him.'

It would be a colossal mistake for a British Prime Minister, in an election year, to rat on one of Britain's best allies in West Africa. Those were the actual words.

Lennox rolled the cigar in his fingers and grinned.

This Prime Minister has been a good leader. He has the makings of a great one. The forthcoming Commonwealth conference will be his chance to show . . .

'What we're very much not saying,' the PM went on, and here, shit him, he was singing from a different fucking hymn-sheet, one written by Sinclo sodding Manners, 'is that the human rights issue's gonna go away.'

'Of course not, Prime Minister.'

'I mean – you know it all, it's all in Sinclo's piece . . .'

Sinclo? Did the PM fucking know the young busybody, or was this simply an example of the Vicar's habit of referring to everyone by their first name?

'We're talking here about torturing journalists.'

'Wouldn't you just love to do that sometimes?' asked Lennox impishly.

He received a baffled, slightly wounded look in reply.

The Elder Statesman rose to indicate that the interview was at an end.

The cigar was still unlit when Lennox Mark was shown out of the Cabinet Room and into the marbled hall. Actually to light up, or to flick ash about the place was a temptation. The cigar had served its purpose, by suggesting that, baby or no baby, the Fourth Estate would if needs be blow smoke in the face of the First Lord of the Treasury; equally that, all things being equal, the *Legion* would show deference to the PM. Hence the good Zinariyan tobacco – yes, fuck it, gathered in by slaves and who cared? – would remain unlit. For the present, the balance of interests was nicely poised, between a Prime Minister in need of a friendly press, and the ambitions of an ex-colonial whose wife would enjoy styling herself a peeress.

The question of Zinariya was, on one level, no more than a useful pitch on which the game could be played out, the *Legion* offering the political puppet the chance to prove himself on the international stage. Besides, they all knew that they were safe. Many of Zinariya's most vociferous critics at the Conference were, as Lennox and the PM both knew perfectly well, tyrants every bit as brutal as Bindiga. Nor did many of them really want to expel the General from the Commonwealth. They wished, if any aid were going spare from Britain, America or the private agencies, to advertise their agonized and shocked consciences. In fact, once their protests had been duly noted in the minutes, when their pompous speeches had been made and their wives had done the hokey-cokey with the Duke of Edinburgh after the State Banquet at Windsor, they were looking to Britain cautiously to retain the status quo.

What Lennox hoped was rather less clear, either to the Prime Minister or to anyone else, was his own dependence on the Bindiga regime. Kurtmeyer (Chief Executive of News Incorporated) and Spottiswood (Managing Director) had both been uttering the same unthinkable warnings for some weeks. Banks making ugly noises – debts unsustainable – share prices plummeting – if you thought last year's circulation figures were bad look at the figures for this year – Blimby bloody useless, Taylor no better – meetings in the City – need to face facts – gravity of situation.

Beyond the possession of LenMar House itself – a questionable asset in a recession since rented office space was hardly at a premium – Lennox Mark had no assets in the UK. This was the stark truth. If measured by the bleak realism of profit and loss accounts, of ledgers, of pluses in one row of figures and minuses in another, then Boss-Man Lennie was no richer than the most junior secretary working on *Legion* Classified.

It was the General who could, with real money, actual dollar bills in suitcases, bail out his old friend. Even Kurtmeyer and Spottiswood were probably unaware of how simply this was true: that the whole glittering media empire of Lennox Mark, the twenty-five provincial newspapers, the TV channels, the dud football club, the glossy mags and the nationals, the dinners for the rich and powerful, the house in Knightsbridge, the glass tower in Bermondsey depended less on the business acumen of its chairman than on the goodwill of a diminutive African army officer, at that moment almost certainly shagging a hooker in his fortified palace outside Mararraba.

There was a much taller man than Bindiga sitting on one of the hall chairs in a contemplative pose. Lennox heard the Prime Minister's secretary address this figure.

'He'll see you now, Brigadier.'

When he stood up, this military gentleman was very tall indeed – six foot six perhaps. Lennox, a good twelve inches shorter, nodded and received a little smile in return.

Lighting his cigar on the doorstep, Lennox remembered the irrelevant detail that Bindiga liked to remind everyone that he was a cavalry officer. As well as being Commander-in-Chief of the Zinariyan Revolutionary Army, he was Colonel-in-Chief of the Lugardian First Lancers. All the horses, unfortunately, had been eaten during the famine of '96.

TWENTY

'Temperatures mild, rising as high as seventeen degrees in the south, with that warm front pushing away to the west, but still gusty and showery and you'll need your umbrella!'

A jaunty jingle followed this announcement which came from Trevor Topling's portable radio.

Mercy, placing a cup of tea beside him, reflected sadly that he would not need an umbrella. He had not been out for weeks.

She was dressed in a black T-shirt with a swooping V-neck, revealing much of her chest. Over this, she wore a pale grey cardigan decorated with geometric charcoal-coloured shapes. The previous day she had taken off work, falsely pleading illness, and had her hair braided at Afro-Styles. It had taken hours – the straightening, the dying of some of the hair golden, the tight plaiting, which had been very painful. She emerged radiant. It was a great success. Brad and Lucius had told her she looked great. Heads had turned in the High Road as she had teetered home. Trevor had not apparently noticed.

'The bishops of the Church of England,' said the radio, 'have issued a joint statement today in which they say that they take very seriously indeed allegations of child abuse among their clergy. The Gay-Lesbian Christian Association has condemned the report, saying that it makes entirely unjust identifications between paedophiles and gay priests. Here's our religious affairs correspondent, Angela Lickorish . . .'

'There's a corn beef hash on the cooker – all you have to do is heat it up and stir it,' she said.

She meant – heat yourself and stir yourself. He sat slumped, motionless, staring ahead.

'He rang again,' Trevor murmured. 'That social worker.'

'Kevin?'

'The boy's been playing truant for a month now.'

'I told you, Trevor – we're not going to worry about that any more. He's nearly sixteen. Even Mum thinks it's best.'

'It's breaking the law,' said Trevor.

'He's got a job – up at this really posh restaurant. I told you that – Diana's. It's in Ebury Street. All the stars go there. He's seen Joan Collins – she had a Caesar salad. Mum says he's so much better.'

Mercy named several other famous people who had eaten at the restaurant.

'He's meant to go to school until he's sixteen.'

'It's only a few months off,' said Mercy.

She caught a glimpse of the pair of them in the mirror over the fireplace, and ran a finger lightly through her new hair.

'. . . an abuse of trust, say the bishops, which cannot under any circumstances be tolerated.'

'He sounded concerned – the social worker,' said Trevor. 'Said that whatever happens, Peter should come to his sessions with him. Said there was a real danger . . .'

Trevor, in the mirror, looked like an old man who was half asleep.

'Yes,' she said. 'Well, I've got to go to work now, love.'

'Where's the boys?'

'They went to school half an hour ago.'

'The Prime Minister is expected to defend Zinariya's continued membership of the Commonwealth today, in a speech to foreign ministers from around the world meeting in Biarritz . . .'

TWENTY-ONE

'Wonders will never cease – a decent article in *The Daily Legion*.'

'You don't mean one by your husband?'

'By you? You must be joking.'

Neither Julia nor Lionel Watson looked at one another as they exchanged these words across the kitchen table.

Julia still possessed a faded beauty in her boyish face. She was nearer fifty than forty, and she spent a lot of money on hairdressing. The dark bob, streaked with silver, framed pale, bony cheeks. She wore very bright red lipstick. People still stared at her beauty in public places, but twenty years of being furious, first with her husband, then with life in general, had left their mark. As she read the paper, she smoked cigarettes with the eager repeated gasps of one who, quite conceivably, believed it to be impossible to inhale oxygen other than through the filter of a Dunhill King Size.

Lionel flinched from his wife's hatred and tried to repay it with indifference. At the same time, he believed she had a perfect right to be angry with him. The only way he could think of making things right for her, since he could not repay her with what she needed – affection – was by maintaining a London house which, even on a journalist's high salary, he could barely afford.

The late Georgian house was not far from Clapham Common. Julia, who ran her own, not very lucrative, interior design company, had been given a blank cheque: no expense had been spared. The kitchen in which they were sitting was stone-flagged. A large deal table stood between the double sink and the Aga. At the far end of the room, a chaste Georgian dining table and eight chairs were reflected in the glass above the white marble chimney piece. All five floors of the house, which had been featured in *World of Interiors* as well as several colour supplements, were comparably spotless and over-considered. She was constantly scouring style magazines for new 'ideas' and the house was often invaded by builders, redecorating rooms which did not need it.

Lionel Watson was a fallen archangel, and Julia had opted to accompany him on his fall. In his youth, after Oxford, he had seen himself as a travel writer and poet in the mode of the 1930s. His first book, *Amazonians*, had recounted an extraordinary canoe journey he had made down the great South American river with a college friend. It had won prizes. A later book, about Tibet, remained a minor classic, an extraordinary evocation of the lives of the people there, deeply read in their languages and religion. He had spent a year travelling rough. He had not cared about money or comfort while he did so. From that experience had come not only a travel book but the first volume of poetry, *Conversations with a Lion* – an allusion to Wittgenstein's saying that if lions could talk, we should not understand what they said.

He had returned to London from his Asian travels thin, brown, gentle, funny. Women fell in love with him easily and he responded. He married the first one to become pregnant, Julia Ingoldsby, a decent, playful woman a bit younger than him. In those days she had a job as an assistant stage designer at the Royal Ballet.

Neither of them had any money. It seemed foolish not to accept any journalistic work offered as a way of paying the mortgage on a small flat in Clapham. L. P. Watson – from the first he had used his initials rather than his first name – wrote reviews, a few short travel pieces for the broadsheet newspapers, and a few longer articles for colour supplements. It was the success of his books which drew him to the notice of newspaper editors. After a year or two, however, he discovered that journalism was much more lucrative, and much less hard work than 'proper writing'.

During one long assignment abroad – a piece on the countries of West Africa, which involved visits to Lugardia, Nigeria, Ghana and Benin – he had an affair, with the woman who had been sent out by the magazine to take photographs. It was a delightful affair – the first since he married Julia. He had not considered it important at the time. Liz Stein, the photographer, and he went their separate ways after only a few months. His children had been four and six when it happened. He was determined not to allow his marriage to founder. Julia knew Lionel so intimately that there was no need to search his belongings nor to discover (as she did, some weeks later) letters from the Stein woman. It clung to him, the obviousness of it, like a smell. The shy way he made love to her, the first time after his return home; his increased intake of alcohol and cigarettes. His spiritual distance from her. Julia had been very much hurt. Lionel had been very guilty. Neither of them had spoken one word on the subject.

He suggested at that time that they should move from the flat, where they lived perfectly comfortably and within their means, into a large Victorian house in Wandsworth which they could only afford if he wrote journalism regularly, rather than occasionally. A volume of poetry – he was reworking some lyrics by Rilke – was laid aside. So, too, was a vague idea that he might write a study of the philosophy of Heidegger.

Both the Watsons often, in their secret hearts, looked back

to the move to Wandsworth as the Fall, the point of no return. Julia had never discussed the matter, but she now, eighteen years on, believed that she could have had the courage then to divorce him, not to depend on his earning power any longer. He for his part secretly believed, with the addled optimism of a man who had long since lost any capacity for accurate moral judgement, that one confessional conversation, when the affair with Liz Stein came to an end, would have 'saved' him; that if he had confessed his sins to Julia, she would have forgiven him and thereby prevented his cascade into womanizing, workaholism, drink and cynicism.

There had been a steady stream of women, and to numb the guilt, he worked harder and harder. He moved steadily down-market, abandoning the travel pages of the broadsheets for 'op ed' pieces in middle-market tabloids. Then – at about the time that Martina Fax's marriage to her proprietor was exciting every journalist in London – Lionel Watson met Mary Much.

Knowing both of them, most journalists assumed that they had an affair – or at the very least went to bed together once. Julia pursued her usual policy of not wanting to know; but in this case she judged an affair between her husband and the editor of *Gloss* to be rather unlikely. Mary Much was a talent scout for the Marks. It was through Mary that the *Legions*, *Daily* and *Sunday*, bought L. P. Watson – an article in *The Sunday Legion* each week, and three articles each week in the *Daily*. L.P. had been a clever man when he was twenty, and he did not stop being a clever man merely because he was thirty-seven. But it was not possible to write with such facility and prolixity without watering the mixture, and in order to delight the fans, he resorted to the expression of wilder and sillier 'opinions' which Mary Much, like a trainer egging on an animal reared by hand, regularly assured him were killingly funny.

Killing they might have been. It had certainly killed something inside him when he went to the *Legion*. Julia, too, had been
harder and colder since they exchanged a house they could
barely afford in Wandsworth for their present abode in Clapham,
which would only be paid for if L.P. dropped dead and the life
insurance paid off the life-consuming mortgage. The children
were away, first at boarding schools – Rugby and Wycombe
Abbey – then at universities – Glasgow and Sussex. Julia sank
into alternate bouts of self-reproach and depression, wondering
who Lionel was sleeping with and telling herself she did not give
a damn. They avoided one another's company. He slept in a
small downstairs bedroom, she had the marital bedroom on the
second floor, a room where they had never, after nine years in
the house, made love. They gave dinner parties about once a
fortnight, and were regarded, by those who came to them, as a
'splendid', 'old-fashioned', 'almost Edwardian' couple who did
not go in for anything tawdry and modern like divorce but who
stuck with one another.

Mary Much, with whom Lionel gossiped on the telephone
for hours each day, had been the presiding deity of the Watsons'
lives for the last decade. Julia referred to her, bitterly, but with
a full sense of the phrase's truth, as 'our benefactress'. She felt
utterly excluded by her husband's friendship with the woman.

Although Mary Much was the editor of *Gloss*, the impreg-
nable queen of upmarket magazines, her real obsession was the
world of newspapers, and she spent all available spare time
discussing them, primarily with her closest confidante, Martina
Mark, but by extension with other members of the Court, of
which L.P. was a key member. Time was, Julia thought sadly
(Lionel had the thought fairly often, too, but he had drifted too
far apart from Julia to be able to share it), that in any one week,
he would have reread one of Plato's dialogues, or written some

poetry, or thought about the Heidegger book, or tried out one of the new novels or biographies recommended in the literary pages. Thanks to his Faustian compact with Mary Much, there was very little time for any of that now. When he was not rattling out his pieces, or drinking with his friends, or seeing his mistress – an affair which, like his marriage, was not emotionally very satisfying – he was entering into the Mary Much obsessions. Chief among these was how competently or otherwise various editors or deputy editors or features editors were doing their job, or how 'good' the other papers and those who wrote for them were.

These judgements were capricious and largely intuitive. They were not usually based on anything so prosaic as how well the paper or magazine in question sold. Mary, or Martina, would decide on a whim that the *Evening Standard* or *The Times* or *The Spectator* was 'completely brilliant'; or, on another whim, that they weren't any good any more. L.P. found himself contributing to these debates with alacrity, longing with a desire stronger than love to ring up Mary Much if he heard some tittle-tattle about the way in which some editor had made an ass of himself.

The strongest feelings, of course, were recorded for the magazine and newspaper executives, and for the journalists, working for Lennox Mark's titles. Time was that the orthodoxy, propounded first by the Martina–Mary Much axis, was that the *Legion*s were essentially gentle, very, very *British* newspapers. What was needed at the *Daily* was a good, solid newspaperman. So they had promoted Anthony Taylor, with his gentle northern accent, his shirtsleeves, his passion for Scunthorpe Athleticals. The last thing they'd all wanted was either red-top cruelty or – God help us – social *pretension*. (They had quite enough of that from Mr Blimby, editor of the *Sunday Legion*, with his clubs, his place in the country, his titled friends.)

Then all of a sudden, Martina had woken up one morning, or Mary Much had done so (did they sometimes wake in the same bed? wondered 'Dr Arbuthnot' with his sprightly malice), and realized that Tony Taylor was a 'thundering bore'. A newspaper was not a vehicle for purveying news. You got news from TV. What a newspaper could do so brilliantly was create an atmosphere, give you a vision of the world. Taylor in his polyester-cotton, Taylor with his famous 'campaigns' – how the Court had groaned at his raising money from *Legion* readers to send a minibus to Mozambique during the floods! Or again, his exposé of those dodgy children's homes in the Midlands. That sort of thing was dead duck journalism. Tinkling with laughter down a dozen telephone lines, Mary Much had given an example of how out of touch Taylor was. He hadn't heard of Nicole Kidman. This lie created itself the first time she spoke it. By the time she had repeated it a dozen times she – and They All – accepted it as part of the canon.

So Taylor had to go – 'good newspaperman' he. For a few weeks, Mary had wondered whether to put L.P. in his shoes – a truly witty appointment, one which would buck all trends. Spottiswood, when Lennie mentioned it, had screamed with rage, and Mary Much had quickly rethought. Martina and she knew which side their bread was buttered. They needed something butch, something macho, something which everyone could see was ironical, something brutal, something from the primeval slimes. They needed Worledge.

And tonight was to be the night. After a 'party' at LenMar House at which Lennie said farewell to Anthony Taylor, there was to be supper at Redgauntlet Road for the Worledges and the Court. No one was much looking forward to this, and L.P. was fully expecting Julia, at the last minute, to plead a sick headache. She had hardly ever been known to enjoy the social engagements generated by his *Legion* life – nor, indeed, to have made a positive comment about any aspect of the newspaper.

That was why it was so extraordinary when she said, 'Wonders will never cease – a decent article in *The Daily Legion*.'

L.P. never read the paper *through*. In fact he had reached a stage of his career where it was no longer possible for him to read: he only skimmed other people's work, though his own articles were endlessly rereadable. His habit of rereading his own stuff was one reason for its tendency to self-parody.

'Sinclo Manners.'

'What about him?'

'He wrote this article about what's happening in Zinariya. It's bloody good – the first bloody thing I've read about the subject in the *Legion* which makes any sort of sense.'

'It's dangerous to make sense out of nonsense.'

'What's that supposed to mean? You haven't read it – I know you haven't.'

'Of course I've read the *Legion* – I write for it.' His weary schoolmaster tone.

'In a surprise move,' said the radio, but neither Julia nor Lionel were listening, 'President Bindiga of Zinariya has said that his country would be well placed to host next year's Commonwealth Games . . .'

'This fucking little man' – she pointed to the picture of President Bindiga – 'allows slavery in the cocoa plantations. The nationalized copper mines have what amounts to a slave-labour force. He lives in a socking great palace with tall Scandinavian prozzies . . .'

'Wait a minute . . .'

'No, I will NOT wait a minute . . .'

'The mystery to me is how that article got printed,' said L.P.

'Perhaps it has something to do with its being true. It's also very well written.'

'Women like him – always do – young Manners. Mary's nuts about him, which makes me wonder whether she . . . but no, she wouldn't have licensed him to rubbish Bindiga. The whole *raison d'être* of the *Legion* is to support Bindiga.'

'You write articles *praising* this man – have you read about the public torture of that homosexual?'

'It's all more complicated than—'

'Than a woman would understand? Is that what you were going to say? My God, to think of the things you're prepared to say for *money*.'

'You're quite happy to spend the money,' he said quietly.

Later – doors had been slammed, he'd been left alone in the kitchen staring sadly at Sinclo Manners's peculiar article – he'd prepared to go out.

'So you'll come to the dinner and not the party,' he called up the stairs to her office. He knew she was in there; he could hear her computer bleeping.

'I'll see you at the dinner – but you won't want to come all the way to Bermondsey for the party,' he said – this time through the closed door on her landing.

She flung open her office door and said, with eyes aflame, 'Maybe I could be the judge of what I do or don't want to do.'

TWENTY-TWO

Lily d'Abo wore her coat and hat. She had her basket ready, and her shopping list. She would go to the Blue Mountain Cash and Carry for Costa Rican plantain, sweetcorn, sweet potatoes and green bananas. Then she would go to the fishmonger and buy some parrot fish, if he had any in today. Then she would go to the shrine and thank Our Lady for Peter's job, and the huge improvement in his character. So, okay, he hadn't passed his exams. But there would be time enough for that. Lily knew that there were many Peters, but among them was a kind, considerate boy who could be nurtured. She wondered whether he would not one day follow in her footsteps and become a nurse. There was a midday mass at the shrine today. Lily would stay on for that, then bring her shopping home. She would cook the meal, and take half of it upstairs to old Mr and Mrs Simpson, neighbours for whom she did occasional good turns. Then she would set out to the hospital. She could work any shifts there, now that Peter was settled in his new work.

'In a surprise move,' said her radio, 'President Bindiga of Zinariya has said that his country would be well placed to host next year's Commonwealth Games in Mararraba, the country's capital. Many have criticized the country's human rights record, and the . . .'

Lily had the radio on continuously, leaving it speaking to itself when she left the flat – a deterrent, she believed, to burglars.

'Yes,' she said to the telephone, and repeated the number.

It was Mercy, who had got to work, and who had rung for a chat. Lily looked anxiously at the clock.

'It's surely better that he should be stable, and well behaved . . . Exactly . . . That's what I say . . .'

It was inevitable that her daughter should have wanted to talk about the whole situation, but it was simply a pity she should have done so when the morning schedule was tight. Lily pictured Mercy sitting comfortably in her office, coffee and biscuits on her desk, and a leisurely day stretching ahead.

'Father Vivyan wants to talk to us about it,' Lily told her. '. . . Because I asked him, that's why he's getting involved . . . I don't know why you won't come and meet Father Vivyan . . . You never come to church any more . . . Father Vivyan says he don't think Kevin has been a good influence on Peter. He says he wants to talk to the both of us about it. I agree with him . . .'

Mercy made the predictable response.

'That's not true – I would not agree with anything Father says. But what good was served by telling the boy his father was . . . I know . . . He's not said one word to me about it. Not a word, love. Maybe he's just bottling it all up inside him. Or maybe he thinks – what's the use a big fella like him, my dad? He's not going to want to confront him, is he? How could Peter get to meet a man like that? . . . I reckon Peter's sometimes a bit more mature than people give him credit for. What can't be done, can't be done . . . I'm late now, darling . . . Okay . . . See you . . . Take care.'

TWENTY-THREE

'In Baban Bari,' said the car radio inside Lennox Mark's Bentley, 'troops have been out all night firing on the crowds. In the copper mines to the south of Bomberra the so-called Happy Band, teenaged youths and young men, have been once again rioting. A small explosive device was detected in the Kanni-Karkara mines, identical to one which exploded in the mine shafts last month killing twelve people. Scotland Yard say that they are investigating reports that a similar device has been found in the Zinariyan High Commission in London, prompting speculation that the Happy Band is linked to terrorist organizations in Britain . . .'

As the Bentley purred into the forecourt of LenMar House, the Chairman rested his large soft fingers on his belly. A late lunch had been unsatisfactory from the theological point of view. Kurtmeyer, with his fucking pocket-calculator and his auditor's reports, had shown no stomach for the rerun of the Ontological Proof, Lennox's own personal favourite among the various 'classic' arguments for the Almighty's existence. At least Kurtmeyer had consented to have foie gras with a fried egg on top as a savoury. (Lennox had had three of these to give him strength for the journey to Bermondsey.)

His plate-glass tower, the visible monument to his own achievement, was most satisfyingly far from the centre of things. No wonder Mary Much insisted that *Gloss* remained where it was when Lennox acquired it, in the old eighteenth-century house off Hanover Square. Not for her, as for all the journalists on *Daily* and *Sunday Legion*s, the punishment of internal exile. It gave the proprietor and his wife enormous satisfaction to know that even by sprinting to Bermondsey station and catching a Jubilee Line train, the Nibelungs (Martina's brilliant word) were a good three-quarters of an hour from Christopher's or the Savoy, an hour from the Ivy. Those who tried to get into London by taxi at lunch-time were sure to be stuck in traffic for an hour and a half. Lennox, Martina and Mary Much all derived particular pleasure that the Would-be Gent (as they called the editor of *The Sunday Legion*) had to spend three frustrated hours in snarl-ups just for an hour or so of eating cutlets with some lords at a club in St James's.

Swooping up in the lift in his glass palace, Lennox's eyes took in the plane tree straining towards the skylights; the cascades of water which fell towards the twin busts, one of his great-grandfather, *old* Lennox Mark, the other of General Bindiga; the open-plan offices stretching for visible yards on all four sides of the building; the swarms of journalists, who were such a constant drain on his purse. The ownership of newspapers gave Lennox an all but orgasmic sense of his own importance. It was just a pity that the price to be paid for this pleasure was having to fund editors, 'celebrity' interviewers like Peg Montgomery, columnists, diarists, all of whom claimed 'expenses' for every luxury in their lives – their fucking restaurant bills, their fucking taxis, probably in some cases their fucking. How much more money could these bastards take from him?

That was one of the questions at the back of his mind as he arrived at the editorial floor of *The Daily Legion* and found himself greeted by the outgoing editor.

'Tony!'

'Lennie!'

Both men pumped one another's hands and grinned. An anthropologist observing the scene would conclude that this was what these strange animals did when two of them aggressively loathed one another. When Lennox had emerged from 10 Downing Street that morning he'd wanted Tony Taylor's guts for garters. If he could have stopped the man's Golden Handshake and cancelled his pension, he would have done so. At the back of the Bentley he had roared and howled at the man via his mobile; about ingratitude and some things not being funny. Martina, when he had rung her, was already on the case, writing a riposte to 'the Captain' as she called Sinclo Manners, and setting out in no uncertain terms why Bindiga was a role model for all other African leaders to follow. This would be published in tomorrow's *Legion*. She would dictate the 'stand first':

We at the Legion *believe in the free debate of important issues, which is why we have allowed an article highly hostile to President Bindiga to be published in yesterday's issue. But, argues top* Legion *opinion-former Martina Fax, those who support the rebellion against West Africa's stablest and most prosperous state are at best naive . . .*

Kurtmeyer had done damage-limitation with the Zinariyan Embassy. Spottiswood had been in touch with the Mararraba office. Assurances had been given that such articles would not appear again. Lennox himself wanted the young idiot who wrote the article to be hung out to dry; but Mary Much had pleaded.

'Go on – make Aubrey's day.'

The tall former army captain would be moved from Features to be an assistant to Aubrey Bird ('Dr Arbuthnot') on the gossip column. It was hardly the fucking Siberian salt mines, which was what Lennox thought he deserved.

There was a ripple as the retiring editor, Anthony Taylor, a tall, thin, cricket-loving man in specs, led the proprietor, six inches shorter, sun-tanned and silver-haired, into the newsroom. A virtue was being made of necessity. Lennox Mark had said he'd be fucked if he was going to hire a special party venue to say goodbye to Tony Taylor. Spottiswood decided that a good newspaperman would prefer to have his send-off in the newsroom itself. It was clear, from the smell, noise and atmosphere of murmurous disrespect among the two hundred and fifty or so who thronged the great open-plan office, that they'd been at the Asti Spumante for about an hour. Over the laminated grey surface of the desks stood a multitude of bottles. Some drank from glasses, others from plastic cups. Canapés had been ordered and arranged. An atmosphere of stale fish drifted from mouths and plates. On the back bench itself, chromium platters of smoked salmon on inch-square brown bread and butter congealed with tiger prawns and cigarette stubs. Some of the plastic cups containing fizzy white wine were clouded with floating filters and deposits of ash.

The proprietor stood on a chair and tapped his tin of Seven-Up. It was inaudible in such a throng, so Tony Taylor tapped a glass. Still the conversation and laughter rumbled on.

'Quiet, please!'

This from Taylor.

'General Bindiga!' called Lennox.

The calling-out of this controversial name brought silence; the whole office had been buzzing for twenty-four hours about the article by Sinclo Manners, and its consequences.

'General Bindiga – my *friend* General Bindiga!'

There were loud guffaws of mirth at this.

Lennox beamed. He had hit a right note. They were going to listen to him.

'My friend General Bindiga is a much kindlier fellow than you'd believe if you read everything in the newspapers . . .'

A great roar of laughter. Peg Montgomery, interviewer extraordinaire, appeared to be choking on a Silk Cut cigarette.

'But he has been known to dispense of the services of his Cabinet and other trusted colleagues in a way that some of us would find, shall we say, a trifle peremptory.'

Yet more laughter. The atmosphere was now such that if the speaker had begun reciting the alphabet or reading at random from the telephone directory, the audience would have rocked with mirth.

'But, my dear Anthony' – and Lennox placed a podgy hand on Tony Taylor's shoulder – '. . . not dispensing so much as . . . sad leavetaking . . . worked on the paper, I believe now for thirty-five years . . .'

'Twenty-nine years – I'm not that old!' called back Tony spiritedly, which caused more laughter from the audience.

'. . . much valued . . . through and through a newspaper-man . . . though many would remember some of Taylor's less than spectacular scoops.'

Lennox had consulted the Court about the wisdom of ribbing Taylor for the innumerable gaffes in his career. His speech was typed out in bold for him by Mary Much, on cards which could be slipped back into his pockets.

He reminded the crowd of the time when, on the say-so of some alcoholic stringer in a tapas bar, Taylor – then Foreign Editor – had been proud to track down Dr Goebbels in Buenos Aires. The man who had committed suicide in 1945 had been the double of the National Socialist Propaganda Minister; the 'real' Dr Goebbels, having escaped to Holland and boarded a merchant vessel, had reached the Argentine, where he had been living for a number of years with a belly dancer.

Helpless laughter. 'Dr Arbuthnot' bent double. Tears of mirth making Peg Montgomery's mascara run.

Then Lennox recalled Taylor's campaign to have Belisha beacons restored. 'How many more kids have to die on the roads?' Taylor's anguished editorial had asked before the Department of Transport informed Tony that Belisha beacons could not be restored because they had never been abolished.

The grin on Taylor's face became decidedly fixed as his proprietor got the staff to laugh at him for not having heard of Nicole Kidman.

'But seriously . . .' said Lennox Mark, 'seriously, and we must be serious . . .'

'Shame!' cried out L. P. Watson as the oration limped on.

TWENTY-FOUR

While Lennox Mark stood on his chair and drew forth such predictable responses from his staff, there stood among them a thirty-one-year-old man whose spiritual agony was so palpable that many who found themselves near him in the throng edged away from him, unaware of why they did so. Some considered him haughty or stand-offish. Many of the women thought him extremely handsome. His face was not that of a naturally sad person, but of a happy man whose heart had become totally desolate.

Sinclo Manners was a tall man, with the ruddy complexion of a countryman, high cheekbones, blue eyes and aquiline nose. He had thick chestnut hair which, when not fiercely brushed back from his brow, flopped over it. The fact that, until five years ago, he had been a captain in the Royal Green Jackets was easy to imagine. (What was less easy to imagine was that he was on the staff of *The Daily Legion*.) Wherever his face had been seen in whatever part of the globe, it would have been quite impossible to suppose Sinclo to be any nationality other than English. This was not merely because of his colouring and physiognomy, but because of the cast of his face, which combined melancholy and comedy in equal proportion. (This accounted for an expression which some saw, quite mistakenly, as 'stuck up'.)

There were two reasons for his unhappiness. First, he loathed *The Daily Legion* and was ashamed of himself for staying on as a member of staff; secondly — his reason for staying — he was profoundly and, as far as could be seen, hopelessly in love.

He was one of those who had decided to give journalism a try, but who had been sucked into a branch of it which, until he entered a newspaper office, he had never known existed. Emerging from the army after seven years, he had imagined himself as a foreign correspondent. On active service abroad he had more than once encountered journalists — in the Balkans, in Saudi Arabia, in Malaysia. He had envied them, and believed they were doing work which he could do well. When he had met these men and women, who were often in disaster areas or war zones, running risks as great as the military, it had not occurred to him to think that journalism was a shaming occupation. No doubt, if Sinclo had played his cards differently, he could have become just such a foreign correspondent. It was still very much his ambition to do so.

When he left the army, he had gone through a period of unemployment and depression, sharing a London flat with old school friends, all of them in well-paid jobs in City firms or lawyers' chambers. Poverty and boredom oppressed him, and he began to lose any sense of self-worth as days, then weeks, passed without any offer of work. He wrote to several newspaper editors pointing out his army experience, and suggesting that he be sent to West Africa. General Bindiga had fought off an attempted coup, but there was in effect a renewal of civil war in Zinariya. Thousands had been killed, but no mention of this had appeared in any British newspaper. Sinclo believed that his first-hand experiences of this African country would make him well qualified to write about it. In the event, only one editor bothered to answer his letter, saying that he could not write articles about Zinariya without a 'story' or 'peg' to hang them on.

Some of Sinclo's friends told him that there was no point in trying to secure a job in journalism unless you knew someone who was already working on a newspaper. Others told him to write some articles and hawk them around. He tried both, and neither experiment was successful.

At the far end of the newsroom now, Lennox Mark was still speechifying about Taylor, the decent but essentially unintelligent editor who was being fired. The ritual of the insulting speech, delivered to the victim before a baying drunken audience, had something of the feeling of a public execution. Sinclo hated bullying. In the army he had always moved in to stop it, actually getting one sadistic corporal court-martialled when he found out what he'd done to his men. Lennox Mark seemed much worse than that corporal. Sinclo had to go back in his memory to school (Radley) to summon up comparable examples of oikish thuggery. He wanted very much to go up to Mark now and punch his face, as he had once punched a Radley boy who was picking on a younger child.

'Not that Tony could ever be accused of being a dedicated follower of fashion.'

Laughter from the sycophants.

The present occasion was making sharply clear in Sinclo's mind impressions which had hitherto been only latent. The mist was clearing and the grotesque edifice was revealed, its gargoyles and resident monsters in all their Brothers Grimm monstrosity. The smoke coming from the nostrils of Peg Montgomery could have been from a dragon's nose. Aubrey Bird (the diarist 'Dr Arbuthnot'), one of the last men in London to affect royal-blue shirts with white collars, was certainly an evil old fairy. L. P. Watson, whose travel books had so impressed Sinclo, was perhaps one of those knights errant caught in the tangles of a briarwood for a hundred years – or was he simply in a snare of his own cynicism? And now, entering ostentatiously late,

tiptoeing as through a minefield, with such exaggerated movements of her long, thin, pointed shoes (hand-made in Paris),
was the Enchantress herself, Mary Much, her silver-blonde bob,
and her long, cool, beautiful face gazing mischievously around,
casting spells as she strode.

As Lennox spoke, *The Daily Legion* was exposed to Sinclo in
all its brutality and power. And it was the power, expressed
through money, of the tycoon which made sycophants of them
all: including Sinclo himself. He was fully aware of that, having,
on the strength of his *Legion* salary, taken out a mortgage on a
flat which he could only just afford. There did not have to be any
rules, telling you things which must or must not be done or said.
There was a perpetual atmosphere of fear, generated by Lennox
and his wife, by Mary Much and by the editors. That was why
it had been so liberating when, a few days before, Taylor
(everyone knew he'd been sacked in spite of his repeated claims
to be taking early retirement) wandered over to the features
desk where Sinclo worked and said, 'Your Zinariya piece –
would you like to tweak it? We'll run it on Monday.'

Sinclo had written his article about Zinariya well over a year
ago. It was after he had secured his desk job on Features, and he
thought he might persuade Taylor to send him to Africa on an
assignment. Taylor had barely acknowledged the article, and it
had sat around in the Features 'basket' for months before being
spiked. Sinclo's boss at Features told him that Zinariya was a no-
go area in the *Legion*s.

'Lennie doesn't ban us from carrying stories about it. He
doesn't need to. Taylor and Blimby are so shit-scared of annoying
him they'd rather not mention the subject.'

Zinariyan topics were therefore handled with kid gloves.
Martina Fax and L. P. Watson in their columns praised Bindiga,
and Lennox himself sometimes dictated leading articles to

Taylor about the General being a latter-day Oliver Cromwell, supporting the liberties of his people by the paradoxical, though time-honoured, method of curtailing free speech, free elections and indeed freedom of any kind. *The Daily Legion* liked Bindiga's 'no-nonsense' approach to homosexuality. (It was illegal in Zinariya – if we're honest, don't we all feel our kiddies would be safer if it were still illegal in Britain?) While not letting readers into the secret that Lennox Mark owned tobacco and cocoa farms where unpaid children worked, *The Daily Legion* opined that the best chocolate and the best cigarettes in the world came from Zinariya. The copper piping in your bathroom would cost five times as much if it were not for General Bindiga. African dictators, like the Almighty, moved in mysterious ways, their wonders to perform. Mary Much, who had taken a shine to Sinclo, said, over one of their lunches, 'I wouldn't write Bongo stories if I were you.'

He'd been impressed by her spy network. He'd never mentioned his interest in Africa to her.

But then, as a last defiant gesture before he left, Taylor had published the article. The office was buzzing with excitement. Sinclo, considered by some a stuck-up bastard, was going to be sacked, or have his arse kicked – this idea caused pleasure to those who invented it, but they were equally impressed by his recklessness. It was seeing his article in print, with the photographs of Father Vivyan, Bindiga, the slave boys, the copper mines, which contributed to this sense of mist clearing, this feeling that he was seeing *The Daily Legion* in its true garish colours for the first time. He was afraid – because like everyone in that newsroom he had become addicted to being overpaid, and did not know how he would live if he were to be sacked. At the same time he tingled with adrenalin: the mingling of fear and joy was a little like going into battle. He looked across at his fellow-journalists: Mary Much was stooping her long, swanlike neck to kiss Aubrey Bird and trying not to dislodge his toupée; Seamus Ahearne ('Creevey' on *The Sunday Legion*) had a face creased with laughter as Lennox Mark recounted the story of Dr Goebbels in the Buenos Aires tapas bar — the face sweated whisky; Dot Saxby, the literary editor, with that alarming low dark fringe of hair and her weird taste in men's double-breasted suits, was edging towards a bird-like girl who wrote medical stories. And through the smoke and the noise and the faces, he felt completely alien. Could it really be the case, he asked himself, that for nearly two years he had been a deputy features editor — not writing articles himself, but telephoning others to write them?

Until he was offered the job, it had never even occurred to him that there was a need in the world for a deputy features editor. The chance to become one arose when he met the features editor at a dinner party. She was married to a school friend of one of his flatmates. She was on the look-out for someone to help at the features desk. He could come along and try it out for a few weeks if he liked. At first he had worked as a dogsbody, fetching 'cuts' from the library. (Many if not most newspaper articles, he discovered, were scissors-and-paste jobs, repeating things which had already been printed somewhere else.) Then Jan, his boss, took her children away for half-term and Sinclo was asked to attend the daily editorial meeting (or features conference as it was pompously called) in her stead. His position as her deputy was thereafter official, and his days had a pattern.

At the beginning of each day, they prepared 'ideas' for the features conference. Then at 10.30 a.m. they trooped in to see the editor and put up these ideas for his approval. The themes could cover any subject ranging from the problem of world terrorism to whether kiddies should eat potato crisps. Taylor usually liked to commission two or three articles on such themes each day. They would be nine hundred words long, and because they were printed opposite the editorials they would be known as 'op eds' or 'leader page articles' (LPAs). Sinclo, who'd developed a fondness for initials and abbreviations in the army, relished this aspect of the job and loved all its private language – blacks (you didn't see these very often now copy was almost always e-mailed), spikes, and so on. After the morning conference, Sinclo would ring up likely writers of the articles they had concocted in outline in committee. One quickly learnt why a newspaper valued a figure such as L. P. Watson, whose appalling facility enabled him to churn out nine hundred words at double-quick speed on any theme, and to adopt any opinion suggested to him by the commissioning editor.

There would then follow lunch – usually an alcoholic lunch – after which Sinclo would read the articles, which were known in the business as why-oh-whys. Then he would have to ring up the writers and sometimes suggest rewrites. This was not usually because of their infelicitous style. Much more likely it was because between the morning conference and lunch-time, the editor would have changed his mind. In the morning, for example, *The Daily Legion*'s view might be that the flood of illegal migrants coming through the Channel Tunnel represented a danger to Great Britain every bit as grave as the threatened invasions of the Nazis in 1940. The researcher would be dispatched to the library for cuts – previous *Legion* articles would be found, which had warned, before the tunnel was built, that it would open the floodgates of immigration. The why-oh-why artist would be primed.

After lunch, however, when the article came in, comparing the refugees from Bosnia or Albania with the hordes of Attila the

Hun, *The Daily Legion*'s great collective mind would be altered. What were these people coming into the country but the twenty-first-century equivalent of the poor huddled masses who created the enterprise culture of the United States? The *Legion* was not offering anyone a blank cheque. If these foreigners thought they could come to Britain and exploit its welfare system then the *Legion* had no pity – they deserved to be booted back on the train and booted back fast. But if they came in the spirit of the great entrepreneurs – why, had not all the most famous American philanthropists started life as poor refugees?

Naturally, the features desk came across the occasional difficult customer who would not adapt their copy in this way. Some pretentious so-and-sos even tried to parade knowledge, and would reel off the names of philanthropic Americans of patrician birth who had never been huddled or poor in their lives. But by six on a good evening the task would be done. The article on immigrants which it had taken all day to rewrite would be spiked and they'd use instead the heart-rending plea of a mum whose eleven-year-old weighed thirteen stone. 'In an Open Letter to the Health Secretary, a Mother pleads – Stop this crisp-eating madness now.' And so, their work would be done, and the wine bar and the London evening would beckon.

'Nicole Who?' Lennox was saying, in an implausible imitation of Taylor's northern accent. This was greeted with a real explosion of laughter. Tony Taylor himself mouthed the words 'Not true'.

It had been a mad way of spending two years, and Sinclo would have relinquished it all willingly were it not for one person in whom he had invested, quite against his will, a hopeless love. No love for a woman had ever made him suffer as he now suffered. And, for all his certainties about the pointlessness of his job, and the moral putrescence of the *Legion*, he knew that he would willingly go into the office as a floor-sweeper if it gave him the chance of daily contact with Rachel Pearl, whose face he could see through the crowd of yahoos, as she sat on her desk top and swung her legs like a schoolgirl.

TWENTY-FIVE

When the face of Rachel Pearl was in repose, she resembled one of those calm, sad Blessed Virgins in the Byzantine tradition. She looked not unlike the young Madonna depicted in mosaics at Torcello. Certainly no face in Western art since those times had such fixity as hers, such calm seriousness. Brows were drawn with the simplicity of the old icon-painters, arched above ink-black glossy eyes. Her nose was small and pointed. Her lips were the focus of her charm. For most of each day, the mouth was pursed and small and prim. Every now and again, however, it would open in the most radiant of smiles. Then her whole face framed with its dark bob would change. The dark eyes became radiant. The straight nose wrinkled. The intelligent intensity melted into hilarity and the intense iconic Virgin became a laughing schoolgirl.

It was one day when one of these transformations occurred to her face that Sinclo Manners fell in love with Rachel Pearl. Such was the depth of his feeling, so completely intense was his misery, that he could form no accurate impression of one vital question: whether she was aware of it at all.

When he joined the paper, Rachel was the only person whom he slightly knew. They had met at Throxton Winnards, the seat of Sinclo's cousin, Monty Longmore. Rachel had been at university with Monty's daughter Kitty – a cousin on whom Sinclo had always had rather a crush. They had a knowledge of this shared world. In the alien world of the *Legion* it was a bond.

It was perfectly usual for colleagues at the *Legion* to lunch together, either in the canteen, or at Bin Ends, the unpleasant little wine bar twenty minutes' very fast walk from LenMar House. The fact that Sinclo and Rachel often lunched together was therefore no cause for remark among their colleagues, who quite often joined the pair for a meal or a drink.

They'd been meeting most days for nearly two years, and yet Sinclo still found her a totally mysterious character. Loving her to the point of heartbreak, he still did not know her. They had told one another the outline of their lives. He had been a soldier, and the son of a soldier from the kind of impoverished and aristocratic background which it was necessary, in an office context, to play down. Rachel was the daughter of two doctors from Barnes. One of the doctors was the great-grandson of Russian Jews who had come to London at the beginning of the twentieth century. The other was the granddaughter of Polish Jews who had escaped the Continent just in time, in the late thirties. (Most of this side of the family had died in Auschwitz.) Rachel had been educated at St Paul's School, and gone to Oxford, where she had read Modern Languages. (It was here that she'd befriended his cousin Kitty Chell – one of those passionate friendships formed between opposites.) She was fluent in Italian, German and French; she had smatterings of Russian, Polish and (from a grandmother) Yiddish. She could read Latin and Greek. She was in all obvious senses much cleverer than Sinclo, which was one reason he feared to disclose his heart to her.

One of her mysteries, to him, was why she wanted to be a journalist at all. To Sinclo, she seemed to take the world more seriously than was quite tolerable, and her decision to immerse herself in the world of the *Legion* must, he supposed, involve her in almost daily lacerations of soul. True, she did not involve herself with news, or gossip, as such. As arts editor, her responsibility was to 'sub' the various regular critics of films, plays and concerts. For the rest, she attended features conferences and put up ideas for articles on, for example, the funding of the Royal Ballet or debates on modern architecture.

Tony Taylor's reaction to such suggestions was a puzzled frown. He would then try to prompt her to produce stories with a 'loose arts peg'. Her apparent desire to take seriously the pretensions – as everyone on the paper, Sinclo included – imagined them of BritArt and conceptual artists brought nothing but contempt from the hardfaced men on the back bench. But she did sometimes surprise them by coming up with some good gossip about some contemporary artist: Hans Busch's love life, for example, or the fantastic sums commanded by this man for his 'installations' and 'concepts'.

Sinclo could see the advantages for her in being an arts editor. (It was said that L. P. Watson helped her to get the job – he apparently was some friend of her parents. Sinclo discounted, as both painful and improbable, the notion that she'd had to sleep with L.P. in exchange for the post: she was much too serious for such a thing to be remotely possible, and besides, he'd quite often had lunch with Rachel and L.P. and their jokey, mildly flirtatious friendship did not strike him as being that of ex-lovers.) The material advantages of the job were obvious. She was only twenty-eight. She had free access on viewing days to all the good exhibitions before the public saw them. Plays, concerts and films could all be sampled for no money. She had an expense account and could travel everywhere by taxi. While her student contemporaries, some of them, were still living in rented bedsits finishing a thesis on a subject so obscure that no one would read it, she could somehow afford her own flat overlooking the river. She was serious, but she was not unworldly. She enjoyed all this, and she dressed with discreet flair and sexy good taste. And yet, when they lunched *à deux*, she would often share with Sinclo her sense of despondency at having fallen into Lennox Mark's 'honey trap'. Yes, it was beneath her dignity to write four hundred words before lunch about the likely contenders for the Cannes festival – four hundred words which were concerned not with the cinematic skills of those discussed, but entirely with tittle-tattle about their love affairs and feuds, their clothes, or their misbehaviour in restaurants. Such work filled her with priggish shame; but, as she liked to quote, 'She wept, but she took.' Intellectual snobbery might make her squirm at her work, but she did not scorn its material rewards. In a metaphor which surprised Sinclo, the first time she deployed it, she scorned the idea of going to work for a more serious newspaper for less money. 'If you're going to work in a brothel, you might as well earn the full whack.'

She had a fascination with money. In one of the conversations in which she had tried to explain conceptual art to Sinclo, she had told him that the huge sums of money which the artists received was part of the point.

'The world's changed,' she would tell him with a strange faraway look in her eyes. 'Money is a very simple way of codifying value. In an aristocratic world, artists needed patrons to produce' – she'd shrug – 'an epic, a mass, a painting. We're not in a world of industrial capitalism, we're in a post-paper-money, post-industrial, post-modern world. The novel which commands the highest advance *is* the best novel. The installation in the visual arts fights for its own importance, its own status, by rewarding the artist.'

'You can't believe that,' he'd said, staring into the glossy blackness of her eyes and hoping against hope that she did not.

When she made these points in conversation – the joke about

working in a brothel, the defence of art which Sinclo deemed pure chicanery – little dabs of strawberry rouge would appear in her cheeks. This blush had come into her face, too, when referring to men who were interested in her. She'd once told Sinclo about the unwelcome advances of another journalist.

'Can you *imagine* anything more embarrassing?' she had asked as these almost consumptive flushes came into her normally pallid face.

(Was it her way of warning him off?)

Sinclo assumed that she had a lover. While he was pains-takingly 'tweaking' why-oh-why articles, and conversing with their authors by telephone, he would gaze across the open plan of the office to her desk where, much of the time she seemed to do little except read novels in French and German. Sometimes when she was on the telephone he would assume, with the instinctive jealousy of the man in love, that she was speaking to her lover though he had no evidence that such a person existed. The lover took shape in his mind in a manner rather comparable to the idea of God in the minds of eighteenth-century Deists. They had no experience of him, but by positing his existence a number of mysterious holes in their universe could be patched. Her air of unattainability, her sudden decision, if she'd agreed to join a group for dinner, to break away at the last moment, her habit of referring occasionally to 'ex-boyfriends' – all these things suggested another life, a shared life with Another. Sinclo feared very much that the love affair was making her unhappy, but although in his fantasy life he was forever 'rescuing' her, he believed it was unlikely that she could ever love him. He some-times wondered if the reason for keeping her lover a secret was that he was famous – Hans Busch, for example.

Whoever it was had not made her happy. She carried about not merely a cynical dissatisfaction with her work, but a much more general melancholy, which was why, when those beautiful smiles dispelled the gloom, the moment appeared magical. During Lennox Mark's speech, Sinclo stared at her, but she either did not see him or chose not to return his gaze. This evening, she looked almost lachrymose. Sinclo wondered whether this expression was caused merely by the essential cruelty of the occasion, which was disgusting him too (the public guillotining of poor Tony Taylor), or whether it was born of that deeper, sadder inner mystery of hers which in his fantasy life he longed to salve.

After the applause, the thumping of desks, after Taylor's own (feeble, embarrassingly) speech, and the cheers, the large room susurrated to the general murmur. By the time Sinclo squeezed through the crowd, several colleagues were grouped round Rachel. A general proposal was in the air that they all should pile into a taxi and dine at a newly opened club in Soho.

'It shouldn't be too bad at this time of night,' said Peg Montgomery. She was considerably older than Sinclo, this doyenne of the Killer Interviewer. He was bad at judging ages. She'd more than once indicated that she fancied him. She smoked so much that her breath was acrid, something of which she must have been aware since she ate Polo mints even while swigging the fizzy wine. She had a friz of dyed blonde hair, and her teeth stuck out, but this was not unsexy. Her breasts were large and round. Her face had extraordinary coarseness, and yet the attention paid to it with make-up on eyes, cheeks, lips, all signalled a disarming willingness to be viewed as a baby doll – the sort of inflatable lifesize porno-doll which lonely men 'use'. Like three-quarters of Peg's male colleagues, Sinclo had often wondered what would happen if he got drunk and had half a chance with her.

He realized, as he piled into a taxi with Peg, that he was not quite as sober as he had imagined. There were four of them in the cab. He felt her thigh squeezing against his, but he took no more notice than if she had been a mattress or a dog. In his reverie, he wished he had been more forceful and got into Rachel's taxi. He saw only her face, intent and serious, somewhere beyond the raindrops of Jamaica Road, the floodlit, sodden Tower Bridge, the hissing tarmac of the Embankment, the wet, cloudy orange sky over Soho, which they eventually reached when a sum showed on the meter which was equal to the amount given to an old-age pensioner each week by the state. It was half past nine by the time any of them piled on to the pavement outside the club; ten fifteen before they got a table. He tried to make his enquiry as casual as possible when he asked what had happened to Rachel.

'What's the matter?' asked Peg, squeezing his arm and refilling his glass with Australian red. 'Aren't we gorgeous enough for you?'

They all laughed. He felt his misery coming out as humourlessness, stuffiness. He must have been drunk, because he found himself reading and rereading the label on the wine bottle 'Wattles McLaren Vale Grenache Shiraz 2000'. His mind left the company. He and Rachel had become 'Rhone rangers', growing wine in Australia. They were dressed rather like pioneers in some American children's story. The outback setting of the winery was bright and drenched with sun. Rachel had that smile on her face.

Peg and two of the men at the table were shouting rubbish about the *Legion* overtaking the *Mail* in the circulation war.

'Lennie's got tricks up his sleeve,' said one of the men.

(All *Legion* employees referred to Lennox Mark as Lennie, though few would say so to his face.)

'I'll get this fucker Worledge to sort out the paper.'

This sentence, said by another of the men in a very poor imitation of Lennox's voice, made everyone yelp with laughter.

'It's still Muchie-Muchie who hires and fires,' said another knowingly.

The positively ancient questions about Mary Much were then aired: whether she was a lesbian, having it off with Martina; whether she was Lennox Mark's mistress . . .

'She gets what she wants *without* doing it,' said another drunken journalist. They were too far gone in drink to be careful of their words because Sinclo sometimes had lunch with Mary Much.

Someone else was asking, 'I wonder what Derek' – Worledge – 'had to do to Muchie-Muchie to get the editorship of the *Legion*?'

It was late by now. Cigarettes had been lit, and congealed fragments of lamb's shank or char-grilled tuna littered the plates of the jaded crowd. They all began to make suggestions. Sinclo felt so utterly bereft, so completely desolated by Rachel's absence, that he filled his glass and decided to join in the talk. His own ingeniously obscene suggestion of what Worledge had been made to do to bring Mary Much to a climax and guarantee his position as editor was filthier than anything dreamed up by the others. It created a roar at the table. As they laughed, he thought that the filthy idea was one he wouldn't mind trying with Mary Much. Or with any woman, come to that. He did not resist when Peg Montgomery slipped her sausagey fingers with their scarlet talons into his trouser pocket.

TWENTY-SIX

In the kitchen at Redgauntlet Road, eight staff worked busily, preparing the evening's entertainments.

'Is that enough ice?' asked Piet sharply.

The Constancios, a Brazilian couple who had been installed in the Marks' service for a fortnight, were not used to being spoken to in such a tone by a mere boy, but for some reason they accepted his authority. Maria José, who had worked in embassies, and big hotels, and who knew how to serve caviar, checked nervously in the ice-buckets which supported the vast mounds of grey, glistening roe. There were only twenty to dine, but this amount of caviar would have fed twice the number. The hired waiters and waitresses seemed equally in awe of Piet's expertise, especially when they had heard the accounts of Helene, the beaky Bulgarian who was now a resident housemaid, and who appeared to be in love with Piet.

On days when Mrs Mark lost her rag, or Frau Fax was being more than usually short-tempered, or – perhaps the worst of all – when Mr Lennox threw food, Piet was a source of strength.

Helene was a young woman with a sympathetic smile. Her thin, sensitive face would have been conventionally beautiful were it not for an enormous nose. Her shoulder-length blonde hair was tied in a pony-tail. The temporary Greek waiter fancied her, but it was clear from the way she spoke about Piet that the Greek did not stand a chance.

'In Africa, he prince – Prince Tuli. His father king. They have big, big palace, many wives, servants, concubines.'

She smiled at the thought. The other servants, as she had told them, had realized that if Piet (or Prince Tuli) so commanded, she would willingly volunteer to become a concubine of his.

'Tuli was only eleven years old when he have wife – it is part of a ceremony, you know, to show, like he becomes man. She, his first wife, she is big lady, very big boobs. Piet, when he was boy in Africa, he was allowed any woman he liked. The king, his dad, sent him to England. He was at Eton. Prince Charles, Prince William, he knew them all – they went to the Drones Club together. But then there was revolution in his country. No way would Prince Tuli be a puppet to General Bindiga like Prince Charles a puppet to Blair. Prince Charles's cock's the size of a shrimp – Piet's seen it in the showers after polo matches. So Piet left Eton and he's working on his own now. He's in disguise – no one's meant to know who he is.'

The others were too polite to question any of this when, with whispered giggles, both salacious and profoundly impressed, Helene had told them. Piet at the time had been upstairs. He had found out Martina's password on her computer, and had been checking her e-mails. In the course of his researches he had found out why Mr Constancio – Pedro – had left his last job. This was another reason why the couple, well past their fiftieth birthday, treated the young man with a certain deference.

So, the servants stared about at the banquet – the caviar, the baron of beef, the huge ham, the great vats of potatoes, the oozing vacherins, the hunks of fruit-cake, looking as if hacked for giants.

Piet's phone rang. Toodle-pip.

'Yup,' he said. 'Okay.'

All admired his beautiful public-school English. You only got that from going to Eton.

'Ten minutes,' he told them. 'Helene – come.'

And he led his willing handmaid into the hall to greet the guests.

'Have they all met her before?' asked Helene.

Piet shook his head and smiled wickedly. In his white coat, buttoned to the throat, and his white gloves, he was magnificently handsome. His long neck jutted from the uniform. His hair had been cut quite short by the man who cut Mary Much. His grey-blue eyes looked from the hall to the drawing room, where Frau Fax, in a cocktail dress, was fortifying herself with a glass of Schnapps.

'The guests of honour have not met her,' he said.

'They are in for shock, no?' asked Helene, but he answered her by placing one of his white-gloved fingers on her lips.

TWENTY-SEVEN

Mary Much was as tall as Esmé Worledge was squat; her ash-blonde bob as expensively chic as Esmé's yellow hair shrieked disaster. Aubrey Bird remarked afterwards that Esmé might as well have come to the dinner with the words SURBITON WOMAN pinned to her back. When Mary phoned L.P. with this gem, the columnist dismissed it as unfair.

'Esmé,' he told Mary, 'was making a post-modern statement. She had come to the dinner in fancy dress. She was posing – as a *reader* of *The Daily Legion*!'

This was a classic. It would certainly run and run.

Certainly, from the moment of their all tumbling through the front door, and handing their coats to Piet and Helene, there was a sense of the new editor of the *Daily* and his nervous wife being visitants from outer space. Aubrey Bird said that to define Derek Worledge you'd say that though he wore hand-made Jermyn Street shirts with the monogram D.W. on the pocket, he wore them as if they were polycotton from British Home Stores. And who ever wore shirts with a breast pocket? As for Esmé, from the top of her cheap blonde hair to the peep-toes of her deeply unfashionable patent-leather high-heeled evening shoes, she was Mrs BHS – Madama Suburbia, Essence of Esher. The outfit would have been more suitable for handing round slices of home-made quiche, or even those little chunks of cheese impaled on tooth-picks, at a Tupperware party than for celebrating the appointment of her husband to a position in the world.

For Esmé's part, fear and loathing battled for pre-eminence as she was led into the large drawing room by the two women, Mary Much so patronizing, as she took her arm, Martina so scornful with that fixed smile. And then – the old lady. Well, as she ventured to say on the way back to Surrey in the car, she did think she might have been *warned*.

At dinner, Esmé prodded the glistening grey sludge on her plate with a timid fork. The black boy had given her far too much. She did not think she could bring herself to eat so much as one granule of it. The sight of Mr Mark spooning it into his mouth made her swallowing muscles freeze.

'Just eat a little,' snapped Derek, as if coaxing a three-year-old. He spoke to her across the table. It seemed an alarming gathering of people – the old, rather effeminate gentleman who wrote the gossip column; the Watsons, evidently not very well matched; the Blimbys (Derek had always said that little Blimby couldn't edit a paper bag – and his wife Sal, a disconcertingly posh-sounding woman, up from the country) . . . None of these were people Esmé knew. She did not expect to know anyone, but such things seemed to matter less on the Sunday red-top which Derek had edited before his appointment at the *Legion*.

Half the table – the Kurtmeyers, Lennox Mark himself, Derek – were talking about the future of the *Legion*. The other half were gossiping, and talking nonsense. Some were reliving poor Mrs Mark's experience of being burgled some weeks before, but they did so in a frivolous tone which Esmé found baffling. Nor did she understand Derek's angry, anxious tone when she sounded sympathetic rather than trying to be clever.

'If anything like that ever happened to me . . .' Her voice trailed away at the horror of it.

'But it didn't,' said Derek. Then, with a switched-on smile, he sycophantically said, 'Martina – you were saying.'

He was sitting between Martina Mark and Mary Much, and both of these women smiled with inscrutable cruelty whenever he leaned over to correct his wife.

Mr Blimby, the editor of *The Sunday Legion*, was a small man with a loud booming voice. His social origins were really on a level with Esmé. Sal's family – he referred to them as Sal's 'people' – had been appalled when she'd come home with a man who only reached up to her shoulder and whose father was a dentist. They had also been appalled that he was a journalist. These views had been modified when Simon Blimby became deputy editor of a broadsheet. The salary enabled them to buy an Old Rectory, and by the time he'd got the editorship of *The Sunday Legion*, Simon was a passable shot, and could, in the views of his brothers-in-law, be mistaken for a White Man.

'Frankly,' he boomed, 'in any contest between a Yardie from Brixton and our beloved Martina, I'd rate the bloke's chances of survival rather low!'

Sal loyally guffawed.

'Zere were tsree of zem – tsree!' squawked Frau Fax like some one-eyed vulture.

'I mean,' said Esmé.

'Just don't,' interrupted her husband. 'Just don't *mean*, will you?'

Then, when she drank some champagne to steady herself, he added brusquely, 'Watch that stuff. Remember!'

In clear reference to some earlier social occasion at which his wife had disgraced him, Derek Worledge imitated someone suppressing a burp.

'I'm afraid if a nig-nog or anyone else broke in on us,' said Sal – thanking Piet with a silent display of dentistry as he came round to fill her glass with Pouligny Montrachet – 'it would be out with the 2.2 and bang, bang. Off goes a woolly head!'

Mary Much sighed at this countrified remark. She had no 'views' – if people wished to be coarse, let them. It was simply that there were certain things, in London, you couldn't *say*. This kind of talk, especially with Piet in the room, was simply not permissible.

'I'm afraid,' Derek Worledge told her, 'that we've all grown too soft. That man who shot a burglar – locked up for murder – that can't be right.'

Mary sighed again.

Piet, the beautiful house-boy, placed his cheek quite close to hers and asked if everything was all right.

'Just wait until Mr Mark has finished his caviar,' she murmured. Then with those long white fingers she touched his sleeve. 'It's all fine, fine. Thanks for everything.'

He shimmied away. So much had been *put* into that one complicit glance between them.

When Martina and Mary had planned the evening, as they planned everything together, they had realized that socially speaking, they were facing a poser. Derek Worledge had been educated in Leeds, where his father was a doctor. He had retained his northern accent through three years at Bristol University and twenty years in London working as a journalist. Something clearly marked him out from the Court. It was not in the simple, socio-economic sense, social class, since Worledge was (and in some circumstances he would be blunt enough to say as well as think it) the equal of any of them. It was something to do with style, the quality which Mary and Martina had in such buckets and which the Worledges did not even seem to covet. Another way of putting it (though none of them would have done so in Lennox Mark's hearing) was that Derek Worledge, alone in that assembly, was following his true inclinations and ambitions. For the others, journalism was a means to some quite detached end.

'I am *Sviss*,' Frau Fax was noisily leaning over to croak at Derek – for she had insisted on being near the new editor at table, and was pursuing a monologue of her own with anyone who would care to listen. He smiled politely, as a doctor's son would in such a circumstance, while trying to stop his eyes playing too obviously over the sight which greeted him: the gaping eyeless socket with its sagging pink and white stringy scars set in that sallow bony cheek; the crooked mouth; the half-built nose. '*Sviss* – from Basel. Ve stood out very strongly against ze Nazis.'

The others – this was it, this was what Martina later agreed with Mary Much – felt slightly – not ashamed exactly, but in need of protecting themselves from the full blast of the *Legion*'s atmosphere. They did so by conversing in an irony which was quite lacking in either Mr or Mrs Worledge. Perhaps L.P. and Aubrey Bird and the others were all smeared with Lennox Mark's own sense of moral failure, his refusal to hear God's word in Africa in his teens.

Martina for her part was impatient with such scruples or introspections. In the various interviews and profiles she had given since she married Lennox, she had freely adapted her age, her past, her nationality. It was more helpful to be Swiss. Her mother had added the attractive detail of her father having been an eminent cancer doctor in whose prestigious clinic many were treated free of charge. No one knew how to check details – this was one of the first lessons Martina had learnt when she made the career switch and became a journalist. Let Lennox worry his fat rich conscience about God. For Martina and her mother, God, if He had ever existed, had been bulldozed out of their lives in East Germany in '45 and she saw no reason to try to resurrect Him when she re-established herself in Frankfurt in '63. She was incapable of sentimentality about money. Such a moral luxury was never hers. She knew from an early age that she had two assets – her looks, and her adamantine character. These could command the highest prices. When she'd moved to London in the year that England beat her country in the World Cup, she did not mess about – she'd moved in at the top of the market. At the end of two years she had made enough for her mother and herself to be able to retire. A client – never mind who – was just as happy as herself to bury the past. No ugly words or threats were ever uttered, but she got her 'break' in journalism with the same ease that had earned her the freehold of a small house in Chelsea.

Martina would let no one, and certainly not Lennox Mark's Christian God, judge her for the way she'd lived. As a two-year old child, she had been carried by her mother through flames – their apartment building on fire, their street a heap of smouldering rubble. The Western Allies showed their gallantry by raining fire on a hundred thousand women and children in Berlin. Then these English and American lovers of democracy showed their devotion to freedom by handing those German civilians who had survived the air-raids into the loving protection of Marshal Stalin and his German stooges.

After the Royal Air Force destroyed their home and their hopes, Martina and her mother (left a widow by the war) found themselves citizens of Communist East Germany. The skinny, undernourished, red-headed infant flowered into a precocious twelve-year-old Martina. Herr Hoffmann, the manager of their condominium and a keen Party member, said he could get waitressing work for Martina after school. She and Frau Fax both joined the Party. Her mother chose to be out in the afternoons if or when the waitressing led to more lucrative activities, first with Herr Hoffmann, then with other privileged Party activists. Between twelve and fifteen, Martina developed looks which could not merely disturb, but could bewitch men. By her late teens, by the time she and her mother had made their decision to escape to the West, she was working the tourist hotels, posing with gullible foreign businessmen or politicians in full view of the hidden cameras.

Then came the moment of choice. You could not trust anyone in Berlin in those days, and even though they bribed someone who said they knew someone who could nobble the guards on the Wall, neither of them had expected their escape to be easy. They actually retraced their steps, crept along the same street where her mother, that night of flaming nightmare in '45, had carried her as a baby. That first night, in '45, they had been among crowds of thousands, as screaming, panic-stricken women and children, many of them in flames, ran in all directions. The second night, eighteen years later, they were alone. The street was dark. The first patch of barbed wire was reached soundlessly, and from the air of desertion in the street, both women formed the hope, or expectation, that the 'friend' had been trustworthy, and their escape assured. They tore their clothes on the wire, but what the hell. Then began the climb up the concrete, the grazed shins, the bleeding palms as they scrabbled desperately in the dark for their freedom.

That first night, in '45, the noise of explosions had been all around them. The second night, of escape, in '63, was silent until the explosive gunfire began, and it seemed all the louder for being directed just at them. Here were no thousands of German women being butchered for the sin of living in the wrong European country. These were just two individuals facing death itself. First, the sniper's shot, just as they got over the top of the wall. Then, as her mother slumped there, impaled on the wire, they switched on the arc lights and steady gunfire followed. It was for Martina the definitive moment of her life.

The world was against them. Somehow, they had slithered or fallen on the Western side of the wall but the lights were still on them from the East and the guns were still firing. She held her mother under the armpits. It looked like they'd shot off her face. In the arc lights Olga's head was just a splash of blood. While the guns continued to fire, Martina dragged her mother (whom she believed at that moment to be dead) across a scrub of urban wasteland. She felt determined to live. The bastards she'd left behind were not going to have her mother's dead body. The bastards she was running to join were going to pay her for the privilege of having her body alive, and pay her handsomely. She'd taken enough shit to last her a lifetime.

Derek Worledge and his wife were absurd, but if they did the trick, lifted the *Legion* from its doldrums, made some more fucking *money*, Martina was prepared to give them a try.

Worledge was built like a bruiser, his neck rolling over his shirt collar, his cruel heavy mouth jutting out as he spoke. Martina and Mary put him through his paces. His voice seemed to be scrambled, like the devices used to disguise a voice on anti-bugging equipment. It came shaken through gravel, this noise.

'Basically, it speaks for England, doesn't it, the *Legion*?'

'*So* true.' Mary Much sucked in her cheeks.

This had always been Mary's line, since she entered Martina's life and they together discovered Lennox, and all the potential which a marriage between Lennox and Martina would provide. The *Legion* spoke for England, and the successful editor of the *Legion*, like the successful Prime Minister, had his finger at any one moment on England's pulse. Martina was never more conscious of the cold winds of East Berlin blowing at the back of her head than when Mary spoke of England's heartbeat. None of them need know of the German past. Mary knew when not to be inquisitive and had never probed. Lennox himself appeared positively gratified by the chance to be vague about origins. Germany, Switzerland, what was the difference?

Perhaps one ingredient in the success of their marital partnership was this dread of England they shared: a respect for an image of England. Mary imitated Derek Worledge's gravelly accent, but Martina could not really hear it: the voice gave her no signals. Lennox had comparable feelings of alienation when such matters as class were aired. His Englishry had been ersatz in Lugardia. The rugger matches had been played on hard pitches at Queen Alexandra College, clouds of blood-red dust came from the sun-caked mud of the pitch if you tried a free kick: none of your genuine oozing black mud of the playing fields of Eton.

(Father Vivyan, he would say, was the first 'proper Englishman' he had ever met; he was never more conscious of it, absurdly, than when the priest, with his record of great valour in the army and his manly bearing, had touched the elbow of an armed policeman at the border checkpoint going into the Karkara mine compound.

'My dear, there's no need for guns.')

That *my dear* – Anthony Eden English, rather than mincing camp – had suggested a world to colonial Lennie. He still felt himself excluded from it. Martina, likewise, did not really under-stand what Worledge was talking about – the rights of the trueborn Englishman to shoot burglars, to keep out foreigners, to retain pounds, shillings and pence as opposed to the hated euro, these he asserted. Just as African-born Lennox and mysteriously born Martina heartily endorsed this man's Little Englandry, so 'Dr Arbuthnot', poor mincing Aubrey Bird, seemed to be agreeing as Worledge laid into homosexuals. He asked if they'd seen a feature he'd commissioned for his final edition of the Sunday red-top he was leaving: six tell-tale signs to see if the vicar's 'one of those'.

'It was a bit of fun,' he gravelled, 'but it had an underlying serious point. I don't mind standing up and being counted. Those perverts . . .'

Esmé pursed her lips.

'These perverts in the Church, for fuck's sake . . .'

Mary Much could number few among her close circle who did not come among the categories of human being excoriated by the editor-elect. Modern artists, Europeans, homosexuals . . . This man saw them as the enemy.

'He is the most *inspired* piece of retro,' she cooed into Martina's ear when they had all gone home, and it was just the two of them again.

'I do hope we know what we are doing,' said Martina.

'With Worledge?'

'Lennie says the money situation is very bad.'

Martina sat at her dressing table. Mary stood behind her stool, a hairbrush in her hand, brushing her friend's coppery tresses. They had learned so well, these two, how to make use of contradictions in life. The brutality of the *Legion*, even when directed against people or things which they liked, was not without its uses. (The conceptual art of Hans Busch was a case in point. The more the *Legion* derided it, the more 'controversial' its appeal in other quarters.)

'How bad?' asked Mary.

'Kurt and Spottiswood say the *Sunday* and the *Daily* will have to merge. They'll lose a lot of jobs, which is a good thing.'

'*Very* good,' cooed Mary.

'But the advertisers will be scared away.'

'*Not* good.'

Mary's long white fingers caressed and massaged Martina's neck. Martina looked at the face of her friend in the glass. Had one of Burne-Jones's models dyed her hair ash-blonde, and dressed in a shapely little black dress and black tights, the effect would have been similar. This intensely worldly woman had a way of looking almost disembodied.

'The Watsons were snappy with one another,' said Martina.

'She was crazy this evening. That moment when L.P. said, Oh Martina's *brill* . . . and before he'd said the word 'brilliant', Julia was tearing at her hair and saying that if her husband told another woman she was brilliant, she would *scream*!'

'Wasn't that awful?'

'And her snapping and snarling at L.P. when they put on their coats to go.'

'I didn't hear that.'

'Wasn't it funny when L.P. asked poor Esmé whether she'd rather be burgled or raped?'

'No, *no*,' laughed Martina, 'he *said*, "I'd rather be raped than burgled – wouldn't you?"'

'Her face!'

'It was true what I said – the police did take samples from my fingers, DNA samples.'

'Will they ever follow it up, do you think?' asked Mary. 'One can usually rely on the police to be inefficient.'

'They haven't taken samples from . . . a certain person.'

'Ah, the beautiful boy!'

'You're not to touch.'

'Aubrey was very smitten with him,' said Mary – and then in the gravelly mode of Worledge, 'The *Legion* will root out perverts!'

Both women giggled.

'Piet isn't a criminal,' said Martina authoritatively. 'It was perfectly sensible of me to see that at once.'

'He did have a knife – you told me.'

'He waved it like a toy. He just wanted someone to take some notice of him. His story is so sad.'

'If we believe it,' said Mary Much.

'We do not have to believe every word people say about themselves. The lies people tell about themselves are often more revealing of character than supposedly accurate memories.'

'So you want to believe he is an orphan.'

'I *do* believe that part – about his mother being dead. I don't know I believe that she was a famous actress. But – being brought up by his grandmother – this I believe.'

There was silence for a while, as Mary caressed and massaged the hair and neck of her friend.

'He's a dangerous game, darling,' she said to Martina's reflection.

'If you say so,' said Martina, 'but as you may have noticed – I have lived dangerously.'

TWENTY-EIGHT

As the boy waited in the shadows, he heard taped human voices on his Walkman and the familiar jangle of his own multifarious selves.

'Don't make me – I'll only make a fool of you.'

'Course you've got to come to the dinner, you silly *cow*. Just don't say anything.'

'I don't know *what* to say.'

'Jesus!'

This exchange took place between Worledge and his wife. She was a cunt and all. That stuff about black boys being more likely to nick something than white boys? That racist filth spewing out of her stinking quim of a mouth? It had been as much as Jeeves could manage, to stop Murderous Moron slitting her throat in front of her fucking husband.

Boys, boys! Jeeves had intervened.

It had not stopped MM pocketing the kitchen knife. They had a good supply of them now. Sabatier. One day, he'd steal that service revolver of Father Vivyan's. Had that in Africa. He'd shown them how it worked. Safety catch. Ammo. The fucking lot, wicked. But his latest thing. He pressed the rewind button.

'Don't make me – I'll only make a fool of you.'

'Course you've got to come to the dinner, you silly *cow*.'

It impressed them that Lennox – or was it one of the broads? Yeah, them more like – had planted the bugging devices. How many more of them existed? The offices of all them fucking fools in LenMar House — they'd be bugged, stood to reason. But this simple little thing. No wires. Just clip it on. You're sorted. It would have to've been the titty-ones who thought of that. They were cunning, that pair of dykes, unlike Mr Fat. How many receivers were there? Lots, probably. He'd withdrawn from the dinner — had to go for a slash, run upstairs, just a quick one. Liked the idea of pissing in *her* toilet. Liked putting his arse where her fanny had dribbled its piss. Nice one. And there it was — on her fucking bathroom table, this little box. He'd pressed ON and fuck-a-duck man, he could hear the whole fucking dinner party — the shit, the total shit with his silly-cow wife — Derek he were called — saying:

'Six tell-tale signs to see if the vicar's an arse-merchant. A bit of fun, a bit of fun . . . Very much tongue in cheek,' he was adding.

It had been a matter of seconds. The receiver was inside his shirt, stuffed it into his Calvin Klein elastic. The mike? Stood to reason it was somewhere on the shit himself, the one with a voice like a concrete mixer. Derek. Felt it easy when the dinner was over, helped him on with his overcoat. Stupid tosser, with a fucking mike pinned to his jacket and he didn't even see it.

Playing the tape back further, Tuli was able to listen to all the things which Worledge had been saying about his hosts before the dinner.

'They do say Martina isn't Swiss at all — some people think her mother got that face from the Gestapo . . . Threatening to say who the dad was . . . yeah, Martina's dad . . . I'm not joking . . .'

The crackling noise made it difficult to hear the next bit but someone had obviously asked who Martina's dad really was.

'Think of her eyes — those cold, staring eyes . . .'

The concrete mixer laughed, and added, 'Great story anyway.'

You could hear the other person repeating his question.

'That's what they say – the Gestapo beat up the old dear because she'd got pregnant by Adolf Hitler.'

'So Martina's . . . ?'

'Great story . . . great story . . .'

There was more stuff, about Mary Much: about men she'd fucked even though she was a lesbian, about how she interfered too much in the newspapers owned by Lennox, about how when he – Derek Concrete Mixer – became editor of the *Legion*, he'd have difficulties with Muchie-Muchie.

'I might have to drive a wedge between her and Len. If I can. If I can.'

When the Guards officer heard Derek Worledge's conceited gravelly voice, he wanted to silence it for ever – maybe with one of those rabbit punches? Like they learned in self-defence? At Happy Band? The Guards officer fancied Mary Much. He liked the fact that Mary wanted to take him away from Martina. He intuited that she had always been doing this, from the start of the 'friendship' between the pair, preying on her.

This was the exact spot, where he now stood in the shadows, where they'd gathered before; where Murderous Moron got the slicer to the little Paki bastard's ear-hole and the Guards officer had had to drawl, Cool it, man, and . . .

That was before Jeeves came. Jeeves had the real cool. Jeeves now controlled them all. He'd promised the kid: he could take his revenge on Mr Currey, bloody pedalo like you read about in *The Daily Legion*. On Lennox, for all he done to their mother. But they must be patient.

Revenge, Jeeves had told them all, is a dish best served cold.

'If it crosses your mind to tell anyone, I can get you sectioned. Locked up. I'm gentle with you. They wouldn't be gentle with you in prison.'

That was what that uphill gardener had told him – the kid still whimpered when he remembered. Mr Currey had told him, You're enjoying this – look at that – nice one! But Jeeves said just 'cause you got a hard-on when they was doing – *that* didn't mean you was a fucking bum-bandit yourself. Murderous Moron would be allowed to finish with Currey. Meanwhile – silence was the Name of the Game, especially now they're wired for sound. Hello – we've got some action.

The mincing figure of Aubrey Bird, the diarist on *The Daily Legion*, came out of the house. They could hear him calling out his farewells. Slowly does it. Safe distance. If he hails a cab, let him go. But that one – you gotta be joking. He's taking the night air: even though it's still pissing with rain, he's cruising. On to the bus – quick, quick, they ran. Just caught the 14, this one's going down Piccadilly. Yes – silly old fucker, though he can hardly get up the stairs, he's going on the top of the bus to see if he can meet with some trade. Rub his horrible little trouser leg against a boy.

He was dressed, Aubrey Bird, in 'shorty' white mac and a little brown trilby hat. He wore a dark blue suit and Gucci loafers with little gold buckles and shiny black leather tassels. And yes, yes! Hyde Park Corner has been passed, and he is finding his way down the stairs again. Nothing doing up there, then. Where now? We're at the bottom of Piccadilly and he's got off the bus, and turned up a narrow street. Brick Street. The darkened doorway of a public lavatory shields him from the rain. The silly old bugger creeps inside.

In Redgauntlet Road, the disappearance of one of Martina's receivers had been noticed almost at once.

'Think – think calmly,' urged Mary Much, who hated it when Martina went into overdrive.

'I am thinking – and I'm thinking I've been a bloody fool. It must be Piet who stole it – who *else*, for Christ's sake . . .'

'Martina – he wouldn't *dare*. He knows that the minute he steps out of line, it's curtains for him – the police, Borstal, prison, even.'

'Suppose he's stupid.'

'He isn't stupid. That night – the night he came – you at once saw his potential. Martina, he's our project – he's so much *enjoying* this, he's not going to spoil it all by pilfering things. No – one of our other guests went round the house while we were eating and . . .'

'Switch it on – switch it on,' urged Martina. 'Then we'll listen. Suppose he still has it switched on – then we'll hear.'

Mary Much murmured, 'God, you're brilliant.'

She had her perv side. In certain company, she loved to get gay men to tell her all their fantasies. Aubrey Bird had told her – she did not know whether this was true – that he liked to take rent boys home and perform surgical operations on them. He had the full outfit – green surgical cap and mask, surgical gloves and boots. Some of them found his renditions of the task so realistic that they had screamed or passed out, when he presented them with liver or sausages which he had ready on a plate but which, in the intimacy of the moment, they believed to have been removed by the scalpel of 'Dr Arbuthnot'.

'And your fist, darling – tell us – what did you do with your fist?' Mary would ask with eager panting intakes of breath.

It was therefore Mary who was first to have her suspicions when she heard the whispered tones which crackled through the receiver in Martina's bedroom.

'Don't let's stay here . . . let's . . . ooh! That's nice. Let me feel yours . . . I'm a doctor . . . Would you like to come and see my surgery?'

'It's Aubrey,' said Mary calmly.

'What did I tell you?' Martina exclaimed. It was one of her more endearing character traits, in Mary's mind, that she claimed prescience for matters which were, strictly, unpredictable.

'Where do you think he is?' Mary asked.

'Hampstead Heath – wherever it is they go.'

Something had clearly been whispered, or grunted, in Aubrey's ear, because they could now hear him laughing, and the atmosphere of sound had changed. He had moved from indoors to out of doors.

'What, here – not *here*?' He was speaking in his quite audible and recognizable voice.

'What was he thinking, stealing a bugging device?' asked Mary.

'He's taken one of the recorder receivers and he's taken a listening device. He's a gossip columnist. Equals spy.'

'Yes – but he's so obviously going to be found out.'

'Maybe he's stupid enough to think he's taken the only mike, or the only receiver.'

'Sh – sh . . .'

'It's cold here,' Aubrey was saying. 'Wouldn't you like to come back to my place? I don't want . . . This is a multi-storey . . . Unless you have a car?'

'They're in . . .'

'A multi-storey car park. I can hear. Sh, sh – what did I *tell* you?'

'No – not here – ooh . . .'

There followed some indeterminate noises of bumps and thumps. They were in fact the laying of Aubrey Bird on the concrete floor of Level D of the multi-storey car park behind the Hyde Park Corner Hilton; the removal of his Gucci loafers; the stuffing of his socks into his mouth, and the rather crude but actual enactment of something which he had up to this point in his life only performed on others, and then in fantasy.

'The sound's gone dead,' said Mary Much with very distinct disappointment in her tone.

'The silly old *bugger*,' said Martina.

Some Italian con artists, who had spent the small hours fleecing alcoholics in a Park Lane casino, spotted the body of Aubrey Bird in the headlights of their Alfa Romeo at half past three. It was they who alerted the man who checked the tickets at the car park exit. An ambulance would come about half an hour later. Some twenty minutes after that, a feral cat who lived in the shadows of the car park, and fed normally on the fish and chips left by the prostitutes there, ate two rather gristly pieces of offal which it found on the concrete floor.

TWENTY-NINE

Rachel Pearl lay alone in her flat. It was in a small apartment block built during the 1990s. The flat consisted of two rooms: a large living room, whose back wall was entirely lined with books, and a smaller bedroom. Both rooms had plate-glass windows which overlooked the river. The Thames had always been interwoven with Rachel's inner and imaginative life since her early childhood in Barnes, and walks along the towpath to Putney or Ham. This eastern region where she now lived had been an unknown world to her until she had landed the job, and her lover had bought her the flat. (It was within walking distance of LenMar House.)

Sometimes her lover came to spend the night there, but more often their time together was a matter of snatched lunch-hours or afternoons. Rachel very much regretted the fact that he was married, but she had learnt for much of the time to blot out this fact. She hated him talking about his wife or children, preferring to think, if not actually to believe, that when he was not with her, he ceased to exist, and plunged into a kind of nothingness until his next reappearance. This treating of him as the genie in a magic lamp who appeared and disappeared at unpredictable moments enabled her to get by, though much of the time she was lonely. She was angry with him for letting her love him, angry with him for buying her this flat and making her not only his dependant but also a creature of *The Daily Legion*.

She had been his lover – on and off – since she was at

university. She had been vice president of the Oxford Union and helped to organize the debates. This House believes England is Done For; this House rejoices in the End of History; this House does not believe in God. Arch, silly undergraduate-ish motions such as this were debated each week in term-time. Rachel's best friend Kitty Chell thought the Union was woefully uncool, and she was right. But – at that age one could spell things out – Rachel had said:

'Kitty, you have your world – I have Mummy and Daddy and Barnes.'

'What world? You don't just mean 'cause Papa's a lord?'

'Partly – no *listen*. It's not just Throxton Winnards' – the large old house at which Rachel had spent part of the Long Vac with her friend – 'or your dad's title – of course it's not. But they are part of it – your parents knew everyone and that's quite exciting. If I say, Oh, L. P. Watson, you don't say, I read his book – you say, Oh, Papa had him to stay, or He goes out with a cousin of mine.'

'Who's L. P. Watson?'

Even at that stage, before she'd met the man, Rachel felt protective of him. She thought Kitty was being mean to pretend not to have heard of him. She admired the travel books and *Conversations with a Lion*: in those days she read the newspapers sparingly, so was hardly aware of L.P. the controversialist.

Every week, three or four show-offs, grown-ups, would come up from London in their evening dress and take part in one of the Oxford Union debates. The week that L.P. came, he was accompanied by an ancient Catholic peer, a 'maverick' Labour MP (this appeared to be an adjective one applied to any MP who had not actually undergone a lobotomy, that is, anyone capable of thinking for themselves), and a lady novelist who doubled as an agony aunt in a newspaper Rachel never read. She had known, during that early and disgusting dinner – grand clothes, cheap wine, filthy food – that L. P. Watson fancied her. He did not try anything on – she would have been disgusted if he had done – that night. He was the soul of politeness, and had shaken her hand after the debate, when he went back to the station. As he did so, he'd said he hoped they'd meet again.

'Perhaps we shall,' she'd said – and she had smiled her radiant smile.

The train had come in to Oxford station.

'Next week?' he'd called through the train window.

When Kitty Chell came back from a party, Rachel had kept her up for hours, wondering whether she was on the verge of something big.

A letter – 'Dear Miss Pearl' – had arrived at her college two days later, asking her to dinner in London. Mon Plaisir. Monmouth Street. Eight fifteen.

That was seven years ago, and loving L.P., as she now did, had become a habit. She knew – moreover, she believed – that sleeping with a married man was a low trick, which could only lead to trouble. She'd not exactly quarrelled with Kitty over it, but her friend's assertion that L.P. was 'exploiting' her, too obvious to be gainsaid, caused a cooling of their early close relationship. When she began to realize that she was not the only woman with whom he committed adultery, she had no friend to whom she could pour out the pain: she hugged it to herself as a guilty secret. She knew that he could not possibly love her as she loved him – else how could he sleep around casually?

One of the worst aspects of the whole affair was that she would never be sure whether her advancement in the world of journalism would have been achieved by her own efforts. She was perfectly confident of her abilities and more than confident of her own intelligence. Whether she would command such a salary (at twenty-eight she was earning the same as a country doctor), she doubted. And his purchase of the flat, which she had accepted, made her feel trapped. She saw her lover with two quite different parts of her intelligence. One part of her nature was able to see that he had almost wilfully ignored his talent – who was it who 'thrust his gift in prison till it died' in a poem? – and chosen to mix with people less intelligent than himself. This figure was a ruined archangel, whom she pitied but also dreaded, fearing that his company would drag her down, teach her habits of drunkenness, philistinism which were alien to her. The other part of her mind, the docile part, was in love with him quite simply, and felt very pleased and proud that she was the secret love of the famous L. P. Watson.

Now, as she lay awake at midnight in her flat, she knew sadly that he would not come: she told herself that she must not now imagine where he was, or what he was doing. Above all she must resist the fantasy, or fear, that he was in fact perfectly happily married; that she, Rachel, was nothing more than his little bit on the side, that at that moment he was at home in bed with his wife, who was still very beautiful, making happy marital love. Such torment was caused by this idea that this alone, more than any other consideration, made her sometimes want to end her relationship with L.P., and to start again with someone else, someone normal, someone with whom she could go about openly, someone like Sinclo, who was clearly nuts about her.

It was at moments like this that she most intensely missed Kitty.

She tried to concentrate on reading. She was doing something she had never done before – reading the *Odyssey*. She had known many of the incidents and stories before – at her primary school, she had even acted a small play based on the scene when Odysseus slays the Cyclops and his men escape the giant's cave under the belly of the sheep. She had never, until actually reading Homer, appreciated how intelligently the story was arranged. In particular, she liked the fact that when the gods came to earth, they came in disguise – so that the bright-eyed goddess Athene (played at her school, she recollected, by a clever girl called Rose) arrived, for example, at the court in Ithaca in the form of a stranger, Mentes, leader of the Taphians. *'Chaire, xeine!'* was Telemachus's greeting to this 'man', not knowing that 'he' was really the goddess who was directing his destiny. (Rachel was reading the Loeb edition: she had forgotten half her schoolgirl Greek, and so she read the English translation and dipped occasionally into the language of Homer him- or herself.)

Hail, stranger! What a brilliant way of mythologizing the strange shape life took, the way that our own lives, and those of our friends, appeared as stories. There were certain key moments of life-changing destiny in the existence of everyone – which could very well, if retold by Homer, be seen as points when a god landed from Olympus in the shape of another human being. At school, she had hummed and hawed about university until her French teacher, Miss Rice, simply told her to try for Oxford. It was a *chance* – but thereafter had come the friendship with Kitty Chell (her most important emotional attachment aged nineteen, far more important to her than boys she'd been 'seeing'); and then – because she was in Oxford – she met L.P., and the rest of her life had been as it had been.

Rachel could not believe in the God of Abraham, Isaac and Jacob, the God of Sinai whom her ancestors, time out of mind, had worshipped. The Book of Job seemed to her a primary atheist text, because the arguments put forward by the one and only God for how He could allow such suffering as Job's were so inadequate. Monism, the thought of one God, one Creator, one

Shaper of human destiny, was not compatible with the idea of His also being one giver of Justice. Jewish history alone (quite apart from the general suffering of humanity) simply was *not* just. If you posited the idea of a God who was like the God of her spiritual ancestors, purity of mind and conscience forced you to an absolute atheism.

Yet, the human sense that there were destinies, patterns, even *purposes*, shimmering and hiding behind Nature's curtain, and behind the events of our lives – the sense that coincidence was sometimes so strong as to be incomprehensible – this made, to Rachel, a very strong *imaginative* case for seeing the world as Homer saw it: for supposing 'The Divine' to be not a single entity, not a Monist conception, but a pluralist one, in which the raging of the sea, or the pains of love, or the gnawing of conscience were in the control not of one God but of many.

As she held the small green volume in her hand and sleepily had these thoughts (Telemachus and Nestor had just reached the palace of Menelaus, and encountered Helen herself, the cause of all the Trojan wars, and now returned to her husband), she heard the key in her lock. (Was Rachel's obsession with the *Odyssey* partly derived from the obvious fact that it was a story of the aftermath of the calamitous consequences of adultery? Yet Helen was not like a medieval penitent. In Homer, she and Menelaus seem like a 'modern' couple, who had lived through the calamity of her elopement, and the ensuing wars, and her return . . .)

'Anyone awake?'

L.P.'s head poked round the door.

She dropped her book – she was propped up in bed wearing one of his shirts – and extended her arms. Rather than running into them, and embracing her, which was what, at that moment, she wanted more than anything in the world, he said, 'Is there a drop of whisky?'

'I'll get you some.'

She swung her elegant bare legs off the bed.

'No need . . .'

But she hoped, once she was upright, bare-legged, beautiful, that he had enough good manners, if not libido, to hold her in his arms. It was evident from his voice that he had already had too much to drink, and his breath, as she came to kiss him, was not simply vinous: the stomach juices had been at work digesting a meat dinner, making his breath into a pungent halitosis laced with fruit.

He was fumbling, in the sitting room, with glasses and bottles.

'I couldn't face going to dinner with the others,' she said. 'I came home, ate some toast. I've got to Book Fifteen . . .'

'Book Fifteen?'

When she had first met L.P. – that first dinner at the Oxford Union, their first date à deux at Mon Plaisir, he had talked eagerly about literature – she'd been impressed by his unaffected interest in, memory of, Corneille. She knew from his facial expression that he was not going to allow her so much as two sentences about Homer, or the thoughts which had been passing through her head.

'Well – big changes ahead,' he said, as he took a swig of whisky.

'Hallo,' she said. She squeezed him, and he squeezed her back in a perfunctory way, while fumbling with his other hand in a pocket. Momentarily she allowed herself the rash thought that he was looking for a condom; but when the inevitable cigarettes came out, she was surprised to discover within herself the sensation of relief. And when he began his analysis of the evening chez Mark, Rachel asked herself with a coolness which she found shocking, whether she was beginning to be free, to wean herself from loving him.

'As you know,' he began, 'Martina wanted me as editor. I'm convinced of that. She wouldn't play games with me . . .'

Oh no?

'It was Kurtmeyer who put a stop to that, I'm quite sure. So they went looking among the red-tops. You see, Lennie and Martina are both the victims of a false *syllogism*.'

He just about managed to say the word without spitting.

'Red-tops make a lot of money. Red-tops are edited by shits like Worledge. Therefore, if you get a shit like Worledge to edit the *Legion*, you'll make a lot of money. But it doesn't work like that.'

'Come to bed, old thing.'

Unable to rise to the courtesies of either interesting conversation or sex, he was doing perhaps the only thing of which he was capable: he was delivering orally one of the famously witty paradoxes which were his hallmark.

'The *Legion* has its own ethos, its own especial magic . . . It even has – or had, until tonight – its own extraordinary power. You know I've often thought that whoever you asked to write for the *Legion*, they'd sooner or later start writing in a *Legion*-ish way.'

'Yeah, yeah, Proust'd start writing in snappy sentences – *A la recherche* would become a why-oh-why . . . Come to bed, baby, it's one in the morning.'

She'd heard this one so often. He used to speak like a man who read books. Now he sounded like a man who was so used to mixing with, and writing for, people stupider than himself that he was in a world where just to know the names of great writers was something for which you expected applause.

'If Dostoevsky' – he paused for the unseen fans to gasp with amazement – 'were asked to write for the *Legion*, he'd write – *Legion*-ishly . . .'

'Come on – bed.'

Socks, shoes, trousers, tie lay in a huddle beside the bed.

'Worledge is a bastard' – said to the pillows – 'going to change that ethos. That special *Legion*-ish. You know something – if Marcel Proust himself . . .'

He was asleep. His head was on her shoulder making her uncomfortable. When she stretched across him to switch out the lamp on his side of the bed, he let out a loud fart.

'Do you know something?' she asked his sleeping form, receiving no reply but snores. 'I *hate* the *Legion*.'

THIRTY

The sodden dawn arrived imperceptibly, the sun invisible in the grey, rain-filled sky over Crickleden.

Ali Hussein jabbed and stabbed at the parcels beside his back door, cursing their weight. Thick pungent armpit sweat filled the shop with a smell redolent of cat pee as he humped the large cellophane-wrapped bales; and after the Stanley knife had chopped, he began the tedious daily task of sorting the different papers into piles, and making sure that the correct number had been sent by the wholesalers.

TRUST ME OVER ZINARIYA PM TELLS COMMON-WEALTH – the *Daily Express*.

LAST CHANCE SALOON FOR BINDIGA – the *Daily Mail*.

For no discernible reason, Mr Hussein thought of the verses in the Holy Qur'an (Part 3, Chapter 3, 46) when Allah gave the glad tidings of a son to Mary. And he recalled that his two younger children, who attended the local primary school, St Mary's, had told him the things their priest had told them: how Mary had known, as soon as she had been told by an angel that a child was in the womb, that a new age had dawned. The mighty and powerful were to be dethroned. The humble and meek would be raised up.

Well, it had not happened. The Husseins had received no compensation for the attack on Ahmet. The boy now hid in his bedroom, afraid to go out. His mother was having a nervous breakdown. Mr Hussein tried to pray for his son's attacker, but when he thought of him, his heart was filled with murderous hatred, a heaviness of spirit which produced nauseous gasps. Mr Hussein tried to recite to himself the opening verses of the Holy Qur'an about being guided along the right path.

The priest, the old man at Mary's shrine, had been to the mosque to pray with the imam. He said, this Father Vivyan, that they were all children of Abraham: but how the mighty were to be toppled from their thrones, this Mr Hussein left to the wisdom of the Almighty.

COPPER PRICES FALL – *Financial Times*.

And the business pages of *The Times* had HOW LONG CAN LENNIE SURVIVE?

The Daily Legion had IS YOUR VICAR A PERV? PERV HOTLINE 0800 *** ***. Mr Hussein respected Father Vivyan who sometimes came into the shop. But he was worried by the thought of his children attending the shrine, which was full of niggers. To think that he had made the long and perilous journey from Bangladesh to settle in Crickleden, leaving behind him his beloved parents, the village where he had grown up, with all its familiar sights and sounds, the mosque where he had prayed, the smallholding where his forebears had tilled the land, just in order to send his kids to school with a lot of black bastards. Mary the mother of the Prophet Jesus conceived her child when still a virgin; such is the power of God who creates what He pleases . . .

The bell jingled on the door. Fucking hell, he had not opened, not officially, and some fucking woman was coming into the shop.

'Good morning,' she said.

Mr Hussein looked up and blinked. For a moment he thought she must be a hooker, making her way home after a busy night. She brought into the shop a sweet odour. Her large lips were scarlet, and she smiled with an open mouth to reveal gap-teeth. Her round, sensual face was framed with gilded, elaborately braided hair. Mr Hussein had an inbuilt prejudice against Afro-Caribbeans. You only had to read the fucking *Daily Legion*, nearly all the fucking crimes in London were committed by black boys – and not surprising if their shameless mothers were all . . . But this woman's intelligent smile stopped the cycle of predictable rant which churned through Ali Hussein's head. Her eyes, one of which had a very slight glide, fixed him with a friendly smile.

'Hi ya! Listen, I know it's early, and you're probably not open yet . . .'

'No, no.' He gestured expansively as if she was welcome, not merely to enter the shop, but, if she so desired, to come and live there. Her short leather skirt and her PVC mac were – extraordinary. Raindrops covered the mac, and her knee-length boots, and on her head she wore a hat with a brim which also dripped.

'. . . I just felt desperate for a fag – if you could sell me twenty Silk Cut, I'd be ever so—'

'Course, lady, for you . . .'

Mr Hussein got to his feet and rummaged behind the counter for the cigarettes.

'You wouldn't let me have a paper, would you?'

She'd placed a crumpled note on the counter.

'That's what we're here for.' He beamed at her.

She took her *Daily Legion* and her cigarettes and went out into the grey smudge of the wet morning.

THIRTY-ONE

By seven thirty, the day was as light as it would ever become. The clouds were lowering and the drizzle was turning to a steady downpour. The light was enough to reveal Father Vivyan's dwelling-place. It was a redbrick house, purpose-built as the rectory at the same date, 1906, as the shrine church beside it. The house was set back from the street behind a shrubbery. By the standards of Crickleden it was a large house, but although the diocese had redecorated it before the arrival of the new priest four years ago, it already bore every sign of Father Vivyan Chell's occupancy. Three camper-vans were parked in the drive, inhabited by a floating population of migrants. At present, they seemed to be chiefly composed of refugees from the Balkans. On the mud patches which had once been a lawn, several large bell tents, army surplus, had been erected, also containing migrants. More of these characters, Bosnian and Albanian Muslims who spoke little or no English, were to be found inside the front door of the house. Although it was never locked, the front door showed every sign of having been kicked, charged, battered and even on occasion lifted off its hinges. One of its panels had been bashed through and replaced amateurishly with some makeshift plywood.

Inside, the visitor unaccustomed to Father Chell's manner of life might have been forgiven for supposing either that the house had been recently gutted by builders in preparation for demolition, or that it had been the subject of criminal attack. For though there was, technically, furniture, it did not seem like a furnished house. Chairs, sofas, piles of bedding, and blankets seemed to have been tossed hither and thither. They were all 'jumble', donated by well-wishers or rescued from skips. In the large room directly opposite the front door, a trestle table was erected, seating perhaps twenty or two dozen people at a variety of makeshift seats, upended tea-chests, deckchairs, office stools, and some Lloyd Loom chairs which were coming unwound, and whose painted cane backs, burst and broken, stuck out in porcupine spikes. Breakfast was being served at this table, two huge tureens of steaming porridge, from which two teenaged black boys ladled portions into chipped bowls and passed them down to the others. Most of those present were boys, aged between twelve and sixteen, but there were also about six unshaven and red-faced 'Gentlemen of the Road', as Father Chell always insisted upon their being called, who ate their porridge with greedy, grateful slurps. Some of these men were sane, and merely enjoyed the total independence which being homeless offered them. Most, however, were in some way disturbed, either by alcohol, mental illness, or a mixture of the two, so that there was a cacophony of sound at the table, with the Gentlemen conducting conversations with themselves or with invisible personages eight yards from their purple noses.

Sitting beside one such, and meekly accepting his bowl of porridge from a boy waiter, Vivyan Chell shut his eyes momentarily in prayer, a silent grace, and then prodded his neighbour.

'Matthew, my dear.'

Matthew was balding, scarlet in the face, and very dirty even by the standards of those sitting round that table. He made a particular contrast with the priest who, though he was dressed in the scruffiest old black jumper and black jeans, with Doc Marten shoes, had, as customary, showered himself at six a.m. and was impeccably clean.

'They never come,' Matthew said desperately. 'They never come – they never . . .'

Vivyan Chell's voice, manner, general bearing was less sacerdotal than soldierly. He did not seem as he sat there like any vicar you'd ever met. He retained all the bearing of a Guards officer; and in his conversation with these waifs and lunatics, he could have been a good-humoured colonel gently ribbing the more disgruntled of the majors or captains in his mess.

'You might not like it if they did come,' he said, his face creased in a smile.

'But they never *come*.'

'Count your blessings. Listen. Matt, my dear, there's something you can do for me.'

'They never *come*.'

'You're not on washing-up duty today, are you, Matt?'

'No, Father.'

Suddenly the wild red eyes of the vagabond focused and he was called to order.

'Well, we've been given quite a lot of new jumble – several boxes of clothes at the back of the shrine. So after breakfast, be a good man. Cut along and help me shift them. They all need bringing back to the house.'

'But they never—'

Vivyan Chell put his arm round Matthew and held his shoulder. He shook him with three jerky hugs.

'Cheer up!' he insisted briskly. 'Cheer up!'

The priest then concentrated on his porridge, eating the contents of his bowl in about one and a half minutes. Then he closed his eyes in prayer once again and rose from the table. He had a busy morning ahead – some sick communions in the council flats; then he had to go to the juvenile court and be a character witness for some young friends who were charged with armed robbery; then he had to come back and say the mass at noon.

Emerging from the dining room he passed Tuli, the young boy who had been sleeping on his floor for the last few weeks, and who had woken that morning, after about four hours' sleep, with his head on Father Chell's knees.

'Father – I must speak to you,' said the boy. There was real anxiety in his voice, and fear in his haunting grey-blue smudgy eyes.

'I'm busy now, dear.'

'Confession, Father, I must go to confession.'

'Tuli, we've talked about this before. You don't have to keep coming to confession.'

'Oh bless me, Father.'

Vivyan Chell reached out towards the boy's head, and for a moment held his black hair in his long elegant fingers. Then he ruffled the boy's hair and laughed. 'Come with me,' he said. 'I have to take Holy Communion to some people this morning. You can come along as my server. Then we can talk about this confession of yours.' They paced off together to the church.

'Can I wear the gear, Father, can I wear the gear?' clamoured Tuli with the insistence of a much younger child.

Vivyan Chell laughed. 'If you like – we'll go over to the church and kit you up. You can be my acolyte for the morning.' From behind, he held the boy's shoulders, breathing the words into his neck. 'You can wear lace,' he murmured, noting as he did so the beautiful way in which the thick black curls clustered about the nape.

It was at this point that one of the young monks who had been saying the dawn mass at the shrine church came into the house.

'Oh, Father,' he said, 'this lady was looking for you.'

'Mum,' whined the boy. Jeeves, Murderous Moron, the Guards officer and Sex Maniac all retreated and dissolved. It was the whimpering child, the one who was so afraid of Mr Currey, and so submissive with him, who looked up at Mercy Topling.

'Mercy,' said the priest. He smiled, but it was a forced smile. 'I wondered when you were going to turn up.'

THIRTY-TWO

It was nearly seventeen years since they had met.

Father Vivyan at once controlled the situation.

'Tuli – Peter.' He smiled, but there was no doubting that he expected to be obeyed. 'Cut along with Father Aidan – is that all right, Father? You can take Peter to the church. He wants a cassock and cotta – he's coming with me to take sick Communion.'

'*Peter?*' Mercy's surprise was total.

'You said I could wear the gear, Father.'

'So you can. Father Aidan here will help you choose what you want to wear.'

It looked as though the boy was hesitating, wondering whether he would allow himself to be palmed off in this way. Then he turned to Mercy and said, 'Mum – look after my jacket.'

'There are pegs in the vestry,' said Father Vivyan.

'There are funny people in this place,' the boy replied. 'Can't be too sure.'

'Have you got something valuable in here?'

Mercy held up the denim jacket.

'Keep it, Mum.'

The younger monk took the boy off to the church. The elder said to Mercy, 'We could take some coffee up to my room.'

Mercy had never been in the house. At the time of the parish mission sixteen years before, the clergy house was being run on conventional lines with a lock on the front door, and two bachelor priests, a vicar and a curate, living there with a housekeeper. As a child and adolescent she had been taken regularly to the shrine church by Lily, but there had never been any reason to cross the threshold of the vicarage. The gaggles of extraordinary-seeming people, the atmosphere of chaos, and the mess were all astounding. Father Chell led her into the room he called the refectory and poured two cups of coffee from a large pot at the table, where several Irish tramps sat eating porridge, and where a couple of young families were conversing loudly in some Eastern European language.

When they had walked upstairs to the first floor, he said, 'We can talk in here.'

Once again, his room was a source of astonishment. A few sleeping bags and bundles of old rags appeared to have been thrown randomly on the floor. The bookcase was the only solid-looking object of furniture, a large item against one wall, with glass-panelled doors. It was bursting with books untidily arranged. The desk, an old door, taken from a skip, and balanced on two tea-chests was littered with envelopes, letters, papers, and scribbles of all kinds. There were two deckchairs facing one another near a small one-bar electric fire at the far end of the room. Above the fireplace an enormous crucifix brooded. It was about half life-size – the great outstretched arms of the young man had veins sticking out.

'I had to come,' Mercy said.

'I thought you'd come sooner. I waited for you to come.'

'I slept last night at Mum's flat – she had to do some emergency nursing in Intensive Care. She warned me that Peter sometimes did not come back at nights, but – *where has he been?*'

'He came here last night – at about one in the morning. He

quite often comes at night, sometimes to sleep, sometimes to talk. He's a fine boy.'

'Yes. Yes, he is.' She smiled broadly.

'But he is not always happy.'

'No.'

'And he is very much disturbed.'

'Oh – I've been so worried. I didn't sleep, and I didn't sleep. I didn't dare ring the police. You know he's been stopped several times by the police? For no reason, as far as I can tell. If you're a tall black boy and you're out on the streets, then they think you're probably a criminal.'

'He's told me about this. It's certainly true. Only when Peter talks . . .'

'You don't always know what to believe?'

'I call him Tuli. It's Hausa. It means "My name is Legion because we are many". It's as if there are many different boys in that handsome head of his. Some of them are frightened, some of them are angry.'

'The school insisted we sent him to this psychiatrist. Well, he's not a psychiatrist, he's a psychiatric social worker . . .'

'I know about Mr Currey.'

The priest now sounded angry.

'We must be careful what we say, Mercy, but I was almost inclined to tell Peter not to go back to see that man. I did not want to upset your mother . . .'

'Mum's tough.'

'I know she is. But – I have my suspicions about Mr Currey.'

'You don't mean he's . . .'

'I have my suspicions. I think you should keep Peter and Mr Currey apart.'

'But this is terrible. A boy like Peter . . . He's *vulnerable*, he's so easily led . . .'

'He is very vulnerable. He is very . . . Peter.' The priest put his hands together and looked at the floor. 'Peter is in danger. I sense that he is in danger.'

There was a long silence. Then Mercy looked up into Vivyan Chell's eyes.

'Do you think he's schizophrenic?'

'I think it's unhelpful to label people. But I think that Peter needs help. Proper help from a doctor. I know a number of good psychiatrists. I could put you in touch with them; or I could tell your mother . . . I knew you would come to talk to me, Mercy, but I quite understand . . . if you do not want to return.'

She sat perfectly still, hearing him out. They both had things to say to one another, but neither was sure that the right words would come from the other, the words which would enable them to speak.

'Mercy . . . I feel that I want to say something to you . . . If I have done something to you . . . something which hurt you . . . I am deeply, deeply sorry. Sometimes our passions are so strong that they are quite literally uncontrollable. Sex makes us into lunatics. But I abused my position of trust . . .'

'Don't say that . . . Please don't say that. I don't think that. I knew what I was doing.'

She smiled in remembrance. It was an absolutely forgiving smile.

'I wouldn't come back to haunt you! I'm not a blackmailer.'

'Just as well,' he grinned – and with an arm he gestured to the mess of the room. 'As you see, I'm not a rich man.'

'Do you remember that day – that day we were alone together – sixteen years ago?'

'Of course.'

'And I was a really, really naughty girl.' She giggled at the thought of it. 'I've been a good girl ever since – I'd never betray my husband. But *then*, then it was different. And I wanted to talk to you about sex, but I think it was because I'd seen you talking to the crowds round the clock tower and I'd really, really fancied you.'

'I don't know about that.'

'But I *did*. I wanted to ask you lots of questions – like, if sex is such a sin, why God makes the appetite for it so, so strong . . .' She smiled at the thought. 'And I wanted to *talk* to someone about the mess I was getting myself into. I was sleeping around. I was sleeping with the boss, and with two or three other guys at the time.'

'I see.' His lips pursed.

'And then I came to see you in church . . .'

'And *that* happened. If you *knew* how I reproach myself.'

'Look – *don't* . . . Look. Do you realize I've never called you by your name. *Vivyan*. I enjoyed it. What we did. I en*joyed it*. I had a great time. Okay . . . It's just . . .'

'Is Peter my son?'

'He's told you about going to Mr Currey? How Mr Currey thought – like, maybe what's wrong with Peter is that he hasn't got an anchor. Maybe we need to know who our father is, even if we never see him. And . . . well, it was crazy, but I believed Mr Currey. I thought I had to tell Peter something, and I couldn't tell him the truth, and I couldn't tell Mum the truth.'

'Which is?'

'Which is that I don't know who his father is – that's the truth. And I blurted out that it was Lennox Mark. And, you know, as soon as I'd said that I was, like, going, I really, really hope that's not true. I don't think Peter even knows who Lennox Mark is.'

Suddenly, as if in his unworldiness a monk might not have heard of a tycoon she said:

'You know who he is?'

'Yes. I know who Lennox Mark is.'

'It didn't seem like it made any impression on Peter at all. He's never talked about it to me or to Mum – I just wish I hadn't told him. And I do wonder . . . You know it says how the sins of the fathers are visited on the children . . . You don't think that Peter is like he is because of me being bad and wicked?'

'You don't think that?'

'Not really. I just worry about that boy so, so much. And he's been such a mystery. You know, like as a young boy he was a lovely kid, but he and Trevor – Trevor's my husband – just rubbed each other up the wrong way. It got so bad at home, Peter had to move out. I don't know where I'd've been without Mum . . .'

The priest leaned forward and cupped her hands in his. Neither of them knew whether this was the gesture of a pastor or of a lover.

'You've been a wonderful mother. You know that, Mercy? Don't reproach yourself. If you ever want any help – of whatever kind – I'm here. Until I came back to England – to this parish – I'd no idea you'd had a child. I did not want to scandalize you or Lily by suggesting that I was the father. But if you need *anything* – money, help, a room in this house for Peter until he's calmed down a bit . . .'

'I hadn't realized you'd become such friends.'

'The door is open,' said Father Vivyan. 'We're like the Windmill Theatre here – we never close.'

She hugged him, and he hugged her in return.

'Father!' Peter was calling excitedly up the stairs. 'Father Aidan's found me . . . Mum! Look what's he's found me to wear!'

He wore a long black cassock and a short lacy cotta. His fine bony head, with its new short haircut, its faint, sharply cut whiskers which made acute accents on the top of his angular cheekbones, and his aquiline nose bore in that light a strong resemblance to the priest's.

'Mum – got my coat – valuable stuff in there!'

'I've got your coat.'

She held it up.

'What's this – a little Walkman?'

She held up the tiny tape-recorder and the mike, which dangled from a pocket.

'I'll take those.' He grabbed them and put them in the pockets of his new robes.

THIRTY-THREE

Mary Much felt drawn from the very first to the irritation value of Hans Busch. She'd sniffed it afar, as others might nose out talent, seen its capacity to expose, even in those who considered themselves all irony, a last-straw quality. *Gloss* had gone big after Hans Busch. After that feature, the lesser magazines and supplements had followed: some with a baffled wonder at his work, others with that satisfying and so, so English mixture of envy and admiration for the sums he commanded. Mary Much considered herself responsible for having swayed the Royal Academy. The latest installation would be erected in the courtyard of Burlington House – not as part of the Summer Exhibition but as the most exquisitely funny commentary on the whole yawn, yawn, let's dip a brush in a pot, daub, daub, draw, draw, yawn, yawn thing.

Martina, anxious to keep up with her friend, had expressed full enthusiasm for Hans Busch – had even begged Lennie to sign him up to design the *Daily Legion* garden for the Chelsea Flower Show. (Poor Martina, Mary said, when recounting this information, it showed she hadn't quite got there.) Martina, aware of the kind of games Mary had been playing throughout their friendship, was certainly not going to do anything so satisfying as to say that she disliked Hans Busch or his work. There were times when that fixed smile, stitched in place by the New York plastic surgeons, had its supreme value. She was certainly not going to say she *minded* that Mary had enrolled Piet in the project. She'd told Aubrey – poor Aubrey, knowing it would be repeated artlessly straight back to Mary Much – that the house-boy would hold his own with the artist.

'Darling,' said Mary, 'he can hold his own, and Hans's if he wants to.'

Poor darling Aubrey and his lickle-ickle accident. (For some reason the conjunction of sex and violence made Mary Much think and speak in baby-talk.) The *Legion* had been told that he'd been *mugged* in a car park. Stabbed. The nature of the injuries was left vague.

But – Piet and Hans! Mary knew that Martina really, really *minded* – which further extended Hans's quite enviable ability to get under every skin.

Both *Legion*s had behaved according to type when, like obedient puppies, they had leapt at the leaked information. Mr Blimby had got his art critic on to the case, and been enterprising enough to create a mock-up of what the finished installation would be like. This imagined projection was photographed beside Rodin's *Thinker*, and the art critic had then delivered a satisfyingly swingeing attack on the blatant commercialism which could create a concept such as this. If Hans Busch were to come up with this idea for free, said the critic, then no one would pay it the smallest attention. Because his works sold for princely sums before they were so much as finished, he was regarded as the prime alternative to art.

Spies at Derek Worledge's brutal features conferences also brought most satisfying reports back to Mary Much about the treatment he meted out to Rachel Pearl. It was bad enough that L.P. should still be wasting time and money on her: but that gorgeous Sinclo could also be breaking his manly, yummy heart over the little pseud was more than Mary Much could stand. Once again, one saw how stupendous Hans Busch was. Hitherto, since Worledge became editor, the Pearl (as Martina always dubbed her) had not suffered as much as the rest of the staff.

That was simply because he did not know about art, and tended to leave her alone. Naturally, the amount of space in the newspaper devoted to exhibitions or plays had been slashed to almost nothing, and her only role as art editor had been to supply the morning conference with updates on the states of various Hollywood marriages. So long as an interesting love affair or bust-up among the stars could be timed to coincide with the premiere of some commercial feature film in Leicester Square, Worledge appeared to be satisfied on what he called the Arts Front.

Hans Busch, however, was another matter. Worledge only heard about him some two years after the rest of London had been 'taken by storm'. It had actually been Esmé who first saw one of this fashionable person's works, photographed in a magazine at the hairdresser's in Esher, and remarked – Worledge had agreed one hundred per cent – that this just wasn't art.

The little Pearly pseud had piped up at a conference in reply to this rant. She'd been brave, bless her. She was, she had said, 'troubled' by the philistinism of Derek Worledge's response to Busch, and tried at first to point out that Busch himself said that his work was not art. That was the point of it. Busch was asking us to reconsider the stereotypical, artificially 'progressive' Story of Art from the Pyramids to Picasso. He was not claiming to be the next thing after Francis Bacon or the next thing after anyone. Okay, he might be an incredibly tiresome, self-publicizing jerk, and the commercialism surrounding his work was nauseating. But, she had wanted to say . . .

Worledge was a man who, during such discussions, knew no buts. When the Pearl had tried to explain what she thought of

Hans Busch's work, during that morning's features conference, Worledge had wrinkled his nose. Then, in an insultingly laddish manner, he had started to snigger, and to look to the others, nearly all men, for support.

The spy said that Sinclo had blushed to the roots of his hair, but he had not dared stick up for his little Pearly Princess. Bright pink flushes had appeared in those sallow cheeks – by Christ, Mary envied the purity of that woman's skin, it just wasn't *fair* – and she'd spoken up for herself:

'I thought we were trying to take the *Legion* in a new direction – I thought we were trying to talk to the twenty-thirty-somethings whose interest in art is a bit more sophisticated than just wanting a block-mounted reproduction of Monet on their walls.'

Mary and her informant had shrieked in unison down their telephones that they bet any money that Esmé and Derek did indeed have a block-mounted Monet in their Esher dining room.

Worledge had apparently erupted:

'Christ Al-fucking-mighty, we're not talking about the fucking *Mona Lisa*! That isn't ART! We're talking about a poof whose mind is so fucking sick he's exhibiting real people going to the fucking toilet! I'm sorry, but if that's sophistication . . . dear, oh dear, oh dear.'

Wasn't he priceless? He had Rachel marked down as trouble from that moment.

As for Martina and Mary, few things in recent years had displayed more clearly their ambivalent relations with Lennie's *Legions* than the two women's joint passion for Hans Busch. They loved the *Legions* for the money they provided. Martina also loved them for the political power they wielded. They, who had accustomed themselves over so many years to live with ambivalence and paradox, positively enjoyed the contrasts between their own outlook on life and that of the two newspapers which paid them to sustain it. The *Legions* themselves, however, were sustained on a multiplicity of vision no less marked, though more crudely self-contradictory. The front half of *The Daily Legion* had increased, since Worledge became the editor, its siege mentality. The Court had been not far wrong when they saw Esmé Worledge as the archetypical reader of the newspaper whom her husband had in mind. The vision of England presented by Worledge in his editorials and news stories was of a plucky little middle class which had pulled itself up by hard work and its own boot-straps, and who watched in horror as its savings accounts, its church, its favourite television programmes and its very methods of weighing and measuring were all eroded by Foreigners, Perverts, Busybodies, and hangovers from the days of Socialism. The Good Guys, paradoxically, were those who had in fact done most to erode the 1950s England of Esmé's imagination: the Good Guys politically were the right-wing Americans, and the big multi-national companies. The Bad Guys were the European Union, the sexual liberals, the would-be abolishers of the pound and the Bureaucrats.

At the heart of the *Legion*, though, there was a paradox. The marketing men knew about it, and so did everyone who came to edit it. The very first *Daily Legion* to roll from the presses in 1887, with the old Roman legionary holding his spear aloft as he still did on the logo, had been a paper directed – as Mary Much liked to say – at Carrie Pooter. It was a paper for women, and so it still remained, in essence. Sloanes read it, nannies read it, secretaries read it on their way to work. Therefore, when they'd skipped through the first twelve pages, and had sporadically taken in all the photographs of asylum seekers living on huge bogus benefit claims; of mullahs in Bradford telling their congregations to slit the throats of the white population; of teenage

West Indian rapists and Belgian bureaucrats tampering with the good British banana, these readers wanted to read the remaining fifty pages of the paper, which were given over to new diets, continental holidays, quack cures for depression, and lurid accounts of the erotic lives of the celebrated. These readers knew that half the couples in England lived together without being married, that many of them were gay, bisexual, of mixed race, of no creed or of many. They knew this, just as they knew that their neighbours and friends and colleagues at work belonged to that mixed and complicated conglomeration of types known as the human race. Everyone lived with the paradox.

The difference was that Mary Much and her friend Martina did not merely live with it, they revelled in its cynical implications. Martina was going to make Lennie buy Hans's latest installation. She almost had it in mind that she would erect it in the Atrium of LenMar House.

She certainly was not going to spare Piet – who had been SUCH A SUCCESS since his arrival as the house-boy and general factotum – to waste the summer being a permanent feature of Hans's work. The most that Martina would allow was that he could be the model chosen for the first week in the courtyard of Burlington House.

So this was what Mary Much was doing, bringing Piet to the studio, to show him the exhibit, and to explain to him, as tactfully as possible, what would be involved.

'You mean, I've got to sit on it?' had been his ironical response. Oh, she could die for that orotund, upper-class voice of the boy's! He looked like a Nubian slave in some painting by Veronese and he spoke like a brigadier in the Coldstream Guards. Mmmm! Mmwah!

Hans Busch's studio was a huge loft just off Clerkenwell

Green. It had formerly been a warehouse for a gin company, long since defunct. He had achieved some notoriety when taking it over by spending half a million pounds having the place gutted and reinforced with stainless-steel girders. The original warehouse had looked too homely, too retro, too love-me. It lacked the appropriate rebarbative harshness. He wanted a place where anyone, even a labourer in the dirtiest dungarees who had been unblocking drains for Dyno-rod, would look too chic, too overdressed. He also, by paradox, wanted a place which was spotlessly clean.

Piet's appearance, in the black Armani suit bought that morning by Mary and an open-necked cream silk shirt purchased for him by Martina, was undeniably striking in such a huge, whitewashed space.

The boy looked around him to see evidence (it was, after all, called the Studio) of the artist's work-tools. On failing to see them, he asked – oh how gorgeously like an Etonian trying not to be patronizing when he spent a week at a local comprehensive, seeing how the other half lived! – 'Is this where you work?'

Busch said, 'Sure.' His accent was a strange *mélange* of the English Midlands and the mid-Atlantic.

Busch was an ugly brute, but this, like the uncharmingness of his installations, was, what Worledge so deliciously failed to see, *the idea*.

He had a shaven head, on which several spots and wens had erupted. The sneer of his lower lip was emphasized by a large stud which suppurated. He wore an open-necked denim shirt from which thick brown body-hair sprouted in unappealing places – the throat, the top of his back beneath his neck. Dirty jeans and large sabots covered the nether man. He smoked cigarettes continually.

'I was looking for your work-tools, a bench . . .'

'This is my work-tool – this is my bench,' said Busch. From the top pocket of his denim shirt, he produced his Nokia mobile and said, 'This does the rest! I order someone else to make me a Perspex toilet. The crap I order from others.'

He smiled.

It was indeed a remarkable, if not entirely original, device. Piet had once been taken on a school trip to the Science Museum in Kensington. In the basement there, among the vacuum cleaners and electric kettles and other exhibits displaying 'life in the home', there was a cross-section of a working toilet with a fully operative fake turd being swooshed into the U-bend to the merriment of the younger children. Busch had merely extended the idea by having a Perspex toilet which could be viewed from all sides.

'Shall we see him sitting on it?' Busch asked Mary Much.

She smiled at Piet and cooed, 'Could you bear it?'

'You mean, fully dressed?'

He smiled back at her, attempting to maintain his insouciance.

'He must drop his pants,' said Busch.

'Could you?' She had put on her poor ickle-wickle-girl cooing-voice and had lowered her mascara-lids to flutter at him.

Piet liked it when she did this, and after a momentary shock he did not mind the idea of the exhibitionism suggested. Indeed, as he lowered trousers and underpants and sat on the Perspex throne he could feel the beginnings of an erection. Let them look, if they liked! Let them look!

Hans Busch appeared to be totally impersonal, unaffected by the sight of the boy on his toilet, until he was conscious of Mary Much's visible excitement.

They were gone – what? Ten minutes? This was presumably

what such people called a quickie. When they returned, their faces were masks of impassivity. They found Piet still sitting there, but with no erection, and everything under control.

'I'll take my pants down, but I'm not going to crap into this thing, you know,' he said good-humouredly. It was as if they were all taking part in a party game. 'I'm not a queer.'

'What will you do when it's exhibited in public?' asked Mary Much.

Piet wondered if they should mention the artificial turd in the Science Museum, or whether to demonstrate so clear a sense of Busch's source-material would somehow place them all at a disadvantage.

'That is part of the point,' said Busch. 'They will come and stare and stare at that Perspex U-bend and hope to see crap. That is the point. Just before they enter the Royal Academy, they will be asking themselves, Am I going to view some crap coming out of a human arse and down the U-bend?'

'God, you're witty,' said Mary Much.

THIRTY-FOUR

Since Worledge had been editor the raffish, jolly atmosphere of the old *Legion* had evaporated.

Worledge was hated and feared in equal doses. There had been many redundancies, several sackings on the spot, and a number of formal warnings issued to his staff.

Worledge found it impossible to work without creating an atmosphere of terror and resentment around himself. Whether as a result of having attended English boarding schools, followed by the army, or whether for some other reason, Sinclo actually found life was now easier to cope with. Like everyone else on *The Daily Legion*, he was miserable; but this, he had come to feel, was how things should be. Pain was a warning. If you put your hand too near the flame, the time to worry was when it didn't hurt, not when it did.

Worledge had caused the shake-up for which Lennox Mark had hired him. The typeface of the paper had changed. The old Roman legionary still stood beside the title at the top, but Worledge had created what he called 'a middle-market tabloid with a red-top appeal'. The front pages most mornings showed female television stars, or film actresses, usually with blonde hair or large chests, preferably both. When blondes could not be found, appalling sexist and racist innuendo enlivened the captions and headlines – CHOCOLATE SAUCE! being the quite gratuitous description of a pair of black tennis players from the United States, both chaste and religious, neither of whom could by the wildest distortion of language be described as 'saucy'.

The staff never knew from day to day whether their jobs would be safe, nor whether they would be doing the work at which they felt confident.

Rumours circulated daily, hourly, about the next candidate for the chop. It was generally assumed that the entire *Sunday Legion* was to be dissolved, but Lennox Mark remained silent, and the discomfiture of poor Mr Blimby (who suffered from a duodenal ulcer and was obliged to eat rice pudding each day in his club) may be imagined.

Sinclo was surprised not to have been sacked for his article exposing the crimes of General Bindiga. Instead, he had found himself transferred to the diary, which, while Aubrey Bird was in hospital, was edited by Peg Montgomery. It was embarrassing to work under someone with whom one had had a functionally successful but not especially enjoyable one-night stand. He found Peg an exacting boss, and it was disconcerting to discover how easily she conformed herself to Worledge's views and ways. As a Diary underling, Sinclo still had to attend a features conference each morning and contribute to the 'input' of ideas.

Tony Taylor had conducted conferences in what, with three nostalgic months to distort them, now seemed models of insouciance and gentleness. Worledge charged into the room and scratched himself like a ferocious gorilla. These back and armpit scratchings were so intense that they sometimes drew blood which seeped through his shirt.

'Ideas, ideas, ideas!' he would yell. Then, with yet greater frenzy, 'Stories, stories – IDEAS!' He sounded like a man thirsting for water after three days in the desert; without an idea or a story, the nervous colleagues round the table were going to make this man die.

In such circumstances Sinclo's notions of suitable subjects for why-oh-why columns appeared as hopelessly woolly as they always were in truth.

'I thought in the light of the fact . . . er . . . er, this story this morning – this Chancellor effort.'

'Chancellor? What's he been fucking up to NOW!' Worledge would bellow. 'Putting up road tax? I don't BELIEVE it! Get L.P. to do one of his pieces sticking up for the motorist.'

'No, er, er, this story in *The Independent* about the Chancellor of Germany saying . . .'

Worledge's face would at this point darken.

'Where did you say he was Chancellor of?'

Merely repeating the word 'Germany' in this company felt like uttering an obscenity to a gathering of nuns.

'Fucking Krauts,' said Worledge.

Sinclo had been stupid enough not to see that the existence of these eighty-two million individuals was a personal affront to Worledge.

There had been talk of protests at that year's Royal Ascot by animal rights activists and Sinclo proposed as his second idea of the morning a fairly straight article by a member of the racing fraternity defending the sport of kings. Worledge did not like this. He sensed that many of his readers, while not actively wishing to bomb turkey factories, nursed sentimental feelings about animal suffering. Also, though the paper devoted several pages a day to racing and football, and frequently splashed (as they said in the trade) with National Lottery winners, Worledge sensed that many readers did not approve of gambling.

Peg, catching the mood of the meeting, had sycophantically suggested a piece denouncing the Queen for having enough money to buy racehorses, and this idea was taken up with enthusiasm.

Sinclo was told loudly in front of the entire conference that he was fucking useless. He rather agreed.

Aubrey Bird returned from hospital looking ashen and old. Everyone had their own version of what had happened to him during the mugging. No one knew the actual truth, though most suspected that he had been cruising and met with a spot of bad luck. Since he was, for official purposes, very firmly still in the closet, Aubrey had to smile and laugh his way through the conferences at which Worledge shouted his coarse, queer-bashing jokes, and he was always being urged to 'hit bum-bandits where it hurts' in Dr Arbuthnot's diary.

Sinclo assumed that it could not be long before he was himself sacked from the *Legion*. Were it not for the daily heart-rending delicious torment of seeing Rachel, he would probably have walked out. His flatmates with whom he shared his sorrows – the bankers and lawyers – urged him to stay on until he was pushed.

'Why give the bastard the satisfaction of leaving him?'

So, he stayed. And one day, he had an invitation to lunch with Mary Much and wondered whether she was going to offer him a job on *Gloss*.

This magazine (Worledge had defined it and *Lips*, in Sinclo's presence, as 'The Two Must-Have Glossies') continued, despite the recession, to make money. (Appealing as it did to the 'luxury' market, it still attracted advertising revenues from the most expensive fashion houses, jewellers, fine art galleries, leather manufacturers.) Though Middle England was passing through a trough in which it felt it could no longer afford conservatories, stair-lifts for the elderly, cheap foreign holidays – all the things which brought in advertising revenue for the *Legions* – Upper England still wanted its crocodile-skin shoes, its diamond necklaces, its Rolex watches, its bespoke female underwear, its expensive scents.

Over this world of fantasy, Mary Much had reigned as empress since the day News Incorporated acquired the title ten years earlier. Sinclo had never got his eye in to the glossy mags, made the mistake of thinking one had to flick through eighty pages of advertisements before you got to the interesting bits, without realizing that these *were* the interesting bits. Partly to extend her power and patronage, and perhaps partly because it flattered her sense of herself as a person of culture, however, Mary Much had appointed music critics, opera critics, even a literary editor to review books. Their lucubrations were to be discovered somewhere in *Gloss* if you burrowed deep enough between the dozens of pages devoted to lipsticks, eye make-up, boots and bras.

On his way to Mayfair, Sinclo wondered whether he was to be privileged to become one of Mary Much's entourage. He had plenty of time to meditate on the theme, since the journey – the brisk walk, nearly a run to Bermondsey, and then the Jubilee Line to Green Park, and then the walk across Berkeley Square – took the best part of an hour. The invitation had come that morning – breathless, cooing, and yet for all its tone of self-deprecation quite peremptory – 'You're probably so busy . . . but if you *could* bear . . .' As soon as he'd bumblingly said, 'Oh no . . . that would be . . . no, of course, yes . . . I'm sure I could rejig . . .' she had said in quite a clipped manner, 'One, then. Come to the office,' and rung off.

Gloss and *Lips* occupied a handsome old Georgian house in one of the streets off the western side of Hanover Square. Its interior, under Mary Much's watchful tutelage, had undergone several transformations since her occupancy of the editorial chair. She had had her Georgian queens moments, when young men in three-piece suits had come to advise about panellings and fire baskets; her sudden change to Swedish minimalism. At present she had, at colossal expense to Lennox Mark, given the house the look of a building being squatted by unmaterialistic persons of good taste. The seagrass and rugs had gone years ago, of course: but now the bare floorboards had been expensively scuffed, and the skirting boards and shutters kicked to achieve that 'squat' atmos. Her own office, from which paintings and flowers had been removed (save for one white orchid drooping in a metallic pot), consisted of a plain bleached oak table and two upright chairs. The grate had been torn out, leaving in the fireplace a cave of uneven, blackened bricks. The panelling and window shutters looked as if they had been given a coat of grey, uneven undercoat in which some incompetent painter had dropped soot.

An essential ingredient in her genius, and there was something of genius in the character of Mary Much, was to make almost every individual with whom she had anything to do believe that there existed between them and her a special shared little intimacy, a whole world of small-talk and jokes which the rest of the world knew nothing about. When Sinclo was shown into her room, she stood, all six feet of her, and put her ash-blonde hair on one side as if she was a floppy rag doll. Then she straightened up and 'became' Peg Montgomery.

'That was a brilliant idea, Derek. I've got a good story here about a soccer manager.'

She was an eerily good mimic. Sinclo, who had come to assume that Mary 'knew everything', thought it quite likely not merely that she knew that he found working with Peg tiresome, but also that she'd heard somehow or another about the one-night stand. He attributed psychic, even magical, powers to her. Although she was clad in a fringed Wild West white leather top, half unzipped, and a matching white leather skirt, both Versace, with pink cowboy boots by Judy Rothschild, there was always something of another time and place. She could easily have been one of those maidens who appeared out of a mist to bear King Arthur to his barge, or emerged from the waters of a lake brandishing a sword, or she could have been Vivien the Enchantress, holding the wizard Merlin in her thrall.

This impression of timelessness was partly the result of her extraordinary resemblance to those round-faced, beaky-nosed girls so beloved of Burne-Jones; partly because her hair, which had been that colour for as long as anyone could remember, was quite ageless, being neither white in the way old people's hair is white nor blonde in the way that most cheap dyes are blonde.

'Diana's' – she named the most expensive restaurant in London, where she lunched almost every day, as if it were an idea that had just sprung to mind. 'Could you bear? Could you?'

It was dismaying, when they were settled at the table, and she was smoking a cigarette over her tiny Caesar salad, to discover that she was not offering him a job on *Gloss*. Instead, she wanted to talk about 'Dr Arbuthnot's Diary' on the *Legion*.

'Peg's an interviewer, not a diarist,' she told him. 'Now *you* . . . you *could* be a diarist.'

Nothing about Mary Much was accidental. He felt their knees momentarily meet beneath the table.

'But it needs to be tougher. That thing about the Kitty Henderson drug cure – it was much too kind, much too bland.'

That was the moment to say that he was a cousin of Kitty's. Afterwards, he realized she had known this all along, and needed to draw forth his tacit disloyalty towards her.

'Charles Henderson's a creep,' she said sharply.

The previous year, Sinclo's cousin, Kitty Chell, had married Charles Henderson. It had been a stormy relationship fuelled by shared tastes in wild friends, alcohol and cocaine. Kitty had lately taken a cure at a clinic in Arizona and Charles Henderson had been stupid enough to tell 'Dr Arbuthnot's Diary' – while Peg was editing – that he and Kitty hoped to have a baby.

'*Trying for a family*' – she said it in a mincing voice. 'Such a common phrase. Such a boring thing to want to do, but they are both bores – know 'em?'

'I do – as a matter of fact, I . . . er . . .'

'Martina wants to have a go at them.'

'Oh, really?'

'You know Martina.'

'I don't, really.'

Mary Much leaned so far forward towards him over the table that he wondered whether they were going to kiss. He put down his forkful of calves' liver, slithered as thin as paper.

'Paranoia,' she whispered. 'Lennie and Martie – ickle bit paranoid. They really think they're . . .'

She made a *moue* with her lips.

'You're not saying they're bankrupt . . .'

'Shh.'

She touched her lip with a long white finger. Then, business-like, she said, 'No, of course they'll be okay, it's a recession. Neither Lennie nor Martie realize that the rest of the world is affected, they think it's just them. That's why . . .'

Her voice sank to a whisper and he had to put his forehead almost against hers to hear.

'It's quite all right now, I've saved you, it was a brilliant piece, brilliant, but that's why they were so angry with you for your piece on Bongo-Bongo.'

It was a while before he registered that Zinariya was being discussed.

'You know that Lennie comes from Bongo-Bongo – very keen on De Blik Men, even more on De Blik Ladies, Lennie . . .'

'Oh, really?'

She nodded enthusiastically, her face animated, her finger momentarily making thrusting copulatory gestures before she picked up her cigarette again from the side of her plate.

'Thinks that old bender monk is buggering things up for him in Bongo – you know who I mean, you wrote about him – brilliant, brilliant – but you know he's Kitty's uncle, the bender.'

'Father Chell? Yes, I did know . . .'

'Frightful old hypocrite, the bender. Calls himself a communist . . .'

'Does he? Father Chell?'

'. . . but swans off to stately homes every other week. Married Kitty Chell to that drip Charles Henderson. One minute telling Lennie how to spend his money, the next going to marry silly little coke-fiends in some . . . Funny that about Lennie and Martie, have you noticed?'

All this was whispered at rapid speed.

'As I say,' said Sinclo, who was as flattered to be taken into Mary Much's confidence as he was disturbed by her malice about his cousins, 'I don't really know the proprietor . . . Lennie.'

'Grand dinners if you call entertaining the Prime Minister grand.'

'I would, wouldn't you?'

'But they don't know people like the Hendersons. Never get asked to Badminton or Chatsworth or Blenheim. The lords and ladies come to their big parties. Love the smell of money, lords and ladies do – but Martie and Lennie aren't really accepted. That's why . . .'

The whisper sank to near inaudibility. Her hair, which was wonderfully soft and silky, tickled his forehead, and the scent of Coco Mademoiselle intoxicated his nostrils. The sound coming from her was so faint that it was almost necessary to read her glossy red lips.

'. . . they so much want Lennie to get his *peerage*.'

'Is that likely?' asked Sinclo, much too loud.

'It's not in the bag yet,' she whispered. 'That's why it's so important that the Prime Minister and he see eye to eye about Bongo – all de other Blik countries are raising such a silly stink about the Bongos hosting the Olympic Games.'

'Commonwealth Games.'

'God, you're clever. Anyway, if the Prime Minister emerges as a hero over Bongo-Bongo, he might reward Lennie with a peerage. So we must keep on attacking Bender Chell.'

'As a matter of fact, I don't think Father Chell is—'

'And Kitty Chell, silly little heroin addict, spoilt brat . . . and her randy old dad.'

'Is Lord Longmore especially randy?'

'Wasn't there an affair with an actress?'

'Yes, but twenty years ago . . .' said Sinclo, trapped into revealing much too much knowledge about the family. Of course she must know he was related to them all.

'That was Aubrey's little weakness, I'm afraid.'

'Actresses?'

She spluttered with mirth.

'One day,' she whispered, 'I'll tell you about Aubrey's ickle accident. What *really* happened.' Her face contorted itself into a mockery of pain. 'Ouch! No – Aubrey's *other* little weakness apart from rough trade is lords and ladies. Very sweet in a way, and it was the old way of doing a diary. But we must have something much more hard-hitting. That's why that stuff about Kitty giving up drugs and trying for a baby was so, frankly, nauseating. We only want posh totty stories if they're getting into trouble . . .'

She cackled. Sinclo remembered the phrase 'motiveless malignity' from some English lesson at school.

'Son and heir drives sports car into the ornamental temple, Lady Esmerelda snorts the top of her head off, the Duke of Posh shags his way through Shepherd Market, that's Worledge's view of the aristocracy. The old *Legion* readers looked up to Posh, just as they looked up to Royals. Now the tumbrils are rolling – not for political reasons you understand, just spectator sport. No one wants to be told that as well as being richer than them and better looking than them and better born than them, the upper classes are also *nicer*. They have to be braying, selfish buffoons.'

Sinclo laughed. He wondered to what class her parents had belonged. She was so entirely *sui generis* that she had outsoared the ordinary borders of social classification.

'There are plenty of braying, selfish buffoons about,' he conceded.

'Look,' she said with sudden earnestness. 'Aubrey's past it. He hasn't got . . .' She sniggered into a napkin.

'What it takes?'

'He hasn't got the balls for the job any more.' And completely silently she mouthed, 'And that's true. LITERALLY.'

Two fingers made scissor gestures.

Sinclo stared open-eyed. He had just enough self-possession not to remark openly that Aubrey Bird was, surely, one of the 'best friends' of this woman who was now destroying his career.

'It's yours if you want it.'

In that moment of seriousness, she could have been speaking, not of Dr Arbuthnot's Diary, but of her heart.

Sinclo closed his eyes. He thought of his ambition to be a foreign correspondent. He imagined himself at a café table in, say, Cairo, with all the newspapers, French, Arabic, English, spread out in front of him as he drank mint tea.

'That . . .' he was lost for words, 'that would be wonderful, Mary,' he said.

'I think you'll find that the priest, the old perv, got thrown out of Bongo-Bongo for being a bender. Write it up. Worledge would like it. I'll get Martina on the case. We'll get rid of Aubrey.'

Aubrey Bird had been Dr Arbuthnot for thirty years. He was a journalistic institution. Getting rid of him, however feeble he might be, was like getting rid of the ravens from the Tower of London. Besides, mindless tittle-tattle about minor aristocrats, and racehorse owners and their chums was Aubrey's *métier*. Sinclo had no interest in it whatever.

'How?' asked Sinclo.

She snip-snipped again with her two fingers, and when her giggles died down she said, 'God, you're gonna be *hot*.'

THIRTY-FIVE

'I just can't believe you wrote this.'

The Daily Legion was folded open on the upended barrel which served as a table at Bin Ends. A long pale finger pointed accusingly at the leader page. The headline was HANS BUSCH – YOUR POTTY OR ARE WE?! The 'stand first' was '*With tongue firmly in cheek, top* Legion *writer L. P. Watson asks whether controversial modern artist Hans Busch's latest work* The Thinker *– a Perspex toilet – is really worth the £1.3 million paid this week by an anonymous collector.*'

The sheepish author slumped on his wobbly chair. He was neither especially proud, nor especially ashamed of the article.

'Darling,' he sighed, 'I don't know what you are making such a fuss about.'

'Don't call me darling.'

'But you are my darling . . .'

'It is so patronizing – we are trying to have a serious conversation.'

'The article is meant to be funny – obviously it fails, unless it's your sense of humour that has mysteriously failed.'

There was silence, time enough for him to wonder for the first time in his life whether this intense and beautiful person in fact had ever, in the eight years, on and off, they had known one another, shown the smallest sign of possessing a sense of humour.

'Lionel, have you forgotten what I am supposed to be?'

L. P. Watson paused and looked at the impassioned, pale face of Rachel Pearl. He was used to being screamed at by his wife because of what he wrote in the *Legion*; his mistress had normally registered her disapprovals and disagreements by silence.

'And the pay-off line . . . it is just, so predictable. Frankly, Lionel, it's not worthy – even of you.'

'Ouch.'

It was eleven thirty in the morning. The features conference had just ended, when Rachel had sent him an urgent e-mail message to say that they must talk. He, as it happened, had much more serious news to impart. His wife had told him that she wanted a divorce. This devastating news made his why-oh-why on the subject of Hans Busch's Perspex lavatory seem a bit trivial; and Rachel's anger about his article seemed, in the circumstances, schoolgirlish.

'It was not Oscar Wilde, it was Ruskin who said that Whistler, not Turner, was throwing a paint pot in the face of the British public.'

'Does it matter?' he sighed.

'Surely accuracy matters.' She prodded the paper furiously. 'You said it was Oscar Wilde . . .'

'Yes, yes.'

She read it back to him:

'*It was Oscar Wilde long ago who accused Turner of throwing a pot of paint in the face of the British public. Hans Busch is throwing a pot of something else – the pot which those of us who are older remember keeping under our beds.*

'It would have had at least a certain style if it ended there, but it's so heavy – "*This isn't art, though it might be something which rhymes with art*" – Lionel, how could you write that?'

'Worledge wrote it, I expect.'

'You're saying you didn't even write this – that you let Worledge tamper with your copy?'

'Sometimes – who cares what appears in our silly little paper?'

'So long as I'm arts editor, I care what gets written about art. You thought you were just writing a jokey philistine article about conceptual art, yawn, yawn – but don't you see just where Worledge was coming from when he commissioned that piece? He intended it as an attack on me . . .'

'Oh, that's a bit self-important.'

She picked up cigarettes and bag and rose from the table without speaking. He did not move to stop her, and swigged heavily from his glass of Shiraz.

'Bye, Lionel.'

Lionel knew that in some mysterious way it was the failure of his relationship with Rachel which had led to the breakdown of his marriage to Julia. There was, of course, no logic in this belief, but it made sense to him, nevertheless. When he and Rachel were in love, when their lovemaking was satisfactory and they were enjoying one another's company, he felt an agonizing awkwardness, a huge condescending pity for his wife whenever he returned to Clapham. This would lead him to be especially solicitous, to ask Julia in detail about her day, to offer to do the washing-up. He would urge her to let him buy her dinner in their local restaurant, or to entertain friends who especially bored him, just to show his conscience how sorry he was for being such a shit. When he and Rachel were failing to get along, by contrast, he was in an unshakeable gloom and allowed himself to be distant, cold and irascible with his wife and children.

It had become obvious to both him and Rachel that their affair had hit the buffers. He felt an old-fashioned gallantry about it; he did not want to hear himself sacking her – he wanted to put her in the position of sacking him.

This she resolutely refused to do. She also inwardly wanted to chuck, and start living an independent existence. For the previous eight years, she had believed him when he said he was unhappy with his wife, did not have sexual relations with her any more; she had believed him when he said he was lonely and sad, and that he needed her companionship. If she did not believe this, she would have had to see herself, since the age of twenty, as something little better than L.P.'s prostitute, and she could not bear that thought. So she stayed with him, not merely out of pity for his condition, as she saw it, but out of need to salvage her own dignity.

She had had a number of conversations with him, over the years, about conceptual art. She knew that he was incorrigibly, deliberately philistine about it. That was not what was at issue. Writing this particular article at this particular juncture must be seen as an insult to her. How could L.P. not see this? Either he had not been listening to her, for the last two or three weeks, when she had told him at such length about Worledge's bullying her to rubbish Hans Busch, and her refusal to do so; or he had listened, and he was still prepared to write this ignorant, condescending article which – in the context of *Legion* office politics – was tantamount to patting her on the head and saying, 'The arts editor of the paper is a sad little pseud, a recent graduate who hasn't learnt that all art is a pretension, that being serious about writing, or the visual or the musical is something we left behind at college with the nerds whose highest ambition was to do a traineeship course with the BBC.'

Looking at her sad, pale, angry face, Lionel knew that this might be a moment when they could split up; he could lose wife and girlfriend in one morning, make a clean sweep. In that moment, there would have been something tempting in that prospect. Coming to work that day, in a daze of confusion and grief, Lionel had felt that he would do anything to stop Julia divorcing him. He wondered whether it would be possible to undo the last twenty years, to become once again the man he had been aged twenty-five or thirty. Why could he not just go back – give up being L.P., wag and cynic, and return to being Lionel Watson, traveller, poet and gentle man of letters?

From where she stood, Rachel saw a balding man with brown teeth who was drinking in order to make himself intoxicated at half past eleven in the morning. She felt furious with him for his attitude of lofty distance.

He looked up at her and said, 'Julia wants a divorce. She told me this morning.'

Immediately, Rachel's anger evaporated.

'Oh, Lionel, I'm sorry. Oh, my poor, poor boy.'

She sat down again at once opposite him and held both his hands in her own. For the first time that day, Watson's eyes filled with tears.

'Oh, Christ – it's all a bit of a bloody mess.'

'And here I was going on about' – her hand swept over the open newspaper – 'this trivia.'

'Trivia is my *métier* – hadn't you noticed?'

'That's not what I meant – oh, I meant, here was I going on about my feelings about Worledge and Hans Busch and . . .'

'I know what you meant.'

'Is it because of us?'

A sly glance peeped over the top of his specs.

The scene at the dining table last night was not going away. It replayed itself constantly inside his head – Julia's face contorted with hurt anger; his teenaged daughter in tears; his son staring at him with hatred before leaving the room and slamming the door.

'And all this time,' Julia had said, 'all this time!'

She'd waved the evidence over the untasted lasagne – some statements from MasterCard, and a bundle of envelopes containing letters which he had always known it was madness to have kept.

The MasterCard statements showed that he regularly patronized a massage parlour in Bermondsey. It was not a fact of which he was either especially proud or especially ashamed. He felt about it as he felt about his journalism. He knew that it could be seen as sad, sordid, possibly disgraceful. He wished, with heartfelt strength, that his wife had never become aware of this degrading habit of his. But – there it was. He was fairly sure that divorce would not have been mentioned merely because of his going to a massage parlour every few weeks.

It was the bundle of letters from Mary Much which provided evidence of something much more damning. Lionel and his wife had been married for twenty years. It now emerged that for well over ten of them, he had been the lover of Mary Much.

'She's been in this house – she's patronized me, she's praised my taste in interior design, my clothes – my God, I'd like to kill her.'

It was the quietness with which Julia said this which alarmed him.

None of this conversation could possibly be repeated back to Rachel. He knew that if she knew about the massage parlours, she would be far more shocked than Julia had been. Julia was a trouper – she probably thought of massage parlours as catering for the ridiculous side of the male psyche, and she was right really. Rachel would be far less tolerant and much more easily hurt. She had often spoken to him of her horror of prostitution and of the men who exploited women in this way. He had always heartily agreed, denouncing them as pathetic wankers. As for telling her the truth – that throughout their affair he had also been sleeping (albeit occasionally) with Mary Much – this was impossible.

'Yes,' he said quietly.

He would never know why he told Rachel this lie, but some of the reason for it was connected with his desire to protect her from the truth. Even as he told the lie, his brain spoke of the appalling risk that she might come round to the house in Clapham, or by some other means – with her humourless desire for truthtelling – confront Julia, apologize to her . . . In that precise moment, however, he was desperate that Rachel should not know about the massage parlours, nor about the Mary Much affair. So, he said that Julia was wanting a divorce because she had found out about his affair with Rachel.

She leaned forward, and he could see in her dark eyes all the things which at that moment he most dreaded – love, undying commitment, and support.

'You know,' she said, 'I know it's hell for you now. And it's hell for Julia. But it's going to be such a relief, sweetheart – not lying any more.'

He made a little grunting noise and found that it was not just that tears were in his eyes: he was convulsed with crying.

'Oh, Lionel. You can call me darling now. Call me darling as much as you like,' said Rachel Pearl.

'Fuck-a-duck,' said Peg Montgomery. She had lured Sinclo to Bin Ends to discuss diary stories. He had kept from her Mary Much's promise that he would soon be in charge of editing 'Dr Arbuthnot' himself. 'Bit early for that sort of thing, isn't it?' She indicated Rachel Pearl and L. P. Watson, who were openly embracing. He remembered as a boy when it became clear, from the laughter of the grown-ups, that his mother and father, not Father Christmas, had been filling his stocking year after year. He had felt enormously humiliated by the laughter, and grief-stricken for the shattering of his faith in something which had been wholesome, innocent, pure. Allied to these feelings was the cynical knowledge that with a part of his brain, he had always known the truth.

THIRTY-SIX

'If he's better – and he's *so* much better, Mum – what does it matter what he gets up to . . . ?'

'I don't *like* it,' said Lily. 'I preferred it when he was being a bad boy . . .'

'Even Trevor notices the difference: though he still thinks he's pinching his Marlboro Lites. Which he isn't.'

'Where does he get those expensive clothes from? I ask him, and he smiles in that strange way. And he doesn't speak in the way he used to. That voice. Sometimes he sounds like Father Vivyan, sometimes it's like he's acting – "Dashed good show" – who taught him to say that?'

'He's got a beautiful voice.'

'Yes, Mercy, he's got several beautiful voices – but what I'm telling you is they aren't Peter's voices.'

'He told me it's a really posh restaurant where he's working. He's always picked up different ways of speaking, since he was a little kid.'

'It don't *feel* right. Like now, he's all religious, and—'

'You surely approve of that?'

'It's not *right*, not all of a *sudden*. I told him when he came to live with me now, I go to mass each Sunday and I want you to come with me. And it was all silence, or "Oh Gram, do I have to", "Oh Gram, I'm tired, don't make me . . ." And now what is it – every blessed moment he's not down that restaurant, he's been down the church. And those nights I worry myself sick wondering where he's got to – he's *sleeping* at Father Vivyan's house.'

'You should have told me, Mum. Those nights he was missing.'

'You've got enough on your plate.'

'I'm feeling optimistic,' said Mercy. 'It could be so much worse. It *has* been so much worse.'

'Finish your coffee.'

'I haven't had a chance to read the *Legion* yet.'

'Bring it in your bag and read it after.'

So it was that Mercy Topling and Lily d'Abo missed an item buried in the paper about the mystery death of a psychiatric social worker, Kevin Currey, 38. From the crowds at rush hour, at the Angel Islington, he had suddenly been pitched in front of a train and died instantly. There had been a number of cases recently of young boys pushing passengers off the platform of underground stations into the path of incoming trains. This death seemed comparable, but no one had seen anything suspicious; no one saw Kevin Currey being pushed. Since his death, it had emerged that Currey had links with various paedophile rings. The schools in south London where he worked claimed that they had received no complaints, but the police had taken his computer and downloaded a large quantity of illegal material.

THIRTY-SEVEN

Tall, bald, cherubic in appearance, Brigadier Courtenay emerged from Crickleden Junction wearing a charcoal-grey double-breasted suit, and highly polished black brogues. He also wore a white mackintosh and sheltered beneath a golfing umbrella.

He had done his homework, as he always did. He would be able to find his way to the shrine without consulting a street map, or otherwise drawing attention to himself, though in that district of London he could hardly fail to stand out, dressed as he was and looking as he did. Nearly everyone he passed in the High Road was black. Since he was in plenty of time, he could take in the drizzly atmosphere, and look in at the windows of shops, most of which were closed. Super Afro Cosmetics looked at first glance as if a scalp-hunter had been hard at work, to judge from the many skeins of hair of various colours and consistency hanging from the walls like tassels. '100% Human and Artificial Hair' said a notice in the window. He noted an Internet café next door; always useful to know where these were. He had lately become an active e-mailer, enjoying this terse and above all silent method of communication. Next to the Internet café was The Gold Shop – Western Union Money Transfer. Cheques cashed. Pawnbrokers. Next to this was a large neon-lit shop front called Silvertime Amusement Centre. Beyond its open door, the Brigadier glimpsed a darkened room twinkling with dozens of fruit machines and one-armed bandits. Next to this was a butcher selling 'Halal Meat – Fair Prices' and next to this was a driving school called The Redeemer's Tuition Centre.

The Brigadier was aware of an atmosphere unknown in England since his boyhood, of Sunday morning being observed. Into the Baptist church near the station, rotund women in large white hats and gloves had been filing in their dozens. The Redeemer Chapel next to the driving school seemed no less popular, and as he wandered along, liking all that he saw, he noted the popularity of the Seventh-Day Adventist conventicle and the Comunidale de Londres Church of Prophecy.

He had read up the previous evening about his own destination.

In the Middle Ages, Crickleden had been a village on the Pilgrim's Road to Canterbury. The Shrine of Our Lady of Crickleden had been a place of pilgrimage in its own right. Henry VI, after his arrest in the north in 1464, had been allowed by his Yorkist captors to come to the shrine and pray, before, with his legs tied under his horse and a straw hat rammed on his head, he had been ridden through the streets of London with the mob hooting and jeering at him. (The monk who accompanied the king often heard him murmur *Owre Ladie of Cryckleden, pray for me.*) Henry VIII in his pious youth had walked to the shrine barefoot, and it was a favourite place for Thomas More.

After the Reformation it fell into disrepair, and it was probably largely fancy on the part of the late-Victorian incumbent of old Crickleden parish church that the few boulders and heaps of rubble found on the site of a proposed new church was the ruin of the medieval shrine. This clergyman was the Reverend Cuthbert Guiseley, DD, a disciple of Canon Liddon, and a keen ritualist. The scheme to build a large brick mission church to cater for the new sprawl of south London suburb became in his mind the 'revival' of the old pilgrim site. To the barn-like basilica, described in Pevsner as 'a substantial stock brick building in Northern French Gothic', had been added, in the north aisle, a 'shrine chapel' in 1906 by the Arts and Crafts architect and metal-worker Oswald Fish. The screens were described by Professor Pevsner as 'Fish at his exuberant best', though he disliked the altar added by Sir Ninian Comper in 1931.

The Reverend Cuthbert, having established this centre of ritualism for the inhabitants of East Crickleden – the Brigadier imagined the original occupants of these two-storey modest villas as clerks who read H. G. Wells and most of whom had no time for outmoded pieties – left for the mission fields of Africa. He was consecrated Bishop of Accra in 1910, and was translated to Chamberlainstown in 1917. It was during his life as a colonial bishop that Guiseley formed the Community of the Holy Redeemer, a small religious order whose rule was based on the Austin Friars of the Middle Ages, but adapted to the methods of early twentieth-century Anglicanism. A firm Christian socialist, Guiseley had very much disliked the colonial atmosphere of Lugardia, which was why he had built his first church out there as close as possible to the copper mines of Kanni-Karkara. (The Holy Redeemer was a church which bore a strong resemblance architecturally to St Mary's, Crickleden.) Not long after that, Guiseley returned to England. He had inherited a large house from his father, Kelvedone Hall in Lincolnshire, and this became the mother-house of his order. At first there were four clergymen. By the time of the Second World War, the order had grown very considerably, with some thirty monks in England, and forty or so in Africa, divided between Lugardia (modern Zinariya) and Ghana. There were now about twenty monks left at Kelvedone and a handful in Cambridge, but the African order was flourishing, with over a hundred monks in Zinariya.

There had been a number of CHR monks who, within the

confines of mid-twentieth-century Anglicanism, had made their mark. The order had produced several bishops and scholars. Kelvedone was a place where many, and not merely the professionally 'high church', went for retreats, 'quiet days', spiritual refreshment of various kinds. There could be no doubt, however, that in the public mind, the most famous of the Kelvedone fathers – as they were often known – was Vivyan Chell, CHR.

The Brigadier was not a regular churchgoer but he counted himself pro rather than anti, and had, over the years, attended innumerable services, at school chapel, church parade and parish churches. He had never attended a church exactly like St Mary's, which, he had been informed, was typical of a certain type of London Anglo-Catholicism.

There were about sixty worshippers, and when a bell rang at the back, they rose to sing a hymn which was familiar to the Brigadier since boyhood:

> *Soldiers of Christ arise!*
> *And put your armour on;*
> *Strong in the strength the Lord supplies*
> *Through His Eternal Son . . .*

A procession made its way up the aisle of the church. First, a black youth carrying a gilded cross. Then another black boy, much more striking in appearance, came, swinging incense from a burner on the end of a chain. This boy was tall and angular with high cheekbones against which little sideburns had been carefully trimmed. His aquiline nose and jutting jaw made the Brigadier think that he could have appropriately been chosen by one of the great Venetian masters to model King Solomon or one of the Magi. The most striking features of this boy were his eyes. They glided to left and right as he made his stately way up the church, taking in those he knew, those he didn't. The Brigadier felt himself being noticed. The boy was not quite as tall as the Brigadier himself, but he was fully six feet. At his side, holding a silver vessel containing unburnt incense, walked a little boy who could not have been older than seven. This child, dressed like his tall companion in black cassock and lacy cotta, nuzzled against the elder boy's legs, and stared entranced as the burning incense was swung to and fro, filling the air with billows of sweet smoke.

It was going to be the Communion service. The Brigadier did not possess quite enough faith to receive Communion. Besides, he felt, given his purpose in visiting the church, that it would hardly be good form to go up and take the bread and wine from the priest who brought up the rear of the procession.

> *From strength to strength go on,*
> *Wrestle and fight, and pray;*
> *Tread all the powers of darkness down,*
> *And win the well-fought day.*

Father Vivyan Chell now came into the Brigadier's line of vision. If he recognized the stranger in church, he did not betray this. He held his hands together, and his eyes were raised aloft, staring towards the crucified figure on the rood beam at the east end of the church.

The form of service was unfamiliar to the Brigadier: one of these modern Communion services, but it was conducted with great seemliness. He noted how devout the congregation was, and what a varied collection of individuals they were — several families looking like Albanian gypsies, respectable West Indians in suits and hats, and a number of Africans in their national costumes. There was great stillness as the passages from the Bible were read aloud. Then came the sermon. In the context of the elaborate ceremonial, the bowings and scrapings as the Brigadier saw them, the informality of Father Chell's mode of addressing the people came as something of a surprise.

The children from the Sunday school sat on the floor at the front, and instead of standing in the pulpit or at the reading desk, the monk walked up and down. The Brigadier was reminded by his manner, though not by his words, of an old-fashioned staff officer briefing a platoon before exercises.

'The Kingdom of Christ! Christ our King! So, Jesus Christ is our King. Does that mean he is a rich man?'

He pointed to a girl who had her hand up.

'Olukemi?'

'No,' said this girl clearly. 'He was a working man, a carpenter.'

'That's right – a poor, hard-working man, a carpenter. And what did his mother say when she knew she was going to have this baby king? Our Lady's song? You remember we had that last week. What did Our Lady say about the powerful people, the rich and the mighty?'

The same girl put up her hand.

'Another person – yes, Olukemi you know!' He grinned but asked, 'Who else knows?'

There was general silence, shuffling of feet, looking at the floor.

'Help them, Olukemi.'

'She said God would put down the mighty from their thrones of power and send the rich people away empty.'

'That's right, right, right! And who was God going to exalt in place of the rich?'

'The humble and meek.'

'Yes! Yes!' said the monk excitedly. 'The rich and the mighty and the powerful have been cast out of God's Kingdom. It is a kingdom for the poor. And what does that mean in today's world? Who are the mighty people today?'

'The Prime Minister.'

'Good, Olukemi, the Prime Minister – but anyone else?'

Several hands had shot up and children began to shout out the names of those who might have been famous in the world of pop music or football. The Brigadier admired the way in which Father Chell bluffed his way with 'Exactly! Splendid! Any grown-ups in the congregation got some ideas about mighty men in this world whom God will overthrow?'

One man called out, 'What about these fat cats, the bosses of big industry with pay of nearly a million pound a year – there's gotta be something wrong there, that's way out of order.'

'While there are still people in this world *starving*,' added Father Chell, 'that's right. And shall I tell you, there's another category of person whom Almighty God would like to bring down a peg or two, and that's the big newspaper barons, the men who make themselves rich by peddling lies in the news-papers – oh yes! They're all as guilty as one another, whether it's *The Daily Telegraph* or *The Daily Legion*. They deserve to be taken from their seats. Yes? Tuli?'

He smiled affectionately at the head server, the tall dark boy with smudge-blue eyes.

'Does that mean we should leave it to God to push the mighty out of their seats, or are we doing God's work when we get rid of them?'

'Thanks for asking that, Tuli.'

The Brigadier wondered whether the boy had thought of the question for himself or whether he'd been prompted to ask it by the priest.

'Today at mass we have a very important visitor,' the monk announced.

The Brigadier's normally rosy face was suffused with crimson.

'Stand up, Professor! My brothers and sisters, this is Professor Galwanga.'

The priest beamed and, by clapping his hands theatrically, he led the round of applause. A bespectacled man wearing a lime-green hat and matching pyjamas rose from his chair and made nervous little bows to left and right to acknowledge the welcome.

'After mass, if you want to meet Professor Galwanga he'll be in the Parish Rooms for coffee and he is going to tell us about Zinariya, his country. The country where I've spent most of my grown-up life. And maybe he'll give us an answer to Tuli's question. Does God expect us to put down the mighty from their seat, or does He do it Himself by magic?'

'By magic,' said Olukemi.

'Now of course, God could send a thunderbolt and get rid of all the bad rulers of this world, all the corrupt financiers, and business bosses and newspaper barons and dictators. He could do that. But that's not the way He does work, is it? What does the Bible tell us?'

The Brigadier noticed that the monk was now talking hastily to prevent Olukemi remembering instances in the Bible when God had intervened in human affairs with fire from heaven, angelic messages or miracles.

'God works through people. God's will is worked by people in this world. So, when Our Lady said that all the hungry people would have full bellies, and all the rich people would be sent away empty, she saw that a new kingdom was to begin on earth. The kingdom of her son, Christ the King – who was true God but also true man – who knew temptation, and emotions, and hunger and illness. From now on, men and women did not wait for supernatural events from the sky. They were not to sit on their hands and wait for God, or the gods, to do things for them. Men and women were to take action for *themselves*. They made things happen. The high and mighty sent to arrest Jesus on trumped-up charges, didn't they? They came at night to the garden where he was praying with his friends, Peter and James and John. And what did Peter do to the High Priest's servant? Yes? Tuli?'

The beautiful, sonorous voice of the blue-eyed server, curiously similar to Father Chell's own voice, said, 'He drew his sword, and cut off the ear of the High Priest's servant.'

'That's right!' said Father Chell. His eyes were gleaming now and his pink cheeks were quivering with emotion.

'There was violence, even in the moment of Redemption. There had to be violence to bring the Kingdom of Peace to the earth! The mighty are very comfortable on their seats, thank you very much, they are not going to come down from them voluntarily. The rich don't say, "We've had our share – now let someone less fortunate enjoy the rest of our wealth." The mighty will only leave their seats if they are dragged out of them – by their throats. When we are faced with the very bad men of this world – with the leaders of big business, with the newspaper magnates, with tyrants like General Bindiga in Zinariya – we can't be citizens of Christ's kingdom and leave it up to God to put things right. We have to be prepared to fight. To fight for justice. Of course we do. We can't stand here at mass on Sundays and pray Thy Kingdom come, and then when Monday dawns do nothing to further that Kingdom. Of course we must fight, and if Christ is our King we must topple the kingdoms of this world by whatever means we have at our disposal. We must put down the mighty, indeed we must!'

And he returned to the altar, placed his hands together and began to recite the Creed.

THIRTY-EIGHT

Helene, the Bulgarian maid, was in tears for the third time that day. She only stayed in this madhouse because she was in love with Piet: in fact, being in love made the misery worse. Her days were now a pattern. Rages and insults from one of the three lunatics would be punctuated by Piet's calming influence. But every time he spoke to her his healing words, she grew to depend on him more, which made the times when he was not with her all the more harrowing. She had been sworn to secrecy about the reasons for his absences. A guerrilla army was poised to take over the African country of which his father had been king. When the war was over, he was going back. First, though, much fighting, many explosions.

Helene saw the unfolding months half in the manner of a dream-vision, half as a film playing inside her head. Piet in camouflage jacket, combat gear, drove in an open jeep in triumph through cheering crowds as he recaptured his capital. African dancing followed. Then, as the lengthy and joyous wedding ceremonies began, his bride, Helene, was carried on a bier to the steps of his palace. In this sequence of fantasy, she was both joyous in her semi-nakedness and self-conscious about the smallness of her breasts. Were they perhaps why her prince, though he whispered smut to her all day long, had not yet kissed her?

The Constancios, the disagreeable Brazilian couple (Maria José had even questioned Piet's story, said he was muddling

Zinariya with Senegal) had not stayed the course. They had returned to the agency, saying that such treatment was not endurable, that they were capable of earning just as much money working for decent people. They advised Helene to get out at the same time, and she had known it was commonsense advice: she knew she had no hope with Piet who (the fragment of her brain which was able to view him clearly) she could see had something 'odd' about him. The Italians sent to replace the Brazilians had walked out the minute Frau Fax deliberately emptied an ashtray on a carpet. Their Filipino replacements (Mrs Mark had vowed never to have Filipinos again but beggars couldn't be choosers) were due to arrive next week. For the time being, the afternoons were 'covered' by Piet and herself, though extra staff was brought in on some evenings. It was when the bell rang furiously and insistently yet again that Helene burst into tears for the third time.

'Three times he ask me to bring caviar. The first, he spill it on the floor – you know how much a jar of that stuff costs? More than both our fees for a month! Piet, listen! He just says, "Clear that up and bring another" – and he's not look at me – he talked in the telephone. And then when I stoop down to pick it up, he tries to come behind me and rub himself. And it is so, so horrible.'

'Small, you mean?'

'How are you saying? What? I don't—'

'You said it was horrible. Was it small? Shrivelled? Not a nice big one?'

'Oh, Piet!'

And she cried some more as the bell rang again.

'Here, cool it – take one.' He held out an open packet of cigarettes. He always seemed to have a couple of packets of Marlboro Lites about his person. He was generous with them, hardly ever smoked one himself.

'I'll go,' he said.

'But he will be angry with you.'

He slowly put another open jar of beluga on a plate, placed the plate on a tray with a tin of Seven-Up. He was aware of her watching him, admiring him, like he was going to walk into a lion's cage.

In fact, the feelings of fear only began when he'd climbed the stairs and was outside his room on the landing. The man was talking. Helene had not mentioned he had anyone with him.

'The thing which even most atheists accept is the existence of some ethical standard outside ourselves. A moral law. They can claim that this came about by purely practical, utilitarian means. But are we really saying that our only reason for disapproving of, say, deliberate cruelty to animals is practical? If someone carried in a cat and suggested, very slowly, killing it with stab wounds, gouging out its eyes, we'd feel revulsion at the deepest level . . .'

Piet knocked on the door.

'We respond in other words to the sense that there *is* a moral order in the Universe. It is a given. There are moral laws just as there are physical laws. And if there are laws, does not this imply— Ah!'

The Fat Man turned in surprise at the sight of Piet. He had been expecting the girl. He was quite alone, padding up and down his room, talking about the existence of God to an imaginary interlocutor. Piet eyed him slowly – the glistening, almost feminine sweaty face; the parachute-sized silk shirt dappled with dark moisture at armpits, nipples and throat. The twenty-five inches of pale grey trousers upheld by huge braces decorated with pink pigs. The boy looked shamelessly at the man's groin. He remembered Mary Much telling Hans Busch what it was like being fucked by this man – it was like having a wardrobe fall on top of you and then feeling that someone had left the little key poking out of the door.

Daddy, Daddy, don't you see – it's me, Daddy.

Keep that child under control, drawled the Guards officer. We might have to act fast and I don't want the child to get hurt.

We're not going in for the—

Murderous Moron interrupted with Kill – kill the fucker. Fink wot 'e done ter yer mum.

As I do often tell you, Jeeves intervened, revenge is a dish best savoured—

'Where's Helene?' interrupted Fat Gut.

'She's occupied, sir,' said Jeeves. 'Still, to put it another way, sir, the house affairs would draw her thence.'

'Eh, what's that?'

'The Bard, sir, has a word for every occasion.'

Fatso had flicked the remote and his eyes were now fixed on Ceefax. Lots of figures. Stock market. *Shit!* World recession. *Shit.* Copper shares plummeting.

'*Shit, shit, shit!*'

'Indeed, sir, but I was wondering if you would care to have a baked potato with your next . . .'

Get him to love you, he'll give you all this – the house, the Moist Woman, the . . . man, you don't have to kill him. Shit, jus' get him to love you, man . . .

'. . . jar of caviar.'

The boy's soothing voice, oddly familiar to Lennox, calmed him, numbed some of the horror caused by the figures and information on the screen.

'You know, I think a baked potato would be just *great*. We're dining with the Leader of the Opposition – it's an important dinner at the House of Commons – the car's coming in . . .' He screwed pig eyes to squint at his Rolex.

Jeeves said, 'The motor will be at the front of the house at ten minutes to seven.'

While the boy was gone, Lennox reflected on Martina's genius extracting this lad from that crap agency. Hitherto, for the last five years, that agency had supplied an unending succession of wastrels, thieves, no-goodniks, spastics who couldn't boil an egg or shake a vodka martini. Then, as if by magic, Martina had come up with Piet. An amazing life story, too, his father a big opera-producer in South Africa, his mother a cousin of Jessye Norman and all set to outstrip her famous kinswoman when disaster struck – a piece of scenery collapsed on top of her during a production of *Turandot* at – a little bizarrely – Johannesburg. Mother and grandmother had brought the child to England, and after attempting to educate him privately for a couple of years, the funds had run out and he had gone into the catering business. Worked for a couple of years in some evidently rather swank restaurant somewhere in Wandsworth. (Len hadn't heard of it, but Mary Much said it was featured in all the magazines the very week Piet told them the story.)

By the time the boy returned to the room with a large, steaming potato, half a pound of Normandy butter on a bone china plate, a bowl of sour cream and two eight-ounce jars of silver-grey beluga, Lennox had switched to the TV news. A demonstration outside the Zinaryian Embassy in London. And there he was again – Lennox Mark's conscience, standing like the grey elongated statue of a Gothic saint in the niche of some medieval reredos, and speaking to the camera.

'Would you say, Father Chell, that . . .'

'It isn't what I say that matters, or what any of us say. But there is a rightness to things. "According to their deeds, accordingly He will repay." And again, "The meek shall increase their joy in the Lord and the poor among men shall rejoice." We are waiting for justice, we are praying for justice, and believe me, justice will come about.'

'But Father Chell, you are a man of God – do you condone the violence in the mines? Fifty people were killed in the explosions in the mines last night. Surely as a Christian . . .'

'It isn't for me to condemn or not to condemn. Listen to what I'm telling you, the days of tyranny in Zinariya are numbered. Thousands of people have died in those iniquitous mines since they were first opened. The Alkawari! party is fighting on behalf of those countless martyrs.'

'Father Chell, thank you.'

The news switched to the Balkans, where some Albanians were shelling a Macedonian village. Talk was of an Albanian terrorist cell having set up a base somewhere in London.

'Father Vivyan,' said the house-boy, standing back and looking at the television.

There was admiration in his voice.

The news item had excited opposite feelings in his boss, who fell on the food which had been brought to him as if its emotional comfort were the keenest of necessities. First, with a fork, he took two large mouthfuls of caviar. Then he knifed a wodge of butter into the baked potato, stabbed it a few times, glooped a dollop of sour cream over the top of that and then raked in the remainder of one jar of beluga. No sooner had he created this feast, and the butter had begun to ooze through the hole, dribbling over the skin of the potato, than Lennox put his face close to the plate and began spading food into it with eager motions, whimpering slightly at the pain caused by the hot potato, while also murmuring with gratified desire as his gullet closed on the creamy comfort. The rhythmic alternation of grunt and whimper sounded more as if he was having sex with the potato than eating it.

'Bad man,' he mumbled through the fluffy Maris Piper, and at first Piet thought Lennox was telling himself he was a naughty boy for being so greedy. (Oh Jesus, was he into that, did Doll-Face Moist have to take the bedroom slipper to his botty? Christ, what a thought, what a botty.) But he was talking of the priest.

'Know him,' said the boy lightly.

The man misinterpreted, took a statement for a question.

'Yes, I know him,' said Lennox Mark. 'Or knew him. Long time ago. Mmm, phhh, oo, pyearcgh . . .' Sour cream dribbled down his chin. 'Bad man, corrupter of youth. Communist.'

'Corrupter?'

'Of youth. I don't mean sexually,' said Mr Fat.

'No?' Piet smiled. 'You should go down St Mary's Crickleden and ask about that!'

Lennox looked up, sharply, and then peered about him – not so much because of the shocking implication of the remark, but because there seemed to be someone else in the room. Quietly spoken Piet appeared to have said these words, but they were uttered in a slightly camp cocknified way, quite unlike his normal voice.

'What do you mean?'

'Father Vivyan?'

Piet smiled once more.

'I've been an altar-boy in that church.'

'Holy Redeemer?' Huge seemed thunderstruck.

Piet paused. While he was working in 16 Redgauntlet Road, he made no effort to suppress the fact that he lived in some (to them) unimaginable suburb. As for his family, the disabled opera-singer who was his mother had been blended partly with figures heard on the radio, partly with his grandmother Lily in Crickleden. Seeing Father Chell on the television screen had called forth recognition, but it was, as it were, a clearly one-way recognition. It was Piet, the suave house-boy, who saw the television, not Tuli, who served Father's mass, and still sometimes went to sleep on his floor and listened to him praying to the spirits.

There was no need, however, for ingenuity or the deliberate exercise of deception. Into that infinitely fertile reserve of stories, Piet was reaching with the ease of a well-versed valet, who could stretch for a coat-hanger inside a closet without even looking, since he knew that the wardrobe contained a hundred suits, all equally presentable.

'It was my mother's idea that I should be confirmed – you know, so I could take Holy Communion?'

He said the words slowly, as if Fats might not understand them.

'I was his altar-boy once, too.'

'You *were*?'

Big Sausage plunged his snout once more in the potato and began to grunt.

Now, this was a very strange moment in the history of Lennox Mark because he had never, ever told anyone this fact in the last twenty years. Martina did not know it – the very words 'altar' and 'Holy Communion' would probably mean nothing to her. No one in his business world knew about his month of holy rapture during his teenage life in Chamberlainstown, or his visit to the Holy Redeemer church. Some of his friends and contacts in Zinariya knew that he'd been acquainted with Father Chell, and the Kelvedone fathers, but none knew of his former sympathy with them.

Piet did not know in specific terms that this was a new moment of revelation for Belly-boy, but he sensed the guard dropping, and moved gently.

'You know what I mean then,' he said quietly.

'But . . . but . . . I thought you came from South Africa.'

'And then to England – to South Crickleden.'

'But – the Holy Redeemer church . . . God, that place!'

He was looking, Grease-pot, upwards, like there was a fucking angel staring down at him from the ceiling.

'That place!' he repeated with this dream-look on his pudge of a dial.

'I know him in Crickleden.'

Then Butter-butt came to life and said, 'You know him now – you've been to his church in London?'

'As I say, sir,' said Jeeves, having sent the camp altar-boy back into the wardrobe where he belonged, 'my mother was desirous of my being confirmed. I believe it's . . . shall we say . . . usual in the clergy.'

'What is? What's fucking usual?'

Piet smiled. 'I have got a tape – if you would like to hear it.'

On the way home that night in the tube, he continued to listen on his headset to tapes of a posh actor reading aloud from P. G. Wodehouse. But gradually, as the train moved further from the centre of things, Piet faded.

At Green Park he changed. Trains. Tapes. Character. He was gyrating now to heavy metal. It was turned up so fucking loud that he felt his ear-drums, like, explode. A real arse-face next to him, reading a *Financial Times*, glared. The noise from those 'phones, their insistent tss-tut-ter-tss-tut-ter-*tsss*, was getting up his foreskin, the shit-mouth. Tuli smiled.

Can Lennox Mark survive the Western African crisis?

The article on which the City shit was trying to concentrate hinted that the Tub of Lard was about to be flushed down the toilet. Share prices in News Incorporated rock bottom. Copper mines – bang, bang. No one buying the *Legion*. Father Chell winning the fight.

'I say,' said Slicker, 'that's awfully loud.'

He pointed, with exaggerated stage gestures, to the pulsating, throbbing 'phones.

'Could you turn it down a little?'

Tss-ter-tar, tss-tss.

Tuli's rhythmic sway turned into a near dance, and he smiled. He'd begun to think of ways he'd finish with Fat Guts. A glutton's murder should be appropriate. Make him eat. There was that electric carving knife in the kitchen. Maybe get the Big Man down the kitchen, and tie him in the chair. Helene could help. Gently rubbing her groin, getting off on her own fingers, she could stand by, waiting at the wall socket to switch on the electricity. Switch on now, Pussy-Helene! Whirr-whirr-rrrrr! Open wide, Big Boy. Taste blade. Tongue off. That ain't no ketchup, man, splatting through the atmosphere. And all the angels of God will sing, Daddi-o, as you tell me what this tastes of, then in, in, in.

PART TWO

ONE

In a black suit, black tie, crispest of white shirts, Sinclo Manners sat in a second-class compartment, rattling westward. He'd noticed a lot of people, mainly in their twenties and thirties, similarly clad, climbing aboard the train at Paddington. It was clearly going to be a large funeral. Kitty Chell's death at twenty-nine had been splashed all over the papers for several days.

Sinclo himself only learnt of his cousin's death when he came upon the oafs on the back bench at the *Legion* holding up a photograph of her corpse.

Worledge, with the thuggish henchmen he had brought with him from the Sunday newspaper he'd edited previously, was, as usual at that hour of the afternoon, pondering between a choice of clichés.

'It's gotta be POOR LITTLE RICH GIRL,' said one of the thugs.

'I want more meat in the headline,' said Worledge's gravelly tones as he lit up his cheroot. 'I want the drugs, I want Daddy's title.'

'He's an old nutter and all, Lord Longmore.'

'GILDED YOUTH? WHAT A WASTE? I mean here's a girl who was an aristocrat's daughter, a good-time girl, she was bright, intelligent, she'd been to Cambridge.'

'Great story, great story,' growled Worledge. 'Pity she was alone when she topped herself. Are we absolutely sure of that?'

'So – SHE HAD IT ALL.'

'Had THEM all, more like.' Lewd laughter.

Sinclo felt anger course through his veins quite uncontrollably, and with a shaking voice he advanced on the editor.

'What's happened? How did she die?'

'Oh, we might have guessed you'd know Lady Kitty Chell.' Worledge's sneer was now habitual when talking to Sinclo. He exuded class-envy and resentment.

'Choked on her own vomit,' said one of the thugs.

'Better than choking on someone else's,' quipped another wag.

'How dare you?' Sinclo erupted. 'How dare you laugh at the death of . . .'

Seeing Kitty's photograph in the pudgy mitt of this oaf was too much. He reached to grab it, thereby creating a moment of school-style scuffle.

'Temper!'

'Just cool it,' said Worledge, evidently furious. Even though the oaf was as much to blame as Sinclo, it was to Manners that Worledge said, 'You've got to keep a watch on that temper of yours. And that's a warning.'

Worledge had been using this phrase with ominous frequency round the office in the three months since he'd become editor.

The thugs assumed, when Sinclo lost his temper, that he had at some stage been Kitty's lover. This was to be expected. What really shocked him, when he tried to get a grip on himself, was to discover how the story had arrived at the back bench of the *Legion* so quickly. Worledge knew of Kitty's death before her own father. The policeman who had discovered her body had immediately tipped off his usual contact on the *Legion*, the seediest of the stringers who helped the crime desk with all the murkiest stories of prostitutes, and many of the most ghoulish autopsies. A sum had been discussed. Money – cash – had changed hands. And all this before the corpse had been removed for autopsy. Sinclo had heard that this was standard practice, but to see evidence of it in the pudgy hands of Worledge's henchman – to see Kitty's pale, shocked, beautiful face, so very scared and so very dead, stuck between the henchman's thumb and forefinger was an outrage.

Sinclo's eyes had met Worledge's and in that moment the two men knew mutual loathing.

Some time that afternoon, Worledge called Sinclo into his office.

'I want you to do the funeral.'

Worledge had a way of smiling which consisted of simply opening his mouth and baring a row of even, orange teeth. There was no warmth in the eyes which glinted behind horn-rimmed spectacles. He watched to see what Sinclo would do. Sinclo was in a state of grief and shock. This would have been the moment to leave a job which he hated and a newspaper which he despised. In some deep place in his heart, he had already taken leave. The moment by the back bench had been a definitive one. He was no longer afraid, either of Worledge's bullying, or of the poverty and insecurity which would result if he was sacked. He was, however, punch-drunk, actually breathless with shock at what he had seen on the back bench. He was therefore only half aware of what Worledge was saying to him.

'I . . . er . . .'

'The Kitty Chell funeral. ARISTOCRATIC HEROIN – what do you think? HEROIN without an E . . .'

'I . . . of course I'm going . . . I'm . . .'

'We'll want all the stories . . . Who's there . . . the ex-lovers . . .' He named several actors, pop stars, aristocratic playboys, some of whom had known Kitty, some of whom (Sinclo was fairly sure) she'd never so much as met.

Sinclo had not managed to say the right words to Worledge. He had not been able to say, 'Kitty was my beloved cousin. Of course I shall be attending her funeral. If you think I shall use that as an opportunity for collecting stories about her, then I am leaving, on the spot, now.' But he'd merely stammered at Worledge, who had sneered back, 'Call yourself a fucking journalist?'

Even by Worledge's standards, the paper the next day had been a masterpiece of bad taste and inaccuracy.

Kitty was variously described as Kitty, Lady Kitty and Lady Chell. Of course, who gives a toss about these things nowadays, but if you are going to use someone's title, why get it wrong? She was described as having been to Cambridge, which was untrue, as being the only daughter of the 'eccentric' Earl of Longmore, eighty-three – in fact Monty Longmore was seventy-three. (She also had two sisters, Marina, who was a nurse in West Africa, and Lizzie, who worked in publishing.) The paper named the actress with whom Monty had an affair a quarter of a century before. Much more damaging than these trivial details, it claimed that Kitty had been a heroin addict since schooldays, had been a criminal to feed her habit even though she was given a huge allowance by the eccentric earl, and that she had committed suicide. Yes, Kitty was what Worledge would have called a poor little rich girl.

It was true that she had received treatment for drug abuse. Since her marriage, Sinclo had not seen much of her, but he was fairly sure that she was clean. Rumours drifted about the family that she had developed various fads, and that she suffered from some eating disorder. Her husband, Charles Henderson, was said to be 'marvellous'. Her death, as an inquest established beyond doubt the day before the funeral, was caused by a rare complication of an ectopic pregnancy. No one could be certain, but it was very probably not related to drugs, or a wild life in her early twenties. It was a piece of quite horrible bad luck. None of the newspapers issued so much as one word of retraction or apology, either for printing the 'great picture' of her dead body, or for the repeated allegations that she had died of an overdose or in the midst of some self-destructive debauchery.

Sitting in the train, watching drizzly Berkshire turn to rain-soaked Wiltshire, Sinclo remembered childhood scenes of Kitty – cantering on Gumdrop, a little black pony which won several rosettes at gymkhanas; or writhing with mirth on the frayed old carpet at Throxton as Lizzie tickled her; or sitting in the Orangery, he the young subaltern about to be posted to Zinariya, and she just starting at Wycombe Abbey. She'd told him about the First World War poets she was studying with the English mistress, and he had wondered whether he was in love with his schoolgirl cousin.

Her wan, elfin, adolescent features were now overshadowed in memory by the horrible photograph of her face in death. Sinclo had been programmed by nature to feel tenderness about a particular physiognomy, and it was only as he meditated upon Kitty's face, and for the first time recognized its broad similarity to the woman with whom he was in love, that he looked up and saw Rachel Pearl.

'Do you mind if I . . .'

TWO

'I thought you'd be travelling First.'

'Er . . . I . . . er . . .'

In fact, the decision to travel Second inwardly assured Sinclo that he was going to the funeral in a purely private capacity, rather than claiming the cost of a first-class ticket on expenses.

'I'm . . . not . . .'

'It's hell, isn't it?' she said firmly.

She had very red lips. Her face was pale as alabaster, her undyed hair as black as her neatly buttoned coat, her leather gloves.

Rachel did not know that she had been seen in the wine bar embracing L. P. Watson. She did not know what effect this had had on Sinclo, because although being generally aware that he was 'nuts' about her, this was an emotional fact which she did not take especially seriously. It was certainly low on her list of priorities at the moment, when her relationship with L.P., and its ending, her career, and its future were all churned up with overpowering grief and shock at the death of her friend. When she had spotted Sinclo climbing on the train at Paddington station, she had not thought, 'There is a man who is in love with me.' Still less had she thought, 'There is a man whose heart was broken last week by the sight of me kissing L.P. in Bin Ends.' She thought, 'There is a man who is the closest thing to a friend in my office, who also knew Kitty.' She had made for him as for a kindred spirit.

Rachel, for all the confusions of her emotional life, was morally a straightforward individual. This had sometimes made her frightening to her friends: it certainly (she knew this and bitterly rued it) was one of the factors in her estrangement from Kitty over the years.

At the University, Kitty and Rachel had been tutorial partners, which meant that almost every week they met in their tutor's rooms and one or other of them read out an essay. In the first couple of weeks, Rachel had bridled at the partnership. She had even complained to her tutor, and asked if it would be possible to be taught on her own. She was told that they would, sometimes, be taken for one-to-one tutorials, but that for her first term, she was to do French literature with Kitty.

Kitty gushed. She treated Oxford, tutorials, life itself as if it were a party.

'You're *so* kind!' – if one lent her a pencil with which to take notes.

'Poor *thing* – can't bear it!' – her interjection, during Rachel's first reading of an essay, on the plight of Racine's Andromaque.

Strangely enough, the two young women had not been dissimilar in appearance. Both had dark hair worn in those days of their late teens and earliest twenties cut very short. Both were beauties, and knew it. Kitty had bright blue eyes which bewitched her admirers. Rachel's eyes were dark. When they both wore black jumpers and trousers, they could be mistaken if not for sisters then for a pair of some kind. Nothing could have been more different, though, than their approaches to relationships, Oxford, work, life. Rachel was passionately interested in her work, and saw no need to pretend otherwise. She wanted to get a First, not as the means to a good job, but to prove to herself that she was as clever as she supposed, and because, given the possibility of getting a degree of any kind, it seemed unthinkable to want anything less than the best. Kitty seemed to have no interest in success of this kind, and wanted, mysteriously, to present herself to the world, and in particular to Rachel, as an airhead with no intellectual convictions or capabilities. In fact, she spoke excellent French, and her German was not bad either. When she stopped gushing and claiming that Hippolyte, as it were, was 'perfectly sweet', she in fact made intelligent comments on almost all the books they read together – though her essays were seldom finished, and did not match the vigour of her talk.

Rachel's Oxford was work, and the Union, where she helped organize debates, and a circle of friends, and two love affairs, one of a schoolboy-schoolgirl kind in her first year with a nice boy she had met at a lecture, the other more serious, though broken to bits when the boy discovered she was seeing someone else – a much older man – in London. She had concentrated primarily on her work, and she had been rewarded with a First.

Kitty's Oxford was parties, parties, parties from the first day. She often stayed out all night. Her friends were almost all at Christ Church and Magdalen. She was promiscuous. She chain-smoked, she lived on her nerves.

After initial sensations of bourgeois revulsion against Kitty, Rachel became very fond of her. She came and stayed for a few days one vacation with Rachel's parents in Barnes and it was a thoroughly quiet, happy occasion. Rachel, too, was asked to stay at Throxton Winnards – an extraordinary experience for one of her background: the great seventeenth-century house with its large old black rooms, its smell of woodsmoke, its guns and antlers and sculptures; and in the midst of it, Lord Longmore himself. The Chells did not go in for country-house living as one might read about such a phenomenon in books. It was more country-house huddling, country-house running for a bucket when the roof leaked, country-house shivering, even in May, around the huge log fire in the hall.

Rachel continued to regard Kitty as a friend, as a very good friend, even when, after Oxford, their ways began to diverge. They continued to meet; but when a friendship has become a matter of arranging to meet, dates in diaries, agreement that next week or the next are 'no good', then it has been silently acknowledged that the old intimacy has gone. Sometimes periods of several months would pass without their meeting. Kitty knew that Rachel was having an affair with L. P. Watson – she was one of very few who had known. Rachel remained, likewise, abreast of Kitty's love life. But as life went by, they confided in one another less and less. Rachel reached a point in her affair with L.P. when she did not want anyone to know how it was going – largely because she did not want to know this herself. Kitty, on occasion, looked deeply ill, and this, again, was something Rachel did not want to ask about.

And now Kitty was dead, and the stark cruelty of this fact confronted Rachel not only as a bitter loss, but also, as by tradition a memento mori should, as a challenge to examine her own life. Kitty's death sealed off her own, Rachel's, studenty youth, and those things which she had done, and not done, with her twenties. Even in bitterest grief, Rachel could not be sentimental about herself. It was illogical to wish that the past could be changed. Therefore she did not wish it. She had known, however, with an extraordinary clarity, from the moment she heard of Kitty's death, that she could not go on living as she had been.

In a bleak way, Rachel felt she owed her new-found freedom to Kitty. Her friend's death had given her back her dignity. She had left the *Legion* – posted her letter of resignation that morning. She had also left L. P. Watson.

The moment in the wine bar, witnessed by Sinclo Manners and Peg Montgomery, had been the beginning of forty-eight hours of intensely painful conversations with L.P. When he had told her that Julia had found out about their long affair, she had felt a confused collection of emotions – relief, excitement, fear. For some time, she had been wondering about her relationship with L.P. She was in love with him, or at least she assumed she was because the situation made her cry a lot and she could not imagine how life would be if he were to drop her. Almost every aspect of the affair had become personally unsatisfactory to her. She suffered all the disadvantages of the mistress of a married man. She could only see him on his own terms, sometimes for as little as a few hours a week. Their relationship had to be kept a secret because of who he was and his position on *The Daily Legion*.

Sometimes, she thought that her hatred of *The Daily Legion*, which grew week by week, was as big a barrier between them as his marriage. He was impatient with her disgust at the paper, and obviously felt implicated in her moral and aesthetic revulsion against the world of Lennox Mark, Martina, Mary Much, Worledge. The L.P. with whom she was in love was a ruined archangel. He was the poet and traveller who had been sucked into journalism *malgré lui*, and she was disturbed by evidences of his revelling in it. His friendship with Mary Much, his hours on the telephone or the e-mail to the editor of *Gloss* should have told its own tale, but to Rachel Pearl, it did not. She was jealous of Mary but, because she felt this emotion to be trivial and unworthy, she had deliberately turned a blind eye to the implications of the friendship.

Similarly, it had suited her for nearly eight years to pity her ruined archangel for being trapped in a loveless marriage. She had, on a few agonizing occasions, been invited to dinner at the

Watsons' house in Clapham, its interiors made by Julia as immaculate as she made the atmosphere intolerable. Rachel, of course, had entered the house merely as a friend and colleague of L.P.'s together with many other journalists of both sexes. No one present had guessed that L.P. was her lover. She had supposed herself to be a pained observer of an unhappy marriage. She had never allowed herself to ask *why* Julia was so unhappy, why she lost her temper so often and so readily with L.P., both at home and at parties.

After the moment in the wine bar, when L.P. had told Rachel that his wife wanted a divorce, they had gone back to the flat and attempted to make love. As had quite often happened in recent times, this was not successful. She had felt all the more tenderly towards him, hugged his naked form, stroked his shoulders, told him she loved him, opened a bottle of rather good white Burgundy, which they drank sitting up in bed. They had both been naked at first, though as the conversation went on, she had put on a dressing gown. She had told him that she would like to meet Julia, to ask her forgiveness, but also to see if she could not explain to L.P.'s wife that perhaps the moment had come when they should all move on. If Julia and L.P. really were very unhappy perhaps it was a good thing that they were getting divorced. But surely it could be done without rancour and without blame. If Rachel was to become L.P.'s acknowledged partner she would like to meet his children, get to know his friends. It would be so much better if she could form some kind of civilized friendship with his wife, or former wife.

L.P. had resisted this plan of Rachel's with uncommon vigour, rising to anger. There was nothing which could be more cruel, he maintained, than for a mistress to write or telephone a man's wife and *crow*. But, she had persisted, Julia was *not* his wife, she was his ex-wife, and the sole reason for this was his love affair with Rachel. Even as she was saying this to her crestfallen, drunken old lover, something like the truth began to dawn on her. He had lied in the wine bar. Julia did not know about his affair with Rachel, or about the flat he had bought her, or about any of it. She wanted the divorce for some other reason.

Over the years, Rachel had heard — because her own affair was such a closely guarded secret that people gossiped freely to her about him — many indiscreet conversations among fellow-journalists about L.P.'s promiscuity. She discounted it, largely disbelieved it, or chose to think, because she knew one important fact unknown to the gossips — the fact that she was his lover — that the other stories were false — that he'd slept with Martina Fax, or with Peg Montgomery, or that he went with prostitutes.

The conversation over the Meursault extended to an acrimonious interrogation lasting the rest of that day. Really, there was no need for any more talk after he had admitted to being the 'occasional' (whatever this meant) lover of Mary Much. When he confirmed that he had indeed slept with Peg, it made Rachel think she might hate him. By the time he was really drunk he was admitting to his habit of going to massage parlours when in need of 'something simple like an old-fashioned housemaid's wank'.

She would go back later, send a van, for the books, the few pictures they'd chosen together, the kitchen utensils — the 'things'. How sad the word was. On the TV news, when the idiocy or wickedness of politicians had forced another great section of humanity into a position where home was a place of dread, one saw them queuing at borders, streaming down dusty roads or railway tracks, many an Aeneas with old Anchises on his shoulders, refugees, old women bundled in prams, fly-blown babies. And always such bedraggled figures in flight had grabbed, quite arbitrarily perhaps, their 'things'. Why in such circumstances of despair had they bothered to take anything at all, unless it was that merely clutching at an object, as a child clutched a comfort-blanket, offered in inconsolable circumstances a faint alternative to consolation? In such a spirit she had left the flat with a couple of suitcases, a few clothes, and gone to stay with her parents in Barnes.

She had no desire to talk about any of this – the end of the affair, nor the decision to leave the *Legion* – with Sinclo. She had chosen to sit opposite him because he had known Kitty – that was all.

'Would you like a paper?' he asked, with a gentle smile.

She tried to smile back, but she couldn't.

PM defends British Arms Sales to Zinariya was the headline in the *Telegraph*. *The Guardian* had *British Jobs or African Lives: The Dilemma for the Arms Trade*. She did not want a newspaper. She felt she might be very happy never to read a newspaper ever again.

WILL IT NEVER STOP? was the *Legion*'s headline, some non-story about the wet weather.

'I'm okay, thanks,' she said.

'Are you sure?'

He sounded so tender. He was looking so kindly at her. She was determined not to weep. He reached across the table which divided them and touched her hand.

She withdrew it instantly with a sharp, '*Please*—'

The train hurtled on through the storm towards Swindon.

THREE

You change at Pewsey for Troon, the nearest station to the Throxtons. It was a two-carriage affair. Normally it was all but empty in the late morning of a weekday. Today, the little train had standing-room only for funeral-suited mourners. Rachel knew that if Kitty had been attending a similar lugubrious occasion she too, like them, would have been engaging in party chatter, but their London socialite voices grated on Rachel's ear. She noted, and realized how keenly Kitty herself would have noted, the varieties of style, ranging from dark City suits (only one man wore a morning coat) to 'Goth' style-statements, Victorian frock-coat and black jeans. Some of the women wore elaborate hats.

The weather was unrelenting. By the time they had all piled into the waiting charabancs and been driven from Troon to the village of Throxton St Martin, the passing scene was invisible, the bus windows steamy and rain-spattered. It was about five years since Rachel had made this journey – with Lizzie, Kitty's publishing sister. Old Monty Longmore, their father, had met them at the station.

All around her now on the coach, the voices were as relentless as the rain. Some were talking of their own lives. Many were rehearsing the coverage of Kitty's death in the papers – some deploring it, others merely assessing it, as though the various sensationalist and inaccurate reports had been reviews of a play or novel.

'She got a good one in *The Independent*,' one voice said.

Rachel shivered when the coach finally stopped at the church gate. The wind and rain were cold, but she felt an absolute spiritual chill at the sight of the hearse, empty of its load, parked beside the churchyard wall, and four undertakers' men sheltering in the lych-gate with cigarettes in their mouths.

She followed the crowd into church and succeeded in shaking off Sinclo Manners. His attempt to paw her on the train had been unwelcome. She wished now, as she entered the ancient medieval building, to be alone with her thoughts of her dead friend.

The coffin, draped with a black velvet pall, was at the far end of the church. There was a smell of lilies and of damp. When attending the weddings of friends (she had never before attended a funeral), Rachel always felt, as in the chapel of her boarding school, the spirits of her Jewish ancestors clustering round her. Both her parents were agnostic and religion had played absolutely no part in her upbringing. She was herself not so much agnostic as a very definite atheist. Not only did her mind reject the notions of a Mind Behind the Universe, a Loving Creator – concepts which seemed unnecessary and indeed quite un-sustainable in the face of the world's suffering – she had a pro-found aversion from the 'religious temperament'. Religions, with their offers of consolations of various kinds, seemed to her to appeal to quite base insecurities and fears. Yet she knew that religions too were tribal markers, and she recognized that the Chells were tribal Anglicans. Their house, Throxton Winnards, had been visited by Charles I, who prayed in the chapel there. Cromwell had besieged the house in 1648, Charles II stayed there after his escape from Worcester. Sir Sacheverel Chell, who fought at that battle, and followed the King into exile, was given a baronetcy. *Pro Rege et Ecclesia* was the motto on their coat of arms, and their loyalty to their High Church religion had cost them. (The earldom did not come until the nineteenth century, one of the Chells – Edwin, fourth baron Winnards, being part of the Young England movement and a friend of Disraeli's, who gave him an earldom with a seat in his first Cabinet.) Many of the Chells had taken Holy Orders. Some had become bishops. One of them – the present Earl's younger brother – was a monk.

The Chells' Anglicanism was something which Rachel recognized (little as she empathized with it) as being deeply entwined with their spiritual roots, rather as she knew, regardless of unbelief, a great sense of kinship with the Warsaw rabbis in her own background. While disliking and disapproving of religion, Rachel also saw that it was one way of trying to acknowledge life's seriousness, and to this extent she had more sympathy with *some* religious persons than with the A. J. Ayerheads.

Nevertheless, the words, both of the hymns and of the readings during Kitty's funeral, struck Rachel as completely alien. A clergyman, presumably the local vicar, read 'All flesh is not the same flesh; but there is one kind of flesh of men, another of beasts, another of fishes, and another of birds. There are also celestial bodies, and bodies terrestrial . . .' This seemed not so much unbelievable as grotesque. And the famous words which followed, about Death being swallowed up in victory, left her cold, shudderingly cold. After a hymn, which was printed on their service sheet and in which Rachel did not join, the old monk, Kitty's uncle, the one who had taken her and Charles's wedding eighteen months before, ascended into the Laudian carved pulpit, and stood, hood-eyed, lantern-jawed, for some moments in silence before he opened his mouth.

'We are here to grieve for Kitty and to pray for her, and to offer her soul back to God, who made her and loves her. That is work – the Work of God. All of us bring our own griefs, our own memories of Kitty. She was my god-daughter. Some of you – particularly if you have read the disgusting things written about her in the newspapers – will think that I did not do a very good job. I have heard about these lying newspaper reports, but I made a decision long ago, which I commend to you as good advice, not to read them. Poor Kitty was always made so unhappy by what she read about herself.

'Kitty was a loving girl, who retained so much of the child in her. The world saw a playgirl. Who is to say that God did not see a girl at play? Sometimes it was pointless, or even dangerous play. Sometimes it was innocent and fun-loving. God does not forbid fun.

'She did much good, and good by stealth. When she came to see me in Crickleden, she would often stay the night, and bed down in a sleeping bag, and wake early the next morning to help prepare and serve the breakfast for my house guests. She spoke unaffectedly and easily with them. There was nothing of *de haut en bas* about her. Perhaps she, and they, understood something which is hidden from people who have chosen to make Money or Success their gods.

'Children have no sense of time, no sense of self-importance, no sense of life as defined by how much money we have made or how many hours we imprison ourselves each day in an office. Kitty and the Gentlemen of the Road were able to see that.

'Kitty died' – the old man's voice broke, but he regained control – 'Kitty died because she was with child, so it is in a sense two deaths that we mourn, two souls for whom we pray. Every thing, every single thing, printed about her – that she killed herself, that she died of an overdose – is a lie, a wicked lie, a deliberate lie. But let us be candid. In any human soul, good and evil are intermingled. In some, demons very obviously do battle.

'Perfect love casts out fear, but none of us can love perfectly. So demons of fear remain. They express themselves in different ways, for the names of the devil are legion, and he is many. Those of us who drink too much, or drug too much or are plunged into the psychological hells of eating disorders are not necessarily more self-obsessed than those who are addicted to different drugs, such as success or power or wealth. Some of us have stared into the pit, and been unable to endure what we saw. Kitty had been down into the pit.'

There was a long silence, and some in the congregation supposed that the monk had finished talking. Yet no one stirred. The church was so silent that you could hear the faint phutt as one of the candles near the coffin spluttered and consumed a globule of wax which had formed itself into a lump near the flame.

'Where is God? At a time of desolation like this, how can we say that we believe in a God of Love? Where is He? Let us remind ourselves what God is not. The world put to death the God who explains things, the Creator God who sewed up the Universe and had an explanation for every blessed mystery. The world put that God to death on Calvary. On Good Friday they said, the God of the Philosophers is dead. How can you reconcile a God of absolute power and a God of Love? You can't. To try is to insult the suffering of innocent humanity. That God is dead. To try to believe in Him is a blasphemy.

'And our faith went to the Garden in the darkness of dawn three days later. Our faith did not find explanations, nor did it find fake consolations. It found a new God. The new God was to be found not in control, but in loss of control; not in strength but in weakness. He was no longer an explanation for what happens, He was now a person – a mysterious person who only the minute before had looked very much like the gardener sweeping the path. That has the profoundest implications for the human race and for human history for as long as it lasts. For we can no longer look to an imaginary God to hand out morality, to feed the poor, to heal the sick, to refashion the world along just and equitable lines. That is our responsibility now, and if it seems like a Godless world, we shall be judged – we, not God.

'The Twelve did not recognize the friend who had been killed, brutally and savagely killed – they did not recognize him at first. But the one who doubted most of all saw, with the eyes of hindsight, that his Lord and his God was to be found not in the highest heavens and heaven of heavens but in a wounded human body: in bleeding hands, and pierced feet, and wounded side. It was in the presence of that abject vulnerability that Doubt was cast aside, and Faith could say, *My Lord and my God!*'

FOUR

Throxton Winnards – it simply takes the name of the hamlet of which it was the manor house – is a seventeenth-century survival. Young Sacheverel Chell had been at the Court of Charles I; his father's tomb in the parish church of Stanton St Leonards shows him kneeling and facing his wife. Various Chell offspring, alabaster renditions of the Children of the New Forest, kneel behind the parents. The tomb, crowned with the coat of arms, is ingeniously embellished with astrological, and heraldic, devices, some of them punning on the surname Chell. (Cockle-shells, scallops and mussels in black marble and pink alabaster cluster around the capitals.) Inigo Jones, who rebuilt Whitehall for Charles I, was undoubtedly Sacheverel's inspiration for the rebuilt Throxton Winnards. Earlier generations believed that the little square courtyard, with its Tuscan columns, and the Italianate arches of its cloistered arcade, was the work of Inigo Jones himself, but this view is no longer held by architectural historians.

Because of the family's loyalty to the House of Stuart, the Chells sank into poverty during the Hanoverian era. This is the reason that Throxton Winnards survives as so unspoilt an example of early seventeenth-century architecture, without additions from later ages of taste.

Since it was an 'important' building, there had been various attempts by well-meaning architectural societies to persuade Lord Longmore to conserve or restore the house. So far he had resisted the offers of English Heritage to – as he thought of it – bugger the place up.

The funeral party, about eighty individuals, walked in the rain up the rutted drive, trying to distinguish between shallow puddles and deep pools. At the first turn of this drive, which was half a mile long, the house came into view, its mellow grey limestone sodden and blotched. Many of those who caught that first view of the house framed by the dripping beeches of the avenue felt a shock of pleasure which was something more than simply aesthetic delight. The mullioned and transomed windows, the great portico with its twisted stone columns, the castellated front are undoubtedly beautiful. But there is a further quality of Throxton Winnards, felt by all but the most insensitive of visitors, that one is stepping back into the past itself. This feeling intensifies as you walk through the portico and find yourself in the arcaded square courtyard. Over the front door in its niche is a crumbled stone bust of the Royal Martyr looking as if carved in Cheshire cheese. His darkened portrait – oil on board after Van Dyck – hangs in the Great Hall, which you enter on passing the front door.

The high walls of this hall, which date from the time of Henry VIII, are panelled in black oak, so that the antlers, horns, spears, helmets, targes and firearms hung on display were only semi-visible glimmering in the chiaroscuro. Local caterers were responsible for the food, which by London standards was unsophisticated – rice salads, ham sandwiches made with sliced white bread, segments of rather tasteless quiche. One of Kitty's sisters and some of her Oxford contemporaries, including Rachel Pearl, were still tear-stained, but for most people in the room, ink-black as their clothes might be, the event took on the atmosphere of any other social gathering. Conversation murmured. And when two or three glasses of Chilean Cabernet

Sauvignon or Chardonnay had been consumed, the noise level
rose. There was even laughter.

Sinclo could see across the crowded room that Rachel, red-
eyed but not actually weeping, was in deep conversation with
Father Chell. He wondered what these two very different
people could possibly be finding to talk about. The tall monk,
clad in his grey habit, was canted over to listen to her, and her
lips were quite close to his ear. It would almost have been
possible to believe – had Sinclo not happened to know that she
was an atheist of Jewish background – that she was, like some
Russian peasant in the presence of a *staretz* or holy elder, making
confession of her sins. The priest was nodding vigorously at
what she said, and then putting his hand against his mouth he
bellowed something back into her ear.

'Sinclo, my dear boy.'

Sinclo found himself face to face with Brigadier Courtenay,
unseen since army days. He was a tall, bald, roseate figure, his
slightly toothless face producing child-like dimples when he
smiled. He was approximately sixty, in Sinclo's judgement, and
therefore belonged to that generation in the British Army which
had no experience of large-scale warfare. After his own
regiment, the Rifle Brigade, was amalgamated with the Green
Jackets in one of the everlasting army reforms of recent times,
he had served in Ireland, and was said to have a formidable
record in dealing with the terrorist cells – a fact which Sinclo
and the younger officers found hard to reconcile with his gentle
mannerisms and uncompromisingly Etonian voice. He had
served for many years in Germany, and a little in the Far East.
He had been with Sinclo in Zinariya when they formed part of
the peacekeeping force during the outbreak of fighting some
eight years ago.

'How very nice to see you, sir!'

'Very sad, very sad,' Courtenay said quietly.

'Kitty was . . .'

'A lovely girl.'

Sinclo wondered what the Brigadier was doing there. Then he recollected a conversation which he had had with him years before, in which it emerged that the old boy (whose mother had been some kind of cousin) was distantly related to Lord Longmore. Perhaps he was the sort of man who enjoyed attending funerals. He had not been a guest at Kitty's wedding, and Sinclo did not remember seeing him at any previous family gatherings.

Still with his eyes fixed on Rachel Pearl, Sinclo tried to frame in his head a polite way of asking the Brigadier whether he was retired. Luckily the question was answered for him.

'I've been more or less bowler-hatted,' he said, 'working for the MOD on various' – he smiled his dimple-baby smile as he selected *le mot juste* – 'administrative problems, so to say.'

Sinclo had never known him well, certainly not well enough to expect any recollection on Brigadier Courtenay's part of his own activities. It was a surprise, then, when Courtenay came out with:

'Still working for that paper?'

Sinclo assented. The Brigadier pushed out a lower lip and shook his head sorrowfully. This wordless gesture made Sinclo feel infinitely ashamed.

He looked across the room. Rachel and Father Chell had been joined by Lord Longmore, who was circulating the party and having a few words with everyone. Seeing the peer beside his cousin Vivyan Chell was to be struck by a paradox which he had noted before at family gatherings: namely that Lord Longmore looked, with his halo of silver hair round a bald tonsure, like a holy old monk, and Father Chell, in spite of the monastic habit, still looked every inch a soldier, with his smarmed-back hair and his face so closely shaven and scrubbed that it shone.

'I tell you what, Sinclo,' said the Brigadier. 'There's something about which I should value your advice.'

'Really?'

'Do you ever eat lunch?'

'On a daily basis.'

'Good. Good.'

The Brigadier's mouth set firmly. It was as if he had been making some very long-term plan which would have been completely upset if Sinclo had confessed to not eating luncheon. Then he reached in his pocket for a small diary.

'Next Monday any good? Lancers' Club? One?'

Sinclo was mildly puzzled by this request and only mildly more surprised by the fact that the Brigadier, who still wore his mac in the house, left at once having made the lunch date. It was almost as if he had only attended the funeral in order to buttonhole Sinclo himself, but the younger man did not think much of these things. His chief preoccupation was now to cross the party and link up with Rachel. He had formed a plan in his head. They would travel back together to London, and, having drunk wine at the party, they would have whisky on the train. The journey time was an hour and forty minutes, and in this time he would uncompromisingly lay his cards on the table. He would tell her that he loved her, and knew that he could only love her, Rachel, and no other woman. He knew that she did not love him, but he knew that she would be happier with him than she was at the moment. He would say he knew about L.P., but that he begged her to consider, if only for an experiment, to allow him to woo her. He did not even demand, at first, that they should so much as kiss or hold hands, he only wanted it to be acknowledged that he was in love with her.

When he reached her side, she was on her own.

'You seemed very deep in chat with the Mad Monk,' he said with a frivolous air he neither felt nor meant. Everyone in the family called Vivyan the Mad Monk, but Rachel's appalled expression revealed she supposed him to be mocking.

'I was asking him about his work. It sounds fascinating, this open house of his. He has refugees, tramps, the homeless, all living there, hugger-mugger.'

'You should see it,' said Sinclo.

'I'm going to,' she said with such intense seriousness and determination that her words sounded defiant: the tone implied that Sinclo had been trying to dissuade her from any such course.

'I was wondering,' he said wildly, 'which train we were thinking of getting. There's one which leaves Troon at four seventeen and then nothing until five seventeen.'

'Oh, I'm not going by train,' she said.

There had been no prior arrangement that Rachel and he should travel together and until she came and joined him on the train down he had not even known she would be at the funeral. He now experienced, however, the most abject, swooping disappointment.

'Couldn't you . . .'

'I've said I'll take a lift from Giles and Palmer – do you know them?'

'I know who you mean,' said Sinclo, and not liking the prospect of travelling back with this pair of art-loving bachelors, one of whom was an Oxford friend of Rachel's and Kitty's.

'No, no,' he said, when she said she thought there might be room to squeeze Sinclo into the back of Palmer's car with Giles and another friend called something like Spence. 'I've got my ticket, I may as well use it.'

They did not say goodbye to one another, and by the time he returned to his solitary bed that night, Sinclo had made himself very drunk.

DRUG GIRL'S FUNERAL: THERE IS NO GOD, SAYS RED PRIEST was the headline on page eight of next morning's *Legion*.

FIVE

Later that day, Worledge sat in his office with his feet on the desk. Two of his thuggish deputies were there, as was Peg Montgomery. Sinclo had been excluded.

'Again?' asked Worledge. The eyes were dead bullets behind the horn-rimmed specs, but the teeth were displayed, the row of yellow tombstones, as he fiddled with the cassette-player. A stubby index finger forced the machine into life again.

An adolescent boy's voice was heard. 'I'll take my pants down, but I'm not gonna crap into this thing, you know . . . I'm not a queer.'

'Tuli – Peter . . .' said Father Vivyan Chell. 'We could take some coffee up to my room . . . We can talk in here . . . I feel that I want to say something to you . . . If I have done something to you . . . something which hurt you . . . I am deeply, deeply sorry. Sometimes our passions are so strong that they are quite literally uncontrollable. Sex makes us into lunatics. But I abused my position of trust.'

'I'm not a queer,' said the boy. 'I'm not a queer.'

It was Peg who broke the silence with her perhaps inevitable 'Fuck-a-duck'.

Worledge's fingers caressed the cassette-player.

'Isn't it magic?' Then his gravelly question turned into that cement-mixer laugh. 'This has gotta be dynamite. Dynamite.'

SIX

All over central London, luncheon was beginning. In sandwich bars and cafés, people had been satisfying hunger for hours. But for the more leisured, with time to spend in a restaurant or a club, the ceremony was only just beginning. In Westminster, Chelsea, Mayfair and the West End, waiters and waitresses gazed at empty tables, the folded napkins, the polished glasses, knowing that within minutes, their clients would be seated at their regular tables, and all the transactions of gossip, business, lust and commerce would recommence. Lunch was the meal, not dinner, over which business was contracted. It was for lunch, not for dinner, that couples tentatively met, to see whether they wished to commit adultery with one another. It was at lunch that secrets were disclosed, for whereas Londoners tended to congregate in fours or sixes in the evening, they naturally formed pairs for the midday meal. Lunch was a conspiracy.

It had always been so for Mary and Martina, who sat at their accustomed window table at Diana's, watching the rain fall on the street, as they had done hundreds of times before. They were lunching very slightly early, since the installation was to be initiated at Burlington House at two thirty, and it was essential not to be late.

The Daily Legion lay between them on the marble-topped table. Mary had noticed that Martina carried the newspaper with her everywhere, like a passport or a meal ticket: in her case, it had been both. STOP THIS HYPOCRISY was the headline. Martina Fax had herself contributed a why-oh-why on the subject of Bleeding Hearts who wished to stop British arms companies exporting bombs, planes and heavy military hardware to West Africa. These know-nothing liberals, Martina had argued, were prepared to sacrifice tens of thousands of British jobs for the sake of their dubious 'principles'. It was not often realized how many British jobs depended on armament manufacture. Martina had included in her statistics anyone who had manufactured a screw, a bolt or an engine which might at some stage of its life come near some weaponry. She had almost worked herself up into the position of believing that the entire economy of the Western world depended on giving to the West Africans the means to destroy themselves.

The second thing these liberals did not understand was that though General Bindiga distributed rough justice, *it was justice*. The Alkawari! party were anarchists. *How would we feel if we had to have Professor Galwanga as our Prime Minister?* The third point was a strange one for *The Daily Legion* to be peddling, since it had, in other areas of life, a rooted objection to 'hand-outs', sponging, indeed to anyone giving anything to anybody else who had not worked for it. Student grants, overseas aid, dole money – these all, in the usual philosophy of *The Daily Legion*, encouraged scrounging and the dependency culture. But in the case of Zinariya, things were a little different. The economic crisis there was not of General Bindiga's making. Anarchists and enemies of the state had caused the uprisings in the cocoa farms, the outbreaks of civil war, and the explosions in the copper mines. It was vital, absolutely vital, that the international relief organizations continued to pour money into General Bindiga's coffers. The policy of sanctions, advocated by the Bleeding Hearts, would hurt those who had most to lose.

This last phrase was a little odd, but Mary Much supposed it was a covert reference to the fact that their daily fare at Diana's – half a lobster each, with a little green salad, and a bowl of aioli into which to dip their French fries, washed down with their delicious concoction of peach juice and champagne – had been paid for by Christian Aid and Oxfam. Certainly, without the General's well-laundered cheques, siphoned from relief funds sent to Mararraba, the future for Lennie's newspaper empire would be bleak.

Today, as was quite often the case, the two 'best friends' were cross with one another. They sat, a statuesque pair for any passer-by to see through the large glass window of Diana's, Martina's smile eternally frozen, her lips as crimson as her hair; Mary Much, whose ash blonde had lately become peroxide, her more mobile features more capable of demonstrating irritation. Of course, she would give her best friend no such satisfaction as to make a scene. They always scrapped over a new toy. Martina thought that Mary had borrowed Piet too often. Mary thought that he would have looked gorgeous in the opening exhibit. As it was, Hans was to open the show.

Martina had been so adamant about it that she had even enlisted Lennie's support. Piet no poo-poo. Such spoilsports. Lennie said that he was determined to get the priest – the old bender. Said the priest had power. Was mobilizing public opinion against the General. Yawn-yawn – Mary believed that one Bongo-Bongo story was much like another in the eyes and ears of the British public; that they did not care a fig for the Bliks and their wars. But Lennie had a bee in his bonnet. Said they had collected so much stuff on the priest they could get him sent to prison. It would not look very good if the priest's chief 'victim', and the chief witness in any future trial, was seen deliberately lowering his trousers in the courtyard of Burlington House.

'We had the diet *so right*,' drawled Mary, more to herself than to Martina. She dipped a potato chip in aioli and sucked its end. 'Spanish omelettes for three days: plenty of potatoes, a few peppers, but something solid. Hans doesn't want squits against the Perspex. Just a good jobby, long and firm, plopping down into the water.'

The taloned hand which was not holding a chip raised a cigarette to her lips.

'Anyway,' said Martina, 'Lennie was right. While the *Legion* is running a campaign against the installation, it would not look very good if our butler was the first to sit on the john.'

'He's your butler now?'

Mary Much smiled as if at a private joke.

Martina said what she always said when she wished to draw a line under a conversation. She took a deep intake of breath and as she exhaled she said, '*Any-way.*'

That was the end of that conversation. They fell to discussion of *The Sunday Legion*.

'Lennie's going to fire Mr Blimby next week,' said Martina decisively. 'With all his staff. The two titles will then run together, only on Sunday the paper will be called *The Sunday Legion*.'

A recipe for commercial and journalistic disaster, thought Mary Much.

'God, you're brilliant,' she said.

SEVEN

'Potted shrimps – any good?'

Brigadier Courtenay was at his small table in the corner of the Coffee Room of the Lancers' Club.

'Excellent.'

The Brigadier held a pencil in his hand, very carefully sharpened. He wrote the words *potted shrimps* on the printed order-form provided. 'Lamb cutlets?'

'Excellent, sir.'

'Tomatoes? Mushrooms? French beans? Boiled potatoes?'

To all these, Sinclo assented. The only surprise was that, instead of offering wine, the Brigadier said, 'We'll have the luncheon-cup: rather good here. A mixture of ginger beer and cider.'

The business of ordering the meal complete, and a waiter having come to collect the written slip, the two men began the predictable small-talk: the advantages and disadvantages of belonging to this particular club, the wisdom or otherwise of belonging to more than one club. Sinclo got the impression that the Brigadier more or less lived in the Lancers'. The Lancers' Club occupied an old ducal house in a small courtyard not far from Albany, just off Piccadilly, between St James's Church and Fortnum and Mason. It was a handsome, large dolls' house, dating from the reign of George II, and the building had been occupied by the Lancers' Club since the 1880s, when the dukes who owned it went bankrupt. A splendid equestrian portrait by Lawrence of the 4th Duke, an officer in the Hussars, commanded the hall, and other portraits of eighteenth-century and Victorian generals looked down from the cream-painted panelling of the Coffee Room. The waiters seemed like soldiers.

'I've been toying with the idea of asking Father Chell to dine here,' said the Brigadier. 'Do you think he'd have a suit to wear? I can't see the members taking very kindly to it if he turned up in his medieval garb!'

'The Mad Monk?' asked Sinclo lightly. 'He must have come here a lot in his youth.'

'Why do you call him mad?'

'It's his family nickname. He's . . . a splendid fellow.'

'He's more than that, I think.'

With great deliberation, the Brigadier took a small triangle of toast and began to spread potted shrimps on to one corner of it. 'I remember in India once,' he said quietly, 'being taken to see a holy man. I was quite young at the time. Didn't know anything about religion or spirituality.' He smiled, the toothless-seeming mouth shrinking into the appley cheeks. 'Extraordinary.'

Sinclo, who was in the position of the Brigadier when young, having neither knowledge of nor interest in religion, did not know which was extraordinary: the ignorance, or the phenomenon about to be unfolded.

'The villagers believed this man – he was about the age you are now – to be an avatar, an incarnation of the Divine. I don't have Hindi – or not much. It wasn't the words the man spoke to me which made such an impression. It was something you felt in his presence. Completely impossible to describe it, but it was real all right. You *felt* it, like an electric shock.'

Sinclo felt ill-equipped for this sort of conversation, so asked simply, 'When were you in India, sir?'

The Brigadier could hardly have been more than a small child when India became independent.

'I feel like that in Father Chell's presence. You could feel it the other day at the funeral – what?'

'It was a moving sermon.'

'That's not what I said. This man has *power*. Ever been down to Crickleden?' The Brigadier was, as it happened, the second person to ask Sinclo this question during the last few days. Worledge had been telling him to check the place out. Worledge had something up his sleeve in relation to the Mad Monk. Of that Sinclo felt certain, though he did not know what it was. The cuttings files on CHELL had been ransacked. Snappers had been sent down to photograph Kelvedone, the Mad Monk's monastery. Sinclo felt the vultures hovering in the sky for the kill, and by some instinct, he felt that the Brigadier was part of this gathering consummation. 'It's a rum set-up down there,' said the Brigadier. 'Absolute shambles. Caravans, tents even, refugees all over the shop. All sorts of odds and sods. But they're all electrified by Chell. Just like that avatar I met when I spent my year with the Bengal Lancers. They have rather good military clubs in India, you know. An excellent one at Kanpur . . . Lucknow – Agra. I remember at the Cavalry Club in Agra, they make a point of only hiring Muslim barmen – no danger of them helping themselves to the booze!'

He sipped his cider and ginger beer mix from a handsome silver tankard. When the cutlets arrived, the two men had been silent for a short while which to Sinclo had felt like about two hours.

'The thing is,' said the Brigadier quietly – 'do help yourself to those potatoes. Rather good.' He stammered very slightly as he added, 'Parmentier.'

'Has something cropped up about the Mad Monk, sir?'

'The thing is,' said the Brigadier, 'and this is very much . . .'
His knife and fork, between each mouthful, were laid neatly
together across the plate rather than being splayed. It was an
affectation which Sinclo had never come across before. The
Brigadier's hands were free, and with them he gestured the
absolute need for secrecy – first by flickering his right hand in
the air, and then by placing an index finger against his lips.

'Of course . . .'

'Only, I know that Lennox Mark has a vendetta against
Vivyan Chell, and that he is preparing an assault.'

Sinclo was astounded that the Brigadier should be privy to
such information.

'Because you seem to be working for *The Daily Legion*, I
assumed you might know this.'

'There is something afoot,' said Sinclo.

He felt an absurd need at this juncture to keep his end up,
not to admit his complete ignorance. He hoped that his
vagueness would suggest discretion, an inside knowledge of
matters too hush-hush to be talked about openly.

'You see, I'm almost bowler-hatted now, but my job at the
MOD, as you probably know, is a continuation of the work I did
in Ireland.'

'Anti-terrorism?'

'There are a number of fairly peculiar characters, shall we
say?' He laid his knife and fork neatly together again while he
chewed the crisp fat of the lamb cutlet with his fingers. The
peculiarity of these characters – presumably bombers and
murderers – perhaps gave him some amusement. 'There are
African resistance fighters. There are various terrorist organizations in the Balkans. There's at least one old veteran of the
Republican movement from my old haunts . . .'

'You mean IRA?'

'It's not the IRA as such.'

'Real IRA?'

'The thing is . . . and I must urge upon you, Sinclo, that this isn't to be repeated to anyone . . .'

'Of course not, sir.'

'A number of these characters – no one can actually point a finger at Father Vivyan, and say that he is *behind* their cells, but about a dozen of them have, at one time or another, enjoyed his hospitality down at Crickleden.'

The two men ate for a while in silence. Sinclo was astonished.

'You see, what we are considering is the possibility that, under the cover of a sort of freelance refugee camp run by the church, Chell is organizing a liaison between a number of these quite disparate terrorist groups. We can't be certain of anything yet. We've nothing to link Galwanga – who is a very dangerous man, by the way . . .'

'Really? I thought people called him the Zinariyan Gandhi.'

'Quite,' said the Brigadier. 'We've nothing to link Professor Galwanga with the IRA and we've nothing to link the IRA with these Albanian terrorists. But Chell was a first-class officer in a guerrilla war in Lugardia as it was then. First class. MC.'

'I know.'

'If anyone could knock some discipline into that ragtag and bobtail, it would be him. And if anyone could teach them to help each other – with expertise, with men, with the actual explosives . . . You see, some of those breakaway Irish cells in south London are sitting on huge arsenals . . .'

'Excuse me, sir, but what would they use it *for*?'

'Sinclo!' The older man smiled at the naivety of the question. 'What do any of these people want? They want power. They can't enjoy power of the kind you and I might enjoy by going into Parliament or rising to a high rank in the forces. So they cause mayhem.'

'You surely don't think the Mad Monk . . .'

'He's a disappointed man, he's an angry man. We don't know anything at present. But what I — what the MOD is very anxious should *not* happen is that some half-baked version of all this gets into the paper. Lennox Mark uses very primitive surveillance devices, as I'm sure you know. Bugs all your offices. Bugs his enemies. He's been bugging this youth who is a rather pathetic hanger-on of Chell's — a black boy. We've got most of the tapes. He's a little nutcase, this child. Psychopath. Ought to be in the bin. We are really close to having a breakthrough in this case. If I am left in peace for four or five more weeks, I think I can break at least three significant terrorist cells in London. But if *The Daily Legion* comes barging in with its hobnailed boots . . . do you see what I am saying, Sinclo?'

EIGHT

Piet had promised the two women that he would meet them at Burlington House, but so far they had not shown. The crowd was quite large. Piet himself waited outside in Piccadilly, but most people had squeezed into the quadrangle to see the large Perspex throne which had been erected in the middle of the space, replacing the statue of Sir Joshua Reynolds. The words SPONSORED BY *GLOSS* were printed in large letters and stuck like billboards around the plinth.

Piet both did, and did not, want the women to be there. He had said too much. He, or some of the beings inside him, had blurted out stuff to Lennox Mark which he now regretted. He'd hoped that nothing would come of it. Then Martina had called him in. She'd been standing, like it was really formal, like it was an interview. Like, she did and didn't remember how he'd first come into that house. Like, how she really *had* something on him and now she was calling in the chips.

Shit, man, you didn't need and go tell them 'bout Father Vivyan. And besides, it weren't Father Vivyan that made you give him head, it was that uphill gardener Currey and he got all he deserved . . . You're a dickhead. Who's you callin' a dickhead, prickhead nigga yerself. What's the harm, they aren't gonna harm Father Vivyan . . .

And the altar-boy had decided to go to confession and tell Father Vivyan *everything*. He'd told him the lot – about the burglary, about Martina and her mother capturing him and making him into their house-boy; about Kevin Currey and what he made him do – that didn't make *him* gay, did it, Father? More and more of this shit, he'd confessed – like how he went cottaging, but not 'cause he was an arse-merchant, wanted to punish them, filthy creeping bastards. That was all right, wasn't it, Father? He'd like to have killed that old bastard 'Dr Arbuthnot', same as he'd killed Kevin Currey. But he wasn't finished with them yet.

Father Vivyan had listened to his outpourings in silence.

'You won't tell anyone, Father?'

'Oh, Peter, oh, Tuli.'

'You won't, Father Vivyan – will you? You won't tell?'

'Dear boy.' Another long silence.

Peter had made this confession sitting on the floor beside Father Vivyan's deckchair in the darkness of the priest's room one night.

'You need have no fear,' the priest said. 'If you make your confession to a priest, he may not reveal what you have told him. Even if you told him you were going to commit a murder, the priest could not do anything which showed to another person that he knew your secret. That's why when a priest hears a confession such as yours, Peter, my dear, a great burden has been placed on him . . . You see, some of these things ought not to be secret. You should have told someone about Mr Currey . . .'

'I'm not a gay, Father, I'm not a poof.'

'Of course not. But even if you were, God would love you no less.'

'Who you calling a bloody poof, Farver?'

'I'm not calling you names, Tuli. And soon I will give you a blessing, and absolution, and God will have put away all your sins. But before I do that, I want you to make some things clear to other people. You should make it plain to the school that Mr Currey was abusing you. And you should tell Mr Mark that you lied to him about me. You see, now you've told me about it in your confession, my lips are sealed. I can never breathe a word about this to anyone. If the newspaper prints the lies you told to Mr Mark as if they were true . . . Do you see what I'm saying, Tuli?'

'Yes, Father.'

'If they print those lies – if they say that I was the one who abused you – I can deny it; but I can't enlist your help. I can't say that you have already confessed to me what truly happened. My hands are tied. That is why, if I had known what you wanted to confess, I should have asked you to confess to a different priest. But what's done is done. Now I want to ask you another question. This bugging device, those tapes . . . where are they?'

'Mum's confiscated them. Threw them in the bin.'

'You are sure she threw them away?'

'Said I had no business with them.'

'You see, Tuli, it is almost certain that there is more than one speaker and more than one recorder.'

'Yes, Father.'

'You understand what I'm saying, Tuli?'

But he had not really been listening. It was all too confusing. He knew, like, he'd opened up a can of worms, but he could not do anything about it now. Jeeves and the camp altar-boy and the more sensible among them were drowned out by their disturbing companions, the hurt little boy and the one to whom he'd gone for help, the Murderous Moron.

Martina and Mary Much were waving at him now. They were getting out of a taxi and waving. They were on the other side of Piccadilly, and he suddenly had the impulse to run, weaving through the traffic which honked and hooted their horns, to stop them getting any closer.

'Should we not be inside the gateway arch, at least?' asked Martina.

'Surely,' said Mary Much, 'and after all the help, Piet, that you gave Hans, don't you wish you were – on display, as it were?'

Piet, half Jeeves, half a shy public schoolboy, smiled and said, 'I think the artist should have first go.'

'After all the help you gave him. He said those engineers you found for him understood *everything* – much better than the in-house electricians. Where did you say they were from?'

'Kosovo,' said Jeeves.

'Look,' said Martina. And from their vantage point on the far side of Piccadilly, they could see the throne. Hans Busch had emerged from a side door and to the cheers of the crowd had lowered his leather trousers and thong and sat down.

NINE

'You're not suggesting that the Mad Monk is . . . some kind of terrorist boss?' asked Sinclo Manners.

There was a pause while, very slowly, Brigadier Courtenay emptied the contents of one teaspoon into his coffee. He did so with the precision of one conducting a chemical experiment. It would have been possible to suppose that by adding one granule too much to his cup disaster would ensue.

'Look, Sinclo, I know that you aren't happy at the' – he jutted out his lower lip, regretful at having to use a dirty word – 'newspaper. But if you are prepared to stay for a little longer, we . . . that is . . . I . . . could *put work your way*. I think you know what I'm saying?'

Sinclo, who had very little idea what the Brigadier was driving at, nodded vigorously.

'Oh, absolutely,' he said.

'You'd probably rather be abroad somewhere – doing a bit of travel writing, sending back pieces on serious subjects to serious – um – periodicals. Foreign correspondent sort of thing.'

Presumably, Sinclo had often voiced this ambition when drinking with friends, with flatmates and colleagues. As the Brigadier came out with it, however, it seemed positively eerie; as if They, the Intelligence boffins, the MI5, had been bugging his mind.

'This job – if you're happy to take it on – could be regarded as an apprenticeship,' said the Brigadier. 'Let's be quite clear what I am not asking you to do. I am not asking you to snoop or spy on Father Chell. As such.'

It seemed to Sinclo that this, exactly, was what Brigadier Courtenay *was* asking.

'But if, having been down to the place – sniffed it out, as it were – you think that you spot danger signals . . .'

'Let you know – is that what you want, sir?'

'I don't want any further communications with you,' said the Brigadier. He stared firmly into the middle distance, not looking at Sinclo at all. He had stretched out his right palm and held it at an angle to the table, making sawing gestures as he did so.

'No notes, no e-mails, no letters, no telephone messages. We'll meet here for lunch once a month, just as we are doing now. The first Wednesday of every month, here, 12.50. If there is any reason why you can't make it, there is no need to write and cancel. Just turn up the following month. If for any reason you need to get in touch with me sooner than the regular meeting . . .'

'You mean if I find the Mad Monk with bomb-making equipment in the vestry?'

'This is serious, Sinclo.'

'I know, sir.'

'I want you to send me one of these typed postcards. Post it to this club special delivery. Then come to the bar and I shall meet you there at six p.m. on the day after you posted it.'

The cards, all identical, were printed with the letterhead of a tailor in the Prince's Arcade. They read, 'Your esteemed order is ready for a fitting.'

'As for money . . .'

Sinclo made the self-deprecating noises which shy men of his class made when embarrassed.

'When you leave after each luncheon, the hall porter will hand you a package. Fair?'

'I don't know . . . it's very . . .'

'You mean, you don't know if you want to do it, or you don't know how much we are paying you, or . . . what?'

'I mean, thanks very much, sir. Everything you have said is clear.'

'Good,' said the Brigadier. But then, almost at once, he added, 'Good *grief*, what's that?'

A rumble as of thunder could be felt: beneath their feet, in their ears, almost in the air. The rumbling coincided with the deafening boom of a vast explosion.

TEN

'Piet is right, we can see better from here – you get a vista,' said Martina.

But Mary Much was dissatisfied. 'We have to be nearer, darlings.'

The crowd, from where they stood in the courtyard itself, could have been watching a wreath-laying at the Cenotaph. There was near silence as they contemplated Hans on his Perspex seat. From where the critics and photographers stood, there would have been visible through the Perspex the equine anus and hairy arse of the artist. He was still. Mr Blimby's middle-brow comparison with Rodin's *Thinker* was actually inescapable. Perhaps the allusion was wittily intentional.

'We need binoculars if we are going to stand here,' said Mary. 'Oh, look, look. Do let's get nearer!'

Unmistakably, the features of the artist had begun to contort. His pallor momentarily reddened, obscuring the pustules on his bald head. Then he went ashen pale and the process of defecation began.

'I can see it from here,' said Mary Much. 'Oh, a real long Cumberland . . .'

But her word 'sausage' was not heard.

There were some survivors. Amazingly, one of the critics who had been standing quite close recovered sufficiently to file a piece for the following Sunday to the serious newspaper which employed him. From his hospital bed, he wrote that when the brown snake torpedoed the pan it had been a Pearl Harbor Moment. English art would never be the same. The story which had begun with the Wilton Diptych and ended with Tracey Emin and Damien Hirst had now exploded. Chaos ruled. This had been Hans Busch's eternal, tragic legacy. There were, indeed, those who contemplated the possibility that this had been the ultimate form of self-expression, the final clash between the Personal Heresy and the Classical Tradition: Suicide as Art. But the Suicide as Art theory, so popular with some critics, did not wash with the bomb disposal team. It was a timed device, almost certainly home-made in someone's garage. Although every window in Burlington House and a number of shop windows in Piccadilly were smashed, it was not in fact a very large bomb. Hans Busch had been torn limb from limb. His head was hurled in the air like a football, and rolled out into Piccadilly. Legs, blood, fingers spattered in a generalized gore as the crowd screamed, ran, fell. On the other side of the street, Piet, Martina and Mary stood rooted to the spot, seeing at first only a cloud of smoke, and a chaos of pain.

ELEVEN

Rachel Pearl was sitting on the rag-rug which lay at the foot of an old man's orthopaedic chair. She was helping the old man to put on a pair of very frayed tartan slippers. He was wincing with pain as she endeavoured, very gently and delicately, to fit the extraordinary red and purple swollen toes, hard with calluses, into the slippers. The small sitting room of his council flat smelt of urine. From where she knelt, she could see more such ugly blocks, brutalist structures erected during the late 1960s. They were constructed of an absorbent concrete so that, in the extremely wet weather which persisted, they looked soaked.

None of these circumstances was in itself especially cheering. Rachel Pearl, however, felt more intensely close to a sense of joy than she had ever done. It was a happiness all the more pure because it was hedged round with grief. She was, acutely and painfully, in mourning for her friend. She was dazed and hurt by the end of her love affair. She was haunted moreover by a dark foreboding about the future. For a few weeks, however, she had glimpsed a vision of how it might be possible to lead a good life, and this accounted for this inner peace, this calm which was, if not happiness, so like happiness. The old man, whose name was Gordon, was talking about his war years. He was not demented, but getting on in that direction; his tales were an unstoppable film-show in his head of military recollection. Sometimes, the stills from this mental home-movie were historically significant. He saw Wavell in a staff car being driven past as he and his mates marched down a dust-track in Abyssinia. More often the visions were generalized.

'The things Musso had done there, love, you wouldn't believe.'

'Such as?'

Gordon winced, either from an agony of mental recollection or from the torture caused by bulbous red feet and arthritic hips.

After a long pause, he said, 'You'd go to the quartermaster and say, "I didn't lose no billycan – if I hadn't put me kit down a moment sooner I'd have caught it the same as . . ."' His face contorted and he made short inhalations of despair. 'Eeeh! Eeh! Oh! Colin, he were called. He were a funny one. No lip, mind. But even the sergeants had to laugh at him.'

Gordon never reached the point of any narrative, never filled out a generalization with a comment specific to the case. Rachel never did hear what he had seen in Abyssinia to confirm his horror of the Italian fascists. Colin, who presumably got blown up by a mine or a grenade, though alluded to more than once, was never explained.

Kitty Chell, Rachel's best friend of student days, was dead. She mourned her friend. Listening to Gordon, she began to guess what it would be like when she was older, when her head would fill up with a whole gallery of the dead, who came in and out of the shadows, often more real than the living.

Gordon lived almost entirely in this twilit mental world. She had visited him three or four times before she knew that he recognized her. Clearly, he did more than this. He had been thinking about her. He had drifted into one of his interminable ramblings about desert warfare. Then he said: 'We never had any time to think of what was going on in Europe, like, where many had it so much worse. I mean, we'd no idea what you lot was going through.'

At first, she had supposed that by the phrase 'you lot', he had meant the women on the home front, the Londoners surviving aerial bombardment; but his eyes, those rheumy, bloodshot old eyes, had suddenly met hers with tearful tenderness. He opened a toothless mouth and smiled, rubbing his stubbly chin. Somewhere inside this old skeleton was a man who had once been her age, who had known young friends, who had been in love, who had nursed hopes.

'Not till we saw them newsreels at the end of the war. In the camp we was, waiting to be demobbed. We'd come home. The Slade camp it were, near Oxford and there were these big . . . The Brigadier, he come in and spoke to us before the show, kind of thing. Magic . . . magic lantern . . . Before they switched it on, he said . . . the Brigadier, he said to us, "Now you're going to find this shocking" . . . And then his voice went all quiet, like, and he says, "Maybe it shows what we've all been fighting for, only we didn't know it" . . . And then he said, and I'm not religious but I'll never forget it, the Brigadier said, "God have mercy on us."'

She knew then that he was talking about the newsreels of the liberated concentration camps, of the walking skeletons of Belsen, the mountains of skulls, shoes, teeth that those films revealed. Was it so obvious, even to this man who had, until this juncture, seemed so totally self-absorbed, that she was Jewish? She was both mildly annoyed, as she always was when people took it for granted that she was Jewish; and at the same time deeply moved.

In the ordinary texture of English conversation, there was so much maddening anti-semitism, ranging from feeble jokes at school to the airy assumptions by so many journalists and enlightened liberals that all sensible people supported the Arabs against Israel in the Middle East. These things enraged Rachel precisely because they were so unthought, so unconsidered; they were in the simplest sense of the word prejudices. But there was also this other thing about England, that since the time of Cromwell it had welcomed Jews, and while they were only in numerical proportion a tiny part of the population, the Jews had played an important and valued part in English life. That, presumably, was why one of her great-grandfathers had come to this country from Belorussia, and why another grandfather had come here from Poland. There was in England, as well as much casual and unthought anti-semitism, a strain of real reverence for the Jews, based, ultimately, she supposed, on religion. (Her English mistress at school had told Rachel, when they were 'doing' *Paradise Lost*, that the author of the great English epic was theologically closer to Judaism than to Christianity and that he had sometimes attended the synagogue in Creechurch Lane.)

After this almost tearful exchange about the newsreel in 1945, Gordon became one of Rachel's special friends.

She had been living in Father Chell's vicarage for nearly a month.

Like everyone in England who read a newspaper, Rachel Pearl had grown up with an awareness of Vivyan Chell. Liberals of her parents' generation could remember his story. He had gone to Lugardia with the British Army, and after some form of religious conversion, he had become involved in the Zinariyan resistance movement. He had gone as a soldier and become a monk. Rachel's parents and their circle were not much minded to love either monks or soldiers. In his books and broadcasts, however, Father Vivyan had spoken very directly and educatively about the post-colonial situation. He seemed to have serious and interesting things to say about Africa – above all, about Africa standing on its own feet, and developing in its own way without having to ape the political and economic systems of Europe.

After he had joined his order of monks (and Rachel was so hazy about these things that she had always half supposed that he was a Roman Catholic), Chell had openly identified himself with the resistance fighters of Major (as he was then) Joshua Bindiga. That had been in the heady days when Bindiga had claimed to be in favour of Freedom for All.

For a while, Father Vivyan had been the only European in Zinariya who was able to retain the respect and confidence of all sides. The old whites hated him and regarded him as a traitor to their cause. But they also saw that he was a completely straight, honest figure, who had been an officer in the British Army, and that he would be useful to them, trying to retain a toehold of white influence in the newly formed all-African government. This was something which Chell resolutely refused to do. (Lennox Mark was the only white man cunning enough to 'buy' Bindiga.) Chell's influence in the newly formed African country was different from Mark's. Lennie was a wheeler-dealer. Chell was open, and candid. Lennie wheedled his way into positions of hidden power. Chell had authority because he appeared genuinely to want to renounce power. (After a month in his house, Rachel understood this better, feeling in Chell the contradictions of a man who wanted to follow a spiritual path of self-denial, but who was in fact heavily addicted to the exercise of personal influence.) Chell had also, in those early days in Zinariya, remained able to speak to the many Muslims in the country. Hitherto, the Christian missionaries had maintained a position of bigoted hostility to Islam. But when General Bindiga made his historic and very public conversion to Islam — with a display of a number of wives on the balcony of the Presidential Palace in Mararraba — Father Vivyan had preached a sermon at the Holy Redeemer church in which he told the congregation that the Muslims were cousins in faith, the sons and daughters of

Abraham. (Since occasionally attending his services in Crickleden, Rachel had heard him tell the congregation of the Shrine of Our Lady that the story of the Virgin Birth was to be found in the Qur'an as well as the Bible; Rachel found his religious beliefs puzzling, even repellent, but this did not stop her being under his spell.)

He had not been slow – she could remember Kitty talking of this, and Monty, Vivyan's brother had spoken of it during their kitchen chats at Throxton Winnards in happier days – to denounce Bindiga. As soon as Bindiga formed his shady connections with international business, and began to exploit the profits of the copper mines, Chell's condemnation had been loud and consistent. On visits to England, he had frequently tried to remind a largely indifferent British population of the horrors which Bindiga was perpetrating. He spoke of an opposition imprisoned or sent into exile, of journalists and university lecturers disappearing by night, of villages despoiled and whole populations massacred in rural areas. Chell – Uncle Viv, Kitty had called him – had been at times the lone voice denouncing these crimes. Monty used to say that it was a miracle that his brother had survived in Zinariya, without either being bumped off or sent into exile like the cranky Professor Galwanga.

Thus had Rachel Pearl heard of Vivyan Chell and of his doings. He had never, though, been to the forefront of her mind. It interested her that he was the uncle of her closest friend at Oxford – but, then, many things about Kitty had interested her.

Kitty's funeral had been a turning point. Rachel had found herself talking to the priest after the service. Some of the words he had spoken during his sermon had made no sense to Rachel (these had been the words about God). There had been, nevertheless, a powerful sense of *Kitty* in what he had said. He had not merely described his niece, he had in some strange way actually evoked her, summoned her up. Rachel had only been living in his house for a month, and she had already formed the impression that there existed a strong spiritual kinship between uncle and niece: that Kitty's waywardness and love of danger and insistence upon her own terms in life were all qualities which he had in abundance. It did not surprise Rachel to learn that Kitty had sometimes gone to kip down in sleeping bags in the south London vicarage and befriend tramps and vagrants. (Rachel had always known, and been puzzled by the fact, that Kitty retained her religious belief.)

So, when she decided that she needed to start a new life, Rachel had decided upon impulse to make her way down to Crickleden, not really knowing what she would find when she got there. She had not telephoned in advance to announce her arrival, or to ask permission to come and stay. She had simply turned up, with one overnight bag. The monk had been coming out of the front door into the rain as she turned into the drive. The shanty-town effect of bedraggled tents and grotty camper-vans was not exactly what she had expected. At the funeral, he had been wearing the semi-medieval garb of his religious order; the image it left in her mind was of French abbeys and cathedrals, visited on holidays with her parents, of pale Normandy sun streaming through lancet windows, of whitewashed aisles, of an indescribable sensation of peace. (These French churches gave her the closest to what she had imagined to be 'a religious experience'.) Father Chell in his robes, speaking of her dead friend in a medieval church, had summoned up such a world, and she had perhaps half supposed that the place in south London where he had described Kitty coming to stay from time to time was some kind of monastic establishment, breathing a similar orderliness and calm. The tall figure who came to greet her on his tarmac wore jeans and a jumper. The mess, and the noise, coming from the camper-vans, the young children running out into the rain, to be called back in raucous voices by Albanian women, the scuffed front door of the house, the packing-cases and the disorder had all seemed at first like an affront. She quickly came to feel that this, precisely, was what they were: though not an affront to herself but to the World on whom Vivyan Chell was waging war. Christ asked his followers to take up their weapons against the World, the Flesh and the Devil. It was in his defiance of the first of these enemies that Vivyan seemed so remarkably clear. It was much more than a bohemian rebellion against the supposed values of his own class. His household, with its floating population of 'hopeless cases', and its variety of somewhat earnest helpers (these included two rather terrified-seeming monks sent by the mother-house at Kelvedone), was making a statement about England. It was saying: 'These people – the asylum seekers, the homeless, the mentally ill, the lonely and the odd – what are you doing for them, oh glorious liberal democracy?'

Until coming to Crickleden, Rachel Pearl would have accounted herself 'right wing' in the political spectrum. That is, she distrusted any forms of 'political improvement'. She found the economic theories of Karl Marx entirely unconvincing; and those societies which had tried to put them into practice had created hells without historic parallel. Even those nations which had merely adopted milder forms of socialism than those advocated by Marx had created restrictions on individual liberty without, it seemed to Rachel Pearl, advancing either individual dignity or material prosperity. The disadvantages and cruelties of a society such as the United States where the Free Market was allowed to operate freely were obvious in terms of urban squalor, poverty, sickness. An economically free society was one where you had to arm the police. But this, it had always seemed to Rachel, was entirely preferable to any of the alternative methods of ordering society yet devised by the human race.

Almost as soon as she arrived in Crickleden, her perspective on these things radically altered. She did not become 'lefty' – the word she always used for collectivism. But she became an out-and-out sceptic about the values of a free society. She realized the simple and obvious fact: that when she had been forming all her political views, from the safety of her parents' house in Barnes, or from school or from Oxford, or from her office in the *Legion* or from her flat bought for her from L.P.'s expense account, she had done so from the perspective of someone with money. 'The world of the happy is quite another than that of the unhappy' was one of the phrases she liked to quote from the philosophers when she was an undergraduate. (Like 'if a lion could talk, we could not understand him', it was one of those phrases from Wittgenstein which made you sound deep if you said it, but which did not require any understanding of philosophy as such in order to grasp it.) It now seemed to her that his distinction between the worlds of the happy and the unhappy was a self-indulgent one. The crucial difference in the world was between those who did and did not possess money.

Rachel knew that by the standards of almost all human beings throughout history she was a person who was quite extraordinarily privileged. Except for a few self-imposed hardships when on holiday, or on school camps, she had hardly ever known a day when she had been hungry. Water supply, opportunities to drink safely and to wash adequately, and heat had always been available for her without her thinking about them.

Christ called his followers to sell all that they had and give to the poor; to deny themselves, to take up their crosses. These were words familiar to Rachel from her reading of literature. She had dipped into the Gospels, though she had never read one of them through. But she had never encountered a human being who had decided to live as if these injunctions were literally true. 'Blessed are the poor' . . . 'The poor have the gospel preached to them!' . . . These texts were crucial to Vivyan's vision of the world; dispossession was at the core of his spirituality. She realized after only a few days that her pampered, comfortable existence – not just hers, that of Western humanity itself – made her, us, strangely vulnerable; that to be dispossessed and to survive gave those who did it tremendous power. A few, a very few, such as Vivyan Chell did it deliberately. Most did it out of necessity. The boys in his house who had fled Zinariya, having been forced to work on cocoa and tobacco farms for no wages; the Irish vagrants; the Albanian refugees, had not made some grand anti-bourgeois gesture by possessing nothing. They were poor because they were poor, and they were not poor as the English working classes were poor – struggling to live in a council flat on the dole. That was poverty, all right, compared with what Rachel had been used to, but it was not the absolute poverty which so many of Vivyan's friends had encountered: real empty bellies; and in the case of the Africans and the Albanians, the experience of living without clean water or even on occasion without water at all.

'As having nothing, yet possessing all things' – these were the words which Vivyan used to murmur about *their* struggle.

She had begun to see the vicarage and its raggle-taggle encampments less as one eccentric clergyman's attempt to do something about the poor than as a paradigm of the world's agony and its future. What she saw was far from reassuring. She valued the order and the cleanliness of her upbringing; the quiet of her parents' house, the soothing possibilities of knowledge which it brought: time and space for reading, for playing the cello, for conversation. The world-disorder shadowed forth by Vivyan Chell's strange holy-pirate kingdom was one where seemliness and space were taken from us. It reminded her of the household in the film of *Dr Zhivago* after the revolution, when the formerly graceful interiors had simply been invaded and inhabited by those who needed a roof over their heads.

When she had arrived, Vivyan had expressed pleasure but no surprise.

'Hello! I'll put your bag in my room for the time being . . . nothing valuable in it, is there?'

She'd said no, because she did not want him to think her a rich airhead who had brought trinkets into such a place. In fact, she had hidden a watch in some rolled-up tights. It was not an especially valuable watch – it cost about five hundred pounds. L.P. had given it to her. By the time Vivyan had finished showing her round the house, the church, the garden, the watch had disappeared. It was her first lesson in communal living and she had said nothing about it.

He had taken her almost at once to the church, told her the story of the medieval shrine, told her about Bishop Guiseley and his order of monks, walked her up and down the aisles.

'Make free of this place,' he had said in his drawly voice. 'It's not for you at the moment – you probably feel it will never be for you. Fine. But don't feel excluded. Come to mass sometimes to see what we're up to. Stay away if you can't stand it. This is my centre of operations. It's the engine room. Plenty of people can sail the ocean without once visiting the ship's engine room, but if you're interested, this is it.'

That was all he'd said about religion, though from time to time he responded to her questions on the subject, not by direct speech but by thrusting a book into her hand. He'd lent her

Bonhoeffer's *Ethik*, which she had half admired, having heard the story of its author, and Simone Weil's *Waiting on God*, which she had liked less.

On that first day, she had been given a quick tour of the house; it was how she imagined a subaltern would be briefed by the major when he joined a new company. 'Refectory – there's a rota for washing-up, cooking and so forth.'

She quickly became aware of his routine. Up betimes. Showered and shaved by six, but after hours of prayer and meditation in the dark. A bowl of porridge taken at the long refectory table with the tramps was washed down by a cup of black coffee. If he had time, he would come in at twelve when a simple lunch was on offer, sometimes helping to dole out the bread and soup to those who attended it. (Most of the campers came to this meal, as did many of the crowds who drifted in and out of the house all day.) The evening meal was served at seven, after the mass. It consisted of good NAAFI food, toad in the hole with onion gravy; liver and bacon; sausages with mash. There was always a pudding, often a suet pudding, and there were large metal jugs of custard. Tea was drunk with this meal.

Throughout the day, Father Chell was available to people. She was not aware of him having any time to himself, apart from the wakeful hours of meditation in the dark, when he sat up on his deckchair. Even then, though he was communicating with his mysterious God in whom Rachel did not believe, he was not necessarily alone, since figures like the peculiar and rather sinister boy, Tuli, would often spend the night in the room, lying on the floor beside the chair. She had even slept the night there herself once during one of the sessions when he had allowed her, or encouraged her, to pour out her heart.

The first time she had begun to confide in Vivyan, she found herself unable to stop. Everything came out, as if she were undergoing therapy, which in a way she was. Apart from the loss of her friend, and her grief, and her agonizing wish to have seen more of Kitty than she had done in the last years, Rachel felt that this death was a terrible lesson.

'I thought, okay, it would be fun to work on a newspaper, and not many people my age are given that degree of responsibility, or, frankly, that much money. So of course I took the job, thinking it would be fun for a bit, but always, at the back of my mind, this thought . . . that one day I would do something . . . serious.'

She told him of her affair with L.P., which had led to her getting the job. Her attitude to this had been a life-choice of a comparable kind: it was not something which she intended to do for the rest of her life . . . No, that was too cynical. She had been in love with L.P. She still was in love with him – if crying when you think about someone is being in love. But she had now seen through their relationship. She had seen how utterly unfair it was to Julia. She had seen the tawdriness of it, the shallowness of her job, her love affair, her life.

'Then Kitty died, and, I know this sounds so egotistical, but I said to myself, my God, Rachel, what if it was you lying there in that coffin? What if you were the one who was dead, and all you had to show for nearly twenty-eight years of life was work on a newspaper you despised, and a love affair with someone who was married to someone else and who had been lying to you both?'

Sometimes, during this first outpouring, Vivyan would say something. In his drawly old officer's voice he would interrupt, 'It isn't egotistical – or not in a bad sense; to lead a good life one must examine oneself. That's Socrates.' Such remarks were spoken in an almost detached vein. His hooded old eyes were half closed, as if he were praying even as he spoke. And he spoke to clarify. It was half like having your fortune told, half like a philosophy tutorial.

He never made false excuses when she said she was guilty. He did not coo. He never by so much as a syllable spoke as if he approved either of adultery or journalism. She was strengthened by his silences, his acknowledgement that wrong had been done, that her life needed to be redirected.

After that first session, he had suddenly decided that she had talked enough. He leaned forward and put his hands on her shoulders. All subsequent sharing-sessions had been much shorter – twenty minutes or half an hour. Then he would bring them to an end by squeezing her shoulders or shaking her gently, or by saying, 'But – hey! You're young. There's work to do!'

'Hey – you!'

She teased him after a few weeks by saying that this should be the title of his memoirs, he said the words so often to different people throughout the day.

When it became apparent to her that he was listening to comparable outpourings of guilt, sorrow, sadness, puzzlement for almost all his waking hours, Rachel decided to limit the time she spent talking to him about herself. She willingly settled down into the life of the household, sleeping in a kind of girls' dormitory in a sleeping bag on the floor, and helping with the domestic chores. She undertook all the visiting which Vivyan or one of his assistants assigned to her. There was old Gordon. There was a Pakistani family whom she saw every other day. Neither the grandmother nor, shockingly, the mother, who was only aged about forty, knew any English at all. Rachel's task was to decipher DHSS forms for them, to accompany them to the doctor's surgery and act as a sort of interpreter, though the notes they wrote for her in Urdu were completely incomprehensible. She also helped to fetch the daughters of this family, three girls between six and twelve, from school. It was her ambition to teach the entire family English. The mother and grandmother, sitting in their saris and thick cardigans in a crammed terraced house, were effectively in purdah and never went out. Rachel tried to tell them about her own family, her great-grandparents and grandparents coming from far away, and becoming assimilated into London life because they spoke English. These concepts seemed frightening to the women; the grandmother was positively hostile to the notion of learning proper English, though the mother of the children clearly wanted to do so.

Only a month had passed since she left the *Legion* but already it had faded; in her head it was an old photograph exposed to sunlight. But now something had happened which threatened to reawaken all the old demons of the *Legion* world. When she had finished helping Gordon put on his bedroom slippers, and when she had propped him in front of the television and helped him eat his Meal on Wheels, she had an appointment to meet a Mrs d'Abo, a West Indian nurse who lived in the flat below Gordon's.

Vivyan had asked her to call on this woman, whom she had often seen in the vicarage. It was evident that something very serious was afoot. His manner was both shifty and pleading with her.

'I'd so much like you to go and speak to Lily d'Abo – you know about the world of newspapers. There's something very painful about to happen . . .'

'What?'

'I'll tell you about it this evening.'

That was all he had said. He had apparently already made an appointment for Rachel to call on Lily d'Abo. She did not know what it was that the woman wanted to discuss with her, but it was ominous that the newspaper past was being mentioned. So it was that as she helped the old man with his shoes and listened to his war memories, Rachel was conscious of a sudden ray of happiness in her heart; but knew it as a burst of sunshine only, before the clouds once more darkened the sky.

TWELVE

Mercy had decided that the braided golden hair had been that little bit over the top. At her next visit to Afro-Styles she had the whole elaborate artifice unwound. The gilded extensions were restored to their skein on a hook. She had her hair blackened once more, and straightened. She wore a V-necked black jumper which showed plenty of bust, and a black and white checked skirt, with knee-length boots.

Unlike her mother, who was used to walking boldly in and out of the front door of the vicarage, Mercy felt shy in approaching the priest's house. Memory of former intimacies with Father Vivyan combined with a natural diffidence when dealing with the clergy. Today was different. Today was much, much worse. Today was hell.

She did not know how she was going to approach him, or what she was going to say. The nightmare of what was beginning to unfold at home was so terrible, so bizarre, that she had been slow to admit at first that it was happening. She realized now that she had been burying her head in the sand for months, even for years. Peter was a sick boy, a lad who needed help, and neither she nor Trevor had been in a position where they could see quite how bad things had become. It was easier to take each problem as it arose – this little incident at school, that moment when the police had complained.

Mercy now saw that it was all part of one big nightmare – the schools which had suspended Peter, or accused him of theft, or arson, or disruptive behaviour; the troubles at home, with Lucius and Brad and Trevor; the terrible death of old Mr Hacklewit . . . Mercy had tried to take each of these problems as quite isolated moments. She had tried to see them as having no connection. She had tried to believe that schools, policemen, members of the public all shared Trevor's perverse desire to *pick on* the boy.

This latest thing, though, was something else.

She had been furious with her mother when Lily told her over the telephone. Absolutely furious. 'Mum, you had no right to keep that from me.'

'I didn't keep it from you. He told me 'cause he didn't want to talk 'bout things like that in front of his brothers. I don't blame him. It's a terrible shock for me . . . after all I thought of Father Vivyan.'

'It's a shock for YOU! Mum! How do you think I feel?'

'When *The Daily Legion* rang me up I nearly fell off my chair. I said, "Father Vivyan's a good man, a holy man." "What," they say, "you mean, Peter's not told you yet?" "Told me what?"'

'Mum,' Mercy had yelled, 'you realize those people are evil, they're out for a story, they don't care about the truth.'

'Listen, I'm telling you. This was *The Daily Legion* who rang me.'

Her mother could hardly have been more impressed if she'd been telephoned by the Archangel Gabriel. She was naive. She liked to pretend that she was a woman of the world, and to say that there was not much a nurse did not know. This, Mercy had long realized, was rubbish. Lily might be physically unsqueamish. Whereas most of us would faint rather than administer a bedbath or an enema, Lily could look upon the human body without embarrassment. But this did not mean that she was anything more than a child when it came to under-standing grown-up relations. She had made a saint out of Father

Vivyan. At every meal Mercy had shared with her mother since the monk returned to England, she had had to sit there and listen to Lily telling her about Father Vivyan: how he'd started a fund to help the mineworkers in Zinariya, how he stayed up all night praying; what he'd said in this sermon or that; how he'd been on telly, demonstrating about the situation in Africa. Mercy was prepared to believe that Father Vivyan was a good man – a bloody sight better man than most of the clergy who just talked about doing good and never did anything. But she did know some of his flaws. She had no idea whether he'd given up his peccadilloes and settled down into a celibate old age, but she had a clear enough memory of her encounter with him during the parish retreat seventeen years ago to know his true character. She'd seen that look in his eye since – when she met him again. He was a randy old goat. He might also be a holy man and a man who cared passionately about his fellow humans, but he was a randy man – who loved women. Of that there could be no doubt. She had the strongest and surest sense of these things.

That was why the things her mother started to say about *The Daily Legion*, and Peter, and Father Vivyan were so absurd. In fact when Lily had first said them, Mercy had just burst out laughing.

'I suppose you think it's funny – your own son, being abused . . . *The Daily Legion* said Father's had a history of it. That's why they expelled him from Africa . . .'

Lily had been full of it. As a nurse, she had already appointed herself as the expert on her grandson's troubles. The evidence all pointed, she knew now, to sexual abuse. The boy's decision to retreat into a dream world; the apparent changes of personality. These were all symptoms of a very wounded person, who had been hurt in a very specific way . . .

'Who've you been talking to, Mum?'

'I don't need to talk to anyone. I can read, you know.'

Never, never had Mercy been angrier with her mother. Even if this grotesque story had been true, who was it who nagged them all to go to church day in, day out? Peter had been a churchgoer for most of his sixteen years, but it was only since living part-time with his grandmother that he had become an altar-server, and started hanging around at Father Vivyan's house.

Peter had not been living with Lily for some weeks now. Since he'd turn sixteen in the late summer, he no longer bothered to attend school, and there was a place for him in the maisonette in Streatham. Mercy had told herself that since he got the job in a restaurant 'up West' he had been so much better.

Now, she wondered quite what he had been up to in all the months that he had supposedly been living with Lily, and keeping out of Trevor's way. Lily, it seemed, had often not been there. She had worked nights at the hospital; she had allowed the boy to stay overnight at the vicarage, because she was so sure that he would be 'safe with Father Vivyan'. Now there was this ridiculous story about Father Vivyan being an abuser of young boys.

Mercy was coming to the vicarage to discuss the way forward. She entered the porch, shook her transparent plastic umbrella and stepped gingerly into the untidy hallway. A young monk approached her and asked if she was lost.

'I'm looking for Father Vivyan.'

'Ah, Mercy . . .'

He appeared at the top of his staircase.

'Step up here, if you would, Father Aidan. Could you bring Mercy with you?'

The younger monk, who was dressed in the full rig, the fancy dress which Vivyan had been wearing on the day of their memorable tryst seventeen years before, led the way into the large upstairs room where Father Chell lived. Her eyes took in the large table by the window, covered with letters, papers and paperback books. A few camp-beds littered the room – they had been put up at angles to one another and there was nothing orderly about them. A large figure of Jesus on the Cross hung on the wall at one end. Father Chell gestured to one folding deckchair and he himself sat down on another.

'The thing is,' she said, looking at Father Aidan, 'it's rather private.'

'I've asked Father Aidan to stay with us at all times, Mercy. I think you know why.'

She realized to her embarrassment and to her extreme surprise that he was angry.

'Vivyan – I've got to talk to you alone.'

'I'm not going to be tricked twice,' said the priest curtly.

'Tricked?'

'Presumably you have a recording device about your person now.'

'Do I look as if I have?'

She had taken off her PVC mac. Her jumper was tight, her skirt was tight.

He smiled sheepishly. She could see him enjoying the sight. She watched his eyes straying towards her breasts and feasting on the sight of her nipples which showed through bra and jumper. She thought what a handsome man he was.

'Well, what I have to say is very embarrassing,' she said, 'and I'd rather I said it to you alone.'

'Father Aidan, I'm asking you to stay,' said Vivyan.

The blushing young monk looked from one of them to the other; but like an obedient junior he did what Vivyan told him and stayed put.

'Look, Vivyan, *The Daily Legion* has been ringing up my mother with—'

'*The Daily Legion*, who presumably paid you a lot of money for a tape-recording of our last conversation,' said Vivyan curtly.

There was silence between them. It felt like an hour, though it was probably only half a minute.

'What did you say?' asked Mercy.

'I said, the newspaper presumably paid you to record our last conversation together. They telephoned me some days ago to ask whether I recalled saying to anyone the following words – "If I've done something to you to hurt you, I am deeply sorry." Words to that effect. They were the words I used to you when we last spoke. In private – or as I stupidly thought . . .'

'What are you saying?'

'You know what I am saying. I am saying that the newspaper telephoned me with what amounted to a blackmail. They asked if I intended to deny saying those words to, as they put it, "a certain person". They then added that they did not suppose – I'm sorry, Father Aidan, but you must stay and hear this – they then added that they assumed I would not deny that I had been intimate with the person to whom I said those words. I hung up on them. I have considered approaching the police, and I have consulted a lawyer. Mercy, Mercy . . .'

'Vivyan. Listen to me. The newspaper has rung up my mother. A woman there has told my mother that . . . I don't know how to say this to you . . .'

'I don't think it is funny. You, evidently, do.'

'I'm not laughing because it's funny. It's bloody TRAGIC.' But she was smiling. 'And it is also funny, come to think. My mother thinks they are accusing you of being a . . . well, of being GAY.'

The young monk looked at his shoes and blushed scarlet.

'How do you work that out?' asked Vivyan.

'Look, I don't know how they managed to record our last conversation. Maybe this room is bugged, who knows? But if you think I'd . . . Oh, how *could* you think I'd do a mean trick like that? That makes me really, really angry, you know, Vivyan! I came here to warn you, to help you, to see what we can all do about Peter.'

'About Peter? What does he have to do with it?'

'Just about everything, I think. Look, let's get out of this room if it's bugged. Let's go for a walk in the rain. You and I have some talking to do, Vivyan, we do, really.'

THIRTEEN

Brad, who was twelve, had been doing well at school, but Peter persuaded him it would be better to take the morning off. The school sucked, Peter could tell them. He'd been there once. Little Lucius had resisted their half-brother's desire that they should both skive off. So it was only Brad who came with Peter. He took his half-brother on top of a bus, and they rode out of Crickleden together through the driving rain into the new world, the cool world which Peter had persuaded Brad was waiting for him if he'd only leave that fucking school of his. Forget 'bout lessons. Who needs fucking teachers, man — did Brad not know they were all ignorant perverts? Shits? Fucking pervert shits who deserved having their dicks cut off and stuffed down their throats?

No, Peter had averred in an altogether more suave tone — so posh, Brad had laughed and thought it was like an act — no, he would teach Bradley all that was necessary. The younger boy and the older boy sat together at the front of the bus. Brad imitated the way that his brother — he was proud to call Peter his brother — pushed his large Reeboks up against the front window, treating the bus seat as if it were some exercise device at the gym. When the conductor came round for the fares, he'd asked for Peter's proof that he was entitled to travel as a child. Peter had raised two fingers. The conductor guy had asked if Peter wanted to be thrown off the bus. And Peter, like, asked who was throwing who off the fucking bus, 'cause if anyone threw anyone, it wasn't going to be some ponce from fucking Jamaica throwing *him*, and the conductor had said he wasn't from Jamaica, and that if they did not pay the fare, he'd throw them off the bus. Peter had then paid, and they'd both giggled and Brad had been proud to say, 'Wicked' as the conductor went round collecting fares from all the other nerds.

When they were alone together on top of the bus – as they were passing through Bermondsey – Peter asked if Brad knew how to fire a Tokarev.

Bradley did not know what a Tokarev was.

'Semi-automatic,' said Peter. 'Lovely little shooter. Used them in the Red Army. Very handy in Yugoslavia for shooting Croat cunts.'

Very slowly, and with the full knowledge of all the excitement he was creating, Peter had then unzipped the front of his hooded sweatshirt and revealed the little Chinese pistol.

'Neat?'

He laughed.

'Where you get that?' Bradley had asked, wide-eyed.

'Two hundred quid, not bad.'

'Two hundred?'

'It was nothing, nigga. You think that's a lot of dough, two hundred? One little watch, that's all I had to steal, one little watch off a yid. She'd wrapped it in her knickers, stupid cunt. I took it out her knickers then shoved something else in – know whadda mean?'

'You got two hundred pounds for a watch?'

'I swapped it, didn't I?'

That was the end of that. The exact processes by which he had managed to exchange a stolen watch for a pistol were either too arcane or too tedious to be entered into with so young a boy as Bradley.

'Like to learn how to use it?' Peter asked.

His half-brother looked at him with a flicker of fear, but a smile of adoration.

'You betcha.'

FOURTEEN

'Are you the lady who interviewed my grandson?'

'I haven't met your grandson.'

'Peter.'

'I haven't met Peter.'

'But you are from *The Daily Legion*? Father Vivyan promised me he'd send on the lady from *The Daily Legion*.'

'I used to work for *The Daily Legion*.'

'Do you know L. P. Watson?'

Rachel Pearl blushed at this directness. For an absurd moment she wondered whether Mrs d'Abo knew what she was asking.

'It's one big open-plan office. You meet them all.'

'Even Peg Montgomery?'

'Even Peg Montgomery.'

'She's wonderful, isn't she?'

This was one way of putting it.

'Her interviews are so' – Mrs d'Abo paused for the right word – 'sympathetic.'

'Mrs d'Abo, I think we're at cross-purposes. I used to work for *The Daily Legion*. I was arts editor.'

'What's that?'

'I organized the reviews mainly – the reviews of films? Plays?'

Rachel felt herself smiling with condescension as though her perfectly intelligent interlocutor might not know what these were.

'I never read those pages,' said Lily d'Abo, evidently not one to indulge in false flattery. 'Sorry about that.'

'No need to be. I don't do the job any more.'

'What have they put you on to then? Reporter, is it?'

'No – no, I've left my job at the paper. I'm not in journalism any more. I've come to live at the vicarage for a while till I've got myself sorted out . . . It's just that Father Vivyan – I don't know quite what's happened, but he seemed to think I might be able to help you. Let me get this straight. The newspaper rang him up and made a number of frankly ridiculous suggestions about him and your grandson . . .'

'Who's saying they are ridiculous?' asked Lily sharply.

'Oh, come on, Mrs d'Abo – Father Vivyan . . .'

'Haven't you been reading these stories day after day in *The Daily Legion*? Priests who had been trusted by their people, by their *faithful* people . . .'

'Yes, but Mrs d'Abo, you know Father Vivyan . . .'

'I feel betrayed,' said Lily calmly, but with very stiff lips. 'It is a terrible betrayal, not just of Peter, not just of the boy, but of all of us, of the whole church, that he could behave like that. A man in his position.'

'Yes, but Mrs d'Abo . . .'

'Miss . . .'

'Pearl. You can call me Rachel.'

'Miss Pearl, I have heard what he said to my boy. The paper concealed a tape-recorder on Peter . . .'

'You think that was a nice thing to do?'

'They concealed a tape-recorder. They have the facts. They have it on the tapes – what he said to that boy. He said he was very, very sorry that he had done wrong to him, and he prayed for Peter's forgiveness. Then there is Peter saying he hopes it doesn't make him a homosexual. Miss Pearl . . .'

'Mrs d'Abo, I . . .'

'I'm a nurse. I've read the textbooks. Do you think I haven't worried myself sick about that boy night and day for years? For years he has shown signs of being – strange . . .'

'It doesn't matter being gay, you know.'

When she heard herself saying this, Rachel realized that she sounded pert, metropolitan, chic; she hated herself for her tone.

'I'm not talking about gay. I'm talking about being mentally disturbed. Peter wasn't like other children. Quite early on, we saw the danger signals but we did not do anything about them, because we could not face up to the consequences. He heard voices, he saw visions. He was usually very charming, and of course when he was the centre of all our attentions, that was fine. But once his mother married Trevor, the trouble began. And when the other boys were born . . . They picked on Peter and they made him worse, and he developed, you know, all kinds of big behavioural problems. I don't want to go into it all with you. But to exploit a boy like that, a vulnerable boy . . . Father Vivyan knew he was vulnerable. I have told him so much about Peter. Tuli, he calls him – it's some African word, it means Legion – because we are many. You know?'

'I don't, I'm afraid . . .'

'It's a story in the Bible,' said Lily, patiently, but with evident scorn. 'You don't know the Bible? About Jesus? It's a story in the Gospel. Jesus comes upon a poor lunatic among the tombs, cutting himself and crying aloud. And when Jesus asks him his name, he replies, "My name is Legion, because we are many." I thought Father Vivyan gave Peter that name because he understood, because he sympathized, because he wanted to help, and all the while, he really just wanted—'

'Mrs d'Abo, think about it. You know what sort of a man Father Vivyan is. He is a good man, a transparently good person.

If you think the same can be said of the people at the *Legion*, then you are very, very wrong.'

'You worked there.'

'I left there. Mrs d'Abo, don't get mixed up with them. Whatever has happened, it won't be made better by getting mixed up with journalists. Whatever is true, they will twist it into a falsehood. They'll pretend they want to help you, but all they want is a story. Please.'

'It's all right for you. You're rich,' said Mrs d'Abo.

This much was true. Rachel had realized already that this otherwise reasonable, if troubled and mistaken person had been sucked into the *Legion* honeypot.

FIFTEEN

Mercy and Vivyan were walking in the rain. She had tried to put up her umbrella but the wind was too strong and in any case it made conversation impossible. She had a headscarf tied over her new hairdo, and the PVC mac, though short and tight, kept out some of the rain. Vivyan wore his long black monk's cloak over his jeans, and when the downpour became heavy, he drew the hood over his head, giving him the appearance of something in *Lord of the Rings*, as they walked up the gradual incline of St Mary's Road, past the Roman Catholic primary school (St John Bosco), past the Hindu temple and the cemetery to the gates of Furbelow Park. The children's playground was empty. The deluge splattered sandpit and swings. Beyond it, a few budgies and canaries screeched their dismay from the pathetic little aviary. Mercy and Vivyan made for the covered bandstand at the brow of the hill, walking in silence, until they reached the spot.

The bandstand was strewn with pigeon shit, chip papers, condoms, used needles. Various cave artists had, with spray or brush, left their messages for posterity on the concrete walls, some in mysterious scripts which would puzzle the palaeographers of a future age; others, in versions of the common orthography, had put on record that CHARMAINE GIVES HEAD, and that WAYNE FUCKS. Still others, with Beckettian brevity, had conveyed their message by single words – SHIT, WANK, NIGGERS, NF. It was a sad place for a conversation, though in her girlhood Mercy could remember coming here for

surreptitious moments of romance, punctuated by no less surreptitious intakes of nicotine. From afar, beyond the neglected
graves of ten thousand forgotten south Londoners, could be
glimpsed the high-rise blocks of Catford on the one side and the
endless streets of Bromley on the other. These, punctuated here
by railway track, there by spires and towers, could look almost
cheering in sunshine. Today they suggested a limitless waste of
life, a humanity which stretched sadly as far as the eye could see,
indulging in its youth in the activities which so obsessed the
graffiti-artists in the bandstand; scurrying, in middle age, to the
bus stops and railway stations which, even in the heavy rain, the
eye could discern, to go to work in London, to pay for the mean
residences which stretched in endless terraces; lying, eventually,
in the cemetery whose identical headstones made their cruel
commentary on the rows of houses of those who were buried
there.

'I'm going to tell Mum about us,' said Mercy.

'Mercy, what would be the point? It would just make things
even more painful.'

'Don't you see, it's all been the most terrible mistake.
Peter's . . . Peter's, well – you know what he's like. You gave
him that nickname, but actually it isn't funny.'

'I never thought it was funny. But . . .'

'If I don't tell Mum . . . about us . . . about you . . . and what
I know about you, she's going to carry on thinking that you
are . . .'

'I don't care what people think,' he said, looking away from
her.

'Oh, yes you do!' she shouted back at him. 'You care passionately. You know what I think, Vivyan? I think you care so
bloody much that you'd rather they suspected you were a child
molester than that they knew the truth – that you were a randy

old goat who just LOVED sex . . . You've got such an idea of
yourself as a saint, as a monk, as a holy man who can put the
world to rights, and you can't bear the truth about yourself.
You can't bear being human . . .'

'I deserve that,' he said with a smile. 'I'm sorry I accused
you of having a tape-recorder stuck to your . . .'

He turned and looked at her. Behind her, rain lashed across
the park. Her lips were slightly parted to reveal her gap-teeth.
The lips were moist with purplish-red gloss. Her throat was
bare, her chest was half-bare, and her large breasts quivered
beneath her jumper.

'Oh, Vivyan . . .'

'I don't think that would solve anything.'

He said this to the top of her head. She had somehow come
very close to him, and was holding him tightly. He wound his
huge rain-sodden cloak around her.

Much later she said, 'We've got to tell Mum that Peter is
our son.'

SIXTEEN

Several weeks had passed. It was the time of the evening mass at the Shrine of Our Lady of Crickleden. Rachel Pearl sat on a chair at the back of the church. She sat in the main body of the church. The mass was being held in the shrine chapel which was on the left-hand side of the church. She preferred it, when she attended these evening rites (as she more and more did), not to sit too close to the other worshippers, nor to take any active part by kneeling or standing or saying the prayers.

A little bell rang, and Vivyan entered, with a server, from the robing room or sacristy, which was to the right of the high altar. She watched the pair cross the church. Outside, Vivyan strode with wide, swift paces. In church, he shuffled slowly, and tonight for some reason she had the macabre thought that this was the unwilling footstep of a man who was ascending the scaffold for his own execution. The server was Peter d'Abo, the boy who had caused all the trouble.

In the ensuing weeks, the trouble had got even worse. Peter's mother and his grandmother had had some devastating quarrel. The parish gossips did their best to supply the details of this terrible dispute, but no one was as yet privy to the details. This was because Mercy had left the parish — returned to her husband and other two sons in Streatham — and Lily had not been near the church since the rumours began. There was talk of Father Vivyan being accused of improper conduct with boys, with women, with men, with all three.

So far, from the *Legion*, there had been an ominous silence, but one development had filled Rachel with foreboding. She had two or three times glimpsed Sinclo Manners in the parish. She had managed to hide, or avoid him on two of these occasions, but on another, with studied casualness, he had come up to her – in the very drive of the vicarage – and asked her how she was.

She had replied that she was well. It would have been more accurate to say that she was emotionally exhausted. Since this trouble over the boy had erupted, Vivyan had been distracted, and there was an atmosphere of great tension and sadness in the house. Vivyan's temper was short and he had several times snapped at her when she had tried to say something helpful or sympathetic. The truthful answer to Sinclo's question was that she was very, very definitely not the better for seeing him. She knew that his presence could only mean that the *Legion* was still pursuing Vivyan.

'Couldn't you think of something better to do?' she had asked harshly.

'I wondered if you'd . . .'

He had stared at her like the goof that he was.

'Maybe you'd like a drink.'

'It's half past ten in the morning. I'm about to go and teach people some English . . .'

'Excellent.'

'How would you know?'

'I mean . . . um . . . Look, Rachel. I've been missing you.'

'You haven't come all this way to tell me that.'

'I have actually.'

'Sorry, Sinclo, I'm busy.'

And she had left him standing there. If there was anything worse than his coming to snoop round the place for Diary stories about Vivyan to put into Worledge's putrid *Legion*, it was his coming over sentimental.

Vivyan and the altar-boy, who were both robed for the part, had begun to say the words of the mass together, and the people were joining in.

'*Father eternal, giver of light and grace, we have sinned against you and against our neighbour, in what we have thought, in what we have said and done, through ignorance, through weakness, through our own deliberate fault. We have wounded your love and marred your image in us. We are sorry and ashamed . . .*'

Rachel was sorry and ashamed, very, for the way she had lived life since university. She was as yet completely unable to see why invoking a supernatural being – either Jesus, or some Bronze Age deity worshipped by her Jewish forebears – could have any bearing on ethics. She had watched the women of the parish before the mass queuing up to confess their sins personally to Vivyan. Presumably they came out of the confessional box convinced that God, or Jesus, had cleansed them of their sins, removed their responsibility for their own actions. She very much disliked this idea. It seemed to her a corrupting one.

Since running away from L.P. and coming to live in Crickleden, she had certainly formed the resolution to lead a better life. She wanted in the weeks or months she spent there to discover the possibilities of a new dignity, a new virtue; to find a life which would bear examination in the Socratic sense of the word. She very much did not want to pretend that she was not responsible for her own actions; nor did she believe that any process of ritual cleansing, or merely saying that she was sorry, would absolve her of responsibility for what had passed. In any event, it was not the supposed offence to God which mattered in what she had done: it was primarily a sin against herself. The years had coarsened her, and she had allowed them to do so.

Then again, by allowing the affair with L.P. to go on so long, she had contributed to the corruption of *him*, and she had added to the miseries of his wife, even if Julia did not know about 'them'. Now that Julia did know about the affair, and about all the others, there was no point in expecting God to take away that woman's dreadful sense of anguish and betrayal.

If Vivyan had not been so distracted in recent weeks, she would have liked to discuss these matters with him. She found a strange contrast between his public *Ethik* and the words of his church's liturgy. Bonhoeffer, whom he seemed to hero-worship, had struggled in his book with the practicalities of how to live out the Gospel in the world. It had led him to the belief that 'pacifism' in Nazi Germany was tantamount to allowing the evil of Nazism to persist. Bonhoeffer was eventually to join those who plotted to assassinate Hitler. He was hanged with piano wire by those who found out. 'Not many professors of theology have been hanged,' Vivyan liked to say. He had heavily scored, in his copy of Bonhoeffer's book, that passage where he wrote, 'If it is responsible action, if it is action which is concerned solely and entirely with the other man, if it arises from selfless love for the real man who is our brother, then, precisely because this is so, it cannot wish to shun the fellowship of human guilt.' Humanity, by its very imperfection, is bound, in its pursuit of good ends, to do things which are not in themselves wholly good – such as shooting a man who happens to be Hitler. Bonhoeffer quoted one of Rachel's favourite plays, where Goethe's Iphigenia is the prig and Pylades is trying to persuade her that 'An over-strict demand is secret pride'. In the temple, she can keep her purity, but outside 'life teaches us to be less strict with ourselves and others'.

This bold readiness to cut corners, not to be precious, in the furtherance of a public good seemed to lie at the heart of

Vivyan's political stance. Rachel did not have any doubt that this so-called 'scandal' attaching to his name had to do with this. She found it completely impossible to believe that he had any sexual life at all. Surely it was all channelled into his work, his mission?

One of the congregation was now reading the lesson, a passage from the Christian Bible. *Bear one another's burdens, and so fulfil the law of Christ.*

These words encapsulated why Rachel found Vivyan Chell such a fascinating man. She could not conceive of what it would be like to share his religious beliefs; and yet his preternatural sympathy for others, his evident willingness to give his whole life to others, to bear their burdens with them and, where possible, for them, these indubitably good qualities were inseparable from the religion. They could not be faked up, and she had begun to feel that somehow they were different from the ideals of personal integrity to which her own humanism aspired.

They were all standing up now and Vivyan was reading the Gospel.

'*And they arrived at the country of the Gadarenes, which is over against Galilee.*

'*And when he went forth to land, there met him out of the city a certain man, which had devils a long time, and ware no clothes, neither abode in any house, but in the tombs.*

'*When he saw Jesus, he cried out, and fell down before him, and with a loud voice said, What have I to do with thee, Jesus, thou Son of the Most high? I beseech thee, torment me not . . .*'

From where she sat in the church, Rachel only had a sideways view of what was going on. She could see Vivyan at the lectern, but she could not see everyone else in the shrine chapel, and at first she thought some strange echo was occurring. The echo said, 'Torment me not, torment me not, me, me' in Vivyan's own voice.

But it was being interrupted by another quite different voice, which cried out, 'Priest! Priest! I'm full of sin! Priest, make me clean, man!'

This voice, which sounded not unlike Louis Armstrong, was interrupted by a frightened little boy saying, 'Leave me alone, Trevor, leave me . . . Don't make me!'

'Priest, cleanse, man, cleanse!'

In spite of this heckling, Vivyan continued to read the Gospel story in his drawly, but authoritative voice. He had come to the moment in the story when the demons inside the lunatic begged Jesus to expel them from the man and send them into a herd of pigs which then cascade down the hill into the lake. The story ended with fear. *The whole multitude of the country of the Gadarenes round about besought him to depart from them, for they were taken with great fear.*

Rachel was still unable to see where the hecklers were.

Vivyan at the altar was holding aloft a little silver dish with a wafer on it. He was saying, '*Blessed are you, Lord God of all creation, through your goodness we have this bread to offer . . .*'

'Fuck you, priest! Fuck, fuck!'

'*. . . which earth has given and human hands have made. It will become for us . . .*'

'Don't make me, Trevor.'

'Fuck you!'

'*. . . the Bread of Life.*'

She could now see that the altar-server, Peter d'Abo, instead of helping the priest to prepare the bread and wine for the mass, was standing in front of the altar and performing a grotesque parody of his actions, pretending to lift up an imaginary paten and an invisible chalice. The voices were all coming from the boy.

In the middle of his praying and preparations, Vivyan suddenly stopped.

He came round the altar to where the boy was prancing about and said, 'Tuli!'

The boy laughed. It was a high-pitched laughter rising to an eerie screech which filled the church, almost making one suppose that a bat or some variety of bird was flapping its way into the high rafters, and round the crucified figure on the rood screen.

Vivyan placed his hands on the boy, who was beginning to shake with convulsions.

'Tuli, dear child.'

'Don't touch me.'

'Tuli.'

'Priest, forgive.'

'Tuli. Peter. Do not be frightened. May Almighty God bless you.'

The scream which followed these words was even louder than the first.

'May God, Father, Son and Holy Spirit, bless you. May Our Lady pray for you and strengthen you. May your holy Guardian Angel protect you. And once again, my dear child, may Almighty God bless you, the Father, Son, the Holy Spirit.'

The banshee-shriek had echoed and faded. The whole building became extraordinarily still and quiet. The rain continued to whir and patter on the church roof. Outside could be heard an ambulance siren, perhaps a police car wailing. Buses and cars continued to change gear at the corner of the old clock at the top of the High Road. So, it could not be said that there was absolute silence. But a palpable stillness had descended, a beautiful calm which had embraced them all. Rachel found herself thinking that the calm and stillness around Vivyan had the cold purity and limpidity of a mountain rock pool.

The altar-boy had crumpled to the floor.

Vivyan continued with the mass. He left the boy where he was on the carpet in front of the altar as he consecrated and distributed the holy bread and wine. When the rite was over, and fifty or so people had trooped up to receive Communion, Vivyan briskly brought things to a conclusion. Only when the last prayer had been said did he turn to the congregation and say, 'Could two of you give me a hand?'

Two people, a man and a woman, stepped forward to lift the inert boy on to a pew. He seemed to have passed into a trance.

'If we could get an ambulance,' said Vivyan, 'just to be on the safe side. I think he is going to be all right.'

At his side, there now appeared two young men whom no one remembered seeing in the church before.

'Mr Vivyan Chell?'

'I'm Father Chell, yes. You're not paramedics? We have a sick boy here.'

'Can we have a word with you, sir?'

'Of course. What about?'

'You might prefer it to be a word in private, sir. We are police officers.'

'Here is as good a place as any for a word.' Vivyan made a sweeping gesture round the church. 'We can sit here, or you can come back to the house if you'd prefer.'

'We should prefer it, sir,' said one of the young men, 'if you accompanied us to the station.'

'Is someone in trouble?' asked Vivyan. 'One of my people?'

'It rather looks as if you might be in trouble, sir. We are not arresting you as yet, but a number of very serious allegations have been made and we would like you to come with us to the station.'

'Allegations? What sort of allegations?'

Vivyan was not demonstrating anger, but he was every inch the officer interrogating semi-incompetent corporals.

'Allegations of an intimate nature, sir. We really must insist.'

'You want me to come dressed like this?'

His hands swept over his purplish altar-robes.

'Of course you can change, sir, but then, if you don't mind, we should like you to accompany us. We have a car waiting.'

SEVENTEEN

The scene outside the church was one of confusion. It was raining extremely heavily. A crowd had assembled on the tarmac forecourt where a police car was parked. The word had spread fast, that Father Vivyan had been arrested. This was not technically true: he was merely being asked to accompany two officers to the police station to 'help with their enquiries', as the jargon had it. Such distinctions easily became lost in the minds of a small but angry crowd; outside in the road, a large white van containing more police officers was in wait, in case things got out of control.

'What you arrestin' him for?' 'He a good man — he done nothin' rang' were among the objections which Rachel could hear people making as they all squeezed through the church door to the tarmac. It was very bright there and it took her a while to recognize that arc lights had been fitted up by a television camera crew, who were filming the incident.

Everything happened so fast. Rachel was not close enough to the priest to be able to say any of the things which, with hindsight, she wanted to say: perhaps they were things he knew, and which did not need saying — such as that she wanted to be near him, that no one was obliged to go to a police station without the police producing a warrant . . . like *What the hell's going on here?*

The police were now coming into the drive from their parked van, and asking people to keep calm, but the atmosphere was the opposite of peaceful. The quite extraordinary calm which had descended upon the church during the mass when the priest had blessed the head of the lunatic boy had been replaced by a collective frenzy. It looked as if one man, whose name Rachel did not know, one of the refugees from the camper-vans, was scuffling with a policeman – perhaps being arrested. It was not easy either to see or to interpret what was going on, since the whole of the tarmac drive was crowded. Vivyan and the two policemen with him were lost in the mêlée. Some of the women had started to cry, and one or two of them were screaming at the police.

'You've no right to take him!'

'He done nothing rang!'

'Move along, please, madam.'

'Who you tellin' to move along?'

'Rachel.'

'Sinclo – what are you doing here?'

It was both reassuring to see Sinclo in that distraught scene, and instantly upsetting.

She said, 'Oh Christ, what's happened?'

'You need to get out of here – I've got a car round the corner,' he said, taking her arm.

'Please let go.'

They were both extremely wet, even though she had only been out of doors for a matter of seconds. She could feel the rainwater soaking her hair, splashing her cheeks, seeping into her clothes. She realized that among the huddle of confused figures, some shouting at the police, some swarming around the police car, which was now on the move, there were photographers. Flash bulbs popped in the driving rain. Through the crowd, she caught a split-second glimpse of Vivyan Chell in the back of the police car. He had slumped, and although his eyes were open, it was as if all the life had gone out of him, and he had been shot or suffered some bodily blow. He held up a book – it was the battered black volume called *Day Hours* which he usually carried everywhere with him – against his face.

'Oh my God, you've set this all up,' she said suddenly to Sinclo.

'I . . . I . . . er . . .'

'This is a set-up of some kind,' she said. She did not know what kind of dirty trick had been played, but it was inconceivable that TV cameras and a lot of journalists should have turned up without something underhand having been plotted. Every hour of the day in London the police turned up on someone's doorstep to take them in for questioning, and the newspapers didn't send reporters and cameras to snoop on the fact. 'I really think you should . . . er . . .' Sinclo's hesitancy, which was part of his charm when he was plucking up courage to suggest lunch, had sometimes warmed her heart. Now it seemed craven, even sinister.

'Just what is going on?' she asked.

'Your guess is as good as mine.'

'On the contrary,' she said furiously, 'you did not have to guess. You were here for the kill. You were here to watch when they took him.'

'I didn't know . . .'

'Oh, come *on* . . .'

'I didn't . . . er . . .'

'What? You just happened to be coming down to Crickleden in your car and you thought you'd look up Father Vivyan . . . Sinclo, he's your uncle for Christ's sake . . .'

'He's a rather remote cousin, actually.'

'I don't care what relation he is – he's your family, and you can do *this* . . .' She gestured wildly to the cameras, the lights, the snappers who were running after the red tail-lights of the departing car as it squelched out of the drive, spattering the puddles at the onlookers, and turned right into the evening traffic of Crickleden High Road.

'You don't really think that, surely?'

'Well – how did you know?'

'I didn't. I was coming down – well, about something . . . something else.'

'Don't tell me you were coming to see me.'

'Rachel, you know what they are saying?'

'Who?'

'The hacks there.' He gestured with the side of his head to the reporters, an anorak-clad gang who were moving among the crowds asking for what they would call quotes.

'He's a good man – he'd never hurt a kiddy,' one woman was shouting.

'So you'd trust him to be alone in a room with one of your boys, would you?' this disgusting person was asking the woman.

'Sinclo – what is this?'

'You know, surely?' He smiled.

'Know what?'

'There've been – er – complaints about Vivyan.'

'What sort of complaints?'

'A boy . . . er . . .'

'Oh, but that's *ridiculous*!' she shouted at him.

'I know . . . er . . . I mean, I . . .'

'You drive all the way down here to join that pack of *ghouls* . . . All right, Sinclo, I don't know if he's your cousin or your uncle, but you've known Vivyan all your life . . .'

'Er . . . much of the time . . . Africa . . . not very long, actually . . .'

'And you know what a good man he is . . . I don't think until

374

I came down here I had completely understood what it might be to live a good life.'

'Oh . . . no . . . splendid.'

'What do you mean, splendid?'

'I mean, he does splendid work – did . . . Mad Monk . . . wonderful.'

'Sinclo, you are a hypocrite.'

'Absolutely . . . I mean, no, no, Rachel, it's not what you think . . . I knew nothing of this . . .'

'You deny you were snooping and spying on him?'

'No, I don't deny that,' he said, suddenly and surprisingly able to finish a coherent sentence.

'Clear away now, please!' some young policeman was shouting.

'You admit—'

'Rachel, come away with me.'

The rain poured down his intense, miserable face. She was not sure whether or not some of the drops of water were tears. It was only afterwards that the curiosity began to eat into her – what did he mean by admitting that he had been spying on Vivyan Chell? When he said the words, she understood them to mean that he was snooping for the newspaper . . . Then again, later, as she mulled over the whole confused ten minutes they spent talking to one another in the rain, she understood his *Rachel, come away with me* to be another embarrassing declaration of love; but had he perhaps just been suggesting that they leave the arc lights and the hysterical parish women and the angry little crowd, and find shelter from the rain in some pub in the High Road? She had not given him time for explanations.

'Go away, Sinclo,' she said, and went back to the vicarage.

Here was a scene of comparable confusion, with photographers going into all the rooms, and snapping the rows of sleeping bags, the many unmade beds, the furniture rescued from skips, the plastic bin bags full of clothes.

Two of the burlier parish workers, one male, one female, were doing their best to get rid of the photographers.

One said, 'If you do not go freely, we shall have to call the police.'

'You go ahead,' said one of the snappers as he pointed the camera at these justly furious people and took their pictures.

Watching the photographers go about their work, Rachel asked herself how she could ever have taken money to work for a newspaper. They barged and shoved and kicked.

'Would you please leave,' asked Heather, one of the parish workers.

A mustachioed little snapper in an anorak ignored her words completely and shouted to one of his underlings, 'What about the kitchen? We haven't done in there.'

The large kitchen, by contrast with some of the scruffier rooms in the house, was always kept in apple-pie order. The floors and surfaces were clean. The high tea which was always served after the evening mass was in the process of being prepared, and various huge saucepans of boiling vegetables were on the vast caterer's stove. There was a pleasing smell of cottage pie.

'Try upending the rubbish bin,' shouted the photographer to his assistant, who shoved past the cooks to a dustbin full of potato peelings, cabbage stalks and empty tin cans. He proceeded to do just that – to upturn the rubbish all over the floor. This gesture elicited the inevitable – Rachel considered, the appropriate – response: Lance, one of the kitchen assistants, a nice young black boy from one of the neighbouring estates, tried to restrain the hooligan who was upsetting the dustbin; another young man, one of the asylum seekers, grabbed the camera from the snapper's hand and hurled it to the ground. He then took a wooden meat-mallet from a hook on the wall and began to smash the camera.

Someone had already called the police – or perhaps the police had never gone away – for several officers now came into the kitchen. They began manhandling Lance, and taking a statement from the photographer about the wilful damage to his property.

'Look,' said Rachel, 'you can't do this.'

'If you don't mind, *madam* . . .' said a WPC. There was heavy irony in her emphasis on the word 'madam'.

'I do mind, and you just can't do this. Those people came into this house unasked. This is a private house. That man deliberately upset potato peelings all over a perfectly clean floor, just so they could take some filthy picture for their stinking paper.'

'So, who's this being so hoity-toity?' said the photographer. He turned and leered at her. Beneath a smudge of revolting pubic moustache the evil smile made a row of uneven orange panatella-smoker's fangs. 'L. P. Watson's little *whore*?'

Some minutes later, Rachel Pearl, the kitchen-helper called Lance and the asylum seeker, a twenty-five-year-old man called Thimjo, found themselves being bundled into the back of a van and driven to the police station.

EIGHTEEN

Just for a change, Mary Much and Martina Fax had abandoned
Diana's for the restaurant at Granville Stoppard, a penthouse at
the top of the store which looked across the dripping plane
boughs to the sodden green of Hyde Park and, beyond, to the
rain-sprayed, opalescent surface of the Serpentine.

The *Legion*, which lay between them, had a photograph which,
as both women agreed, could have been anyone. They meant, it
could have been anyone being arrested, since it was of a man
holding a book against his face while he slumped in the back of
a police car. The pictures inside were a little better.

'How *can* people live like that?' Martina asked, scratching
with a scarlet talon at a photo of the upended rubbish bin, and
the tea-leaves and potato peelings all over the vicarage floor.

'Darling, it's no worse than you and Lennie, the week before
you *got* Piet!'

'It's looking like that *now* again!' She added, 'Now Piet's
stopped working.'

Mary Much just murmured, 'Piet' gently and mournfully,
almost to herself. She was wearing a white leather trouser-suit
and a very pale pink mohair jumper. Somehow, with her newer,
shorter hair, whose peroxide suggested that some electrical shock
had been administered to her entire system, she had lost some
of her Arthurian-enchantress qualities and now resembled one
of the more alarming intergalactic dominatrices in science fiction aimed at an adult market. Martina, in all ways more

378

conservative, retained her coppery hair, and since without further surgical attention she would have been unequipped to alter the perpetual mirthless smile, she left it be, that same impressive combination of crimson gloss and orthodontic reorganization. (Martina wore a neat little green CD suit which revealed her pin-like legs.)

'He was – is – a little strange, that boy,' said Martina, 'but it was clever of me – wasn't it – to *get* him?'

'Darling – you were a genius.'

Martina clapped her hands together excitedly and said, 'Darling, we must order.'

At Granville Stoppard they didn't do the lovely mango and peach thingy they served at Diana's, half and half with Dom Perignon. The women risked the Buck's Fizz but agreed it wasn't a patch. At least there was lobster and there were chips: a consoling constant when one had worries.

And they *were* worried. About Lennie-Wennie's mun-mun, or lack of it. About the situation in Africa. About the boy. Martina had lived life on a high wire. Lennie had not, and he did not always have her knack of jumping sometimes, as from the Wall, quite literally from one zone of danger to the next, nearly always to her own advantage. To have *got* the boy was genius. Martina's fears, and Mary's, had been aroused quite early on, though they had not been voiced so much as mimed, with screwy gestures of fingers to the side of the head and in the case of Mary, who still had facial muscles, hilarious, squinting evocations of idiocy. But what did one *do* when he started to say he thought Lennie was his dada?

This unanswered question, unanswered by all, was joined in a queue of unanswered questions in the minds of Martina and Mary Much. Then they had discovered – both discoveries more or less coinciding – that the boy had stolen one of their teeny recording thingies, and that he knew the ghastly old bender. The monk who made Lennie's life such a misery with all his communist rubbish about boo-hoo let's feel sorry for the slaves, miners, whatever they were supposed to be.

Martina's instincts, what Mary called her Martennae, said, Stop! Too risky. Too many things to go wrong. It was clumsy old Len who charged ahead. They'd perhaps told him too much about the boy – his quite preternatural capacity to adapt, his willingness to do and say what was required. But this was a high wire on to which Martina would not have, herself, advised Lennie to tread, this Old Bongo Monka Benda stuff. Might there not be a reckoning? An establishment of the facts? A discovery, at the most simple level, that the tape had been doctored by some expert in surveillance acquired by Kurtmeyer; that the boy confronting some old bender happened on one occasion and the old priest apologizing happened on some quite different occasion, when he was speaking – rather awkward fact, this – to a woman; to a woman – even more awkward fact – who had obviously been the old man's . . .

It was facts which were troubling: facts, and the specific. Both women had spent their lives avoiding both, and so it was no surprise that they had triumphed in the world of journalism. They had learned so well together to cultivate their natural gifts for remembering, yet not remembering. They had instinctively known for so long what to say and what to keep hidden. Both in all likelihood had censors in their brains which edited events as they happened, allowing some to be altered, others to be eliminated from the records. Perhaps some such witty but unspoken irony had led them now to lunch in this very store, Granville Stoppard, where, thirty years before, the two women had first met.

In those days, the cocktail bar on the top floor had been a

recognized place to meet the more discerning client. Martina had been in practice before such helps to work as telephone numbers left in kiosks. Whether she would have sunk so low in any event was a good question, since it had never been her habit, once she had arrived in England, to touch anything but the upper end of the market. The lunch-time crowd in the bar at Granville Stoppard were the richer businessmen, lawyers and foreign visitors. For the really pricey ones, she relied on contacts, introductions, word-of-mouth reference – in those days no Cabinet minister or bishop would want to try even so discreet a venue as Granville Stoppard for viewing the goods.

Naturally, the shop had its reputation to keep up, and very occasionally the young women were asked to move on. Perhaps Martina had unwontedly had a glass too many. Perhaps her words – forgotten now in form or detail, though their sense was recalled vividly enough – had been too unsubtle. Whatever the reason, her interlocutor, who turned out to be a store detective, had asked her to move on. Leave the shop. Nothing so obvious as a scuffle occurred, but she could still recollect the shame as he had accompanied her into the lift, and down to the ground floor, out through Make-up and towards the glass doors. Beyond, she recollected, the Knightsbridge day was surprisingly bright – much brighter than the artificially lit world of the bar from which she was being excluded. Well-heeled hippies, long-haired men in flared trousers, droopy girlfriends in flowery T-shirts. Gandalf Lives! All You Need Is Love. Oh no, darling, she had thought, all you need is lolly, as the Beatles fucking well know.

But as she and the store detective had advanced to this bright early-seventies world, it was the fracas in Make-up which drew all eyes. A young woman – in those days just a few years made a difference, and this frail Marianne Faithfull lookalike was significantly younger than Martina herself – was being rudely stopped by the store detective.

'I never said I'd paid for it . . .'

'And you left the store . . .'

'Like I said . . .'

There was not a cockney accent, but the basically middle-class voice attested to its aspirations, its imaginative home at that era – namely, Stones concerts, parties which lasted all night, happenings in Covent Garden piazza presided over by John Peel . . . So the words were on the edge of 'loik Oi said', but nothing like so cocknified as that. It was the way Mick, Marianne, all that crowd spoke. This was no member of the exalted crowd, however, but someone on a par with the shop girls and the store detective. Mary Much in those days did indeed work in a boutique, half a mile away down the King's Road. It was only months since she had moved out, for good, from her parents' semi-detached in Reading. She had come into Granville Stoppard quite regularly to steal clothes. It was easy if all you lived on was dope and black coffee and your body was thin as spaghetti. Sometimes, she could get two or three Mary Quant dresses on, one on top of the other, before scampering out of the shop. She sold them at a 'nearly new' place between the department store and the boutique where she herself worked.

'Like I said, I came over faint. I just stepped outside to get some air.'

'But you are still wearing . . .'

'I know I'm still wearing . . .'

'Would you step this way, madam, I'd like you to come into the manager's office.'

All in an instant, Martina had taken the situation into her own hands. She spoke in English, but with the thrill of it all, her words were inverted.

'With me, come – please.'

She had reached out, and taken Mary Much's hand. The Marianne Faithfull, who literally did have a garland of flowers in her hair, had immediately recognized the gesture. Partners in different crimes, and hand in hand, they had run out into the sunny afternoon. The screams of the store detectives, the pursuit of them, had been ineffectual. The taxi had come to their aid at once. And they had driven off in the direction of Park Lane, still holding hands on the back seat.

Nothing had happened on that afternoon. That is to say, the affair which developed between the two women was a thing of much, much later in their story. They had merely held hands and giggled, as they got away. Martina had wanted – this she told Mary in later years – to take her back to the flat in Park Lane (where she worked – but these words had not been used) and make love to her there and then. But instead, they had gone to a chi-chi little Italian café in North Audley Street, not far from the American Embassy, where the (in Martina's judgement) silly people had demonstrated against the Vietnamese war. They had not even exchanged names on that occasion – just drunk their coffee together for perhaps twenty minutes, and talked of nothings, and giggled. Martina was in her late, Mary in her early, twenties.

When, some years later, they had 'met', the recognition had been instantaneous. It had been at a party. Mary Much, who had won the *Vogue* talent competition, was working on that magazine. Martina, after a year slogging it out in Features on the *Legion*, had begun to write her spirited column – the voice of young womanhood.

The success of their relationship, the deepest thing in either of their lives, was that they had never prised it apart with too much questioning, or too much confidence in the power of truth to make them free. On the contrary, both had enough experience of life to know that the truth would have landed them in prison. It was a lifetime's habit, in both cases, of adjusting the truth which had enabled them to reach their present plateaux of contentment. So it was that Mary met Martina for the first time at that party, and neither of them in thirty years had ever made any allusion to the previous encounter in the department store, nor of Martina's rescue of Mary from arrest, nor their ride, shaking with girlish laughter, in the taxi. All that was given, understood, and forgotten. Mary's past was what she chose to make it – as far as anyone else was concerned, she began life when she won the *Vogue* talent competition. Martina the journalist had already transmogrified her past. The one-eyed old lady with whom she shared her apartment and her life was now the widow of a Swiss medical professor, heroic in his attempts to rescue unfortunates from the Third Reich – when they came his way – and who had sadly died when Martina was in her infancy. The Basel childhood of impeccable Zwinglian rectitude, with maiden aunts, was a mere sketch, an allusion, if the past was ever referred to: one does not wish to bore people by talking about oneself all the time.

Thus it was the two women had got by, knowing and not knowing. The affair had had many ups and downs. They were never publicly a couple, though all thought of them as inseparable comrades. For long stretches, when one or the other had men in their lives, the bedroom side of things went into abeyance. Both women had known, from the acute jealousy suffered during such periods, that they could not risk quarrelling with one another. The pain was bad enough to be mistaken for love. It had outlasted Mary's much-needed affair with the Duke (needed because sometimes a woman in her position requires not just the jewels but the cachet, something sturdy to put in the inner curriculum vitae which she secretly peruses); it had outlasted, and in its complicated way was entwined with, Martina's marriage to Len. Certainly, their feelings of jealousy about the new boy were not going to get in the way of a love as old or as twiningly persistent.

'What if Piet denies the story? What if the Old Bender makes him deny it?' There was real panic in Martina's voice.

'No smoke without fire, darling. Won't people think that?'

'What if the Bender sues? He's grand – he's really a lord . . .'

'Monty Longmore's his brother,' said Mary Much, as if to explain everything. She let out a long breath, and somewhere in the middle of this smoky exhalation, words began.

'Whatever happens – front pages like this . . .'

She tapped the crappy headline.

'FATHER FAGIN,' said Martina. 'What's that meant to mean?'

'Fagin's a character in a musical, darling. "Food, glorious food."'

'No one under sixty's going to know that. We made a mistake with Worledge, darling.'

'We' meant 'you'. Mary Much heard all the aggro in Martina's tone. She knew every nuance and echo of meaning in her speech patterns.

'It's not too late . . .' she said, with vivid garrotte-mimes, placing her two hands round that neck whose incipient broiler's scrawn was so fetchingly concealed by pink mohair polo.

'We always thought Mr Blimby had more class,' said Martina, to the middle distance.

'L.P. won't be pleased.'

'L.P.'s a mess.'

They ate a few more chips and smoked another ciggie apiece.

'So, when Kurtmeyer closes down the *Sunday* and the two titles merge . . .'

'Bye, Worledge!' Mary Much's voice had become high-pitched, girlish, a thirties flapper waving to a subaltern going away to war by train. 'Byeee . . . !'

'And Piet?'

There was a long silence.

'You know poor Hans?' asked Mary Much. It was the first time since the explosion, and the calamity, that the friends had been on the verge of confronting the mystery.

Martina's scarlet claw came towards her lover's face. For a split second Mary feared that like a vengeful Fury she was going to scratch, but a fingertip merely came to rest on Mary's pink lips. Mary kissed, then gently nibbled it.

NINETEEN

'Philosophers scorn the argument from design,' said Lennox Mark. 'But take something as complex as the optic nerve. Now a Darwinian will tell you that it evolved. *Gradually.*'

He forked in *pommes de terres dauphinoises*.

'Was it Lloyd George who said that in politics you can't cross a chasm in two leaps?'

Mr Blimby stared, wondering whether this was some kind of trick question. He had heard about these theological conversations, but he had never been intimate with the Chairman, and so had never been subjected to one before.

'It's the same with Creation,' said Lennox. 'No way can you persuade me that the optic nerve *evolved*, for fuck's sakes. Have you ever examined the complexity of that goddamn thing?'

Mr Blimby was shy to admit a failure to have done so. He had heard the rumours, just as everyone else had. The two *Legions*, the *Daily* and the *Sunday*, would merge. The staff of the *Sunday* would be ditched. That shit Worledge would become editor-in-chief of the whole paper; someone else, possibly L.P., possibly another, would edit the 'comment' section of the *Sunday*. He, Blimby, would be chucked out.

He had not dared to tell his wife about these rumours, but she, of course, had heard them, down on the Sussex farm. She had leaned her bum against the Aga and said, in that hard, direct manner which he found so terrifying: 'If they're sacking you, make sure you don't accept less than half a million.'

He knew that there might well be newspaper proprietors who were able to hand out sums like that to departing editors. He also knew that Lennox Mark was not such a proprietor. Sal's utterly unsympathetic, calculating remark sounded like a threat. He felt that unless he brought home half a mill at the end of the week, he would be facing more than just dismissal as editor. Would he mind it if she ditched him? Certainly, he would miss neither her, nor his teenaged children, who towered over and intimidated him. Both children — Henry at Eton, Fiona at Marlborough — had caught from their mother and her parents the sense that Dad was not *quite*. If allusion had to be made to Grandpa — Simon's dad — they always said he had been a 'medic', rather than a dentist. Simon had even heard Sal at dinner parties guffaw, 'That's what I got for marrying a surgeon's son.' Simon felt himself despised by all of them, not merely because of his size and manner but because they were unconvinced. The loud braying voice, which he had adopted when an undergraduate at Trinity Hall; the supposed enthusiasm for shooting; the aristocratic friends at his London club . . . none of them could disguise the fact that he was a grammar-school boy whose father was a dental surgeon. In no other world but Sal's bogus, snobby county set would this harmless fact have been shaming.

It would be a relief, in a way, to be ditched, and to start all over again. But Mr Blimby was fifty-one, and starting would not be easy. He would not miss his wife and children at all; in fact, he detested them. But he would deeply miss the shooting week-ends; the overnight stays in grand houses; these (he did not kid himself) would evaporate without Sal to stage-manage them.

He knew that he had made a hash of editing the *Sunday Legion*. This was because of his various adopted personae, that of the would-be gent despised the newspaperman. He had therefore tried to produce a Sunday title which would appeal to his stuffier country friends. The deadly-dull result partly explained the catastrophic decline in circulation. He knew that it was only a matter of time before he was sacked.

But this way of doing it – this ordeal by food and theology in the Savoy Grill – was more than he could stand. He had tried to match the proprietor course by course. When Lennox ate steak and chips for his first course, Mr Blimby had smoked salmon. Then there was a fish course – they both ate lobster salads. Then they ate the roast of the day – it was lamb today. Lennox told the man carving the joint that he had not given enough fat to Simon Blimby. By now, Mr Blimby was wondering which would come first, his being sick or his being sacked. It was at times like this that he cursed his size. Men of more normal dimensions could presumably simply eat more. At five foot two inches, and of a delicate build, he simply could not take as much food as larger men.

'What are we expected to see with,' Lennox was asking, 'if it takes tens of thousands of years to evolve an optic nerve? No, no. This is a clear case of a device of such complexity that it is merely perverse to suggest that it was other than *designed*. And if designed . . . then . . . Shoot me down, Simon, shoot me down!' he urged suddenly. 'Tell me I'm wrong . . .'

'Sal and I are keen supporters of our local parish church,' said Mr Blimby after much clearing of his throat, 'and therefore of course – of *course* we subscribe to the Creeds.'

'What you ought to say,' said Lennox; his eye stared disapprovingly at the large fatty morsel which Mr Blimby had tried to conceal beneath a cabbage leaf on the side of his plate. 'You haven't eaten . . .' he said. 'May I?'

As he ate up Mr Blimby's food, he explained to the small man what he should have said. A natural process, even one as complex as the construction of the optic nerve, did not imply the existence of anything *personal* behind it.

'God himself doesn't have to be personal. Did that ever occur to you?'

'As I say, Sal . . . the parish . . . the Church of England.'

'Christ, someone ought to put a bomb under the Church of England,' said Lennox.

'As they did under Hans Busch.'

Mr Blimby harrumphed at his own witticism.

'I liked your coverage of that,' said Lennox. 'The *Sunday* wrote an excellent leader – was that you?'

Mr Blimby bowed his head in acknowledgement. The leading article in question had in fact been written by a young graduate in the leader writers' office who would be fired when the two papers merged.

'Anything we said in the past about not liking the fellow's art . . . rule of law . . . support the police . . . No, it was a nicely balanced piece, including the sting in the tail, that a man like Busch, who was trying to put into concrete form the nonsensical post-modern philosophies of Foucault, had in a sense died as a martyr to his own beliefs. Had he not been an open admirer of Genet and the philosophy of crime as rebellion? No, it was a learned piece. What should I read if I wanted to start reading Foucault? He might have some interesting things to say about religion. No?'

Mr Blimby stared open-eyed. No one had prepared him for this. He had thought it would just be the sack; then he'd be brave enough (or not) to murmur the name of Sal's family solicitor in Lincoln's Inn Fields who might 'discuss terms'.

'This story about the monk,' said Mr Blimby gingerly, 'Father Vivyan Chell . . .'

'I'm glad you raised that. You see, when the two papers

merge – and let's cut the crap, Simon, you know why you're here.'

The proprietor wiped his plate with a piece of bread. He belched very gently, placed a napkin to his lips and sipped his Seven-Up.

While the waiter cleared the table, Blimby was brave enough to say that he did not have room for pudding. Lennox Mark ordered double plum duff.

'Cream or custard, sir?'

'Both,' he said curtly; his manner denouncing the tomfool character of the enquiry.

'We're here because of the *Legion*. We both want it to survive. The merger of the two papers is long overdue. I meant to do it when Tony left the *Daily*. That was what my instinct told me to do.'

He often referred to Martina as his instinct in such sentences as the one he had just spoken.

'It won't be easy for you . . .'

Blimby saw that this was his moment to mention the solicitor in Lincoln's Inn.

'Well, I've enjoyed myself at the *Sunday* . . .' was all he could feebly manage.

'That will make it all the harder for you to sack them all – your colleagues. That's what I'm asking you to do. If you think you've got the balls for it,' said Lennox. 'Ah, lovely grub!'

He began to spoon in plum pudding and custard with eager speed. Anyone watching him would guess he had not eaten for days.

'If you think you can sit down and tell them all in the newsroom that they are fired . . . and I'm sorry to say that I can't offer them generous redundancy money. Kurt's done the necessary with the lawyers. We've been through each and every contract . . .'

The miraculous, the joyous nature of the news began to dawn on Blimby. Through every part of his small frame he felt joy, like the sap rising in springtime in a miniature shrub.

'And Derek?' he asked mischievously.

'Derek has frankly . . . let's put it this way. He's not a *Legion* man. You mention the Hans Busch explosion. You see, he just made the paper look bloody ridiculous. One minute he's lambasting the guy as if he was Satan. Then, when he's blown sky-high, he's the marvellous avant-garde artist Hans Busch. Then there's the Father Vivyan story. He's badly bungled, badly. It's a bit of a hot potato, that one. I can't fill you in on the details, I'm afraid. I will, but . . .'

'But Derek . . . Derek will be going?'

'We can't sack Derek,' said Lennox, looking shiftily at Blimby. 'We can't afford to. But I'm making him your deputy on the new joint title.'

All the pride and pleasure which Blimby had been feeling during the previous five minutes evaporated at once as the horrible fact dawned. He and Worledge, who had led quite separate lives producing two quite different newspapers, would now be working together on a daily basis. And, since Lennie had made him Worledge's boss, he would have to live with all Worledge's resentment and hatred. He stared blankly ahead of him.

'I hope I can live up to your expectations,' he said weakly.

'Sure you can, Simon, sure you can.'

Lennox lifted his glass of Seven-Up and clinked the one glass of claret which he had bought for his luncheon guest. 'Here's to the future of the *Legion*!'

TWENTY

'You'll find him very much changed,' said Monty Longmore. 'I can't describe it to you.' He shoved a glass of Chilean Cabernet Sauvignon across the kitchen table.

'You mean he's depressed?'

'He even looks different.'

Rachel sipped from her glass.

'This stuff's delicious.'

'Isn't it? It's from a Rothschild winery. Discovered it at the Beefsteak. Told our local offie in Pewsey. Now we drink nothing else. No, the dear old thing . . .' He reverted to his brother. Rachel had never been close to Monty, but whenever she had been to stay at Throxton with Kitty, he had been kindly. They had gone for walks together in the park, and they both enjoyed bridge.

'We talk about something like this being a blow. It's as if he's been hit by something. I wondered whether he'd had a stroke, but he won't see a doctor. The first week he was here, it was as if he was on holiday. He was positively high. As if he hadn't taken in what had happened. Said he'd not had such a rest since he became a monk. Refused to have a bedroom, of course, at first. Said he'd just sleep in a chair in the library. Mrs Thorn put a stop to that nonsense. Shoved him in the King's Room and he slept for hours. We thought he was dead. Full of jokes and fun when he woke up. Lizzie and Jontie and the children came down that weekend. Charles came, too.'

'How is Charles?'

'Charles is . . .' The father-in-law of Charles Henderson smiled wanly. 'Well, we all miss Kitty.'

'Yes, we do.'

'Less than five quid a bottle, too, which can't be bad,' he said, tapping the bottle of Los Vascos. 'Viv, though, was life and soul. Played with the children. Romped about. He's always liked that sort of stuff much more than I do. Perhaps he'd have been happier if he'd got married . . .'

'Perhaps happiness wasn't what he wanted in life.'

'It's what we all want – surely . . . Well, when the children went back to London, the house went quiet. You know what the old dump's like when no one's about. You remember that week you came down with Kitty. You were swotting . . .'

'We were doing revision, or meant to be.' Rachel laughed. 'We were so cold, we got in bed together with all our clothes on and a bottle of . . .'

Her words were interrupted by a shuffling of feet on the stone-flagged kitchen corridor. This was in itself a distressing signal. The long strides of Major Chell MC had been reduced to this slipper-shuffle.

'Anyway, there's plenty more of this stuff, so drink up,' said Monty, emptying the remains of the bottle into Rachel's glass.

'I say, doesn't a man get a drink in this place?' asked Vivyan. Looking at Rachel, he said, a little shyly, 'Hallo, old thing.'

She had expected, from Monty's warning, that Vivyan would be paler and thinner. If anything, he had put on a little weight and, whether as a result of country air or nightly potations in the kitchen, he had gained some colour in the face.

She got up and did something she had never done before but which, she realized, she had very much wanted to do. She kissed him. As she did so, she saw a flicker of fear in his eyes. He had lost some authority. He was now a man on the run. He responded to the kiss as if it was indicative of something other than affection: he looked fearful that she knew more than she was letting on; coming as she did from London, did she bring more bad news, more threats of police investigation or intrusions by the press?

'How have you been?' She was trying very hard not to cry as she asked the question.

'We read aloud to one another, don't we?' said Lord Longmore. 'Neither of us can stand the telly. I wanted *The Heart of Midlothian* again – do you remember, Mother read it to us?'

'Mother could do Scottish accents,' said Vivyan. 'Monty's rendition of Jeanie Deans was too much of a penance. We're on *The Eustace Diamonds* at the moment.'

'Good.'

'Some of it's good. Some of it's rather twaddle,' said the monk. 'Ah. At last.' And, being given a large glass of red wine, he gulped it greedily.

'Now,' said Monty. 'Since we have company, I've done some cooking.'

'Oh, good!' with a strange faraway sadness in his eyes.

After the lamb cutlets with tomatoes, which were eaten in the kitchen, the three of them went back to the little drawing room, which smelt pleasantly of woodsmoke. For Rachel, it was a room, with its frayed Aubusson carpet, its Reynolds of Sir Montague and Lady Chell, circa 1770, its rosewood bureau, its charming Adamesque commode, its family photographs scattered over the dusty grand piano, which evoked most powerfully her friendship with Kitty, and the hours they had spent there playing Scrabble or gossiping about their boyfriends. Monty settled in a low armchair beside the fire, from whose arms horsehair sprang in huge tufts. Vivyan, who seemed to be wearing some borrowed clothes – presumably his brother's – an old grey suit whose trousers were much too short, and an open-necked blue shirt, sat beside Rachel on the sofa. All had mugs of coffee.

'The Bishop has graciously written,' said Vivyan.

Monty looked up anxiously, as though he would prefer these things not to be discussed. It was unclear whether he feared that the subject would depress or excite his brother, or whether he disapproved of talking about it in front of a comparative stranger. Viv chose not to see his elder brother's admonitory glance.

'Very kind of him. Says I can say mass. I have been doing so anyway. It did not occur to me that I wasn't allowed to – in the chapel here. He says, the Bishop, that I can't say mass in public, or hear confessions or preach. In short, that I am suspended.'

His mouth tautened as he said these, to him, manifestly extraordinary words.

'General Bindiga constantly tried to shut me up; he never dared to. Lennox Mark would like to shut me up if he could . . .'

'Chance'd be a fine thing' – these words from behind *The Times*.

'But in the end, it was the dear old Church of England that managed to gag me.'

'But it's so unfair,' said Rachel. 'Can't you appeal? Can't a lawyer . . .'

'Oh, lawyers!' He sighed. 'At least here I have an altar, and I can say the office. I'm still a priest.'

'Why is it important to say mass if no one can come?' she asked.

'I go,' said the voice behind the newspaper. 'Except when he gets up at five a.m. to say it in Swahili or some bloody language.'

'I sometimes say mass in Hausa. I don't know Swahili . . .

Why do I do it? It gives a strength which nothing else does . . . You don't want to hear all this.'

'I do.'

'If you ask me, do I understand the mass in the same sense that we were taught by the novice-master all those years ago?'

'What's a novice-master?'

'When I joined the order, I had to go to our mother-house at Kelvedone for two boring years. First I was a postulant: that's when they test to see if you are capable of bearing the rigour of monastic existence. Then you start the training proper and you are a novice. The novice-master trains you. He's your personal trainer, if you like. He's preparing you not only to be a monk but to be a priest. In our community we were all made to read books – oh, Gregory Dix, *The Shape of the Liturgy*. I wonder if it's still read? We were taught a really very mechanical view of the mass; you know, it had to be said and done in exactly the right way.'

'Did they teach you that it was really the Body and Blood of Christ?'

'Well, that's the essence of it.'

'It sounds like the Catholics. Sorry. You have to understand, Vivyan, I was brought up as a Jewish atheist and I'm . . .'

'And you still are?'

'Yes.'

'Well, I'm very nearly one. Not a Jewish one, but an Anglican one. You can't see the total unfairness of life, the absolute arbitrariness of suffering, the triumph of evil and injustice, without being an atheist. And certainly most of the arguments for the existence of God are ropy, to say the least.'

'They don't stand up *at all*,' said Rachel vehemently.

'Maybe they're not meant to.'

'Meant by whom?'

'Maybe our forebears felt by instinct that there were gods or that there was one true God. This instinct formed itself into religion, or several religions. It's after people have practised a religion that they begin to make religious philosophy and try to make sense of it all. The rituals come first, the philosophy second. Those deep instincts that goodness is not something we invented for ourselves, that it is *there* independent of our ability to attain it, irrespective of how many people deny it. You could have the whole Third Reich with all its power and all its deadly attractiveness designed to tell you that it was a good thing to send a child to a gas oven; but every single person on this planet would *know* that it was evil. That's what makes me hold on. We did not invent the rules . . .'

'But Bonhoeffer, in his *Ethik*, seems to be saying something subtly different. Isn't he saying that the truly good person must be prepared to sacrifice some pure, unsullied notion of his own virtue – tear up the rule-books, in fact . . .'

'Rule-books are not the same as the Good,' said Vivyan. 'Bonhoeffer was hanged because he followed Christ. That led him to do what was illegal, what was bad in the shame-culture of Nazi Germany – he was prepared to abandon his own purity, to that degree, yes. But he never lost hold of his idea of good and evil. It was the authorities who had lost their moral sense, as they always do. Christians are always anarchists, always against the system. We're not saying Joshua Bindiga is as bad as Hitler, and we're certainly not saying that Lennie Mark is as bad as Hitler. But they are both *bad men*, because they knew what the Good was, and they have let themselves lose sight of it.'

'Aren't you just saying . . . no, that's not fair. I was going to ask what made you so certain that you were right and they were wrong.'

'Rachel – I've seen the slave boys, I've seen the welts on their backs where they have been repeatedly beaten, I've seen their fathers and uncles half-starved and dying from overwork in the copper mines. I've met men and women who have been tortured . . .'

'Okay – I know.'

'And you know? Lennie Mark is not quite a lost soul. Hey!'

He had suddenly become animated by an idea.

He stood up, and she was reminded, by his gaunt, overexcited features, of those moments in the Sherlock Holmes stories when the great detective is at last on the trail of the truth, though bumbling Doctor Watson does not yet see it. Was this why she was in love with him (or whatever she was)? Because Vivyan Chell reminded her of Sherlock Holmes?

'Hey!' he said.

'What?'

'The boy – the poor, disturbed boy. Peter. You are the go-between. I did not see it before now. You could go to Mercy. Ask her the story. Tell her I said that I don't mind how much you are told. There are things I can't tell you, and things I can't say, my dear. I hope you understand that. But equally, that poor disturbed boy needs help. And he needs rescuing from any further exposure in the media. And funnily enough, Lennie needs rescuing from himself. How do you get on with Lennie?'

'I've hardly ever met him.'

'But he was your proprietor.'

'I never really got to meet him.'

'Astonishing. It's late. Tomorrow, I'll tell you about Lennie. But will you do this for me, Rachel?'

'I'll do anything for you, Vivyan.'

'Done,' said Lord Longmore, throwing down the crossword puzzle on the other side of the fireplace. 'Time for bed.'

TWENTY-ONE

Mary Much was fond of quoting Lord Beaverbrook's doctrine that one of the secrets of running a successful newspaper was, from time to time, 'to put a ferret in the cage'. It meant that a happy paper such as, under Tony Taylor, the *Legion* had broadly been was not necessarily a good paper. Nor was a mini-dictatorship, such as Worledge had run for a few disastrous months, conducive to good journalism. Everyone agreed, however, that the appointment of two men who detested one another, Worledge and Blimby, to run the new combined titles had been an inspired idea. The jolly, pointless energy which the *Legion* had possessed under Taylor, and the savagery which it tried to adopt under Worledge were combined, under Blimby, to produce a winning formula. Day after day, the *Legion* was breaking stories, attracting attention by its opinion columns, its gossip, its bold new layout, its photography.

The carnage – Mr Blimby called it cutting out dead wood – of two hundred and fifty redundancies affected the lives of the journalists themselves but was barely noticed by the readers. 'Dr Arbuthnot' – a page which had been 'drifting' since Aubrey Bird's accident in the multi-storey car park – was now being edited by Seamus Ahearne ('Creevey' from the old *Sunday Legion*). He bullied his three young assistants, ripped up their copy, swore, drank, sweated: now half the world seemed addicted to the tittle-tattle he purveyed. The sports coverage was said by those interested to have improved immeasurably.

The rough politics remained roughly the same, but the hiring of a new young political commentator made the paper look serious.

It was by no means clear which was the ferret – Worledge, or Mr Blimby. Worledge had scoured his contract when he heard the bad news. The very last thing he had wanted to do was to work under Blimby. His lawyer had to tell him that the contract did not entitle him to the huge redundancy he'd hoped for. In the event of the *Daily Legion* and the *Sunday Legion* merging, it said, he would be offered at the same salary a post commensurate with his abilities. Working as deputy to Blimby was a personal humiliation but he could not claim it was the sack.

The two – perhaps they were both ferrets – snarled at one another inwardly but they maintained a studied politeness. Each man felt forced by the reorganization to prove to the other that he was not as incompetent as the other supposed. Worledge reined in his cruder prejudices. Blimby, to prove to Worledge that he was a real man, despite his voice and stature, insisted on the paper being tougher. Stories which he would have deemed beneath his dignity when editing the *Sunday* – TV personalities found in brothels, errant clergymen, implants in the chests of famous actresses – now consumed his interest. He wanted to get there before Worledge in all these traditionally red-top areas of concern. Equally, he hugely enjoyed going to Number Ten and bellowing to the Prime Minister the terms on which the new *Legion* would be supporting him for re-election. The shopping list was a catalogue of incompatibilities – low taxes, and a huge increase of spending on health. Defiance of Europe in every single resolution of the Council of Ministers, while expecting Britain to be seen as a Big Hitter in the European Game. Support for Bindiga against the anarchists. Determined to be more bullish than Worledge, but with a sharper, more intelligent edge, Mr Blimby pored over every 'opinion' piece, and had developed the habit of making all the columnists (except, of course, Martina Fax) alter their copy.

The 'Father Fagin' story had faded away like smoke in the previous fortnight. Everyone agreed that Worledge had bungled it. There were rumours that the boy in question was mentally unbalanced. It was quite possible that the story would go away altogether were it not for a series of quite unrelated chances. Blimby dined with Martina and Lennie and Mary Much one night: he gave them dinner at his club. (The joy of being the editor of a daily was that he only needed to go back to Sal at weekends, if then; he had taken a small bachelor pied-à-terre in St James's.) They'd discussed a wide range of issues, and it was only at the end of the meal that the subject of Zinariya arose. Some liberal paper had carried an article that week about opposition to Bindiga mounting in Britain, and it had strongly hinted that the allegations made against Father Vivyan had been part of a smear campaign. The article was written by Rachel Pearl – not a name familiar to Mr Blimby, but Martina filled him in.

'She's an embittered Jewess. You know how they can be bitter?'

Mr Blimby had crumbled his Stilton with an embarrassed air.

'Vengeance is mine,' said Lennox. 'That's the Jewish God for you.'

'She used to be L.P.'s squeeze,' supplied Mary Much.

The eighteenth-century portraits in the Coffee Room of Mr Blimby's club stared disapprovingly.

'He dropped her – she's just taking her revenge on the *Legion*. How pathetic can you get?'

'How's L.P.'s life these days, would you say?' Mr Blimby enquired.

The two women looked at one another.

'He's a bloody fool,' said Martina.

'It's *tragic*,' moaned Mary Much. 'Who'd ever've thought. I *mean*, L.P.'

'What's he done now?' asked Blimby.

Mary Much mimed exaggerated yawns.

'So boring. Jokes not funny,' supplied Martina in case he hadn't understood.

'You should watch him,' said Mary. 'Maybe there's a case for using him a teeny bit less.'

'He's spreading himself too thin,' boomed Mr Blimby, as if he was the first to have noticed the phenomenon.

'But his bimbo's article wants smashing on the head,' said Lennox Mark. 'If we can't make that story against Father Vivyan stand up, we're going to look like cretins.'

'It'll stand,' said Martina.

The dinner happened during a week when there was not much in the way of news. True, a civil war in the Congo had killed two million; the Israelis and the Palestinians were engaged in further exchanges of conflict; there was a threatened nuclear war between India and Pakistan and the economy of the Argentine had imploded. But none of these tragic events seemed sexy enough at morning conferences to be made into stories. At the next such conference, Blimby looked down the table. Ahearne, always a bit groggy before eleven, Peg Montgomery, L.P. and the rest stared eagerly towards him. Blimby knew what they said about him behind his back. He knew that Mary Much's nicknames for him, the WBG or Titch, were in common circulation. But since he had become the boss, and sacked two hundred and fifty people, the survivors looked at him with timid respect. No one, he kept telling them, was indispensable. Journalists – a phrase of which he was proud – had a 'sell-by date'. Those who had survived the purges were on their mettle and they produced better stuff in consequence. (By 'better', Mr Blimby meant crueller.)

'Peg?' he roared at the next morning's conference. 'What interviews have you got for us?'

With a distinctly wobbly cigarette, the Killer Interviewer named the star of a television soap opera.

'Is this going to shake the nation?' Blimby enquired.

'The show is watched by fourteen million people,' growled Worledge.

'The point is,' said Peg, 'it's the first time in the show that a married man has come out as a gay.'

'Is that something we want to encourage?' barked Blimby.

'Good point,' grovelled Worledge, who never watched the programme and had not known that this was the reason for Peg's interview. She floundered and began mentioning a TV cook known for alcoholism, a TV 'impressionist' whose second marriage was near its end, and a plucky TV weather-girl battling with breast cancer.

'Don't you expect our readers to do *anything* except watch the fucking TV?' shouted Mr Blimby, and he produced Rachel Pearl's *Guardian* article from a folder.

TWENTY-TWO

'Soup?'

'Please.'

'Pea soup?'

'Wonderful!'

'Then sausages, onion gravy, mashed potatoes?'

'Yes, please.'

'And, a little cabbage, I think,' said the Brigadier, writing the word out in full with his sharp pencil on the pad before him.

'That's our plan of battle,' he told the waiter, handing him the pad. 'And we'll have a little of the . . .'

'Luncheon cup, sir?'

'Yes, please.'

It was the third or fourth such luncheon. Sinclo had begun to find them a reassuring punctuation to life.

It had come as no surprise when Blimby gave him the sack. Now that Rachel was no longer in the office, he had come to loathe everything about his job at the *Legion*. The day after he had collected his P45, he had gone down to Crickleden to offer his services as a volunteer at the vicarage. It was the Brigadier's suggestion that he did so. He had hoped to use it as an opportunity to make things right with Rachel, but she appeared to have left at the same time as the Mad Monk.

All sorts of rumours ran round the parish. Some said that Father Vivyan had been sacked for paedophile activity. Others said he had eloped with Rachel. Some said the police had tried to frame him for political reasons. Sinclo no longer knew quite what to think. He discovered, to his dismay, that he was more painfully in love with Rachel than ever. The fact that she now believed him to be some sort of low-level gutter journalist who had set up the arrest of the Mad Monk, arranged for the presence of television cameras, etc. made him anxious not merely to put her straight, explain the true state of things, but also to lay his heart at her feet, tell her that he knew she wasn't in love with him, but that he would wait, be patient, hope for love to grow . . . Even as he said the words in his head, their hope-lessness, their actual absurdity, was quite clear to him, but he could not stop himself loving, and hoping.

'So what have you been doing down in Crickleden?' asked the Brigadier between his first two slurps of the (quite excel-lent) pea soup.

'A certain amount of football,' said Sinclo. 'They have some seriously good players.'

'This would be the Happy Band?'

'That's right.'

'All black?'

'Well, no. Most of the indigenous Band are black, of course, the Crickleden boys, but there are about eight Bosnian kids who are also really good.'

'Albanian?'

'Yes.'

'Just footer? Nothing . . .' The Brigadier peered carefully at his soup spoon as if it contained some rare specimen of pond life.

'There's this fellow, Thimjo. He's about my age, I suppose, late twenties, early thirties.'

'He's not in the youth club, surely?'

'He's not, but he more or less runs the Happy Band. He does teach them some pretty sophisticated survival techniques. I don't know if he got it from the Mad Monk, or whether it's his own idea. But a couple of nights a week, those boys are learning martial arts from him which would be deadly stuff if they were the SAS, quite frankly. And there's another thing. He has an armoury.'

'How do you know?'

'I've got into his camper-van. One evening when they were all at supper, I broke in. There were about twenty weapons in there – some of them taped to the top of the Formica cupboards in the little kitchen arrangement, others stuck to the underside of the bunk beds. Pistols mainly.'

'Tokarevs?'

'Yes.'

Sinclo had told himself by now not to be surprised by the Brigadier's omniscience. Sometimes, however, it was hard not to be surprised.

'There are dozens of these semi-automatics in circulation,' said the Brigadier. 'Some are old Red Army issue, others are slightly more modern, made in China. You think he's teaching the boys how to use them?'

'They don't need much teaching. This is Crickleden, not South Ken.'

'Quite,' said the Brigadier and ate silently for a while.

Then the older man added, 'You see, if you think about the little disturbance which we overheard after our first lunch together . . .'

'The Hans Busch explosion?'

'I think the reason Special Branch haven't come up with anything on that is quite possibly very simple.'

'Go on.'

'It's possible,' said the Brigadier, 'that there's nothing to come up *with*. You see, when we were working against the Irish, we had something to *go on*. There were *some* – not many, but *some* – of the Republican leaders that I almost came to like. Some of them were first-class commandos, and very brave. And you knew where you were, to a certain extent. To a *certain* extent. They had an objective – it was some form of Socialist Republic of a United Ireland. They knew they'd never get it, exactly, but they knew that if they went on bombing, they could destroy the Orange case: they could make the notion of a divided Ireland, and six counties ruled by the Protestant elite, seem *implausible*. They were entirely successful in this aim. Triumphantly so. Now they are part of the Joint Assembly there. And they knew that the first requirement was to destabilize, to undermine the confidence of the British Government. Again, in spite of our best endeavours in the Armed Services, the Republicans were totally successful. We kept telling every Prime Minister – Callaghan, Mrs Thatcher, Major – that we could manage. If all this was was a terrorist war, we could contain it, even win it. But of course, the political will wasn't there on the British side, which was why the IRA and friends were so successful. Now these people – the Crickleden mob . . . I think we can assume in some way they were responsible for blowing up Busch.'

'Behind it.'

'As it were,' drawled the Brigadier.

Partly out of nerves, partly because he found it genuinely funny, Sinclo almost spluttered his remaining mouthful of soup.

'The Irish were exposing the lack of political will in the British for a purpose. What if these chaps just want to expose the emptiness? As PMs go, you can't get a much emptier vessel than the present incumbent.' The Brigadier's eyes momentarily looked at the ceiling and he smiled to himself. 'What's going on in Crickleden, like so much of the other crime in London, it might just be empty anarchism, you see. Motiveless in a sense.'

'What about your theory that the Mad Monk is waging war on the last remaining vestiges of capitalist society, or some such?'

'I don't think I quite put it like that, my dear fellow.'

'You thought he might be a mastermind?'

'He's driven, isn't he? Or he was, until this latest fiasco.'

'Well, we always called him the Mad Monk.'

'You don't have any sympathy with religion?'

Having finished his soup, the Brigadier leaned back and put his rosy head on one side. He contemplated this lack of interest, as a curiosity. Or so it seemed as he smiled at his young friend.

'That's true, I suppose,' murmured Sinclo apologetically.

The first time he had ever lunched with the Brigadier, the old boy had compared the Mad Monk to some holy man he'd met in India. Evidently, there was some sense in which the Brigadier took religion seriously. Yet this was a matter about which Sinclo felt bold enough to speak up.

'It's all hooey, surely? The legends and so forth? Don't all religions prey on the unhappy feelings of people, their fear of death, their loneliness, their dread of rejection, and offer them consolations? Isn't that what the Mad Monk has been doing all his life? On one level, he's been doing good. On another, he hasn't cared to mix with his social or intellectual equals. He has preferred to play God, first in an African shanty town, then in an armpit like Crickleden, with old ladies and nutters and poverty-stricken immigrants coming to him out of desperate need. Have you see the notices he's put up in that shrine place – all about the Virgin Mary being worshipped there in the Middle Ages, and so on?'

'I did read them when I went down to the morning service one Sunday.'

'Rum stuff – I mean, you expect that sort of thing in Spain or Greece, but Our Lady of Crickleden!' He began to laugh again.

'You're not saying that Vivyan is a hypocrite, are you, an out-and-out fraud?'

'Of course not, no, no – er . . .'

'What then?'

'I just think . . . Ego-trip's an awful cliché, but I think . . . he's been on the most colossal ego-trip all his life. And he can't see . . . how it looks . . . And I think it's possible . . . Well, sometimes families see things other people don't see. We always called him the Mad Monk. Suppose he is off his trolley? Suppose he's organizing some gang of boys to cause mayhem in London? Suppose it has something to do with his feelings of anger against Lennox Mark?'

'Or Lennox Mark's feelings of anger against *him*,' said the Brigadier. 'What enrages me is that *The Daily Legion* – of course you couldn't stop them, my dear fellow, but they came up with all this nonsense about *boys* . . .'

'Is it nonsense?'

'We don't know, do we? And thanks to the newspaper wading in, we might never know.'

'They seem to have gone quiet for a while,' said Sinclo.

'For a while. As you say. Ah, here come the sausages.'

TWENTY-THREE

They'd sent Peg Montgomery. That was how important this thing had become. Lily d'Abo was a level-headed professional woman when faced, in the wards, on a day-to-day basis with life-and-death decisions. In family life she had always been a woman of robust common sense. But when confronted with a journalist whom she had been reading for years, over her Club chocolate orange biscuits and morning coffee, her judgement left her.

Instinct began to fight back almost at once, but Lily, reflecting afterwards on her day with the famous interviewer, could see how it was that men and women whom she'd hitherto despised for their lack of willpower could be led astray. Gamblers who ruined their family for a foolish speculation on a horse; philanderers who wrecked their career for an afternoon with some painted lady; drunks, exhibitionists, compulsive eaters.

'Why don't you take a grip on yourselves?' That had been Lily's question. She knew by the time she'd parted from Peg Montgomery that sometimes a grip was impossible to sustain.

She knew, for instance, even as she was agreeing to it, that it was a mistake to allow a journalist to come with her when she went for an interview with the Bishop. Some things, obviously, were better kept private.

'It's kind of you,' Lily said, 'but for this – seeing the Bishop – I'd better be alone. It's so – it's so *personal*. It's not just to do with Peter, it's my whole family, it's my faith itself . . .'

She never, afterwards, attempted to justify herself. She

despised self-justification. She did recognize, however, that her weakness and confusion sprang not simply from the fact that she was star-struck – *Peg Montgomery* in Lily's own flat! – but because for weeks she had been in a state of miserable shock and grief. It was a form of bereavement. She had not felt so lonely or so tired since the news came of her mother's death in Nassau in 1977.

The thought that, for all those years, Father Vivyan had been nothing better than one of those child-molesting homosexuals you read about in the *Legion* made Lily uncontrollably angry. People spoke of suffering as a blow. They spoke of being knocked sideways by bad news. Well, she'd been hit, bruised by the shock. It disturbed her very depths, those deep places in her heart where she had never imagined that dark or doubt could come. If *this* could happen, then not merely the Church but God Himself was a sham.

She thought of the periods, sometimes ten minutes, sometimes half an hour, when she had sat in silent prayer with Father Vivyan in his room. She thought of the hundreds of his masses she had attended. She had supposed him to be one of the saints, just as much of a true saint as Francis of Assisi or Vincent de Paul, whose statues stood on either side of the cast-iron grilles leading into Our Lady's shrine. You could feel God in Father Vivyan's presence. And if this man . . . with her boy, her grandson . . . Even while he was dressing the boy up in a cassock and cotta and telling him how to serve mass . . . how to hold the censer . . . All her idols crumbled. It was not just Father Vivyan who had fallen. God Himself was the last idol.

None of this could be said to Peg Montgomery. She sensed that the famous journalist was not in tune with things of the spirit. On the other hand, it was impossible not to remember the woman's triumphs. That crooked cop – fourteen years inside, after he'd been exposed taking bribes from drug traffickers, prostitutes, strip-joint proprietors. Or that surgeon: fifteen babies had died at his hospital in three years. Later, when the scales had fallen, Lily would see that Peg Montgomery had not contributed anything to the downfall of the crooked cop or the negligent surgeon. She had merely moved in on the stories and sensationalized them. The surgeon was unmasked because the parents of one of the dead babies complained to the local health authority; the rotten copper was unmasked by an internal investigation in the Met. But in each case it looked, from the way the *Legion* printed Peg's 'exclusives', as if she had single-handedly uncovered abuse. Lily, when she had contacted Peg Montgomery for advice, had felt that this journalist alone could punish the Church with a sufficiently glaring spotlight.

During that period of despair, Lily had written to the Bishop, to *The Daily Legion*, to her local MP. The Bishop had telephoned, himself, personally, and she was impressed by that. There were things she needed to talk about to him. After all, a bishop was first and foremost a priest. She could talk to him about her sense of spiritual desolation since all this began.

'Perhaps another day . . .' Lily was saying. 'Perhaps if you came and talked to me . . . if I went to the Bishop . . .'

'First things first, Lily.' Peg switched on a gleaming smile. There were dolls who could be made to smile by pulling a string in the middle of the back. Peg's on-off gleams of sympathy were similar. 'You rang me – you rang *The Daily Legion* because you wanted your story told clearly, truthfully . . .'

'I did . . . I know I did . . .'

'And we both know that without the support of a big organization – like the *Legion*, frankly – the private individual hasn't got an earthly. Not against the big guns. It's like the Lotley story.' Someone pulled the string again and the puppet grinned to the audience. That was the other odd thing about Peg. Though she was only speaking to Lily, she had the demeanour of someone making a speech to a theatre full of fans. Her cigarettey voice was posh, but not aristocratic like Father Vivyan's: it was smart, Kensington posh. She had very bright lips and her face looked much older than it was (fifty?) because of the nicotine-induced wrinkles.

'And money, frankly,' Peg was saying. 'Now all I want you to do is sign *this* and then I can have the pleasure . . .'

It seemed to Lily quite incomprehensible, when she looked back in the weeks and months which followed. She must have signed some contract or agreement, selling exclusive rights in her story to the *Legion*. It was hard to imagine how she had done so; she had never before felt the allure of money. But when she saw the cheque – £10,000! – this produced, on top of all the other sensations of shock, its own extraordinary effect. She went to pieces, began to spend it, in her thoughts, dividing it between the three grandsons and Mercy. Ten thousand!

'. . . no more, frankly, than you deserve . . .' Peg was apparently saying. As soon as the contract was signed, folded, snapped into her handbag, Peg was on her feet, exploring the flat – into Lily's room, Peter's, with its posters, its tapes, the toilet.

'Could I be awful . . . ciggie?'

Strings pulled. Grin. Mascara fluttered. And when a few puffs had been inhaled – she puffed so desperately, Lily wondered if she'd ever breathe out – 'The *Legion* will look after you. This is a *Legion* story now . . .'

Instead of the expected bus ride to see the Bishop in his office, there was the car, with a driver.

'Now, you aren't to let yourself be brow-beaten,' said Peg. 'They're very good, those Anglican oh-aren't-we-so-liberal *men*, at being old-fashioned *bullies*? You know?'

So, the words never quite came. In the car, they talked about Lily's work as a nurse, about Mercy's other two boys. (Afterwards, Lily swore to Mercy she hadn't told Peg some of the stuff: said she must have got it all from somewhere else. She knew, though, that she *had* been indiscreet, ridiculously so, even feeling, for an hour or two after the cheque was safely in her handbag, that she *owed* it to Peg to spill a few beans.)

When a young priest opened the door, Lily had truly intended, at once, to come clean, to say, 'This is a journalist.' She felt ashamed to do so – it was only a step away from admitting that she had just accepted £10,000 for her story. So she kept quiet, as the young priest, the chaplain evidently, showed them both into the Bishop's study.

And there he was, a half-balding bland figure with specs, pale grey suit, purple shirt and pectoral cross.

The chaplain announced their names, simply their first names, Peg and Lily, as if they came as a pair. And while the Bishop sat them in chairs on either side of the fireplace, Peg was asking, 'Is it the eighth deadly sin if I smoke?'

The Bishop's faint frown conveyed obvious distaste. On the other hand, this was a very delicate situation. He could hardly deny to visitors in obvious distress whatever relaxant they needed. For a second or two, his expression suggested that he might be brave enough to forbid smoking, but he soon relented into a forced smile.

'Of course – we must find you an ashtray.'

Then, the inevitable palaver ensued; the chaplain coming in with an ashtray, the requests, 'Tea or coffee?' At last the Bishop could say, 'This is a very serious situation, and a very sad one. And, Lily,' he put his fingers together and studied his blotter, 'what I want to say first is – I have been praying for you, I'm here for you. I don't want you to feel let down by the *Church*, Lily.'

All Lily's High Church prejudices had been prepared to keep herself at a distance from this Protestant in a suit; yet now she felt herself heaving, sobbing – and out came all her disappointments with her tears.

'He's taken . . . he's taken . . . my *vision*,' she sobbed. 'Such a vision of *goodness* I had in that man . . . and he was a good man . . . such a good man, I thought . . . and he knew Peter was so vulnerable . . .'

'Peter . . . is your grandson, no?'

'. . . and to fix on Peter . . . when he knew he was like he is . . . not quite . . . It's so, so unfair. Mercy, my daughter, makes it worse, says Peter's lying, and comes up with a story of Father Vivyan at a parish mission . . . making improper advances to *her* if you please, and as if that make a thing better . . . first de mother, den de son. I'm telling you, when we trusted him, we trusted . . .'

Peg sat smoking, while all this was being half articulated.

'It's hard . . . very hard for you,' said the Bishop.

'You bein' so kind, too.' Tears splattered Lily's lap as she spoke.

Now the Bishop got up and sat on the arm of Lily's chair, placed a hand on her shoulder.

'We trusted . . . we arl trusted dat man . . .'

'I know, I know.'

He massaged her shoulder.

Peg stubbed her Marlboro with the decisiveness of a good director watching a hard story of human sorrow turning into schmaltz. She did not quite shout 'Cut!' but she did interrupt, with her mascara fluttering as a call to order.

'This is all very well' – there were nerves in her voice, which the Bishop detected – 'but saying sorry and let's all hug one another's not going to undo the fact that a criminal offence has been committed. This is a clear case of sexual abuse . . . abuse of trust – and I'm sorry, Bishop, but the buck stops here.'

There was a silence before the Bishop spoke.

'I'm sorry, but who are you?'

'I'm Peg Montgomery.'

She uttered the words calmly, with the certainty that they could not make more impression had she said, 'I'm Field Marshal Montgomery of Alamein.' The fact that the Bishop did not recognize the name made her visibly furious.

'Are you some friend of Mrs d'Abo?'

'Peg Montgomery. *Daily Legion.*'

'A journalist.'

The invisible hand and string yanked a smile for the gallery, and the mascara fluttered to the invisible audience. She shook out her blonde curls and reached again for a fag.

Lily moaned, 'I . . . I . . . I . . .' but no words came forth. She might have been giving utterance not to the first person pronoun, but to the primeval shrieks of astonished grief – *Aiai, aiai* – spoken in Greek tragedies.

The Bishop had stopped stroking Lily and had sat down again behind his desk. His fingers drummed his blotter.

'Now, look here,' he said. 'I was under the impression that this was a pastoral visit, and that Mrs d'Abo wanted to speak to me in confidence. We didn't want any of this to get out and become . . .'

While he toyed between 'tittle-tattle' and 'common gossip' as suitably contemptuous terms, the smoke-breathing Peg went on the even-more offensive.

'You bet you didn't want it to get out! You think you can palm this woman off with a lot of flannel about Jesus loves you when we're talking about a man who's been abusing children for years – okay, so he doesn't limit his attentions to the children if he can get his hands on the mothers. We're talking about *crimes* – no, I'm sorry, Bishop – and we're talking about a cover-up . . .'

'Tea and bikkies!' chirruped the chaplain, entering with a tray.

'Graham,' said the Bishop, 'will you escort this person to the door, and will you also telephone for the police? We have an intruder, you see.'

'That's not a very good idea,' said Peg. The smile now made no pretence at mirth; it was simply a signal of menace.

Lily had managed to speak. She was saying, 'I'm sorry. I'm *so*, so sorry.'

'You've got questions to answer,' said Peg, shaking a ballpoint pen at the prelate.

'Not to you, I haven't. To you I have nothing to say. No apologies. No explanations. Got that? Father Chell has been suspended from his parish. That is what the Church did – it shows how seriously we take Mrs d'Abo's allegations. Lily, I repeat what I said to you – the Church is here for you, we are praying for you. But you're not going to help your cause *at all* by bringing in *The Daily Legion*.'

'You mean you're going for a cover-up,' insisted Peg.

'I mean that the police have found no evidence against Father Chell, and if they don't press charges then he can go back to his parish. Frankly, I'm inclined to think this has more to do with his witness against General Bindiga – in which I'm right behind him – than it has—'

'Please, please . . .' Lily was still crying. 'We'll go.'

'I think you can see who your real friends are,' said Peg; once more the histrionic effects of her words were slightly spoilt by the tremolo. 'Not an all-male, all-white conspiracy of silence, but a paper that's prepared to get to the truth . . .'

'Will you please leave . . .'

'. . . stick up for a boy who's been abused . . .'

'. . . Graham – please show this person—'

'Go – go – go!'

TWENTY-FOUR

The next morning, Mrs Thorn asked to speak to his lordship alone. Monty Longmore knew that there was something seriously amiss when he saw that she had not removed her brown overcoat. She did not belong to the hat generation, quite, and light raindrops had settled on her thick grey hair like dew on traveller's joy in the hedgerow.

'Is it still raining?' Monty asked, inconsequentially.

'Hardly so you'd notice,' she said, in a hard, unforgiving tone. The weather was to be pushed well to the margins of conversation; probably excluded from the agenda altogether. On most mornings, Mrs Thorn and Lord Longmore could spend five or even ten minutes dwelling upon its changing faces, and wondering whether there had been a wetter year on record. (Not, according to the Radio Two man who jabbered non-stop to Mrs Thorn in the kitchen.)

'Well, you'd better come into the office,' said Monty, sensing an important occasion.

The estate office was colder than the kitchen, much. It was a predominantly brown room. Large brown Victorian shelves, vaguely Gothicized, followed the high wall from frayed Turkey carpet to yellowing dado. The shelves contained files in boxes, ordered with some neatness. Dates of long-vanished twentieth-century years were written in faded fountain-pen ink on the spines of these records. There was an abundance of telephone directories. Above them, works of reference, such as a *Burke's*

Landed Families for 1926, several *Whitaker's Almanacs*, *Who's Whos*, *Debrett*. There were also books about pig breeding, and several bound volumes of a magazine for poultry breeders, their spines long ago faded. In a corner, lying against these shelves, were a number of air rifles in brown canvas cases. There were also croquet mallets. On an opposite wall were photographs, one of King George V in the uniform of C-in-C Armed Forces, one of Praze, who had been gamekeeper at Throxton in Monty's and Vivyan's boyhood, and one of their father in a tweed cap, taken at some agricultural show.

A black and white photograph of Kitty in a cardboard mount leaned on the chimney piece beside a pipe-rack, and a picture of Vivyan surrounded by African children in the Louisetown township. The one of Kitty was taken when she was twelve. She was wearing a velvet riding cap and grinning as she held the bridle of Gumdrop, the pony with which she had just won a gymkhana. On the wall in frames were photos of some of Monty's father's horses – Blaze Away which had won the St Leger in the 1920s, Dusty Answer, which came third in the Derby, and Harvest Home, a winner of innumerable minor races at Wincanton or Newbury.

All these fading sepia images in their oak frames added to the air of Dutch chiaroscuro into which Mrs Thorn, with her brown overcoat, blended and brooded.

Normally apple-cheeked, she was now blushing, to the roots of her wiry hair. Words which would never normally have come into Monty's head when thinking of Edith Thorn (whom he had known since she was a child) came now: hard, peasanty, flinty. The sense of hostility which she gave off was quite over-whelming.

She opened a large clasped bag and produced a copy of *The Daily Legion*.

'You'll know why I've come,' she said curtly.

'No, no . . . Mrs Thorn, I . . . er, no, I've no idea . . .'

'What's in there,' she said, not as a question, but as a statement.

'What *is* in there?'

He could guess the kind of thing; he did not want to see in detail.

He said feebly, 'May I?'

Peg Montgomery was a name which meant nothing to Lord Longmore. He had never heard of her. Her features, smiling winsomely under a blonde perm, at the top of her page, were totally unfamiliar. His newspaper-reading life was limited to one broadsheet, which in his view had been getting steadily more common, and less informative, since he had first begun to read it as a young man of twenty. He now limited himself to a quick perusal of its front page, a careful scanning of the death column, a little look at the letters, before concentrating on the crossword puzzle. This he usually managed to finish in about half an hour. The whole world of the newspapers, the world which was all-in-all to Mary Much and Lennox Mark, the world which had dazzled and affrighted Rachel for seven years, was completely unknown to Monty Longmore. He had seldom read the vulgar papers before his children grew up; and once Kitty had become, for quite arbitrary reasons as far as her father could make out, one of the characters endlessly written about in the gossip columns, he made it his business actively to avoid looking at them, even if he saw one lying on the table opposite him in a railway carriage or in the smoking room of his London club. The sight of the things had become too painful to him.

'It's page fifteen, as if your lordship didn't know,' said Mrs Thorn.

He murmured, 'Please.' The tone was so bitter – and it was

years since Mrs Thorn had called him 'your lordship'. (They had reached the quite pleasant truce of him calling her Mrs Thorn and of her calling him nothing, or occasionally 'sir'.)

While his eye took in the words on the garish page, Mrs Thorn was talking.

There was a large picture of Lily d'Abo, evidently very distressed, staring out at the top of the page. Inset into this was a photograph of her daughter, wearing a very revealing T-shirt and a short leather skirt with the caption 'Have Mercy, Father, for I have sinned.'

On the other side of the spread there was a huge picture of Vivyan. He looked haggard and rather seedy, with a worn-out donkey jacket over his cassock. Inset into this page was a picture of his bishop, wearing a mitre.

'WE DIDN'T WANT ANY OF THIS TO GET OUT. Bishop admits cover-up to top *Legion* writer Peg Montgomery.'

'I mean,' Mrs Thorn was saying. 'I'm sorry, my lord. But . . . with kiddies . . . even if they be piccaninnies, and their nigger mothers 'n' all. I'm sorry, my lord, but so long as that man . . . your brother . . .'

I went to the bishop for spiritual comfort. From the minute I stepped in the door I was greeted with hostility. I tried to share my hurt with him, the hurt which Reverend Chell did to me, my daughter, my grandson.

BRAVE GRAN LIL SHARES HER HURT WITH THE *LEGION* IN AN EXCLUSIVE PEG MONTGOMERY INTERVIEW.

'You seriously believe all this?' asked Monty. He was appalled by the newspaper item, but far more appalled by her credulity.

'There's no smoke without fire,' she said. 'Either he goes, or we go.'

'We?'

'John feels the same.'

Mr Thorn, keeper, groundsman, odd-job man, was pivotal to the running of life outside at Throxton, as Mrs Thorn was to the life of the house, in so far as it had a life.

'Judie' – Judith Cross, a woman who came up from the village to do charring three days a week, and who helped out at table if there were guests – 'she feels the same as me. More so, she's got little 'uns of her own at home to look after. Well, *I've* got grandchildren.' She said it with such anger that anyone hearing her might suppose that Lord Longmore had just suggested roasting them for his dinner.

'I know you have, Mrs Thorn. I know. But surely, you must see that . . . serious as these charges are against my brother, he *denies* them. Isn't the fairest thing to do to wait and see whether there is the smallest truth . . .'

'Like I say, there's no smoke . . .'

'I'm sorry.' He said it quietly, but Monty was actually very angry with her. Afterwards, he felt that his anger was caused by the fact that this red, stupid face, with all its hatred – its almost open hatred – was not only for Vivyan's sin, but, Monty felt, for him, too, and perhaps for his whole class. This had a most profoundly disconcerting effect on him. He asked himself for the first time, What would happen if the story was true?

'Well,' he said, 'if you feel like that, then you have no alternative but to stay at home until my brother . . .' This was a sentence which could have started better. He had hoped that Vivyan was here indefinitely. He did not want to say 'until my brother is arrested and put on trial', but that was the outcome which suddenly and horrifically he envisaged. Sadistically, Mrs Thorn let the words die on his lips.

He began again. 'To stay at home until further notice,' he said.

'We're not handing in our notice this week,' she said. 'John 'n' me thought as how it was only fair to let you consider it. But with Jude having kiddies – quite apart from *our* feelings, it wouldn't be right for us to go on coming here while *he's* here.'

'I'm sorry you feel like that. But, very well,' was all that Monty said. While she was performing the office of house-keeper, Monty would never have risen and opened the door for her, which was what he did now – as if she were a visitor in the house.

'I, too, of course,' he said hotly, as he led her through the dark shadows behind the main staircase, and out into the stone-flagged hall, past the huge, highly polished refectory table and the brooding Dobson of Colonel Chell and his sons before the battle of Naseby, 'I too will be considering your position. Quite honestly, Mrs Thorn, I don't take very kindly to your insulting insinuations!'

The glass in the huge inner front door rattled as he slammed it behind her, and he watched her stout legs and trainers beneath the brown coat squelch across the sodden gravel.

In the incomparable harmonies of the Anglican chant, the choir of Westminster Abbey was singing the daily psalms.

'My God, my God, look upon me; why hast thou forsaken me: and art so far from my health, and from the words of my complaint?'

All over London, the clergy of the Church of England were reading the words silently, or muttering them quietly at the back of their churches. And in St Paul's Cathedral, only a mile or so east of the Abbey, another full choir took up the melancholy Hebraic poem, lamenting the silence and absence of God.

'O my God, I cry in the day-time, but thou hearest not: and in the night-season also I take no rest . . .'

Sweating, and aching with hunger, for it was twenty minutes

since he had eaten a beefburger in the car, Lennox Mark sat at the back of St Paul's, luxuriating in the words and the sound.

All over London, the voice of prayer was lifted up. Domes, towers, steeples and pinnacles soared through the wet, cloudy air in token of the human faith in some beyond. From minarets in Mile End Road and Regent's Park, the muezzins called the faithful to prayer; from brick bellcotes clattered the Angelus; from temples, Hindu, Bahai and Buddhist, the collective human mind strove towards the Absolute and the Infinite. Great Nature, both amorphous and complex, enfolded this multiplicity of consciousness, of which they were a mysterious part, this million-minded awareness of Being itself, this human race. Pigeons, starlings, jays and magpies took wing through the rainy sky. Seagulls settled on rooftops, telephone wires, drainpipes. The drains and gutters themselves, alive with bacterial forms, amoebic vitalities invisible to the naked eye, gushed on to the indifferent paving-stones and tarmac. Trees, grass, mud, heavy with moisture, simply *were*. Urban foxes cowered by dustbins; cats, feral and domestic, dogs, rats, voles, mice breathed and moved and fed without the need to project their mentalities into the indifferent surroundings, or to look for personality in the vast impersonal processes of the natural world.

'But be not thou far from me, O Lord: thou art my succour, haste thee to help me . . .'

Lennox Mark's certainty, as he heard the choir sing these words, that there was a God, benignly anxious to promote his own personal wellbeing, was based upon not experience but his own processes of mind. It stood, as far as he was concerned, to reason. And now, God had blessed him, and given him what he and Martina had yearned for. That very afternoon, Lennox Mark had been to the College of Arms, a short walk from St Paul's, to discuss the finer points. He had wanted to be Lord Mark of

Kanni-Karkara, but Garter had said that though, in the days of Empire, some of the new peerages had been associated with colonial territory, it was no longer deemed appropriate. Lord Mark of Knightsbridge sounded a little too much like a department store. LenMar House was, broadly speaking, in Bermondsey, but there was already a peer of Bermondsey and, it would seem, of Southwark. Garter, with what degree of seriousness it was hard to tell, had suggested looking to the river for inspiration. The stretch of Thames by Cherry Garden Pier was known as Lower Pool. Lord Mark of Lower Pool was the 'working title'. He was a little anxious about what Martina would have to say about this.

But the great thing was that he had made it! He was no longer Lennie the fat boy who could not make friends; Len from an obscure African country and an ersatz public school; sausage roll Len who prematurely ejaculated, and could not get religion out of his system.

'*His Lordship will see you now.*'

Henceforward, secretaries would say this to everyone who walked into his office – editors, politicians . . .

Waiters would murmur, '*Your Lordship's usual table . . .*'

It was all in the bag. The Prime Minister had announced it in the Birthday Honours List. Lennie would take his seat in the Lords in only a few weeks, during the Bindiga State Visit. The General had graciously consented to come for lunch at the House of Lords with Lennie's sponsors, with Martina and her mother, and witness the arcane performance as, robed in the fur of a threatened species, and swearing allegiance to the Big White Chieftainess, he was led, with much bowing and mumbo-jumbo, to his place among the tribal elders.

There was a rightness about this, a fittingness, a justice which corresponded to his religious view of the world. Yet, ever-gnawing in his mind was the opposite thought . . . The choir sang it: '*For he hath not despised, nor abhorred, the low estate of the poor; he hath not hid his face from him, and when he called upon him . . .*'

What if he really had been running away from the true God all his life? What if the voice of Father Vivyan was the voice of God? Why all this stuff about the poor? Couldn't God stop talking about the poor for just ten bloody minutes?

'*The poor shall eat and be satisfied . . .*' sang the choir.

Lennox felt within him one of those surges of rage which made him hurl food at servants. He stood up roughly, and with a great scraping of the chair against which he had been leaning, and without further ceremony he walked noisily from the Cathedral. It was a long walk, and he reckoned he was about ten minutes away from the next fix of junk food. Since the car would not be expecting him for another twenty minutes, he might have even longer to wait outside in the rain. But he could not wait in this place any longer. That frantic restlessness had come upon him, that sense of panic.

As he left the Cathedral, a university-educated voice was saying through the loudspeaker, '*Here begins the fourth chapter of the book of the prophet Amos: Hear this word, you cows of Bashan, who are on Mount Samaria, who oppress the poor, who crush the needy . . .*'

The traffic outside mercifully drowned out the noise of it. Ludgate Hill, for all its churches, looked down at an essentially secular world of Londoners who were as indifferent to the poor as was the wind and the rain. Cafés, shops, cars and buses: the sight of them restored in him the sense of the normal, where the poor lurked ignored in doorways and sleeping bags.

The cries to God of the godless city rose up unheard in the rain-soaked sky. Yet in some couple of thousand or so of the many millions of consciousnesses in London, God did speak, and was heard. This was not the quiet sense, enjoyed momentarily

by Lennox and now evaporated, that his life had a shape or purpose or pattern. In these cases, an actual voice was heard. In the
Mile End Road, in a mosque, an imam heard his God distinctly
telling him to massacre Jews and unbelievers. In the convent
behind Marble Arch, the nun kneeling before the altar in a
posture of perpetual adoration heard Jesus speak to her of the
peace which passes understanding. In Number Ten Downing
Street, the Prime Minister, anxious about the crisis facing the
Commonwealth, was assured personally by God that General
Bindiga's visit to London would be a great success, a sign of the
PM's personal leadership. God used to address the Prime
Minister by his first name, but recently, perhaps as a mark of
respect, he had started to call him 'PM'. And clamouring for
attention, through the cacophony of voices inside Peter d'Abo's
head, God spoke of the need to collect guns, knives, weapons
for the coming struggle.

Ed Hartley, thirty-nine years old, married with two children,
had only one blemish in his unstained career. Five years earlier,
as the sports reporter for a TV company, he had travelled to
Holland to report a football match. While there, in a group of
other male journalists, he had gone into the red light district of
Amsterdam for a night on the tiles. Having drunk too much, he
and the lads had ended up in a nightclub with some lap-dancers,
who had sold him a number of drugs, including some tabs of
acid and a small amount of cocaine. Two of the tabs and some
of the cocaine were still there, in a tiny envelope in the top
pocket of his shirt, when he awoke the next morning in his
hotel.

It had been a foolish episode but not, as he supposed, anything significant. He knew that when he went home at midday,
he would take the Gatwick Express to Victoria, and then travel

by the suburban line to Dulwich where his wife and two sons (both at Dulwich College) would be awaiting him.

He had no interest in drugs, and since his early twenties (when he had enjoyed clubbing) he had hardly ever taken any illegal substance. It was a misplaced frugality which had made him unwilling to do the sensible thing and flush the contents of that envelope down his lavatory in the hotel. The same habit of mind which made him pack in his sponge-bag free samples of shampoo from the hotel bathroom made him believe that it was a waste to throw away these substances, even though he felt no particular urge to take them himself. So, they remained in his shirt pocket. It was one chance in a thousand, but the customs stopped and searched him at Gatwick Airport. He knew that Carol, his wife, would be furious with him. That went without saying. She was a chartered accountant who worked for a large firm in the City and was hoping to branch out into the sphere of personal financial advice. The boys went to the best school for miles in radius, and since their earliest years Carol had dinned into their heads that only fools took drugs. Now their father, an overgrown schoolboy aged nearly forty, whose 'career' was watching stupid boys' games, had been found with the sort of drugs you associated with juvenile delinquents.

Ed's chief worry, from the first, was not the drugs, but the girls. He did not mind how many lies he told Carol about the drugs. What he did not want her catching on to was that, whenever he got the opportunity, he was unfaithful to her – not in a way which he considered serious, but as a matter of habit. If in the course of work he found himself away from home for the night, staying in a hotel, he would regularly try and pick up a girl, or, failing that, go to some sleazy dive. He did not often go so far as to pay for a prostitute, though this had not been unknown, especially if he was away from home for more than a week, as had happened during the Olympics. He knew that this habit of his, if Carol found out about it, would end his marriage, and he loved Carol and the children. So he fabricated some ridiculous story about being approached by a man in the bar of his hotel and offered the drugs. Carol had insisted that he attend a drug rehab course, and she secretly began to wonder what normal man allowed himself to be picked up in bars in Amsterdam by other chaps. She had looked out ever since for secret signals of Ed's (non-existent) homosexuality.

The drugs incident at Gatwick had the most damaging effect on Ed's career. He was charged with illegal possession by the police and given a two-year suspended prison sentence. It cured him, for ever, of the idea that recreational drugs would add to life's pleasures, and it even brought a temporary halt to his routine, and habitual, philandering. But the worst thing was that he was obliged to give up his job as a TV reporter. ITN were ruthless about this, and applications for similar jobs, even with BBC local TV, were turned down flat. He eventually got a very junior job on the sports desk at the *Evening Standard* and gradually worked his way back. He was good at his job, passionately interested in football, cricket, athletics – most sports, in fact, except racing. He was a reliable and quick worker. He was clubbable and well-liked among the other sports journalists. When Blimby took over as editor of the new *Legion*, he asked around to discover who would be a suitably dynamic new man to run the sports desk. Several friends had recommended Ed.

That was now some months ago, and it really looked as if his life had recovered from the terrible mistake at Gatwick Airport two years before. Then, completely out of the blue, when he was in the middle of sketching out the pages for the following day's *Legion* and comparing photographs of a fast bowler with those of a tennis champion, the telephone rang. Scotland Yard.

Ed had frozen and begun whispering, frantically, into the telephone. It was an open secret, his idiocy over the drug-smuggling, but he had not overtly mentioned it to Blimby when he got the job, and he did not want it referred to. Like everyone who had ever fallen foul of the law, in however minor a way, he reacted with feelings of guilt when confronted by the police.

They asked him if he could come down to see them. They did not specify over the telephone what it was which they wished to discuss. Ever since his night in Amsterdam, Ed had been possessed with the irrational fear that something would happen in the lap-dancing club – some explosion, some murder, some-one would strangle one of the girls – and the international police would, by some process of magic, be able to interview everyone who had ever patronized the place. He imagined a uniformed officer turning up on the doorstep of his house in Dulwich and spreading out black and white stills of Dutch prostitutes on the kitchen table. He imagined the boys – Gavin and Hugh – coming into the room, and Carol's unforgiving eyes falling on fishnet tights and bare tits.

Although he took particular pride in the layout of the sports pages – having supervised each and every page personally since taking his job – Ed had left the offices of the *Legion* in a hurry, and gone down to Scotland Yard, taking the Jubilee Line to Westminster.

The questions they asked him were incomprehensible. At the time of his arrest, he had given the police samples of blood and urine. They had evidently stored his DNA records. The police were interested in the fact that Mr Ed Hartley had recently been appointed chief sports editor of the *Legion*, whose proprietor was Mr – they begged his pardon – Lord Mark.

A while ago, back in February, Lady Mark – Mrs Mark as she then still was – suffered an intrusion at her house in Redgauntlet

Road. The police were not at liberty to disclose how, but one of the intruders (there were three of them, at least) had left traces from which DNA samples could be taken. This DNA data, when fed into the computer, matched the DNA of Ed Hartley. The police were not accusing Mr Hartley of being the intruder. He did not match the descriptions of any of the men who had been to the house that night. What was not in doubt, however – they had the scientific evidence to prove it – was that one of the intruders was someone close to Hartley. Could his sons provide alibis for the night in question?

This line of questioning threw Ed into a panic. He had heard himself stammering, felt himself breaking out into a sweat with quite inarticulated sensations of guilt. They had something on him – but what it was, he could not say. He assured them that they must be making a mistake, that his sons would not be capable of violent crime or burglary – they were being educated at one of the most expensive schools in south London. Nevertheless, the police did insist on following up their investigations, and visited the house in Dulwich. It was then that Carol, indignant on her boys' behalf, and everlastingly suspicious of Ed, insisted that her husband 'come clean'.

'You know what it is they are asking – you must know something you're not telling them.'

That had been her line from the first. Clearly, with her obsessive memory of the (non-existent) man in the bar at the Amsterdam hotel, Carol supposed that the DNA samples left at Lennox Mark's house were somehow or other linked to her husband's secret gay life. Her own, unscientific, belief was that a drop of Ed's semen had been found on one of the burglars' jackets or trousers. Since he had got a very good job again at the *Legion*, Carol had been fond of Ed, and their marriage had been unwontedly happy. All that now evaporated once more. They had rows, either directly or indirectly, about the DNA evidence, even though neither of them knew what this evidence could possibly be. Late at night, their sons, from the privacy of their bedrooms, would hear Carol screaming at Ed that if he was as innocent as he said he was, he'd write to Lennox Mark and ask for *him* to clear the whole thing up with the police.

It was by no means obvious what there was to clear up. Nevertheless, Ed had made several attempts to see the Chairman in his offices at LenMar House. So far, none of these efforts had been successful. After he'd rung Lennie Mark's secretary three times asking for an appointment, Blimby had asked him, 'Is everything all right?'

'Fine, fine, thanks.'

'Only, I gather you've been trying to see the Chairman. Hope you're not trying to bankrupt the paper by asking for a bigger salary!'

Tiny Blimby made that harrumphing bellow of his.

You couldn't keep secrets in that bloody building.

TWENTY-FIVE

48c Kinglake Road,
Streatham,
London SW16

Dear Lennox

I have tried several times to ring you, but of course, it has always been a secretary and 'Could I ask what it's concerning?'

Lennox, you know what it's concerning, but I can't tell it to a secretary. Believe me, I am only trying to get in touch with you because I want what is best for Peter, for my son. I don't suppose it will ever be possible to undo all the damage which Peg Montgomery's article in the *Legion* last week has done. The stuff about me was a load of rubbish for a start and if I was into suing people it would probably be a libel (slander?). But that's not what it's about, Lennox.

Lennox, you know what happened between us seventeen years ago, and I haven't asked for anything from you. You offered me money – remember? – and that wasn't what it was about, either, believe me. I just felt so hurt by that at the time.

Lennox, I've got to see you. You understand that, don't you? Think what this is doing to me. Peter is a very disturbed young man. He can certainly be a danger to himself, and I am beginning to be afraid that he will be a danger to others. Since all this has blown up, he has gone missing.

I don't know what to believe any more.

Is it true he has been working in your house? We were told

he was in some posh restaurant. Then he said he was working for you, but he lives in a world of dreams.

Please, Lennox. I'm not asking for money, I'm not asking for publicity. But you know why I'm asking to see you, and it's not fair to palm me off, it isn't.

Mercy Topling

346 Lincoln's Inn Fields

Dear Mrs Topling

Your letter of 17 July has been forwarded to us by our client. Our client acknowledges that you worked as a stenographer at *The Daily Legion* from July to December 1985. You worked as his assistant. When you left the paper, you approached our client with a number of imputations which he strenuously denies. He offered you a sum of money as a goodwill gesture, and it was in no way intended to confirm your story. You rejected that money.

Our client wishes you to know that he believes your story is highly defamatory. Any attempt to repeat it, either in letters to himself, in telephone calls, or in conversation with others, will result in his feeling obliged to prosecute you.

Yours faithfully

Squibble Illegible

PP Oliver Golightly
Signed in the absence of Mr Golightly from the office

Lennox

This is frankly disgraceful. Look, you know what I am talking about. It is PATHETIC to drag lawyers into this. In my previous

436

letters, I have only referred in a very tactful way to You Know What. But, Lennox, we are talking here about the life of a boy – MY SON – OUR SON!! You know that while I was working for you, we had an affair. I am not claiming any money. I am not pretending you took advantage of me. We were both grown-ups, I knew the facts of life. But, Lennox, I became pregnant and I'm telling you that Peter is our son. I don't care what the law says, you have a moral obligation to help me find him.

Whether you had anything to do with that Peg Montgomery article in the *Legion* or not, Lennox, my mother was fooled into giving that interview, and what it says is frankly CRAP. Father Vivyan is worth ten of you and you know it. He is not a child molester. I could tell you more if you would only let me meet you.

Since that article appeared, Peter has gone missing. Lennox, he could be YOUR son and the article appeared in YOUR paper.

I am just asking for ten minutes of your time. If you're so bloody high and mighty you can't see me, then I'm asking for your help in finding Peter. I don't think you understand what I was saying in my last letter. Lennox, Peter is mentally disturbed. He has not been diagnosed as schizophrenic, but whatever it is, he needs help.

Please, please do not palm me off with another lawyer's letter. This is so cruel. You don't know what this is doing to my family, Lennox.

M. Topling

Dear Mrs Topling
You will see from the enclosed documentation that we have this morning, from Her Honour Judge Marcelle Rosenburg, in the High Courts, obtained an injunction to prevent you from

attempting to write, telephone or have any further contact with our client. He vigorously denies the statements you have been making about the nature of your relationship. We repeat our warning that if you continue to repeat these allegations, we shall be obliged to prosecute you for criminal defamation of our client's character. We need not remind you that the consequences of being found guilty in such a case would be the imprisonment of the defendant and the confiscation of her assets.

We remain your obedient servants.

Yours faithfully

Signed in Mr Golightly's absence while fishing in Ireland

'He's worried. That's for certain.'

'Lennie?'

'Mmm, darling.'

Martina and Mary Much were at their usual table at Diana's. The usual aioli, the usual chips, the usual lobsters, the usual cigarettes.

'Everything all right, your ladyship?' asked the waiter.

Mmmm, that felt good.

Mary had been surprised by the extent to which she had minded, really minded this: Martina's excitement about the peerage. All manner of deep, atavistic national pieties came up, not to the surface, but close to it.

She sometimes wondered whether Martina had forgotten that it had all been her idea, her marrying Lennie.

'It was a surprise,' Martina was saying. 'I didn't think Lennie was into that sort of thing . . .'

Her frozen, sewn-up *moue* moved by a fraction, and she laughed.

'Blicks?' asked Mary Much brightly.

'I meant sex, actually,' said Martina. And then, as she let out a long blast of smoke from her nostrils, she looked up at Mary and smirked.

My God, Mary thought, there was a bit of self-pity in that smirk, a bit of fucking pathos. This woman was asking her to sympathize with her because she did not have to fuck the great heffalump, whose idea of conversation was cricket scores and theology and whose appetite for food was so much stronger than it was for – one. Christ, this really did take the biscuit.

Mary had always hated the way her best friend's scale of morality revolved round self-pity. Okay, boo-hoo, she'd been a poor little slut in East Berlin, and she'd dragged her mother over the Wall like a sack of potatoes. Martina spoke and behaved in a way which suggested that this unmentionable and unmentioned fact gave her carte blanche to behave absolutely as she liked. That really got on Mary's tits.

They had never mentioned to one another that they had first met when Mary was a shop assistant and Martina was on the game, sitting in the bar at the top of Granville Stoppard getting squiffy and hoping she'd meet her sugar daddy. But this fact, though never mentioned, of course determined the subsequent course of their friendship. When they had both in their different ways got their breaks, when Martina Fax had become the trenchant columnist and Mary Much the aspirant Queen of the Glossies, then they were emotionally ready for friendship. Martina had the staying power, the brains, the guts to carry herself from triumph to triumph. But even she would not have had the idea of bagging the proprietor if it hadn't been for Mary Much's 'Don't go to bed with him, God no. Marry him, darling.'

By 'don't go to bed' she hadn't meant never go to bed with

him. But if they hadn't, they hadn't. That was their business. Mary wanted very much to tell Martina that she wasn't missing anything. Instead, she discovered, cold and fully formed like a statue made of ice, the thought of how she wanted to live the next five to ten years of her life. She wanted Lennie to pay Martina off. She, Mary Much, decided it was her turn to become Lady Mark.

'He was all for seeing the woman.'

'The Blik Lady?'

'The nigger,' said Martina, picking up a chip, dipping it in aioli and then putting it down.

'There'd have been no harm, surely?'

'Are you mad? He really did it with her — he did it. Can you imagine that? I asked him where — in an hotel? At the Savoy? He said, in the office — *in the office* — in hotels, several times, apparently. Perhaps that is what he has been into all these years, since African days. Niggers.'

Mary Much knew exactly what Lennie was 'into'.

'Lovely article this morning, darling,' she said, patting the *Legion* which, as always, lay on the table beside them.

'Was it okay?'

'It was, in the circumstances' — Mary smiled — 'very broad-minded of you.'

Since coming to live in this country from Switzerland [Martina had written], *I have been proud to call myself British. Proud because this country was based on decent values, treating everyone as equal, regardless of race or religion.*

But in the criticism of General Bindiga, I have heard something which is downright ugly.

Under the cloak of saying they disapprove of Zinariya, many so-called English liberals have been simple racists.

The issue is quite clear. If you don't support what General Bindiga is doing, you are a racist. He is the only man in his country who is on the side of decency, law and order. He is trying, against enormous odds, to keep the industrial and agricultural life of his country going against the assaults of communists and terrorists.

Those who attack Bindiga use words — like 'savagery' — which they would never use of a white man . . .

'It's true,' said Martina, pompously.

'He's really coming to the ceremony? At the House of Lords?'

'Lennie's being introduced to the Lords during the General's State Visit. We're going to have the General as our guest of honour at the lunch.'

There was something so breathtakingly pompous about this that Mary almost wondered whether it would be possible to take Lennie away from his wife before the Bindiga State Visit. Probably not — even if they forced a quickie divorce. Still, it was useful to know that they had never — ever-wever? — *done it.*

'So, you never knew he was into . . .'

Martina did not need much prompting. She was, by her standards positively forthcoming.

'I'm amazed,' she said, 'that he has ever done anything which could have made someone, even a deranged nigger, think he'd made her pregnant.'

'What is he' — ickle-wickle giggle — 'what is he into, then?'

Mary thought that in Martina's sigh of a reply, she heard her whole life-history. It was not said in the tone of a wife. It was the voice of a bored prostitute who carried within her brain a menu of uncongenial activities which her clients might or might not wish her to perform.

'Can't you guess? Just oral. Basically, with Lennie, if you can't eat it, it doesn't exist.'

Mary's curiosity about other people's sexual lives knew no bounds; but she knew when, in the conversational warfare of best friends, to hold back, when to seize an advantage by apparent indifference. She longed to know just what the opaque phrase meant – did Lennie still 'eat' in the sense described, or did such behaviour belong to his early days with Martina? Did she just sit there, filing her nails or watching television with that frozen, bored expression on her face, while he slurped and grunted between her legs? She did not imagine that Lennie had ever got Martina to eat *him*. That was too much to expect.

'Darling, that shirt of yours . . .'

Martina named the designer.

'I know, but on you – you can get away with it – it's just divine.'

Before Martina had a chance to feign too much pleasure, Mary Much added, 'It looks so much better than the little coat you were wearing yesterday. Frankly, that wasn't you, darling.'

TWENTY-SIX

The allotments spread out higgledy-piggledy over a tract of land, some four acres, adjoining the sprawl of the cemetery. In fine summer weather, they made a comforting sight in this largely uncomforted area of south London. Smoke would rise from carefully contained bonfires, signs of something like domesticity. Each small patch of land was different, tokening the independence and freedom of those who cultivated it, and the variety of purposes which the allotment served in the lives of Crickledenians. Some of these patches, let out to tenants on a yearly basis, had been cultivated by the same families for generations, stretching back to the Second World War when this patch of wasteland was first planted, in the campaign to 'dig for victory'. Such plots were in effect smallholdings, with onions, potatoes, lettuces, beans, peas springing obediently from the well-sifted black soil in regimented rows. Other allotments, the diversion of younger vegetable-growers, were sometimes planted more haphazardly, with failed experiments – unstaked sunflowers, canted like drunken giants to the earth; slug-eaten courgettes; artichokes which had bolted or run to seed. Some plots were given over chiefly to flowers, a summer long, from early sweet peas to late chrysanthemums, of blooms to be taken home as bouquets. The more favoured plots boasted sheds, and here again, the variety of human requirement and character was announced by the difference between, on the one hand, brand-new, fresh-creosoted prefabricated efforts delivered by van and set down that season, and sun-bleached wobbly constructions whose few panes of glass were thick with the cobwebs and dust encrustations of the years. Some of the sheds were strictly functional, sentry-boxes containing the bare essentials of horticultural tools. Others, beside the spade or rake required to stick in the earth and use as a makeshift coat-hanger, were almost more like inland beach-huts: little kingdoms where tea could be brewed, newspapers perused, cigarettes smoked, dreams dreamed. The presence in a few huts of day-beds and mattresses was suggestive in some cases of afternoon naps, in others of discreet romantic liaisons.

But for months now, the allotments had been a desolate paddy-field, as rain followed rain. Many gardeners had not even planted this year; the weather was so unfavourable that there had been no weekend when the ground could be dug, and forked over, or the vegetables planted out. In consequence, in many patches, nature had taken over. Grass, briar, varieties of wild clematis, sorrel, and rosebay willow herb rampaged where runner beans or globular dahlias might, the previous year, have provided their splash of colour. Japanese knotweed, aggressive and abundant, strayed from neglected plots to those areas of land which a few doughty gardeners had attempted to cultivate. The efforts of these brave individuals had been all but destroyed by tempests. Canes had no sooner been erected into ingenious tripods to train the trailing bean or pea than near gale-force winds blew them over. Any plants poking more than a few centimetres above the soil were flattened by storms; and so much rain had fallen that root artichokes, potatoes, carrots had all rotted; radishes had swollen to grotesque, but tasteless proportions.

One such gardener who had defied the weather, and tried to dig and turn the squelching, recalcitrant soil, to sow and to plant in the resultant mud patch, was Solomon Farr, a seventy-five-year-old man who had been a devotee of the allotments for half a century. Sol had been a fireman in the days of steam, working for the LMS railway before it was taken into public ownership, and then for British Railways and British Rail. When he retired he was a guard on the Southern Region. He had been as dismayed as all his generation had been by the decline of the railways. The allotment had been his consolation, particularly when his wife had become ill. For weeks now, he had not been seen. The police had searched his own allotment hut, but they had not scoured the whole four acres, nor opened every hut in the place. Afterwards, they were criticized for this rudimentary negligence, but, in their defence, it had to be said that no one had seen him for weeks, either at the allotment, or anywhere else. Only when the fine weather came, and a couple called the Fentons once more resumed their routine of going to their hut on the allotment to drink tea from a Thermos flask, were the remains discovered. It was an unsolved murder; apparently without motive. Hardly anyone had known Sol, except his wife – now in residential care, with her hip, and, since the news was broken to her, showing signs of confusion – their daughter, who did her best to visit her parents but lived an awkward journey away in Hemel Hempstead, and a few neighbours. Like many, perhaps most, men of seventy-five, Sol Farr had kept himself to himself.

The concealment had been done with some skill. Joan Fenton, sixty-seven, a housewife, had been the first to complain of the smell, but her husband, Pat, a solicitor's clerk in Greenwich until retirement two years previously, had assured her that all the huts smelt damp – it had after all been raining for the better part of twelve months. It was the scuffling of the rats which persuaded him that he was wrong. Once they began to suspect what had been placed beneath the floorboards of their hut, Joan had warned him not to go on. Pat, Pat, she had urged, ring the police – don't look, Pat, it might be . . . Joan had known how her sentence would end, so she had not ended it. But Pat, stubborn as ever, wouldn't take advice, not from her, chance'd be a fine thing, and had gone on, wrenching and prising and swearing at splinters in his thumbs until the plump, insolent gnawing rats had been revealed, scampering over what remained of Sol Farr's face. Whoever had done that, Joan always said afterwards, had Pat's stroke to answer for as well as the old railwayman's murder. But they never did find out who had done it. And that, anyway, belonged to the sunlit period of Indian summer after this story is over. We find ourselves in the allotments when they were Crickleden's wetlands; when paths were liquid mud, and when the planks laid down in parts to facilitate walking were themselves slimy and hazardous, when canes, plants, bushes and leaves were splattered with a sooty black ooze.

TWENTY-SEVEN

Rachel Pearl had called at the vicarage, at Mrs d'Abo's, at Mercy Topling's house, but none of them knew the whereabouts of Peter d'Abo. Odder, given the painfulness of the circumstances, none would admit that they did not know. Mrs d'Abo was withdrawn, crushed, hesitant.

'I say arl I garter say,' she had repeated several times.

The same misconception was apparent in the daughter's much more aggressive response to Rachel's enquiries.

'Don't you think you people have done enough?'

'I'm sorry. Which people?'

'So you *should* be sorry . . .'

'Look, Mrs Topling – Mercy . . .'

'I'm not helping you – is that clear? I'm not telling you *anything*.'

The scene, at the Toplings' maisonette in Streatham, was one of unrelieved desolation. Trevor, the husband, was slumped in a chair, on one arm of which a metal ashtray over-flowed volcanic quantities of stubs and grey dust. His brown crinkly socks stretched useless before him. He looked as if he had no intention of getting up from that posture. He stared, wordless, into the middle distance as his wife spoke out, spoke up.

'This whole thing has just got so out of *hand*. Talk about a stitch-up!'

'*I'm* not stitching anyone up.'

447

'You know who he was working for? All the time, he'd told my mum he was working in a posh restaurant and he was working for *your boss*.'

'I don't have a boss.'

'Oh yes you do.'

'Look, if you think I'm a journalist . . .'

'Like that other one – ever so smooth, handsome, posh. He's good-looking, I'll give him that. Now he's staying at the vicarage, saying he wants to "help out" – when we all know he works for Dr Arbuthnot's Diary. I mean, just how stupid do you think we are? Okay, pretty bloody stupid if you judge us all by my mother.'

'I'm not a journalist. I used to work for *The Daily Legion*. I don't any more.'

'That's just what he says.'

'Who says?'

'That public schoolboy, the one I said – he's good-looking. Lovely hair.'

'There's been a terrible misunderstanding.'

'Too right there has.'

'I'm not the person who . . . Look, if you'd just *listen* for a minute, I want to help Vivyan. I know I can clear his name, but we must get hold of your son . . .'

'You know what they started saying now?'

'Who?'

'Peter – before he left. Lucius. Brad.'

She pointed at her husband.

'I *know* that man – he's not a child-molester. That's what I mean by it all spiralling out of control. First we find that Peter's working for Lennox Mark. Then the accusations start flying around – first it's Father Vivyan. Then it's *Trevor*. They actually accused Trevor . . .'

'Your other two sons, they said that Trevor . . . ? I'm sorry, I don't follow this . . .'

'Peter put them up to saying it, I'm sure of that. I'm not saying Peter's blameless, but what I am saying is that he is vulnerable. This whole thing's made him worse — stands to reason it would, someone like him. Someone in his condition. But where's a social worker when you need one? We had one — Kevin Currey — he was on Peter's case, though if you ask me he made it worse not better. Then — nothing for weeks. Then we heard, it was terrible, he'd met with an accident. I still think they should have put another social worker on Peter's case. As for what that paper has done to my mother . . .'

TWENTY-EIGHT

The cemetery wall divided growing plots from burial plots. In many places, though, its jerry-piled stock brick had collapsed, so that amid the brambles it was hard to know where the allotment ended and the huge municipal graveyard began. Since the turn of the nineteenth and twentieth centuries, south Londoners had been mulching the acreage. The sodden paths where unswept leaves were squelched into mud led to a variety of graves – headstones, marble crosses, angels with outspread wings – but the attempts to suggest individuality in death had as the years went by produced an impression of sameness. Here and there, gestures towards grandeur had been essayed. A terracotta bas-relief, a miniature obelisk, even a pyramid could be found among the undergrowth. And down one edge, beyond the nondescript slabs, was a row of mausolea resembling a parade of little houses, made of marble, or granite. The family name would be carved over the jamb of these bizarre edifices: SOSKICE – WHEELER – AMLOTT. None of the nobility lay here. The vaults represented the sense, here of a prosperous grocer, there, 'SPINELLI', of a restaurateur, there of a doctor, here of a factory-owner, that, if they had to lie in death with the anonymous rows of their clients and employees, whose very names were now illegible on skewed stone, they might, these richer ones, continue, even in death, to mark themselves out, to cut a dash. Inside, as you could see if you peered through the grilles in the doors, the dead, in their coffins, were stacked on shelves up the wall in an arrangement reminiscent of the old *couchettes* in transcontinental trains. These vaults were themselves in various stages of decay and in many of them the locks on the doors were broken. Some of them had been boarded up by the local authority, but to those with a mind to penetrate, there was not much difficulty in wrenching a board, cutting some wire or forcing a bolt. Some of the cave artists who had adorned the bandstand in the adjacent park had been here spray-painting their allegations about the auto-eroticism of characters – Del, Leroy, Jake – themselves already as anonymous as the forgotten dead who lay in multitudes around.

Since the police raids on the camper-vans in the drive of the priest's house, a number of the young men had found these vaults a suitable temporary abode. The police had found many rifles, machine-guns, pistols, but not all, and luckily O'Sullivan, their contact in South Norwood, still held on to the bulk of the explosives. Without Father Vivyan, their possession of this arsenal was, besides, if not quite pointless, then without any immediate reason or justification. For most of the young men, the fun consisted in the accumulation of the weaponry, the secrecy of it, the combat training, rather than in any specific goal. Tuli, the young lunatic, had tried to persuade them that they should take revenge for the priest's arrest – perhaps by the assassination of some well-known local figure, or by blowing up a police station. But this was crazy talk. The priest had been arrested – then the police let him go. No one knew where he was, though one of the young monks said Father Vivyan was ill and had been taken to the infirmary in his monastery. The Kosovans, together with their rag and tag of newly accumulated friends – a Bulgarian called Grigor who had smuggled himself into England buried in a vanload of tomatoes, a mysterious figure called Enver – had dispersed. There was always somewhere else to run to.

The vicarage, quite apart from the presence of police smiles like the man Manners, who was now working for military intelligence, was no longer a good place to be. The two young monks who were running the parish had put locks on the front door, and bolts on the back. The Gentlemen of the Road were directed to a hostel which the monks had set up in the parish hall, run by the volunteers who slept in the vicarage. There were some immigrant families being accommodated in the drive, but no illegals, no seekers.

It was Thimjo, in effect their platoon commander, who had seen the necessity, before they all dispersed, of finding somewhere local to store the remaining armaments, and, vitally important this, of finding an individual who was prepared to act as the arsenal's custodian. The ideal person would be one who was not afraid of solitude, not afraid of sleeping rough. One of the tramps would probably have fitted the bill admirably. Then came the newspaper articles. And suddenly the boy wanted out. Tuli needed to take cover. To go underground. Tuli wanted to hide, Thimjo wanted a guardian of the armoury. The huts in the allotments were an obvious place to hide both boy and guns, at least until the weather improved. After several days of watching, it had been decided the allotments were safe. They had commandeered three huts. One of these had been emptied of rakes, forks and spades and filled to near bursting point with weapons. Another had made a good enough place for general stores – stolen tins of food, a camping stove, rudimentary cooking implements. There was even a toilet in a small brick enclosure, but after one of the Albanians pulled the chain too roughly, this broke and the pan soon became blocked and stinking. In the largest of the huts, a number of them stretched out in sleeping bags and slept – until the old man came and found them. After they'd concealed him beneath the floorboards, they completed the risky job of moving the guns back to the mausolea.

TWENTY-NINE

She had told her over and again, but there was no chance of Rachel persuading Mercy. The last few months had obliterated Mercy's trusting nature, destroyed her capacity for optimism. The boy's madness — no point, any more, in beating about the bush, this was what it was — had infected all of them. Mercy herself, whose gift for happiness through thirty-eight years had derived from her certain, laughing knowledge of her own sanity and good sense, had, even she, begun to be tainted by it. The boys had, after a childhood of football, videos, fun, lost sight of their own boyishness and learnt to be conspirators, to play at criminality, to swear. Their accusations against their own dad had poisoned the atmosphere.

Lily, silly Lily as Mercy had so often meanly (though in the secrecy of her own thoughts) dubbed her mother, had performed the ultimate madness of talking to the press, and thereby she'd made it impossible for Mercy to talk to *her*. Mercy wasn't being vindictive. She hoped, believed, that one day she'd be able to talk to Lily again, but just for the moment — no. It was not a question of forgiving her mother, it was that Lily had projected them all into a narrative which was not real. You couldn't go into that story, even to contradict it, without taking off into lunacy.

So, outgoing, smiling, laughing Mercy had become cautious, half-paranoid and angry. She did not really believe that Rachel Pearl was not after her for a story. There was, anyway, more going on here. Mercy half disbelieved Rachel's story that she was a reformed journalist who merely wanted to clear Vivyan's name and, if possible, help Peter. The half of Mercy which believed this story resented it. She sensed that Rachel was in love with Vivyan, or obsessed by him in the way that so many of his devotees were. Rachel obviously, therefore, resented the stuff in the *Legion* about his having made advances to Mercy. What wouldn't Rachel do – this Mercy thought – for what she had seen and *had*?

Mercy's caginess with Rachel concealed, therefore, a multitude of thoughts. Rachel had worked on the *Legion* – she knew that Peg Montgomery cow, the nice boy who was living in the vicarage: for all Mercy knew, she'd been one of the girls who'd had her bottom pinched in the lift by L.P. She resented this woman with her pert, knowing, educated manners, presuming to be the one who 'saved' the priest – saved the boy.

'He doesn't have,' Rachel was pressing in her enquiry, 'some special friend, a girlfriend maybe, where he's staying?'

'I've told you. I don't *know* where Peter is . . .'

'He must be feeling . . . my point is, he must *know* that the stories in the *Legion* were untrue. All he has to do now is *say so* . . .'

That 'all' was annoying. Mercy looked at Rachel, took in not merely her neatly cut hair, her pallor, her seriousness, but also her need to sort and tidy and boss. Mercy wanted to scream: 'It's my boy you are talking about – my *son*! And possibly his *father* – and you're talking about the situation as if you could just bustle in and *sort* it.'

'Of course,' Rachel said, 'if I hear anything, I'll let you know.'

Mercy made her voice deliberately vague; she said, in a sort of sigh, 'You won't find him,' but she couldn't keep from this assertion a certain edge, a hint of aggro.

Rachel picked up on this.

'Oh, I'll find him,' she said, with gritted determination.

THIRTY

Who you fucking kidding. You told Mr Fat. That's how it . . .

Now wait a minute before you start . . .

Told Mr Fat it was Father.

Yeah, I was . . . I was frightened.

You'll be fucking frightened before I done with you.

. . . before you start attacking him, wait. Quiet. Calm . . .

. . . Blessed Mary ever Virgin, Blessed Michael the Arch-angel . . . through my fault, through my fault, through my own most grievous . . . oh and I served Holy Mass, I confessed it all . . .

You tell him a loader shit, man – you were both getting off on it, you know that – confession – loader shit.

It was Mr Currey who . . .

No uphill gardener get near my ass I'm telling you, mate. You hear me – no bum-bandit – if you say, if you so much as say – see this knife? Remember the Paki – slice, slice? Remember that revolting bit of shit, that poof in the multi-storey? Took his balls off for him, dun I? He's lucky – no listen . . .

We shouldn't, you shouldn't have told Mr Mark it was Father Vivyan when it was Mr Currey –

Listen, fuckface, will you? I'm telling you he's lucky I never cut his cock off 'n' all for him, know what I mean.

A custom, if I may say so, sir, more honoured in the breach than in the observance.

If you say so, Jeeves. I say, Jeeves . . .

If you would like one of my snifters, sir . . .

. . . through Jesus Christ our Lord, by whom and in whom and with whom . . .

In the darkness of the WHEELER family mausoleum, Peter d'Abo sat cross-legged in a black plastic bin bag, the best way to keep dry. The blanket round his shoulders was damp. He lifted aloft the bottle of vodka, half-empty. 'Looking up to Heaven to you His Almighty Father . . .'

Often, when swigging, he became a priest at the altar, drinking from the consecrated chalice. At such times, his head filled with an image, as vivid as a film, of Father Vivyan, his closely shaven cheeks, his high colour, draining the sacred cup and then wiping it with a white cloth.

He thought, on such occasions, of the mass when the priest had blessed him. Had he been crying out? Shouting? Or had the priest simply known of his need for such a blessing? He remembered the heat which passed from the priest's hands into his head as he placed his hands on him, and the sensation of calm, hypnotic calm, which followed.

She'd been there that night, the woman from the *Legion*. All the trouble started – Rachel she was called – when she came from the *Legion* and started to live in Father's house. Jew. All the newspapers, all the TV stations, all the media in the world was controlled by the Jews: *The Daily Legion*, Radio Five Live, Hollywood – they wanted to get inside your head. He'd seen her looking at him, that Jew – seen her looking. She wanted more than what they all wanted. Didn't just want him to fuck her stupid, fuck her ass, fuck her face – that was obvious, any stupid fucking cunt could see that – she wanted more. Wanted inside him, inside his head. Wanted to seize the controls, work the dials, hack in. And that was where she was going to be disappointed, that little yid. He'd heard Mary Much and Martina talking about her, knew her game. Whore, they'd called her.

He'd give her whore. Knew her type. Fucking spy. Spying on Father Vivyan. Everything went wrong once she came. The police raids on the camper-vans. The arrest of Father Vivyan. The dispersal of the guns. Shooters. Nice shooters. Good word, shooter. Give a shooter to Lucius and Brad, get them to shoot fuckface Trevor. Take it to school. Take it into a classroom. WHAM! Fuck, man . . .

Grant by the mystery of this water and wine . . .

He wiped his mouth on a sleeve and screwed up the bottle again.

. . . that we may come to share in the divinity of . . . Tuli!

Yes, Father?

Tuli! Can you hear me?

Yes, Father. Speak.

You see that big shooter?

You mean that one there, Father?

Those Uzis are toys – pea-shooters. I mean the machine-gun.

Is that you, Father Vivyan?

The machine-gun. It's on the coffin just behind you. What's in that coffin?

Bones, Father.

And?

He laughed, for a while uncontrollably.

A skull . . . Some old geezer's skull. Nice ashtray, Father. Stuffed it with butts – in the eye-sockets, stuffed it full of butts.

And?

Ammunition.

Bless you, my child. What is the ammunition for?

You tell me, Father – are you God or Father Vivyan?

I am God. You must tell me what that ammunition's for, what that machine-gun is for . . .

Killing!

The boy was shouting now, out of the tomb to the driving rain, smiling ecstatically, as the quiet calm voice continued, the unmistakable, upper-class English voice of God Himself.

Kill Mr Fat. Kill that shit who left Mum and me when I was a baby. Shoot the yid who wrote 'bout Father Vivyan 'n' me. Kill, shoot – fucking kill.

Yes, my dear. If any of them come for you, you must kill them. Is that clear? Kill them.

Yes, O Heavenly Father.

THIRTY-ONE

On the bus-ride, changing at Catford, Rachel did not concentrate on her book. She stared through the raindrops on the window, thinking of Vivyan, and his absolutely maddening character. It would surely have been possible to refute each of the libels in *The Daily Legion*, and, moreover, to have used the services of a lawyer to get the paper to publish a retraction, and to offer substantial damages. Instead he was determined to maintain the silence of Christ before Pilate. He had refused to deny the story, even to Mrs Thorn. When that disagreeable woman had offered her ultimatum to Monty, Vivyan had smiled, agreed that she was free to withdraw her labour until he left the house, said he would go. Monty had protested. The telephone calls had been made, however, and within a few hours, the elder brother was driving the younger to the station at Troon.

'Had to buy his ticket, of course – the bloody ass won't carry money. He has to cross *London*, for God's sake.'

'It's King's Cross – the station for Kelvedone?'

'That's where he *said* he was going.'

'I want to find that boy before he does,' Rachel had said.

'My dear, do you think that's wise?'

She had left for London herself that afternoon. Telephone calls to the monastery yielded no information. Unsurprisingly, given the amount of unwelcome press coverage received by one of their number, the monks had refused to give anything away. They would not say that Father Vivyan was there, or not there;

that he had arrived or hadn't arrived; that he would be staying or leaving. After two or three attempts to speak to different monks (who was head man? Searching her memory from Chaucer, she'd asked to speak to the Abbot – there wasn't one), Rachel found that the cunning men of God had diverted all calls to an automatic answering service.

She was maddened by his failure adequately to defend himself. She was more maddened simply by *him* and it was difficult to articulate this feeling, to bring it into focus. What she had witnessed in action at Crickleden – Vivyan's miniature Kingdom of God, in which the ordinary self-protective securities were not observed – was unlike anything she had witnessed before. No locks, no personal property, no privacy: this had shocked her at first. Then she had asked herself whether his refusal to be self-protective was separable from a demand – *Hey, you!* – to be noticed. Was his Christ-like life lived for others anything more than an ego-trip? How were they helped, all those waifs and wanderers, among whom she had been numbered, who had come to Father Vivyan to talk, to share their inmost lives with the man who sat in the deckchair, listening, listening? Yet she knew she had herself been strengthened by her time in the vicarage. It gave her confidence. Her old fears, when still at the *Legion*, of losing the security of job and flat, her pathetic addiction to L.P. – she'd been cured of these. Security was no security. That was a lesson learned and she had learned it, apparently without imbibing any of that – another reason for being maddened by Vivyan – that damned religion.

Crickleden was the same: the clock in the little Festival of Britain–era clock tower at the end of the High Road was still stuck at quarter past eleven. The halal butchers were still a focal point of loud conversation in Urdu. The artificial hair still hung in skeins in the windows and along the peg-boarded walls of

Afro-Styles and in Iceland the same zomboid shoppers pushed the same trolleys of frozen food. The rain continued to fall on the just and the unjust. It was only in the vicarage drive that change was discernible. There were still two camper-vans, but they no longer had a detritus of belongings littering their environs. And, as she squelched to the front door, Rachel noticed that flower-beds had been weeded. Two new green wheely-bins had been installed beside the creosote fence. And most remarkable of all, the front door – a new front door of hideous fireproof thick ply – was locked. A tidy notice informed the visitor that soup and simple meals were served 'AT THESE TIMES AND ONLY AT THESE TIMES' in the adjacent church hall. Those in need of accommodation were likewise directed to the hall.

It was nice to see a friend when Lance opened the door. He was the young Jamaican (dreadlocks, a thin, intelligent face) who had shared with Rachel the distinction of being arrested on the night of Vivyan's arrest. (Both had been released the next day with a caution.)

THIRTY-TWO

Lance had a sensitive face which conveyed at once, without words having to be spoken, that great changes had come upon the place since Father Vivyan had departed.

'He's been suspended by the Bishop, but the police aren't pressing charges. They've nothing on him,' said Lance. 'Obviously . . . Meanwhile, we try to keep things going. The soup lunches . . . the teas . . . Father Aidan's organized dormitory accommodation for thirty in the parish hall.'

'But he's put locks on the doors.'

'Yeah, well' – Lance shrugged – 'that's kinda inevitable, isn't it?'

'Lance, I'm looking for Peter.'

'Yeah?'

Lance continued to smile, and to look at his mug of tea.

'Peter d'Abo,' she added.

'Yeah, well.' He laughed gently.

'I gather he's gone missing, but surely someone can find him? His mother, his grandmother – neither of them seem to know where he is.'

'He's sad,' said Lance slowly.

'The point is . . . it could be so easily cleared up, this whole sorry mess,' she said briskly. 'I feel that if someone could simply get hold of Peter and say to him, "Look, we're not blaming you, but you must issue a denial, you must tell the police, the newspapers, everyone, that you were not telling the truth, that Vivyan hasn't . . ."'

'Yeah, well . . .' Lance laughed gently.

'I don't see what the problem is with that,' she said earnestly.

It was irritating to her that he merely looked back at her and smiled.

Then Sinclo Manners entered the room.

It was awful to see the goofy expression on his face.

There had been times, when they were colleagues together at the *Legion*, when Rachel had found Sinclo an almost reassuring figure. Then, as far as she believed or could understand, he had sold his soul to the devil and organized the police raid on Vivyan. That was how it had seemed at the time, and she had not seen any need since to revise her judgement.

'Sinclo.'

She resisted the obvious question, and did not ask him what he was doing there.

She saw in his face an abject love which at this particular moment was merely irritating.

Lance said, 'Rachel's looking for Peter.'

'Ah . . . er . . . of course . . . splendid.'

'What's splendid?'

'I mean, not at all,' he said, blushing.

Rachel had been in love before, but she had never been in the mental condition which she knew to be afflicting Sinclo. Eight years ago, she had been girlishly overexcited by L.P.'s attentions, but there was no period of unrequited love. All too soon, and too readily, as she now believed, she had become L.P.'s lover. It was only later that love began to cause her pain, when she suffered acute jealousy of his wife and other lovers; and when she began to see that whatever the direction taken by their love affair, it could hardly avoid making her suffer.

This adolescent, medieval troubadour routine, this loving from afar, was just too embarrassing. It was all the more irritating when it came from a man who she believed was responsible in some measure for the present misery. Had he not come to Crickleden in the first instance as a spy for 'Dr Arbuthnot'?

'It's not, necessarily . . .' he began. 'I mean . . . Peter d'Abo, gosh.'

'I've tried to tell her,' said Lance.

'Neither of you have tried to tell me anything. You have tried to keep me in the dark and you have both succeeded triumphantly,' she said.

'We don't know ourselves, do we?' Sinclo asked mysteriously.

'Know what?' asked Rachel.

'Anyway,' said Sinclo, 'splendid. Lovely to see you. Lovely. Are you staying?'

'I've gotta go,' said Lance. 'If you're coming back later?' he asked Rachel.

She hummed and hawed.

'Anyway,' said Lance, 'see you around.'

'Thanks for the tea,' she said.

He said, 'Take care,' and she was left alone with Sinclo.

They sat, as they had so often sat in wine bars and restaurants, looking at one another across a table. She saw a man who was good-looking, not completely idiotic, of good family, kind. She had a strange thought. She thought, If we lived in a culture where there were arranged marriages, I could do worse than to marry this man. He is in love with me. It would probably be nice to make love to him. But she did not love him. Whatever the mysterious thing called love was, whatever had been making her so unhappy for the last eight years with L.P., it did not exist with Sinclo, and she doubted whether it ever would.

'Are you here writing a story?' she asked.

'I was sacked by Blimby,' he said with a laugh. 'Good thing, really. Can't blame him. Can't say I miss the work. Thought I'd come down here and work as a volunteer . . . Take a leaf out of your book.'

She did not want any leaves removed from her book; she disliked the sense of being followed.

'Oh, Sinclo.'

'What?'

'What a mess.'

'Have you seen Vivyan?'

'Who wants to know?' she asked with immediate suspicion.

'No one. Me. I just wondered . . . I mean, it seems a reasonable . . . There was some story, probably absolute rubbish, that you'd . . . Throxton . . . probably rubbish.'

'Yes,' she said unkindly.

She actually liked Sinclo, and in other circumstances she would be prepared to be more friendly, but this was not what she wanted now, or here.

'Well,' she said, 'that was a nice cup of tea.'

'Don't go,' he suddenly said.

'I think I'd better.'

'Rachel.'

She knew with a sinking in the stomach that he was about to be embarrassing.

'I know you think I was somehow behind the arrest of the Mad Monk . . . of Vivyan, and I do assure you . . .'

'I don't think that necessarily.'

'It isn't true . . . Rachel, the thing is . . . I know you have always known this, but I just wanted to say . . . You once said it was terribly embarrassing when someone told you they were in love with you, but . . .'

'Please, Sinclo.'

'I know I haven't got a hope . . .'

'Please.'

'I've never felt like this before about anyone.'

'Like what?'

'In love,' he managed to say.

It was quite sweet, and quite flattering, but this was the sort of conversation you expected to have when you were in your teens, at latest in your first year at university. And yet, as he said the ridiculous and predictable words, she found herself suffused with happiness. After all the anxieties and unhappinesses of the last two or three months, these words made her happy.

'You don't mean that.'

'Of course . . . no, no . . .'

'You see, you don't mean it.'

'I'm deadly serious, Rachel. I mean this . . . I . . . love you.'

She wanted him to go on and on saying it. She could not hear the words often enough.

'Oh, Sinclo,' she said. 'Do grow up.'

And she ran from the kitchen.

THIRTY-THREE

There are so few monks and nuns in the Church of England that the members of the various religious orders (a diminishing band) constitute something of a freemasonry. They all know, or know of, one another and their various houses. When in need of somewhere to stay in central London, Vivyan Chell, since he first became a monk, had retreated to a religious house behind Westminster Abbey. There is no secret about the existence of this place, and yet, like the existence of the religious life itself in England, it is not much noticed. Tucked in a narrow street just opposite the old gate into Dean's Yard, it houses about six monks, who chant the liturgical hours, who celebrate mass, and who are available for those who wish to see them.

As soon as it became clear that he could not stay on with his brother at Throxton, Father Vivyan had made for this place. He could have gone back to his own monastery, Kelvedone, the large Victorian house by the North Sea. He knew it was fairly unlikely that any journalist would be sufficiently clued up to pursue him there. But some might. No one, he was fairly sure, would think of looking for him in Westminster.

He fitted into the lives of the other monks silently, and anonymously. Indeed, it was impossible to tell from their demeanour whether they knew of the articles which had appeared in *The Daily Legion*. They seemed to know about his having been suspended from the parish, since their Superior asked him, on the first evening, 'Now, what's the position about you saying mass?'

That was the only allusion to his 'troubles'.

Chell had replied that he was allowed to say mass but that until the suspension was lifted, he could not do so in public, so he was unable to help out in the little chapel, either with mass or confessions.

It was some years since he himself had been to confession, and he wondered whether he wished to do so now. Only after he had been in the cool, silent house for a few days was he aware that he was approaching one of those personal crises in his life, after which he would be different. There had been the moment when he had joined the army. There had been the Call in Africa, when he had been aware of the presence of God. There had been a number of other, minor moments of strange certainty about his own destiny, which corresponded in his mind to Hamlet's 'Sir, in my heart, there was a kind of fighting/That would not let me sleep.'

Such a strange moment had occurred when he knew, after a lifetime in Zinariya, that he was going to leave Africa and accept the job in Crickleden. But something further was in prospect, of that he felt certain. He sensed it, like a hunter. It was not, therefore, cowardice which made him hold back from going to confession. The moment was not yet right. When he did so, or if he did so, he would confess things which he had not perhaps himself personally confronted. Naturally, he would confess to lust – though since his return to England, until the embrace of Mercy in the park, there had not been any lapses. What he was waiting to see, if he did lay bare his soul with the absolute honesty required of the exercise, was how much would be left of his religion, his actual belief.

He knew that the last time he had confessed – to another of the monks, just before he left Africa – he had been shocked to discover that he was confessing a lack of faith. By this he did not mean that he had spent much time weighing the various arguments in favour of the existence of God. These spurious mental exercises had always seemed to him an obvious waste of time since you only had to look at the lives of saints to see that religion flourished in spite of argument. Human minds of supreme intellectual distinction, such as Bonhoeffer's or Simone Weil's, embraced Christ as readily as did the monk's simplest parishioners. What he meant by faith, when he confessed to its lapse, was the preparedness to live as if God were really there.

All his life as a priest (and before that, as a soldier) Vivyan's difficulty had been a lack of trust of others. He had found it difficult, sometimes impossible, to delegate responsibility to others. He had wanted to be the king of his own show.

Belief in God would surely entail a preparedness to live quite passively; to live as if what came to us was sent from Heaven. We would not necessarily strive to make things happen. This was the real area of doubt and difficulty for him. It was not so much the obvious difficulty of believing how an omnipotent God could possibly be loving, or how a loving God could allow suffering. These were intellectual games which, for men and women of faith, were overcome by the way they lived. The thing which a man of such bursting energy as Vivyan Chell found most difficult was what one of the spiritual writers had called 'abandonment to Divine Providence'. When actually faced with a choice between letting God control events, and seizing control of them himself, Vivyan was not sure that he would really trust God, any more than he would trust the dozens of parish helpers, curates, voluntary aid workers, NCOs and others whom in the course of his life he had under his supervision.

Take therefore no thought for the morrow: for the morrow shall take thought for the things of itself. Sufficient unto the day is the evil thereof.

There was something unequivocal about this, and he had

never been able to be the passive, quasi-Buddhist type. In Africa, he had felt fulfilled, because he had always been able to organize, to make things happen, or seem to happen. He had hugely enlarged the parish schools, raised money from overseas for the hospital, and campaigned first in favour of the nationalist victory of Bindiga, then, when his tyranny began to make itself manifest, against the corruption, and the enslavements. Chell had not been very successful, but he had known some success. And he had taught, in season and out of season, that Christians were not men and women who allowed God to do everything; they did God's work for him.

Was this true? Or was it really a poetic way of describing humanism? Did he not believe, really, that what had made Christianity such a powerful force in the world, from its earliest days, was not its theories about God but its ethics? Here was a religion which actually thought it was important how you behaved! The Jews had always thought that, but for the Gentile world in Rome it was a novelty. Within weeks of Constantine making Christianity the official religion of the empire, there were orphanages established in Rome. Before that, unwanted children were piled up on street corners, the way the eco-logically tidy in the West today pile up used bottles, rags or newspapers.

The myth of God made Man was really an example of the extraordinary human capacity to project our dreams into the universe. It really meant Man made God. All that we cherished, all that we deemed to be Good, we now recognized was something we could do for ourselves; and this applied not simply to good deeds, but to the spiritual life. The story of the Ascension, of Jesus actually taking his human body back to Heaven, and re-entering the Godhead with his flesh and bones, was not a fantastical piece of science fiction: it was not a story about the first man in space. It was a myth about what had happened to human religion after the coming of Christ.

But now the myth was discarded. Even the Church did not really want to understand its own myths, and for the ignorant majority, the Christian story was simply a set of unattainable ideals ('sell all and give to the poor') or unbelievable tales (water into wine). How was it possible to go on being a Christian in such a world, unless one seized the initiative, recognized what was happening, and did the works of God for him? Fed the hungry? Put down the mighty from their seat?

It was with such thoughts as these that Father Vivyan Chell wrestled in the silence while he stayed with his fellow Anglican monks in Westminster. He thought, too, of his disgrace, and the pain which had been caused to the parish, and to his brother. Because he had heard the boy's confession – and knew just what a muddle of evil and madness was churning about in that child's skull – he could not tell anyone about it. He accepted this as his punishment for his years and years of leading a double life as a monk, while actually being the lover of dozens of women.

The disgrace weighed on him, as heavy as a cross on his shoulders. He knew now how impure had been those decades of his enjoying a heroic public image. Father Vivyan, the voice of Oppressed Africa! Father Vivyan, the modern saint! This was what *The Daily Legion* had taken from him. The untruth of the stories could never be proved. He had become one of the ridiculous people – presenters of TV shows, drug-crazed minor aristocrats, exhibitionist politicians – who got into the newspapers. The loss of dignity involved was awful. He felt himself changed by it. He was slower, older. His digestion and sleep were disturbed.

At the same time, just as he could not be passive in his belief in God – or 'God' – nor could he be acquiescent in the injustice brought to pass by the lies and tittle-tattle of *The Daily Legion*. It was only right that the truth should be made to prevail – and for people to know what this poisonous newspaper, and ones like it, were up to, in defending lies and supporting evil.

Sometimes, when he thought about *The Daily Legion*, the anger became so intense that he thought he might suffer a seizure. Then he needed physical activity. There was a small garden behind the monastery, where the Superior allowed him to dig and sweep, but there was only a limited amount which could be done in the continuing wet weather. When darkness fell, he walked – sometimes for hours at a time – down to the river, along the Embankment, pacing beside the wide, angry brown flood with rainwater soaking his head.

Somehow, instinct suggested that he should avoid walking out in the light, though there was little enough light in London these days. Dawns rose in a half-hearted wet pall of grey, and it had been weeks since there had been any brightness in the sky. Everyone walked rapidly through the rain, with their heads buried beneath upturned collars, hats, newspapers, umbrellas. When the truth of this fact slowly dawned on him, Father Chell began to venture forth by daylight.

It was on one such day, mid-morning, that he found himself walking with long strides, seemingly purposeful, but in fact quite at random, across Victoria Street, down Storey's Gardens towards St James's Park. Deluge had softened to a light drizzle, and the park was beautiful in its autumnal way, the leaves now on the turn; ducks, moorhens, flamingos all enjoying the wetness. He strode down Birdcage Walk, in the direction of Buckingham Palace. Military music could be heard. It was something which always had a powerful effect upon him, recalling not only his early days as a soldier, but also his childhood and schooldays. It was only as he came near to the Palace and the

Queen Victoria Memorial that he recognized the flags on the innumerable poles which lined the Mall. They were, alternately, the Union Flag of Britain, and the copper-orange, green and red tricolour of Zinariya, with the cluster of cocoa-leaves in the middle.

There had been obvious reasons why, recently, Father Chell had not felt inclined to look at the newspapers. The monks with whom he was staying did not appear to possess a radio and none of them watched television. He had been out of touch with the world for a seemingly indefinite period.

The band was playing 'The British Grenadiers', and in spite of himself, the Christian monk (who was wearing not monastic rig, but black jeans, jumper and dark blue duffel coat with hood up) felt his throat gulp with emotion. Patriotic emotions could not easily or perhaps usefully be defined, any more than religious emotions. Yet, when he heard music like this, Vivyan Chell would have been able fairly simply to define why he found it so moving. It was because he believed, with a very deep part of himself, in the fundamental decency of his own country.

He knew that terrible things had been done by the British Army, and by the British Empire, with its Amritsar massacres and its battles of Omdurman and its atrocities during the Boer War. He nonetheless believed that these aberrations, terrible as they were, were not to be compared with the horrors perpetrated by the Russians or the Germans on their own people, and on others. When the great test came (will you resist Hitler or will you let him take over the world?) there was one nation, and only one nation, in the whole world who answered unequivocally that they would go on fighting. The hammy old rhetoric of Churchill was so moving because it was literally true. The British had been prepared to fight on the beaches and never to surrender. In Vivyan Chell's lifetime, the British armed forces, in an overwhelming proportion of instances, had been used to defend the defenceless, to resist tyranny, to stand up for that which was good against evil.

This was what he found so moving when he heard a British military band playing in the drizzle outside Buckingham Palace, and there was something else which was moving about it too. Whereas his religious beliefs were shared by only a tiny number of his fellow-countrymen, he believed that his pride in his country and its love of liberty and fair play was shared by countless millions of Britons.

He quickened his pace, therefore, and went to join the crowds watching the band.

They were tourists, nearly all of them – Americans, Japanese, Germans. Father Vivyan suspected that they had come to see a spectacle without having any marked sense of what this spectacle might be. Three open landaus were being pulled down the Mall by prancing black horses, and accompanied by the full helmeted escort of the Household Cavalry.

Once, as a young soldier, Vivyan had met the Queen. She was about five years older than he was. He had a recollection, therefore, of a beautiful young woman, small, with a radiant smile and very clear skin, like that of a country girl who had been out riding. She had come to Knightsbridge Barracks when he was posted there, and he did not spend more than five minutes in her company. She had asked him a question about horses. It was, in its way, a very predictable encounter. What he had felt in her presence, however, was awestruck. He had tried to explain this to people at various junctures in his life, and he found that when he was talking to older Britons or to Africans, they did not need any further explanations. It was only younger people who did not understand. His niece, Kitty, for example, who was in many ways an intuitive and sensitive girl, had said, 'Honestly, Viv! I thought you were meant to be a socialist, and underneath it you are simply an old snob!'

This was not what he felt at all. He was not proud of himself for having met the Queen, and he did not revere her in the way that snobs might be excited to meet a duchess. He felt awe, partly simply because she was the Queen; but also because he had an almost mystic sense of her great personal goodness. She possessed an aura. Whether he had imposed this upon her in his imagination, he did not know, though he had subsequently heard of others who felt the same about her.

He had often seen photographs of her since, of course, and he had seen her on television or newsreels. As it happened he had never actually set eyes upon her from that day until this morning, when he saw her passing down the Mall in an open landau in the drizzle. At her side was the figure of President Bindiga.

The State Visit was under way. In spite of all the protests from friends of the opposition Alkawari! party, all the anger of the other African Commonwealth countries, all the reservations of the European Union, Britain was welcoming to London a man who had been responsible for genocide, torture and slavery. Little Joshua! Joshua Bindiga! Vivyan Chell's protégé from the parish school in Louisetown! Little Joshua, on whom Vivyan had pinned such hopes, and who had gone so horribly to the bad. There he sat beside the Queen. Opposite him was some flunkey or equerry. In the following landau was the Duke of Edinburgh and one of President Bindiga's wives, a six-foot blonde Danish girl who was waving shamelessly to the tourists. Behind, the Duke of Kent, for some reason, and a trio of Africans, one of whom was Stephen Obiko, the Zinariyan ambassador.

There now occurred to Vivyan Chell a moment of revelation which was comparable in intensity and importance to his Divine

Call in Africa. The horses trotted past, their bridles and furniture jangling. As always, they and the soldiers were beautifully groomed and trained. The band played the old stirring tunes. The Queen, no longer a radiant young woman, now looked like an old frump made out of pastry, grumpy and about to crack into floury powder.

The generalized feeling of unhappiness about England, which Vivyan Chell had been experiencing since his return from Africa, now crystallized into a moment of truth. That decent, brave, good place of his childhood – that place which fought for the underdog, and stuck up for liberty and justice in Europe – now seemed a mean, ugly, filthy little fraud of a place. Even its corruptions, putrescent as they now appeared in his eyes, were pointless. England had not been taken over by some alien ideology of Stalinism or Nazism. It had simply died and gone rotten. It was pointless. The figures who had gone past in their landaus were all equally pointless. There was no difference between the wrinkled old Queen and the Danish tart.

'Murderers! Boo! Boo! Killers!'

He was yelling at them and waving his fist. Did little Joshua, his pupil, hear him or see him? Or had the royal entourage already trotted by, towards the Palace?

Vivyan Chell turned away. When he had accepted the job at Crickleden, he had done so – he realized this now – because he thought there was something left in England worth salvaging. He thought that it was possible to set up some small corner where the old values, the values which his parents and grand-parents took for granted – kindliness and goodness and Christianity – could be practised, where the poor could be nourished and rescued from the system.

He felt, as he paced along, an intensely personal anger with the Queen herself. He was in a sort of dream-state, for he now saw in his head a replay of the ceremonial trot-past. Instead of wearing an unbecoming tweed coat and hat in too-bright colours, she was dressed like the most dissipated and desperate old madam in a cheap brothel. She wore only a basque and crotchless fishnet tights. You could see tufts of grey pubic hair at her puckered armpits and round her pussy. Her fat old wrinkled arms wobbled as she waved and called out, in her parody of an upper-class voice, 'Looking for business, ducky?'

'No,' he said earnestly to her, 'but you are. Copper business, cocoa business, funny business. If you had half a conscience, woman, you wouldn't have sat in a landau with that murderous little Joshua! Admit it, woman – you only want to preserve yourself! You haven't thought what is good for this country – you haven't even begun to think through what was worth preserving and what needed changing! You call yourself a head of state – a Christian head of state – Supreme Governor of my church!'

He stopped for breath. He felt himself gasping for breath.

If I had a gun on me, he thought, I would have done Jesus's work and shot your selfish old head off.

Everything, in the previous five to ten minutes, had gone; everything which he had previously stood for in life now seemed farcical to him: his belief in English decency, and in the Church. Everything stank. Bindiga was the national treasure, just because the City did not want to lose money investing in copper futures or cocoa futures. The truth was non-existent. *The Daily Legion* was the Bible. God was dead and Lennie Mark was his prophet.

These crazy thoughts, born of grief-stricken disillusionment, only lasted a few minutes as he walked and walked. He found that he had paced beyond Victoria and was somewhere in the Vauxhall Bridge Road before he had formed a plan of action. He no longer worried about the Bishop or the newspapers or the regulations, which had hitherto restricted his movements. He knew the complete falsehood of the allegations against him. Empowered by rage, he decided to return to his parish. That was where he belonged.

He begged at Charing Cross until he had collected money for the tube, and tea at the other end. The placards for the evening paper spoke of minor demonstrations against the State Visit, and rumours, in Bindiga's absence, of a *coup d'état* in Zinariya.

THIRTY-FOUR

Rachel set off for the cemetery. It was good to get out of the vicarage. The effect of Sinclo's declaration had shocked her. He had been showing her a safe, warm, cosy place which would have been a trap, a servitude. Already, even as she heard his stammered declarations of love, whose signs she had been reading in his face for a couple of years, she could see the future. It would not be a bad marriage. Unless (this sometimes happened, she knew) a perfectly nice-seeming man turned out to be some variety of domestic monster, she would be linking her destiny with a kind person. As she had, in the vicarage kitchen, been powerfully aware, it would be perfectly agreeable to go to bed with Sinclo. It was possible that the cliché would come true that 'love would grow'.

She knew, however, that to make such a choice at this stage of her life would be the reverse of life-enhancing. And in this knowledge, she felt that she knew a little of what it was which attracted her to Father Vivyan, and also what it had been that she had loved in Kitty. They lived dangerously. By this, Rachel did not mean that they lived suicidally: rather, that they lived as if there was more to life than creature comforts, stability, common sense. Kitty was a failure, Vivyan a partial success, in the quest for a life which was both interesting and useful to others. Rachel's key moments, her guiding inspirational perceptions about how she wished to conduct her life, came from Kitty's funeral, and next from the ending of her affair with L.P.

They were both negative inspirations: they showed her what she did not want. She did not want, if she died tomorrow, to have been only a journalist on a cheap paper; she did not want to define her life in terms of whom she slept with.

Her honest, clever parents had hoped that she would choose a career for herself after university. This had not happened: she had not become, like Mum and Dad, a doctor – or a civil servant, or a lawyer or a banker. This was the modern disease in England. None of her generation wanted to enter professions or to be part of the old society. They all wanted to live inside their dreams, and they supposed that this would be easier if they were in nebulous, boring jobs connected with the 'arts' or newspapers or publishing. In fact, as she realized now a bit late, she could have led a more independent life of dreams, and pursued the inner life with more dignity, had she possessed the independence which a professional career would have given her.

She had already begun, inside her head, to consider pro-grammes of retraining. A crash course of science A levels would only take a few months, and enable her to get into medical school by the following year, if she wished to pursue the long road of being a doctor. Or she could go in for charity work overseas. Or she could go back to university and become a scholar, possibly do a PhD in philosophy. As yet, the thoughts had not focused, but they had begun. A new life was beginning, and to step back from this and opt merely for the security of being loved by Sinclo would not be the right choice. She knew it would make her happy only for a matter of months. Sooner or later, she would become resentful of him, and begin to notice that she was cleverer than he was. These things mattered.

One of her thoughts was simply to take the civil service exam. There were many things wrong with England – she agreed with Vivyan about what some of these things were; in other areas, in particular his distrust of finance, wealth, the big institutions, she disagreed profoundly. No one had ever been born on this planet whose mindset less resembled Plato's; she thought that the great philosopher's mingling of mythology with actuality was one of the most corrupting factors in the history of Western thought. But she agreed with Plato in one of his 'myths', namely that of the good life only being liveable in the well-ordered society (preferably, literally, a Republic). This well-ordering depended on a sound economy, a fact which Vivyan with his crazy Christian fear of money resolutely refused to see, and it also depended on efficiency.

A life devoted to attempting in some small area of British society to iron out inefficiency would be a good life. That was what would inspire Rachel Pearl to join the civil service. It was absurd that in one of the richest nations on earth, the trains and buses did not work properly, the hospitals and schools were in chaos, the political system was so rightly by some reviled and by others disregarded.

Equally, a life devoted to the decent and efficient working of some area of money, a life in which she herself helped a financial institution to generate the wealth which would pay for this well-ordered society, this would be a good life.

In the background of her new life, whatever it was — whether a medic, an aid worker, a civil servant or a financier — Rachel would keep alive the life which had been so threatened, in her latter days with L.P. and the *Legion*: the inner life. She would keep up her languages, by reading German and French novels, Italian poetry. She would struggle with difficult books of philosophy, and try to read science. Poor L.P., who had begun his adult life as a clever person, someone who was aware of life's imaginative possibilities, had deliberately shut down.

The row they had about conceptual art now seemed entirely typical and revealing. Of course, there was no need for him to like, or even to understand, what Hans Busch had been up to with his meretricious installations. What had been so shocking was the drivel he wrote about it in the newspaper, in which he did not seem to think it mattered when his article confused Oscar Wilde with Ruskin. Everything about L.P. had grown stale and flat. He was corrupted, visibly, tangibly corrupted.

Leaving the *Legion* had been like escaping some land in science fiction or mythology where the inhabitants were being lulled into a stupid lazy dream by money. The Sirens or the Lotus Eaters came to mind. Some of the more interesting employees of the paper actually hated themselves for taking the money. And to give him his due, this was Sinclo's position. This, more than the fact that she and he had friends in common, was what had drawn Rachel to Sinclo. He made no bones about being ashamed of taking Lennox Mark's expenses and salary. L.P., the archangel with furthest to fall, must have been fuller of self-hatred than any of them; but he had nulled his own sense of it by making everything into a cynical joke, a joke which had begun as sharp wit but which was now a predictable series of party-trick paradox.

That marvellous feeling, if you have been drinking too much and you go on the wagon for a few weeks, drinking nothing but pure mineral water: that detoxification of the entire system, this was what Rachel had been undergoing, spiritually, since she told herself she no longer needed the *Legion*.

She was sure, too, that it made her cleverer, not being there. Her detective powers greatly exceeded Sinclo's, that was for sure. When she left him to his blushes in the kitchen, she had asked around among the tramps. Any ideas about the where-abouts of Peter d'Abo? With most of the old men, she had drawn a blank, but then one of them, a very thin old Scot with purplish cheeks through which the veins ran like rivers in a map, had said, 'Ye'll be from the polis?'

'No, I'm not from the police. I'm a friend of Father Vivyan's.'

'That young mon up at the manse . . . Sinclair . . .'

'Sinclo?'

'I'd say he was from the polis . . . He's the main reason they a' went awa'.'

'The Albanian boys.'

'Them and the Michaels. We had the polis dune tae find a' the guns and a' . . .'

'And . . .'

'They funed what they wanted tae find — if ye ken what I mean.'

'They found a lot — that's what I heard.'

'Mebbe . . . mebbe . . .' He laughed. 'I reckon he's a military mon — that young Sinclair.'

'He was in the army, yes.'

'I said sae, tae Jock, but they dinna ken . . . I were in the army m'sel' . . .'

'Really?'

'Och, aye . . . The polis dinna find mair than a fraction . . . In those caravans — they were jus' a few . . . I'm tellin' ye, they took it all awa' and hud ut . . . That's whair the puir lune is the noo . . . dune amang the tombs . . . like the puir lune in the Gospel . . .'

Rachel did not ask the old Scots soldier how he knew these things. She was not wholly convinced that they were true, but it was surely worth a look, down in the cemetery.

She had become gripped by the idea that before she started her new life — her useful, dignified life — she would clear up the mess and confusion surrounding the Father Vivyan affair. It would make an atonement for her years on the newspaper. She would find the boy who had made the allegations, and, with gentleness and firmness, she would confront him with his lies. Then she would ask him, in the presence of lawyers, to withdraw the allegations. If, as seemed likely, he was more than half crazy, she would do everything she could (here, her parents would be able to help) to get him the best medical care. Once the truth had been established, a chapter of life would be over. She was beginning to understand why she had come to the parish, and how this strange episode in her life could be turned to good purpose.

In mittened hands, she held a rain-spattered A to Z map. She had come up the hill from the church, crossed a main road beside a 1960s primary school. She passed on one side of the road some flats, and on the other one of those down-at-heel parks with which outer London was scattered, places which at their opening must have seemed so full of hope, with their bandstands, their Swiss cottages, their aviaries and marigold-beds, and which now in their neglected state were emblems of what England thought of itself. Everything there meant for adults – the flower-beds, the birds, the cafeteria – had been handed over to vandals; the only new thing on which any money or thought had been expended was the ugly adventure playground which, with its rubber tyres hanging on chains from wooden climbing frames, its ropes and nets and shit-strewn paddling pool, could well have been an exercise ground for the younger apes at a zoo in some uninteresting European country such as Belgium or Luxembourg.

Beyond the park were the allotments – again, all decayed. Forgetting the year-long monsoon, Rachel intolerantly saw in this scene of desolation confirmation of her view that modern Britons were too lazy to pick up a spade and fork.

But another squint at the map confirmed that she was going in the right direction. Beyond the allotments, she saw the endless rows of graves.

THIRTY-FIVE

Tuli was half asleep when he caught his first sight of her, coming down from the top of the cemetery. She was the first person who had been into the cemetery that day. Sometimes, if the rain let up for a bit, dog-walkers came, and sometimes sex maniacs prowled about for a bit. Tuli had already sentenced at least one of these men to death inside his head. Sentence would be carried out next time he dared bring his filthy, pot-bellied, leather-coated little body into sight.

The queer in the multi-storey: how he'd begged for mercy! They'd come off as easy as a wog's ear. God had been pleased. Well done, thou good and faithful servant. But now the war had started, and there wasn't gonna be no more gentle stuff, no more fun and games. Revenge, that was the name of the game.

Jeeves could forget his fucking dish tasted cold, they were ready for something hot: vindaloo, coming right up, sir.

Just listen to me, my son.

Speak, Lord, for thy servant heareth you.

Lay not thy knife to her pussy.

No, my Lord.

Keep her as the apple of thine eye.

Yes, my Lord.

Keep her in prison.

Yes, my Lord.

No guns, yet. If the Jews come to get her back, then you will

486

have to kill her – you understand? She is the one who landed you in this shit – are you listening to me?

Yes, O Lord.

Where did she land you?

In the shit, God.

And where did she land your nana?

In the shit, my God.

By publishing?

By publishing lies in my father's house. In my newspaper. In the newspaper which I should own. When I marry Madame Pussy.

When you marry?

Martina?

That's right. But first you must obey me. You must keep this one under supervision. She came as a spy. It was she who came down to spy on Father Vivyan, on me, on your God.

Yes, my Lord.

It was she who wrote lies about your nan in the paper.

Yes, my Lord.

It was she who blasphemed against your mother. It was she who made Mercy seem like a fucking whore.

I'll kill her for that.

All in good time, my son. At present, you must keep her here. You understand? You must keep her here – and no one must know she's here. This is the most important thing I have ever asked you to do, my son. Do you understand?

Yes, God.

Keep calm . . . For yea though you walk through the valley of the shadow of death, I am with you, my rod and my staff will comfort you.

He looked up. The woman was now about a hundred yards away. She was wearing jeans, trainers, and an anorak with a hood, but, guided by the Divine Voice, he could easily recognize her as the cow from the *Legion* who had come to work as a fake volunteer at Father Vivyan's house. She was looking this way and that. Sometimes she turned her back on him, and walked in the wrong direction entirely, stupid bitch. Sometimes she turned back, and walked towards him, and seemed to be looking in his eyes. Sometimes she disappeared, and he realized she was searching in some brambles or behind a tomb. Now she bobbed up again, and she was only fifty, thirty yards away. And now their glances had met, and her intense, bright eyes, as radiant as they were dark, lit up with recognition. With infuriating slowness, she made her way towards the doorway of the mausoleum.

Remember, said God, capture but do not kill. Maim if you must, torture if you like, but do not kill.

'Hi!' she called. 'Hi! Peter! You remember me? Rachel? Father Vivyan's friend?'

Bertie Wooster said, 'What a nice surprise! What are you doing in this neck of the woods?'

THIRTY-SIX

Vivyan Chell reached the vicarage about three-quarters of an hour after Rachel left it. His vision of the Queen as a raddled old prostitute, of England as a pointless, amoral cauldron of putrescence, now possessed him totally. He had been in a very similar overwrought conditions on the day that he won the Military Cross for valour. Adrenalin coursed into his circulation. His heart beat so rapidly, and with such vigour, that the front of his frayed black jumper pulsated visibly. An extraordinary energy, like the energy of anger, but more controlled, both governed him, and exuded from him.

When the young monk, Father Aidan, opened the front door to him, he mistakenly thought that the Father (as the younger monks all called him) was angry because they had reintroduced locks, and covered the broken door-panelling with plywood. Only when he recollected the moment, as he was to do many times in the course of his life, did Father Aidan realize that if Vivyan was 'in a fury', then this was true in a mythic, classical sense. The man, like the Maenads in a Bacchic orgy, appeared to be in a frenzy which soared above petulance.

'What is this?' He jabbed at the lock with his finger. 'Get it off! At once!'

While the young monk was running for a screwdriver, the elder strode into the dining room, Odysseus regaining his palace from the suitors, Beowulf striding into Heorot to banish the monster. In the corner of the dining room, there was an

489

innovation. Television had been installed and, even at this afternoon hour, it was switched on, with a programme giving live coverage of Parliamentary reports. Several young men, Vivyan's Zinariyan friends and lodgers, were gathered around the set. They were not normally addicted to *Their Lordships' House*, as the programme was called. If they had become accustomed to watching daytime TV, then golf or snooker, tedious as they might be, offered more chances of entertaining interludes than the glimpses of empty red-leather benches, a somnolent Lord Chancellor on his woolsack, a few bishops in rochets and chimeres, quiet as chess pieces, being harangued by a stout life peeress on the subject of the regulation of pension funds.

This afternoon, however, was different. A new peer of the realm was being introduced to their Lordships' House. With many boos and hisses, the Zinariyan boys had already watched the new Lord Mark, supported by two former Prime Ministers, one Labour, one Conservative, being put through the arcane rituals of the place. Clad in robes of scarlet and ermine, there was Little Len, bowing and swearing fealty to the Old Whore, as, in his frenzy, Vivyan now considered her. The young Africans, who had hitherto in their year in London seen only the modern face of Britain – its petrol fumes, street crime, fast food and muggings – were now made aware, by the images on the television screen, of the primitive and ritual nature of tribal hierarchy which still persisted here. This man, for all his dependence on modern techniques of communications to make his millions, on plate-glass towers and computerized newspaper production, wanted nothing more than to drape himself with dead animal skins and, mumbling imprecations to the spirits, make obeisance to his tribal chieftainess.

After the mumbo-jumbo was done, his lordship came out of

the Palace of Westminster, most improperly still wearing his robes. He stood to be photographed on Palace Green, with the two old Prime Ministers, his pert, smiling German wife, and a very tall blonde woman who looked slightly sinister, whom none of them recognized. Some thought she was attached to Lord Mark. Others wondered if she was one of the Muslim Scandinavian wives of the President. For, yes, there was Bindiga himself.

'President Bindiga, there are many people in this country who are worried about the human rights record of Zinariya . . .'

A reporter cast out these formulaic words.

Lennie Mark, slow and measured in his new-found aristocratic dignity, was telling the microphone, 'I am proud of my adopted country, Britain; I am proud of my native land, Zinariya. Every country has a duty to defend its citizens against terrorism, and I am glad that Britain supports the President in his perfectly legitimate fight against those who, by violent means, would seek to overthrow the rule of law in Zinariya!'

Mary Much sucked in her cheeks. Bindiga grinned. Martina's perpetually stitched *moue* cast its doll-like smile on the world.

'He's at the Embassy?'

This was Father Vivyan's question.

'He and two of the women . . .'

'Those women?' asked the monk.

'We don't know who the blonde one is. We just know he's staying with two of his women at the Churchill in Portman Square. It's for security.'

The young man grinned.

'Is Thimjo on alert?' asked Vivyan, at last no longer needing to speak in a hushed voice, or in code.

'Thimjo is in hiding.'

They spoke in agitated, repetitive sentences, trying to tell the priest all that had happened since he was 'taken away' (this was how they understood it). Many of the Happy Band had dispersed. The plans to disrupt the Bindiga visit, if possible to assassinate the General while he was in London, were in chaos.

'Well, we must get them out of chaos!' asserted the priest.

Everyone now began to talk at once. Some told Vivyan about the police raids on the camper-vans, and the seizure of weaponry. Others spoke of the Happy Band going into hiding. Others spoke of their fear that there was a spy in the vicarage. Some spoke of the arsenal of weapons which they still had left. And while they all talked, and Father Vivyan tried to make them speak one at a time, Sinclo had taken out his mobile phone.

Lance heard him and shook his dreadlocks in disbelief. At a time like this, when the atmosphere in the house had suddenly become electric with menace and fear, the English public schoolboy was telephoning his tailor.

'My suit is ready for fitting, but there's no time to send a card . . . There's no time,' he was saying.

There was a silence.

'Yes. Yes . . . yes, my esteemed order . . . There's no time any more . . . I would guess . . . yes. I'll get down there.'

Lance came up to him and said, 'Look – when you've finished ordering clothes – oughtn't we to tell Father Vivyan that Rachel's gone in search of Peter?'

So it was that Lance told Vivyan about the young woman's visit, and her quest for Peter, at just about the same moment that one of the Zinariyan freedom-fighters was telling the priest where they had stored the remainder of their armoury.

THIRTY-SEVEN

'Who told you I was here?' the boy asked.

'No one told me exactly.' She smiled. 'I just thought I'd see if you were here.'

'So, who's following you?'

'No one's following me! Hey, aren't you getting wet? I am.'

'Got a bag.'

'Yeah, well!'

She grinned nervously. Then she added, 'We could go for a coffee, if you felt like it.'

'No coffee here.'

'I didn't mean here – I meant in a café.'

Tuli looked down. Wrapped in his dripping bin bag, and hooded, he could have been a very beautiful young monk lost in contemplation.

'At least you've got a shelter,' she said. His failure to respond to her was disconcerting. Back at the vicarage, although he had often seemed a strange boy, he was always polite. That was what had made his mad outburst, half an hour before Vivyan's arrest, all the more disconcerting.

'Have you been sleeping here? Peter?'

'Want to see?'

'Okay.'

He gingerly stood up, so as not to get too wet from the drips all over his protective plastic bag.

She was reassured to find his sweet smile lighting up his face.

'You crawl in,' Jeeves was saying to her.

This, she knew as she was doing it, was a stupid idea.

'There's more room than you think,' he said. 'Just keep on crawling.'

From behind her, when she had penetrated the confined space of the mausoleum, she heard him say, 'They're coffins.'

'I can see,' she said.

There were three coffins on one side of the little building and four on the other, grey with mould and dust.

'I think I've got the idea,' she said brightly. 'I'll come out now.'

'I think not,' said Jeeves. She could hear the smile in his voice, but she could not see his expression very clearly. His form was silhouetted against the entrance, which he filled. She could see the gun he was holding.

'Lie down,' he told her.

'The floor's wet.'

Jeeves had been replaced by a cockney voice, which could hardly articulate its anger.

'You'll lie down,' this voice said. 'Lie on one of the coffins. Or we get nasty, innit?'

THIRTY-EIGHT

There were several red helicopters in the sky, and any quantity of vans – police, military, ambulances – screeching and wailing through the streets of south London towards Crickleden Cemetery.

Sinclo waited in the agreed spot.

In the previous quarter of an hour, he had ceased entirely to be a failed journalist, or a wanderer with no idea of his place in the world. He had returned in heart to being a soldier. By running at the double, he had reached Furbelow Park in less than ten minutes. Even knowing the army as well as he did, he was surprised as well as impressed by the expedition and precision with which the whole operation was managed. One of the red helicopters landed near the tennis courts. Three figures emerged. Two were uniformed SAS officers, who ran at once to the crumbling wall dividing park from cemetery. The other, tall, bald and unmistakable was Brigadier Courtenay. He waved. There was something almost genial about the wave, something between a salute and a halloo!

'He's just the other side of that wall in a mausoleum. He's in the sights of about six guns,' said the Brigadier to Sinclo. 'You're not to worry. She'll be all right.'

'She?'

'You're not to worry – but he's got Rachael Pearl as a hostage.'

495

THIRTY-NINE

Rachel was bound round the ankles with some rags, and round her wrists with a length of plastic-coated rope of the sort used for washing-lines. The cord, which was very tight, bit into her flesh and impeded the circulation – one of the reasons, apart from abject terror, that she felt moments of merciful wooziness, as though she might pass out, or wake and find that the previous quarter of an hour had been a bad dream. The corners of her lips were bleeding, she could taste the blood. Her tights had been used to gag her very tightly. Her trousers were wedged over her head, and she could only breathe with some difficulty. At first she had whimpered, vainly hoping that the pathos of the sound would excite his pity, but it merely made him worse. He had not raped her. But she had felt the blade of a knife being run up and down her thighs – first the blade, then the sharp end – not enough to cut, but enough to leave the unmistakable knowledge that he was running the knife closer and closer to the top of her legs.

She felt that she could perhaps bear the pain if he (or was it they?) would only stop talking.

'Wot? Never seen one of them before? That's pussy, that is.'

'Who's saying I never seen it?'

'You did, if I may say so, sir, seem a little surprised at all that hair.'

'Don't touch.'

'I wasn't.'

'Yes, you woz. I said don't touch.'

'Almighty God, unto whom all hearts be open, all desires known and from whom no secrets are hid . . .'

'You could shave it – scrape the beard off. Don't seem natural, a bitch wiv a beard between 'er legs.'

'What wiv – what wiv do wa cut 'er?'

'Excuse me, sir, but the Stanley knife, if I may say so, is hardly adequate to your purpose.'

'I could pull some of it out.'

'Cut some other bit of her. Cut her foot off.'

'See that – you never seen it before. Admit it!'

'Course I have.'

'You're all talk. You only done it with Mr Currey. All the rest was talk, wunnit? You never 'ad a bitch.'

'Don't know what you mean.'

'If you weren't a poof yerself, you'd give her one.'

'Hail Mary full of grace, the Lord is with thee . . .'

'You could cut off, say, a couple of toes. Post them to her mum. Get a loada dosh. They're all loaded, Jews.'

'Make her beg for mercy. Tuli, Tuli, make her beg for mercy.'

'Or a tit. Not a toe. A tit. Cut one of them off.'

'I want my mum. I want Mummy,' said the little boy.

FORTY

In the first Book of Kings, the prophet Elijah inveighed against King Ahab and Jezebel his Queen. Elijah ran before Ahab's chariot to the city of Jezreel, 'when the heaven was black with clouds and wind and there was a great rain'. Vivyan Chell had preached many a sermon about the prophet Elijah. Ahab's question to the prophet – 'Art thou he that troubleth Israel?' – was the question which all the powerful people of this world should scornfully ask of the Church, of today's prophets and martyrs. If Christians were not troubling to their fellow-citizens, then their Christianity was lukewarm. So he had preached. So he had lived. And now in his frenzy, in which he was no longer sure of his God or his faith, but he knew very clearly his enemy, Vivyan ran like the prophet through wind and rain.

What passed through his head felt like the calculations and practical considerations which must always engage the intelligence of the good officer in the field. He was calculating how long it would be, after Thimjo got the message from the Happy Band, before their joint operation was successful: a simultaneous series of explosions in the House of Lords, the Churchill Hotel, Portman Square, and the office building in Bermondsey. It was imperative, moreover, that the arsenal at present stored in the cemetery be moved, and the reserve troops mobilized.

But although these calculations appeared to be passing through his brain in the rational pattern that he had been trained as a soldier to follow, they were really shapes in his head, stories he was telling himself. As he ran, he heard the actual explosions of former times, the sound of battle during the Lugardian civil war when he was wounded forty years earlier. In his head, these blended with the no less real explosions which he had not heard, those in the copper mines set off recently by the Happy Band.

Elijah the prophet ran in the rain before the chariot of the corrupt king of Israel. Elijah the prophet was the type of all religious witness against the corruption of the sinful state; he was the archetype of holy anarchist, the forerunner of all organized rebellion. He was Archbishop Romero standing out against the American-paid right-wing gangsters who were running Salvador; he was Bonhoeffer loading his revolver to shoot the Führer; he was Becket denouncing Henry II. Elijah the man of God had withdrawn into the desert and been fed by ravens. He had also taken lodging with a woman of Zarephath, who feared that if he lived under her roof, he would consume her last meagre supplies. And yet, so long as the man of God was with them, the barrel of meal did not waste, nor did the cruse of oil fail.

And she said unto Elijah, What have I to do with thee, O thou man of God? art thou come unto me to call my sin to remembrance, and to slay my son?

Panting with overexcitement, and with his heart now thumping louder than the noise of his Doc Martens on the pavements, the man of God ran, through the cemetery gates and up the broad drive which led to the mortuary chapel.

The guns were firing in his head, the mines were exploding at his feet; and yet he thought of his women of Zarephath, their welcoming breasts, their revealed energy, as nakedly, so often, he had filled them with his justice like mountains high-soaring above. And he thought of Nontando, his large-breasted Zinariyan wife in all but name; and he thought of Mercy Topling during their unforgettable encounter, her thighs, her fingers, her *smell*.

The enemy were here. But yea though I walk through the valley of death I will fear no evil, for thou, Mercy, art with me, and my rod and staff will comfort thee.

As he ran towards the mausolea which edged the northern wall of the cemetery, his keen military eyes at first took in the distant horizons, the smudge of rain-sodden Catford and its high-rise blocks. Only a second or two later did he focus on the mausolea themselves, and in particular one of them. At first he thought he saw a monk carrying a dismembered human body.

What he in fact saw, and now recognized, was Tuli, Peter d'Abo, hooded in his dark cagoule, and draped not with the monastic scapular, but with black plastic bin liners. In his arms was not half a young woman, but a woman whose head was covered with cloth, and whose top half was swathed, but whose legs and waist were naked. It was not possible at this distance to be sure at first whether or not the body was dead. Then the legs kicked.

Tuli had a hostage.

The whirr of helicopters was not part of Vivyan's fantasy. Two red choppers hovered over the graveyard. As he stopped in his tracks, the priest turned and took in at least six shielded figures, armed and in camouflage gear, kneeling at strategic points around the cemetery.

The Brigadier was talking through a megaphone.

'Stand still! Both of you, stand still!'

'Tuli,' called Vivyan. 'Put her down!'

'Chell!' – the Brigadier's voice once again. 'That was an order. Stand where you are. Repeat, stand where you are.'

The boy was shouting something, but it was not possible, above the noise of the helicopter, to know what he was saying. He was holding something to the woman's waist. Disobeying the bellowed commands of the Brigadier, Chell walked slowly forward towards the boy and the woman. He felt in the pocket of his donkey-jacket and released the safety catch of his own revolver. Only a few yards further, and he could hear the boy.

'Come any closer and I shoot!'

One long arm was round the woman's neck. He was dragging her like a sack. The other arm, it was clear now, held a small gun, which he sometimes held to her head, and sometimes jabbed roughly at her pubic bush.

'She's the one who betrayed you, Father! She's the spy!'

'Tuli, put her down!'

'I'm telling you – she brought all these soldiers, these planes and choppers, she's . . .'

Vivyan could not hear the last part of this sentence, as the helicopters swooped lower. A burst of gunfire from one of them narrowly missed him.

'Tuli, I beg you, put her down!'

The boy was now close enough to be in Vivyan's sights.

The helicopter swooped once more.

Vivyan ran towards the boy and the woman. As he did so, another burst of gunfire came from the helicopter. There was also gunfire from some graves behind him. He felt a thud in his right shoulder-blade, as if someone had punched him hard. The blow was enough to make him fall, but as he did so he looked up and had the quickness of mind to produce his pistol from his pocket.

'I'm killing her for you, Father. I'm killing her for . . .'

Vivyan was spreadeagled on the path; not immediately in great pain, but greatly weakened. He tried to raise himself on one knee, and to call out, 'Tuli. My son, my son!'

The child smiled. Vivyan was close enough to see those smudge-grey eyes, and to be sure, before he fell back, that he had landed a bullet straight between them.

FORTY-ONE

The dawn had broken simultaneously with the monk's death. That was about half an hour ago. And now, Mercy stood outside the house, under a large portico, watching the golden light streaming through white, earth-hugging cloud, touching the variegated oranges and yellows of the oaks and sycamores in their autumn splendour. Beyond the front lawn were fields, where, in billows of mist and sun-sparkling dew, cows peacefully grazed.

It took weeks, months perhaps, for her to take in those moments after Vivyan's passing. At the time, she was in a state of hypertension which precluded the possibility of noticing, exactly, how she felt. Everything was odd, so that she accepted it, as if it were a dream.

After Vivyan had died, they had drifted out of the infirmary, each having made their private farewells to the corpse. The monks were still praying over it. Lord Longmore, who was staying in the house, must have gone back to his room. Mercy was helped from the infirmary bed by the tall old guy, the Brigadier, whose touch gave off no sexual hint whatever. Rachel had left the room with Sinclo Manners – a young man that Mercy had, for some months, marked down as gorgeous. They had found their way out into the corridor. It was a huge place. Later, trying to reconstruct it in her mind, or describe it to friends, Mercy found herself saying that it was a cross between a hospital and a school: a long corridor led from the infirmary, which had been built on to the back of the old mansion. Then you found yourself in a cavernous Victorian hall, painted white. There was a big statue of Jesus in the hall, with his arms outstretched. And over the fireplace there was a painting of the geezer who'd founded the place, an old bishop with a beard.

It wasn't what she'd have thought of, if you'd said the word 'monastery'. There was no Gothic cloister, no pointed arch in sight. Instead, by the huge front door – as big as the door of the town hall where Mercy worked in her dull clerical job – stood the tubby, crazed figure of little Len, shouting and swearing at the young monk who had let him in.

'I'll go where I sodding like!'

That had been his response when the novice had told him, 'You can't go down there!'

Was he too late? Of course he was too late, if he'd hoped to see Father Vivyan alive.

Mercy was aware at the time only of raised voices, of an older monk coming to see what all the fuss was about, of exchanges of dialogue. 'You don't understand, Father! I've got to see Father Vivyan, I've got to see Father Vivyan!'

This was Len. He was like a junkie bursting into a pharmacy to demand his fix.

'There's so much I've got to . . . I must . . . I must!'

'Father Vivyan died a few moments ago!'

'But he can't . . .'

Something was murmured which Mercy had not heard.

Apparently, the older monk led Len off to the infirmary, where he was allowed to see the body. It was months later that she heard of what had ensued there: Len had run into the room, and ripped the sheet off the corpse.

'You can't do this! You can't be dead! We never . . . Oh, Jesus, we never . . .' He could not finish the sentence. It was not clear what he never did. Was it like Henry II, in a film she'd seen once with Trevor in happier days, when the knights had been to murder Becket, and the king repented of the evil he'd done to the saint? They never would know. Three months later, Lennie was to meet his own death: a stupendous heart attack at the top of the escalator in LenMar House. He would cascade downwards, rolling past the swooping plane tree and the cascade, to die prostrate at the feet of a commissionaire. They never would find out whether it was guilt that brought on the attack, or knowledge of his impending ruin, or simply one heap of fries, one slice of Dundee cake and Vacherin too many.

Mercy was aptly named. Her heart was broken, but neither in the moments at Kelvedone after Vivyan died nor in the weeks which followed could she find it in her heart to blame any of them. Lennie had behaved like a total and utter bastard towards her. But now that Peter was dead, she wondered what Lennie, or anyone else, could have done to save her son. She had known for years that he was not quite right; tried to hide it from herself; then when this became impossible, tried to stop loving the boy. She had seen what his – how could she describe it? His illness? His condition? – had done to himself, to the family, to Trevor, to Brad and Lucius, to teachers, to her mum . . . She could hate the effect it had, but she could not hate Peter. Her beautiful, mysterious boy! She thought not of the bad, recent times, but of the attractive child he had been. In those days, the dreams and the fantasies and the different voices had all added enchantment to life.

'Who are we today?' she'd ask him, when he was three, four, five.

'I'm not Peter, I'm a wolf!' or 'I'm not Peter, I'm an angel!' Those had been the insistent boasts of her little man, as she toddled him to the shops, or pushed him on a swing in Furbelow Park.

'Peter, come here!'

Silence. He would ignore her totally, until she had selected the right 'personality' to call. Only when she had remembered to call for 'Wolf' or 'Angel' or 'Batman' would he heed her voice. Mercy came to feel that though she loved sex, and men, and people, and Trevor and the boys, and her mum, she had never been 'in love': not in the way people were in books or films. Her heart had been prepared for all eternity for one great love: her love of Peter. And so it would always be. She could love no one else as she loved that boy.

That was why, though she felt numb with sorrow in the days after his death, and she was to pass from this numbness into an everlasting mourning for her son, she could feel no bitterness: she could see so clearly, as the years went on, that the devils in him would only have moved from triumph to triumph, creating havoc of all kinds.

Father Vivyan had understood this. He had not killed Peter. He had killed the demons. Though it was a peace of infinite sadness, Mercy was now at peace as she had not been for more than a decade, since the first intimations of Peter's character had been manifest to her.

And, oh, she was lucky to have been with Vivyan at the end! The good fortune which led her from Mum's flat in Crickleden to the vicarage and to the ambulances . . . the whole muddled scene of how it had happened . . . she could not recollect how one thing led to another. All she knew was that she was *there*. She had held her dead boy in her arms before they took him away for autopsy. And somehow she had stayed beside the wounded Vivyan and come with him and Rachel Pearl in the ambulance.

She had wondered, Mercy, about the relationship between the monk and this beautiful young woman. Instinct told her, correctly, that it had not involved sex. When Mercy sat beside the bedside of the dying old man, she had wanted him so much, wanted every bit of him one last time, wanted his voice and his comfort, but wanted what she had found down there beneath the monkish sheets, oh boy, oh man. They'd watched, the poof monks, as she'd gently massaged him, but they couldn't really stop her, and it made her happy that while they commended him to Jesus and Mary he'd died with the biggest hard-on in the world.

The sun rose rapidly over the monastery grounds. It was, she said to herself, more a stately home than a monastery, the sort of place she and Mum liked to visit for day-outings. And the Brigadier was there, offering her, and Rachel and Sinclo a lift back to London. It's all right for you, she thought, you've got each other. And then, she found, she hadn't just thought it, but said it, blurted it out. And into Rachel's pale, tear-stained cheeks came two little blushing strawberries, and Sinclo said, 'Have we?'

'Now,' asked the Brigadier, leading the way to his car, 'who's going to sit in the front?'

Mercy volunteered to do so.

The Brigadier drove the Land Rover efficiently, gently, down golden lanes, past roundabouts, out on to the motorway. No one spoke. But when the big car swooped towards London, Mercy looked in the vanity mirror to catch a glimpse of the pair on the back seat. Sinclo had put his arm round Rachel Pearl, and she was nestling her head on his shoulder, and holding his hand.